Janet Ross

Three Generations of Englishwomen

Vol. 1

Janet Ross

Three Generations of Englishwomen
Vol. 1

ISBN/EAN: 9783337398996

Printed in Europe, USA, Canada, Australia, Japan

Cover: Foto ©Andreas Hilbeck / pixelio.de

More available books at **www.hansebooks.com**

Memoirs and Correspondence

OF

MRS. JOHN TAYLOR, MRS. SARAH AUSTIN,

AND

LADY DUFF GORDON

BY JANET ROSS.

IN TWO VOLUMES—VOL. I.

WITH PORTRAITS AND ILLUSTRATIONS.

LONDON:
JOHN MURRAY, ALBEMARLE STREET.
1888.

LIST OF ILLUSTRATIONS, VOL. I.

INTRODUCTION.

Mrs. John Taylor, the first subject of these Memoirs, was a remarkable woman, whose house at Norwich was the resort of many of the most cultivated men and women of her day, whose friendship was prized and valued by them. She brought up her children with an unflinching love of truth and a horror of debt. Not ashamed of being poor, she attended to all the small details of daily life, in the midst of which she found time to read and appreciate philosophy and poetry, and to think for herself. The Taylor family for several generations has produced men and women distinguished by literary and scientific ability : they and their forbears belonged to the Presbyterian party, and disliked the Independents almost as much as the Tories. It is a saying in Norfolk, that if a collection were made of the works of the Taylors of Norwich, it would form a respectable library.

Of Mrs. Taylor's seven children, Sarah Austin was perhaps the handsomest and the most gifted ; the extraordinary vigour of her mind and body was occasionally almost overpowering, but it stood her in good stead during a long and not over-prosperous life, and was tempered by an excellent judgment and a very kind heart. No one ever appealed to her in vain ; and in her old age children always flocked round her with delight to hear

"Puss in boots," or one of Grimm's fairy-tales, so well and graphically told. I have made a selection among the mass of her correspondence, but I fear that (in the French letters particularly) much has been lost by translation. All Mrs. Austin's letters to M. B. St. Hilaire are in French, those to M. Guizot are in English.

Many have spoken of my grandfather Mr. John Austin's eloquence—I remember it well. To the end he always preserved the upright carriage his early soldier-life had given him, and when we lived at Esher I cannot forget how he used to stride over the commons which divided us from Weybridge.

"Here," says my grandmother, in her Preface to his work on Jurisprudence—"here he entered upon the last and happiest period of his life—the only portion during which he was free from carking cares and ever-recurring disappointments. The battle of life was not only over, but had hardly left a scar. He had neither vanity nor ambition, nor any desires beyond what his small income sufficed to satisfy. He had no regrets or repinings at his own poverty and obscurity, contrasted with the successes of other men. He was insatiable in the pursuit of knowledge and truth for their own sake; and during the long daily walks which were almost the sole recreation he coveted or enjoyed, his mind was constantly kept in a state of serene elevation and harmony by the aspects of nature, which he contemplated with ever-increasing delight, and described in his own felicitous and picturesque language, and by meditation on the sublimest themes that can occupy the mind of man. He wanted no excitement and no audience. Though he welcomed the occasional visits of his friends with affectionate cordiality, and delighted them by the vigour and charm of his conversation, he never expressed the smallest desire for society. He was content to pour out the treasures of his knowledge, wisdom, and genius to the companion whose life was (to use the expression of one who knew him well) 'enfolded in his.' Thus passed twelve years of retirement, rarely interrupted, and never uninteresting or wearisome. His health was greatly improved. The place he had chosen and his mode of life suited him. The simplicity of his tastes and habits would have rendered a more showy and luxurious way of living disagreeable and oppressive to him. Yet none of the small pleasures or humble comforts provided for him ever escaped his grateful notice. He loved to be surrounded by homely and familiar objects, and nothing pleased him so much in his garden as the flowers he had gathered in his childhood. He had a disinterested hatred of expense and of pretension, and though very generous and quite indifferent to gain, he was habitually frugal, and respected frugality in others, as the guardian of many virtues."

Of Mrs. Austin's remarkable talents I need not speak ; her letters will show what she was, and how her judgment and advice were sought by many of the eminent men of her time.

Her devoted friend, M. Barthélemy St. Hilaire has been good enough to write down for me his recollections of her, which I here translate :—

"It was in 1840 that I first knew Mrs. Austin, to whom M. Victor Cousin presented me. She was still extremely handsome, and her complexion, which she preserved till the day of her death, was dazzling. Her vigour was extraordinary, and she was calm, although full of life and gaiety. Her conversation was delightful, intelligent and abounding in solid good sense. At that time she was accompanied by her only daughter, Lady Duff Gordon, and her son-in-law, Sir Alexander, both extremely handsome.

At Paris, Mrs. Austin had a *salon,* which she kept admirably: as she was poor, intellect alone was the attraction and the ornament of the house, and all that was most eminent among the foreigners who passed through Paris eagerly sought to be received in her humble apartment. There also the most illustrious Frenchmen of both the Conservative and the Liberal parties met together, and, thanks to the mistress of the house, the most diverse opinions were discussed without acerbity, and to the profit of all. If any obtained admittance who were unworthy of these pleasant and useful reunions, they were eliminated without harshness ; and I have seen executions of this kind done with perfect tact, yet with a moral vigour which, without any fuss, was most efficacious. The *salon* of Mrs. Austin was a centre where France, England, Germany, and Italy met, and learned to know and appreciate each other. Mrs. Austin spoke all four languages. Her power of work was wonderful, quite virile. She was an excellent Latin scholar, which stood her in good stead when she published the posthumous work of her husband on the Roman Law. Her mind was perfectly balanced and fortified by serious, hard study ; and to everything she did she brought an attention and a maturity of judgment which few men possess in so large a measure. Mrs. Austin was intimate with all the remarkable intellects in

England. She presented me, among others, to Lord Lansdowne, Mr. Layard, Mr. J. Stuart Mill, Grote (Mr. and Mrs.), etc., etc. I went with her to see the Misses Berry, then very old ladies, witty, and delighted to talk with a Frenchman who reminded them, particularly by his pronunciation, of the society of the eighteenth century, in which they had shone in their youth. I also recollect a visit to Mr. C. Greville, then crippled by gout, but whose conversation sparkled with intelligence and admirable taste. Mrs. Austin knew the Duchess of Orleans, who consulted her about the education of her two sons ; and in 1864 I saw the young Princes at her house at Weybridge, after their return from America. They treated her with filial respect.

Mrs. Austin did me a great service—she taught me to know England. In 1840 she found me imbued with all those international prejudices so damaging to both sides. When I knew her better, she often made me blush ; and, to cure me of my folly, she invited me to visit England and judge with my own eyes. In 1849 I went to Weybridge and enjoyed her cordial hospitality. My conversion was rapid, and I returned charmed with and full of admiration for England, and repeated my visit nearly every year.

Mr. Austin was worthy of his wife, but his qualities were entirely opposed. Intensely nervous and often ill, he loved solitude, and even in his own house no one saw him until dinner, at which he did not always assist. Sad by nature, and a deep thinker, he spoke little, but when he did it was with extraordinary vehemence and eloquence. A pupil of Bentham, and intimate with all the friends of his master, he began by embracing all Bentham's doctrines, even his irreligion; but later he modified his opinions, though he always preserved the most entire liberty of thought. When he first went to Weybridge, he considered it right to tell the clergyman that he would never see him at church. He did this to avoid any appearance of scandal, and to preserve his own independence; but he took his share in all the charities and charges of the parish. Deeply versed in law, he was for some time Professor at the University of London, and became known by a remarkable work on the connection of Morals and Jurisprudence. He was a corresponding member of the Institute of France and of the Academy of Moral and Political Sciences. When he died, he left a mass of valuable documents collected for his lectures at the University. Mrs. Austin arranged and published all the manuscripts left by her husband, aided by the advice of his legal friends. This publication redounded to the honour of the author, and of her who assumed the difficult task of editing a work bristling with difficulties and learned quotations.

When Mr. Austin was sent to Malta on a mission by his Government, Mrs. Austin occupied herself with the education of Maltese women, and did immense good. She often talked of her scholastic occupations, and of their success. Returning home, Mr. Austin's health being very indifferent, they withdrew to Weybridge, where Mrs. Austin eked out their small means by her pen. From prudence she confined herself to translating, though she had all the faculties that go to produce original work. But, as she often told me, she feared by publishing anything of her own to expose herself to criticism, and she always considered it improper in a woman to provoke a possible polemic, which generally ends in a manner disagreeable to herself.

The last years of Mrs. Austin's life were devoted to the publication of her husband's book. She worked with vigour and method, and a scrupulous attention which allowed no fault to escape her. The learned friends she consulted had, I am sure, few corrections to make. She died of heart disease, at the age of seventy-three, preserving the freshness and beauty of her complexion to the end of her life. The expression of her face when dead had something sublime and angelic. The calm of death often produces this effect, but I never saw it so marked as in her."

Lucie Duff Gordon, the only child of John and Sarah Austin, inherited the talents of her parents. Of her beauty I should not be considered a fair judge, but one who knew her well writes to me :

" Can I, how can I trust myself to speak of your dear mother's beauty in the phase it had reached when first I saw her? The classic form of her features, the noble poise of her head and neck, her stately height, her un-coloured yet pure complexion, caused some of the beholders at first to call her beauty statuesque, and others to call it majestic, some pronouncing it to be even imperious. But she was so intellectual, so keen, so autocratic, sometimes even so impassioned in speech, that nobody, feeling her powers, could well go on feebly comparing her to a statue or a mere queen or empress."

Forced by illness to leave the home she loved and the society she shone in, the last years of her life were passed in Egypt. My mother's generous spirit and sympathy for everything and everybody oppressed or suffering won the hearts of the Arabs in an extraordinary way. Her own letters will tell the rest.

It remains for me to thank H.R.H. the Comte de Paris, Madame Guizot de Witt, Mr. Gladstone, M. St. Hilaire, Colonel Gatt, Mrs. Simpson, and others, for allowing my grandmother's letters to their parents or themselves to be published, and for permission to print their own letters. I must also express the obligation I am under to Mr. Macmillan for allowing me to reprint extracts of my mother's 'Letters from the Cape' and 'Letters from Egypt'; and last, but not least, thank my grandmother's old friend, Mr. John Murray, for the great help he has been good enough to give me.

JANET ROSS.

October,

1888.

CONTENTS TO VOL. I.

CHAPTER I.

MRS. JOHN TAYLOR.

CHAPTER II.

CHAPTER III.

CHAPTER XX.

CHAPTER XXI.

CHAPTER XXII.

CHAPTER XXIII.

CHAPTER XXIV.

CHAPTER XXV.

CHAPTER XXVI.

CHAPTER XXVII.

THREE GENERATIONS OF ENGLISH WOMEN.

———◦◦———

CHAPTER I.

MRS. JOHN TAYLOR.

Norfolk and its illustrious names—Dr. John Taylor—Mr. John Taylor and Miss Susannah Cook—Mrs. J. Taylor's Letters to Miss Dixon—Mrs. Taylor and her friends—Mr. J. Taylor a poet—Death of Mrs. Martineau—Mrs. Barbauld's 'Tribute.'

IT has been said, " I have seen more of the county of Norfolk than of its inhabitants, but of that county I may remark, that, to the best of my recollection, it contains more churches, more flints, more turkeys, more turnips, more wheat, more cultivation, more commons, more cross-roads, and, from that token, probably more inhabitants than any county I have ever visited. It has another distinguishing and paradoxical feature—if what I hear is true—it is said to be more illiterate than any other part of England ; and yet I doubt if any county of like extent has produced an equal number of famous men."

The mental activity which distinguished Norwich during the latter half of the last century and the beginning of this, was very remarkable ; and although provincial, and occasionally affected, was certainly far above the average of country towns. William Taylor, the German scholar, to whom Mrs. Barbauld wrote— "Do you know that you made Walter Scott a poet? So he told me the other day. It was, he says, your ballad of 'Lenore' that inspired him;" Dr. Sayers, the Martineaus, the John Taylors, Mr. Amyot, Dr. Rigby, Dr. Reeve, Dr. Alderson, and his daughter Amelia Opie, the Stevensons, the Gurneys, and Dr. Enfield, make up a goodly list of talent; and this slight but imperfect record of some of the names of which Norwich is justly proud, may be supplemented by an extract from a speech of the late Lord Houghton at a Social Science Congress in that town :—

"I know no provincial city adorned with so many illustrious names in literature, the professions, and public life; those of Taylor, Martineau, Austin, Alderson, Opie, come first to my recollection, and there are many more behind; and there is this additional peculiarity of distinction, that these are for the most part not the designation of individuals, but of families numbering each men and women conspicuous in various walks in life."

My ancestor, Dr. John Taylor, was born in 1694, near Lancaster. His father, a timber-merchant, was a member of the Church of England; his mother, a Protestant Dissenter. John Taylor adopted her religious opinions, and is described by Dr. Parr as a "defender of simple and uncorrupted religion."

In 1733, he was elected to the charge of the Presbyterian congregation in Norwich, and some years later he published his controversial work, 'The Scripture Doctrine of Original Sin,' which called forth violent answers from Drs. Watts and Jennings. Dr. Taylor replied in a 'Supplement.' In 1745, appeared his 'Paraphrase to the Epistle to the Romans,' and soon afterwards he published one of the first collections of sacred tunes, with an introduction on the art of singing. In 1754, Dr. Taylor brought out his great work, 'The Hebrew Concordance.' Two years later, the University of Glasgow conferred on him the degree of D.D. In 1757, Dr. Taylor was named divinity tutor at Warrington, where he died in 1761.

Richard, the eldest son of Dr. John Taylor, married Margaret, daughter of Mr. Philip Meadows, Mayor of Norwich, in 1734. Her sister Sarah married Mr. David Martineau, grandson of Gaston Martineau, who fled from France at the time of the Edict of Nantes. Both sisters were left widows at an early age, and one had eight, the other seven children, to whose training they devoted themselves. Harriet Martineau was a granddaughter of Mrs. David Martineau. A daughter of Dr. John Taylor, Sarah, who was very beautiful, married Dr. Edward Rigby, a Lancashire man, who was educated at Dr. Priestley's school at Warrington, and afterwards studied medicine under Mr. Norgate at Norwich, where he settled. Dr. Rigby was a good classic scholar, a naturalist, and an enthusiastic and practical farmer.

The second son of Mrs. Richard Taylor, named John, after his grandfather, was put to school at Dr. Akers's, at Hindolveston, whence he was removed on the death of his father in 1762, in order—though only twelve years of age—to help his mother in business. Three years later he was apprenticed to Messrs. Martin and Wingfield, manufacturers in Norwich, and in 1771 he entered, as clerk, the banking-house of Messrs. Dimsdale, Archer, and Byde, in London, where he spent two years, and during that time occasionally wrote poetry in the *Morning Chronicle.* On returning to Norwich, he became a yarn-maker, in partnership with his brother Richard. In April, 1777, he married Susannah, youngest daughter of Mr. John Cook, of Norwich—a handsome and gifted woman, whose energetic character and liberal opinions, joined with great kindness of heart, made her a centre of the circle of remarkable people who frequented the provincial Athens. She possessed the pen of a ready writer, and her literary faculty was inherited by her daughter, Mrs. Austin, and her granddaughter, Lady Duff Gordon.

In April, 1777, Miss Susannah Cook wrote the last of a series of letters describing her " Jaunt to London," and a visit to Bath and Stourbridge, to her friend, Miss Judith Dixon. She announces her return to Norwich, adding :—

" Think how this pleasing agitation is increased when I reflect upon the excellent young man to whom I am soon to be indissolubly united !—when I consider that my state in life is shortly to undergo a total alteration, and that new duties are coming upon me which require my most serious and constant attention. You are too well acquainted with Mr. Taylor's merit to render any encomium needful ; you also will perceive, without my pointing them out, the many agreeable circumstances attending this affair. At these, I know, you rejoice. May we all continue united by the sweet ties of friendship."

After a wedding-tour in the North of England, Mr. and Mrs. John Taylor settled among their friends and kinsfolk at Norwich, and in her sensible sententious way she writes early in 1780 to Miss Dixon, who was "seeing the gay world" in London :—

"My time, you know, has of late been so much engrossed by domestic cares and employments, that very little of it has been devoted to literary pursuits. Satisfied, however, with reflecting that it is better to be useful than accomplished, I endeavour to fulfil, in the best manner I am able, the various duties that lie before me, and in the meanwhile enjoy, with double relish, an interval of leisure. My heart thanks you much more than any words can do for the interest you take in the welfare of that little creature who engages so much of my attention ; but you are ever kindly solicitous about all the concerns of my friends. Nay, more than this, you seem to enter into the exquisite feelings that actuate the mind of a parent. Indeed, my dear Judith, they *are* exquisite ; and while we regard in the present helpless object of our cares, both the companion of our riper years, and the support of declining age, it is no wonder if we are thankful for the inestimable gift. Perhaps he may not prove what our sanguine hopes presage ; but, as I see no harm in it, I indulge the agreeable idea."

In the following year Mr. John Taylor went over to Ireland for his business, and the young wife writes to her "sweet friend," who is staying with Dr. and Mrs. Barbauld at Palgrave :—

"It is not to every one that I would expose my weakness in making a trip to Ireland a matter of such consequence ; but in these situations it is not so much the degree of danger that affects us, as the value of what is exposed; when the treasure is immense it signifies but little that the hazard is trifling, for the mind magnifies bare possibility and dwells upon those ideas which it ought to avoid. I am sure of meeting with every indulgence from you, and therefore freely own that I have felt fears which in another I should have laughed at. You are enjoying the choicest of pleasures, my dear Judith, and you know how to prize them. If ever one might acknowledge being envious without a blush, it would be for such society as Mr. and Mrs. Barbauld; but I don't envy you, I wish only to be a joint partaker in your enjoyment. Give my most affectionate respects to them both. Your good father and mother are so kind and attentive to me that my thoughts are turned from my domestic loss to the comfort I feel in good friends; scarcely a day has passed without one of them calling upon me, and they have felt the same anxious impatience for a letter, and the same benevolent pleasure when it was received, which they always do at every event in which I am so much interested."

Mrs. Taylor went to visit her husband's relations at Diss in September, 1783, and relates how—

"Mrs. Barbauld drank tea with us. She is in good spirits, and her conversation as charming as usual. Mrs. Barbauld told me she had received a letter from you, and we agreed that you had no occasion to fear being too romantic—there is too large a portion of discretion and of solid judgment in your composition to suffer your imagination to be led astray. I have frequently been disappointed in the character of women, on this account. Those who are capable of enjoying the pleasure of knowledge, are apt to be intoxicated with it, and to transplant the high-wrought ideas which they acquire into situations where they have no business. This is a great error, for we must frequently change both our modes of thinking and acting, and adapt them to our circumstances. For this reason a romantic woman is a troublesome friend, as she expects you to be as imprudent as herself, and is mortified at what she calls coldness and insensibility."

In 1784 a third son, Edward, was born, who inherited his father's taste for music and his fine voice. The following year Judith Dixon married Mr. Beecroft, and Mrs. Taylor writes to congratulate her young friend on attaining "happiness of the same kind as my own;" she adds :—

"I have long felt this conviction with regard to the conjugal state ; it is in that intimate union alone that a woman feels herself safe, respectable, and happy ; and she finds that the constant desire of giving pleasure to her husband makes even trifling affairs of some importance. This affords that stimulus which is so necessary to keep the active mind from weariness and lassitude, and when evils come, arms it with additional fortitude to resist their power. May as much happiness be yours as this life can afford."

In the old-fashioned parlour in St. George's, Colegate, might be heard the most brilliant conversation, as eminent people of every opinion gathered round the hospitable, unpretentious fireside. Mr. John Taylor, though strongly attached to the faith of his forefathers, and a staunch Whig, was of so kind and genial a temper that party spirit or religious prejudices never interfered with his friendships. There might be seen Sir James Mackintosh, the most brilliant and popular man of the day, to whom Madame de Staël wrote, "Il n'y a pas de société sans vous." "C'est très ennuyeux de dîner sans vous ; la société ne va pas quand vous n'êtes pas là." Sir James Smith, the botanist ; Mr. Crabb Robinson, the philosopher of the Unitarians, and the cherished friend of all the distinguished people of the last century, and the first half of this ; Dr. Southey, Mr. Wyndham, Sir Thomas Beevor, the Gurneys, Dr. Enfield and Dr. Rigby, Dr. Alderson and his charming daughter Amelia Opie, and Mrs. Barbauld, who "prized and valued Susannah Taylor's affection beyond all others." Dr. Sayers, who lived in an old house near by, in the Lower Close ; and the Sewards, Dr. Parr, and Mr. Smith (grandfather of Miss F. Nightingale), were constant visitors. His eldest daughter, talking of the excitement prevailing in Norwich when the news of the fall of the Bastille was first known, said to the present Mr. Henry Reeve, " Don't I remember your glorious grandmother dancing round the tree of liberty at Norwich with Dr. Parr ! "

Mrs. John Taylor was called, by her intimate friends, "Madame Roland of Norwich," from her likeness to the portraits of the handsome and unfortunate Frenchwoman ; and Miss Lucy Aikin describes how she darned her boy's grey worsted stockings while holding her own with Southey, Brougham, or Mackintosh. The latter had a great admiration for the quiet Norwich housewife, and writes to her :—

" I know the value of your letters. They rouse my mind on subjects which interest us in common : friends, children, literature, and life. Their moral tone cheers and braces me. I ought to be made permanently better by contemplating a mind like yours, which seems more exclusively to derive its gratifications from its duties

than almost any other.   Your active kindness is a constant source of cheerfulness, and your character is so
happily constituted that even the misfortunes of those
who are dear to you, by exciting the activity of your
affection, almost heal the wounds which they would
otherwise have inflicted."

He dwells affectionately upon her goodness, her fidelity
in friendship, and her " industrious benevolence, which
requires a vigorous understanding, and a decisive character."

In 1786, another son, Philip, was born, and two years
later the first girl, Susan, was hailed with great delight.
In 1790, the last son, Arthur, came into the world, and
three years afterwards, Sarah, the youngest child.

Every family event was celebrated by Mr. John
Taylor with a poem, for amid his manifold occupations
he found leisure to exercise his poetical talents.   One
of the most stirring songs I know celebrating the
dawn of the French Revolution was written by him on
the back of a letter announcing the fall of the Bastille
in July 1789.   'The Triumph of Liberty' was not
acceptable to the Tory Ministers of the day, but the
Duke of Sussex made Mr. Taylor sing it at a great
dinner over which he presided at Norwich.   Party
spirit ran high in the old town in 1796, when Mr.
Windham, who had been returned six years before as a
supporter of Whig principles, became the friend and
coadjutor of Burke, and both Mr. and Mrs. Taylor took
an active part in trying to deprive him of his seat in
favour of Bartlett Gurney.

In 1798, Mr. Taylor's aunt, Mrs. Martineau, died ; he
was much attached to her, and wrote to a friend :—

"My aunt was a woman whose head and heart procured her the respect and esteem of all her family and friends. She possessed a strong discrimination of character, and there were few persons whose soundness of judgment better qualified them to give advice. Her affections were warm, and her piety fervent, yet rational."

Mrs. Barbauld, on this occasion, wrote 'A Tribute to my honoured Friends of the Families of Martineau and Taylor,' from which I extract the following characteristic lines :—

"No bitter drop 'midst nature's kind relief,
  Sheds gall into the fountain of your grief;
  No tears you shed for patient love abused,
  And counsel scorned, and kind restraints refused.
  Not yours the pang the conscious bosom wrings
  When late remorse inflicts her fruitless stings.

  Living you honour'd her, you mourn her, dead;
  Her God you worship, and her path you tread;
  Your sighs shall aid reflection's serious hour,
  And cherish'd virtues bless the kindly shower;
  On the loved theme your lips unblamed shall dwell;
  Your lives, more eloquent, her worth shall tell.

  For me, as o'er the frequent grave I bend,
  And pensive down the vale of years descend,
  Companions, parents, kindred called to mourn,
  Dropt from my side, or from my bosom torn,
  A boding voice, methinks, in fancy's ear
  Speaks from the tomb, and cries, 'Thy friends are here!'"

CHAPTER II.

MRS. JOHN TAYLOR bore a great affection to her young friend Henry Reeve, and missed him sadly when he went to study at Edinburgh. He was a sort of adopted son in their house, and she writes :—

" I rather envy Mr. Frenshaw when I see him mending pens, and poring over small print ; my eyes are somewhat more bedimmed than usual, for they overflow now and then in spite of myself. Cowper says, in his address to his mother's picture :—

> " 'Where thou art gone,
> Adieus and farewells are a sound unknown.'

In this odd world they seem to be the most common of all words. To be sure, partings and meetings give variety to our existence, but I am now grown so dull as not to want variety. If I could wish for any, I must be contented to have it all secondhand. And so, when you have seen London, and the Lakes and Edinburgh, all of which I know, and have seen in former days, you may tell me what you think of them."

In another letter she says :—

" Nothing at present suits my taste so well as Susan's Latin lessons, and her philosophical old master. . . . When we get to Cicero's discussions on the nature of the soul, or Virgil's fine descriptions, my mind is filled up.   Life is either a dull round of eating, drinking, and sleeping, or a spark of ethereal fire just kindled.

There is no surer way of becoming acquainted with our own mind than by the effect produced upon it by the conduct of others ; if we can tolerate vice and folly, we may grow fond of them in time.   Perhaps you can bear witness to the truth of another remark, that people generally wrap themselves up in a solemn kind of reserve, and particularly those who have taken upon themselves the task of enlightening the world.   It is to be accounted for from the jealousy and fear of losing a reputation once acquired, by the unguarded frankness of colloquial intercourse.   Be it ours, my dear friend, merrily to philosophise, sweetly to play the fool.   Strange counsel to a young man in a grave university !"

In 1802, the *Edinburgh Review* first appeared ; Jeffrey, Brougham and Sydney Smith were its founders, and Dr. Reeve, who had just taken his degree at Edinburgh, contributed to the first numbers.   Mrs. John Taylor took great interest in the Whig review, and in the midst of her many household duties finds time to review the reviewer.   She writes :—

"Mr. Hayley's style wants that majestic simplicity with which such a character as Cowper's could have been portrayed.   He thinks it necessary, too, as Mr. Jeffrey observes, to praise everybody.   This is so like the misses who call all their insipid acquaintances 'sweet,' and 'interesting,' that it makes me rather sick.   A biographer is good for nothing who does not give those touches, those lights and shadows, which identify his characters. On this account I do not like a remark of the reviewer that Mr. Unwin's little jealousies of Lady Austen might as well have been passed over in silence. If the weaknesses of excellent people are to be concealed, how shall we form an accurate impression of human nature ? "

Again she writes to Dr. Reeve :—

Nothing can operate more powerfully against the attainment of excellence in every species of composition, than the indiscriminate praise and false tenderness which prevent those writers who are capable of higher degrees of improvement from endeavouring sedulously to aim at greater perfection, or which lead those who are incapable to trouble the public at all. I have been witness to such extravagant praises bestowed upon inferior compositions, especially in London, that I rejoice in the more hardy criticism of our northern metropolis, not from a desire to depreciate, but from a conviction that the more completely both books and characters find their proper stations, the better it will be for society. I think the ' Edinburgh Review' contains just, but not ill-natured, criticism.

If I were inclined to make an appeal for any person who has fallen under the lash, it would be for Robert Southey, whose experiments in poetry I acknowledge to be, many of them, fantastic and extravagant ; but they are the experiments of a man of genius. . . . I think we ought to be grateful to literary pioneers."

In February, 1807, Mrs. Barbauld invited the young Sarah Taylor to stay with her, and Mrs. John Taylor wrote a series of admirable letters, sensible, thoughtful, and motherly, to " dear Sally."

" If I was to write to you as often as I think of you, it

would be almost every hour. Even at your early age, the great points of moral conduct must be understood, and I think I may safely trust that they will in no instance be deviated from by you either in thought, word, or deed. But a character may in this respect be irreproachable, and yet fail to be amiable. Now as the world in general cannot search to the bottom of our hearts, they must judge by external appearances, and therefore obliging, attentive manners must be added to rational acquirements, if we wish to obtain the good opinion of those with whom we associate. Perhaps as effectual a way as any to acquire these manners is to think (what is really true) that you are under an obligation to all who take notice of you ; and if you feel gratified by their attentions, you have it in your power to gratify others by acting in the same manner towards them. Don't think that you are to receive all and give nothing ; this would not appear fair dealing if it was applied to the little presents by which girls prove their goodwill to each other ; and it cannot be so in the general intercourse of life. Nothing leads more to this partial offensive behaviour than the general tendency there is in young people to talk only to young people, to be dumb and stupid with those who could tell them something valuable, and flippant and noisy with others from whom they can learn nothing. A bad style of conversation too is acquired by this practice, for girls deal too much in forcible expressions which bear no proportion to the object they relate to, and which, delivered with the emphasis with which they are accompanied, become quite ridiculous. How often have I observed the young describer of some insignificant circumstance at a loss for words to finish a detail, merely because every powerful expression was exhausted in the beginning of the recital. Yet perhaps a more interesting account from another person, or even a sublime passage from the finest author, will scarcely excite a languid remark. These strong expressions used upon common occasions, and the frequent exclamations which accompany them, are among the leading faults in the conversation of girls. Another great source of offence is a love of contradiction—not a love of discussion, which is the great pleasure and privilege of a rational being, nor yet the wish to set another person right—for this is very laudable—and you have sense and discrimination enough to see the difference. One good effect which I promise myself from your present situation is, that you will be less with girls of your own age, and that you must occasionally hear admirable conversation. I hope that without teasing Mrs. Barbauld you will avail yourself of the high privilege of being in the same house with her, where a mind so exquisite as hers must sometimes give out hidden treasure ; but they will not be bestowed upon the insensible, the indolent, or the ungrateful. Pray improve your Italian and your French by every means in your power, and extend your acquaintance with English authors as much as possible."

Other admonitions as to her wardrobe follow, and a letter written in March contains quite a political treatise to her daughter of fourteen :—

"With what can I begin my letter better than with congratulations upon the late triumph so delightful to the friends of humanity from the abolition of the slave trade ? I rejoice also at your being in a house whose dear inhabitants feel and have ever felt upon this subject in a manner so worthy of themselves. Ask Mrs. Barbauld to permit you to read those fine lines addressed to Mr. Wilberforce when some of our senators, instead of feeling that glow of virtuous indignation which is now so predominant, laughed at the recital of cruelties and ridiculed the advocates of the oppressed negroes. Nothing is so gratifying as the idea that virtue and philanthropy are becoming fashionable, and I am almost tempted to hope that this is now the case. The day after I read the noble speech of Lord Howick, Mr. Fawkes, the Solicitor-General, Mr. Roscoe, Mr. Wilberforce, etc., I·could not rest without embracing those friends who were most likely to feel as I did. It is strange, and it is lamentable, that people should ever be reduced to such shifts for conversation as to slander each other when there are so many noble and interesting subjects to be found. I often think with great satisfaction of your answer to Miss Tasker's remark about scandal, and I hear with peculiar pleasure that you seem to enjoy and take a share in the choice society with whom you have now the happiness to converse. Among your other readings you should from time to time read some of Mrs. Barbauld's works, and you would be the more sensible of the high privilege you enjoy ; for indeed, my dear child, to have free access to a mind which has produced so many fine and exquisite thoughts, may well be called so. How kind she is to suffer you to read with her, and how much will it contribute to form your taste ! The employments of school, of the needle, and various interruptions have hitherto prevented that regular attention to the English classics (with us) which I have so much wished for. A comparison of the French and the English is still better, and therefore to read Boileau and Pope with Mrs. Barbauld is just what I should have chosen. The character of girls must depend upon their reading as much as upon the company they keep. Besides the intrinsic pleasure to be derived from solid knowledge, a woman ought to consider it as her best resource against poverty. I went to Mr. Thomas Martineau's yesterday to see the two

Mr. Cokes, Sir Jacob Astley, and Mr. Windham pass by. When the first part of the procession had reached this spot, the last had not entered Magdalen gates—so you may judge of its length ; indeed, the unseating of our old members has been much more like a triumph than a defeat to the Whig party, for the accusations of ministerial influence were disproved, and the treating was as much on one side as the other ; but Mr. Windham has again lost the favour he was regaining amongst us by the part he has taken about the slave trade. Mr. Coke's open, benevolent countenance had an expression of drollery in it when he was waving his hat for his brother, as much as to say, This is quite new and diverting. To add to the effect, their bare heads were all covered with the snow, which fell very thick just at the time of the chairing. I could not squeeze into the Shire Hall to hear the speeches, which was a great disappointment to me."

On the 29th March, 1807, Mrs. Taylor writes in answer to a birthday letter from her dear Sally :—

" I have this day lived fifty-two years in the world. The principal difference between my feelings on the day that gave me birth and yours, are that you look forward and I look backward ; but, my dear child, you will one day look back as I do, if your life is preserved as long, and then what will contribute most to your comfort ? Certainly not the things which have administered to the decoration of the body and the gratification of the senses, though all these are innocent in a certain degree, but the stores which the mind has treasured up, the kind actions we have performed, and the just ideas we have acquired as to the real end and business of this life and its reference to another. I have nothing to expect on the score of merit, having never come near my own ideas on the subject of duty—but I bless God that I feel every year an increasing interest and pleasure in the happiness of my fellow-creatures, and a growing desire for information of every kind. My question about No-one has indeed brought out something—in the first place an answer, which, as you say, for ingenuity is worthy of Mrs. Barbauld, and those four lines so like herself, and in their application to you the most satisfactory to me of anything that could be said of you, because no quality that could be ascribed to you can be so valuable as the kindness and absence of selfish feeling which those lines imply. Preserve and cultivate such dispositions, and you will be a comfort to me indeed! Even intellectual improvement, that great distinction of a rational being, stands second in the catalogue of what your tender mother wishes her dear child to be remarkable for—may general kindness be the first. I told Reeve of your construing the Ode of Horace after Mr. Barbauld; he says it was a great feat, and I am very proud of you for it. You will do yourself much good by committing some to memory, and upon the whole I think your time has been admirably employed. I have not yet read the Curfew,' but I intend it very soon. Dr. Alderson showed me Mrs. Opie's 'Epilogue.' Of the 'Prologue' I shall take particular notice. I rejoice at the opportunity you had of a personal knowledge of Miss Baillie; how much I have wished for that pleasure!"

CHAPTER III.

Marriage of Dr. Reeve and Susan Taylor—Dr. James Martineau's
Recollections of Mrs. J. Taylor—Mrs. Taylor's visit to London
—Uses of such visits—Mrs. Opie—Visit to Yarmouth—Uses
of Vanity and Emulation—Bath—Tavistock—Recollections of
Mrs. J. Taylor by Mrs. Wilde—Mrs. Taylor's conversational
powers—Meeting of Taylor and Martineau families—Sarah's
engagement to John Austin—Death of Mrs. J. Taylor—Basil
Montague on Mrs. J. Taylor—Sons of Mr. and Mrs. J. Taylor.

SALLY TAYLOR returned home in June, and soon afterwards her sister Susan was married to Dr. Reeve, and
the young couple settled in Norwich. In August of the
same year Mr. Taylor, whose family affections were very
warm, assembled thirty-five members of the Martineau
and Taylor families under his roof; and, although
suffering severely from gout, contributed his usual song
in honour of the occasion. Apropos of these gatherings,
Dr. James Martineau writes to me :—

"I retain a vivid remembrance of your great-grandmother, Mrs. John Taylor, as a very remarkable woman.
She was, I believe, one of the contributors to the budget
read at the meetings, held at intervals of a few years, of
the Taylor and Martineau families, the descendants of
two sisters, who at last were upwards of seventy in
number. These papers consisted of essays, poems, and
dramas, the latter being acted by the younger members
of the two families, and I well remember taking a part
when a boy.

An amusing picture rises before me as I think of your great-grandmother. It was the duty of every materfamilias, in those days, to sally forth on market days, before breakfast, and lay in the needful stores for the larder. My mother used to take me with her to help with the porterage of her purchases. We went pretty early, but on the way were almost sure to meet Mrs. John Taylor on her return from the market-place, bravely struggling with her own load, without any boy to help her. Yet she would never pass us without stopping for a friendly chat, often running up into grave and stirring themes. And I remember how my boyish sense of humour was touched by the effect of so much eloquent discourse from the lips of the old lady, weighted by her huge basket, with the shank of a leg of mutton thrust out to betray its contents. So vivid is their remembrance, that, if I were an artist, I could draw the group, and even fix the very spot where I have seen it stand."

In 1809, Sarah went to stay with her brother Richard in Shoe Lane, and Mrs. Taylor writes :—

" I hope you and your brothers really do enjoy each other's society, and that you can get a little study, and a little literary talk ; from both of them you may always be gaining curious and critical information. When this taste is once acquired, it gives one a new feeling about books—converting many which would appear dry to the general reader, into sources of the greatest entertainment. Why are the readers of those works which make their appeal only to the imagination and the feelings so destitute of resources in the decline of life ? Because the imagination and the feelings undergo changes or diminutions, while the understanding (as long as our faculties continue) is always acquiring a stronger desire, and a higher relish for intellectual food."

A letter written in 1811 is very characteristic of Mrs. Taylor's energetic character.   She says :—

"This is the great use of a journey to London, not to beget a fastidious indifference or dislike to the degrees of inferiority which we observe elsewhere, but to judge between them, and make out a standard for ourselves. I have seen the most excellent actors, I have heard the most eminent musicians, I have associated with the most ingenious and cultivated people, and the ideas I have acquired from them are treasured up for ever in my mind.   I do not repine that I cannot continually do the same, but I do repine when I miss an opportunity from negligence, indolence, want of decision, or of energy.   I drank tea at Mr. William Taylor's yesterday, to meet Annie Plumptre, Pitchford and Dr. Wright, Mr. Brightwell and the Dalrymples.   Mr. Taylor was very eloquent in his own peculiar style."

Again the affectionate and anxious mother writes :—

"I send a register of events to encourage you to do the same.   I gave my concert tickets this evening to the girls in Surrey Street, feeling no inclination to go without you.   How I wish to know what you have been doing, but I hope I shall hear to-morrow, and whether you feel as if you could enjoy yourself.   Mrs. Opie treated me with her company three hours last night.   She read me some charming songs she had been writing, and was quite herself.   I have been wishing since you went away that you had taken more silver with you—it is so difficult to procure change in London.   I think I shall send by Mr. John Staff all the shillings I happen to have.   They will be acceptable, I am sure.

Systematic visiting is a great consumer of time, and in general it affords but little recompense.   The art is, not to estrange oneself from society, and yet not to pay too dear for it. The experience you have had is considerable for your age ; by a more rigid plan with you I might have spared both you and myself some pain, but you would have known much less of life. The way to stand well with people is not to make them feel your consequence, but their own, and while you are conversing with them, to take an interest in whatever interests them. By many little innocent and even laudable methods we may gain goodwill without ruining ourselves by expensive entertainments, or giving up too much valuable time. Never sacrifice this desirable thing, goodwill, for the sake of admiration—the one is a gaudy flower, the other a useful evergreen. I drank tea at your sister's with the Gurneys of Earlham, and Mrs. Opie, and Mr. Houghton ; they all dined there. Mr. Madge is better, and now that we are generally alone, conversations fit for rational beings constantly occur. One afternoon he and Mr. Houghton met ; the latter said he had a rich treat, for the merits of Wordsworth and others were discussed, passages read, and fairly appreciated. I am glad you have the Life of Sydney, as I think no book would suit you better. In him the chivalrous character appears in its highest perfection. What a contrast to the libertinism of the French Court, or to that of our own in the time of the profligate Grammont ! "

Sarah went to Yarmouth, and her mother writes :—

" What I am most anxious to know is, whether you steer clear of scrapes and difficulties : whether upon an impartial review of yourself there is a tolerable degree of satisfaction in what you have said and done ? I am not afraid for you in those cool moments when nothing occurs to drive reason from her throne, but in periods of excitation, which are so frequent in youth (*that* being the peculiar season of excitation), then, if possible, consider ! I always compassionate all girls who have had their vanity fostered as much as I condemn them. To make this same principle of vanity not only harmless, but to turn it to the useful purposes for which it was implanted in the mind, it is only necessary to examine its nature and consequences. Like curiosity, it is wanted as a stimulus to exertion, for indolence would certainly get the better of us if it were not for these two powerful principles. Personal vanity is the antidote to slovenliness; but if it leads only to a love of decoration without inducing a habit of attention to the good order and neatness of our garments, it does not answer its genuine purpose. With regard to the mind, nothing is more admirable than the way in which a feeling contemptible in itself is made to answer the noblest ends. Superior acquirements are a passport to superior company; but while we are taking measures to introduce ourselves to the notice and favour of those who are justly placed upon an eminence in society, we are insensibly laying in a store of gratification when the pleasures of society diminish, and our resources for happiness must depend chiefly upon ourselves. As soon, however, as we begin to feel more jealousy than delight in being surpassed, we must call in question the nature of our feelings; we must convince ourselves that it is only by being surpassed that we shall naturally be stationary; and that mind must always grovel in the dirt (whatever its natural powers may be) which takes more pleasure in looking down than in looking up, or for the poor ambition of being at the top of inferior associates, sacrifices the noble desire of profiting by the example .of superior ones. Mr. Southwell lent me 'Sketches of Character.' I suppose many of them are portraits; but if such is fashionable life, how contemptibly insipid! The Grimshaws must be fancy pieces, for there are no such citizens' wives and daughters now-a-days. Indeed, I think it is among the middle classes everywhere that true elegance, as well as information, are to be found. The one cannot exist without the other; but certainly the Cockneighs are notoriously devoid of both."

In March, 1812, Sarah Taylor went to stay with her cousin, Mr. Peter Martineau, at Bath, and her mother writes :—

"There is a probability that we shall lose Captain Cockburn. He has offered to go to the Isle of France, for fear he should be sent to the West Indies, or to any station disagreeable and unhealthy. I hope means will be found to provide for the dear little boys of our family without making soldiers and sailors of them. Let them be chemists and mechanics, or carpenters and masons, anything but destroyers of mankind. This is not very chivalrous, but I hope it is something better. Arthur has promised me a letter as soon as he could 'unpack his memory.' What an admirable one I have had from Lucy Aikin about the society of Edinburgh ! "

From Bath, Sarah went to Tavistock with her brother John and his wife, he having undertaken the management of various mines in Cornwall and Devonshire. Mrs. Taylor writes a gentle remonstrance to accompany a "scolding letter" from her husband for Sally's remissness in writing :—

"Dear Sal,

"Nothing would have prevented my writing to you sooner except the daily expectation of hearing from you ; but as your letter to Susan has relieved my mind from the anxiety I felt lest Nanny or you, or something or somebody, was not well, I can sit down with composure to tell you how we are here. It is curious to observe what different views we sometimes take of the same thing. You do not express any consciousness of having been deficient in your epistolary duties, while we were wondering and fretting and exclaiming to all inquiring friends, ' What can the matter be ! ' However, as I am afraid your father has written you a scolding letter, I will not fill my paper with matter so unwelcome, only premising that, according to the rules of Aristotle or Longinus, the mind of the reader requires (in all important narratives) a beginning, a middle, and an end. I have had your beginning and your middle, but the end (which relates to your crossing Dartmoor, probably in storms and hurricanes) is still to come. You must give Henry Staff some good advice when you come home. I have no influence over young people who do not love reading. The character of Mrs. W. Taylor in the Norwich paper I send, was written by Dr. Sayers. I hope you will not lose your relish for reading. Nothing else will serve through life, and nothing will obtain us so much credit, even with those who cannot avail themselves of its advantages. Make my grateful acknowledgments to Mr. and Mrs. Harness for all their kindness to you."

Mrs. Wilde, a daughter of Mr. P. Martineau, has been so good as to send me her reminiscences of Mrs. John Taylor about this time. She says :—

"When I was seventeen I was again at Norwich, and then it was that I was so much struck with her wonderful conversational powers. One day I was sent to her with some message from my mother. It was a Saturday —market-day—I was shown into the humble sitting-room. Two farmers were talking earnestly to her, whilst she was industriously at work. I sat quietly by, but soon got interested in the talk—such conversation as I seldom had heard before.   When they were gone, I found that it was to Mr. Coke of Holkham and Lord Albemarle that I had been listening so attentively.   It was their habit on a market-day to indulge themselves with a talk with the clever old lady.   Then on a Sunday she used to excite our envy ; we used to see her nodding all through Mr. Madge's good sermons, when afterwards she would criticise every part, whilst we who had been listening with eyes and ears open, could remember so very little."

In August, 1814, there was another large meeting of the Taylor and Martineau families ; forty-four members assembled at Bracondale, the residence of Mr. P. Meadows Martineau, but the joyous song with which John Taylor celebrated the event was soon turned to mourning by the death of his son-in-law, Dr. Reeve.

To Sarah, his youngest daughter, this was an eventful year.   She had for some time been attached to Mr. John Austin, and at length her engagement to him was sanctioned, after considerable opposition from her parents.

In 1819 there was another great family meeting, for which Mr. John Taylor's eldest brother Philip came over expressly from Dublin.   The muster was so large that the Hall Concert-room was borrowed for the occasion.   Sixty-five Martineaus and Taylors sat down to dinner, and old Philip Taylor read an address, exulting in the " firm union of hearts which now obtains among us.   Had our early moral discipline been neglected, had envy, selfishness or inordinate ambition been allowed to grow up among us, and especially had we been suffered to learn the polite lesson of not knowing our

From a drawing by H. Meyer.

own relations, except when perfectly convenient, we should have been scattered asunder like chaff before the wind."

In June, 1823, Mrs. John Taylor died. Always regardless of her own comfort when she could promote that of others, she pursued the even tenor of her way, doing what she conceived to be her duty. No regard for her own ease, no pain or illness, could subdue her resolute spirit. Mrs. Barbauld wrote, " Susannah Taylor is not to be forgotten by those who knew her."

Basil Montague says of her in the Life of Sir James Mackintosh :—

" Norwich was always a haven of rest to us, from the literary society with which that city abounded. Dr. Sayers we used to visit, and the high-minded and intelligent William Taylor : but our chief delight was in the society of Mrs. John Taylor, a most intelligent and excellent woman, mild and unassuming, quiet and meek, sitting amidst her large family, occupied with her needle and domestic occupations, but always assisting, by her great knowledge, the advancement of kind and dignified sentiment and conduct.

Manly wisdom and feminine gentleness were in her united with such attractive manners, that she was universally loved and respected. In ' high thoughts and gentle deeds ' she greatly resembled the admirable Lucy Hutchinson, and in troubled times would have been equally distinguished for firmness in what she thought right. In her society we passed every moment we could rescue from the Court."

The sons were all distinguished in their various lines. John, the eldest (born 1779), whose boyish taste for mechanical pursuits had been encouraged by his mother's birthday present of mathematical instruments and a turning lathe, was appointed manager, at the early age of nineteen, of the Wheal Friendship mine, near Tavistock. The first tunnel executed in England, through Morvel Down, for the Tavistock Canal, in 1806, was made under his direction. Uniting a remarkable power of governing bodies of men and attaching them to him, he was perfectly just, and scrupulously veracious. One of the most indulgent of men, he had a great dislike of gossip, detraction, and angry discussion, and though through life he remained constant to the religious and political opinions which were hereditary in his family, it was without any intolerance or narrow-mindedness. He died in 1863, at the age of eighty-three.

Richard, born in 1781, became a printer. He had literary and scientific tastes, and was largely employed in printing works in dead languages and on scientific subjects. As editor of the *Philosophical Magazine* he was known to most men of science in Europe. *Punch* alluded to his size :—

> " When Corporal Taylor stalks the streets
> A walking corporation."

He died in 1851.

Edward, the third son, was born in 1784. He inherited his father's love of music, and became Gresham Professor of Music in 1837, holding the post until he died in 1863. Mendelssohn and Spohr were his intimate friends, and it was at his solicitation that the latter wrote ' The Fall of Babylon,' in 1830.

The fourth son, Philip, born in 1786, was an inventive genius of a high order, his process of using oil as a substance from which gas for illumination could be easily prepared, was erected in Covent Garden Theatre, in several large factories and breweries, and in the Imperial Library at St. Petersburg. In 1818 he took out a patent for the application of high-pressure steam for evaporating processes. His house at Bromley was a centre for scientific men of all nations. J. B. Say, Clément Desormes the eminent chemist, Biot the biologist, Gay Lussac, Mallet of the Ponts et Chaussées, Paul Seguin (who made the first railway in France), Baron von Humboldt, Brunel, MacAdam the road-maker, Michael Faraday, Rennie, Maudslay, and Charles MacIntosh were constant visitors. Philip Taylor died in 1870, at Marseilles, where, in 1836, he had founded the Cie. des Forges et Chantiers de la Méditerranée.

Arthur, the last son, born in 1790, became printer to the City of London. His favourite study was archæology, and he was a member of the Society of Antiquaries.

Of the Taylor family, the Duke of Sussex said that they reversed the ordinary saying that it takes nine tailors to make a man.*

* Generally attributed to Sydney Smith ; but Canon Howes of Norwich was present when the Duke said it, and I have it on the authority of his daughter, Miss L. Howes.

CHAPTER IV.

MRS. AUSTIN.

Sarah Taylor—Books read as a girl—Her engagement to John Austin—Mrs. Barbauld's lines to Sarah Taylor—Visit to Creeting Mill—Mr. Fox on Mr. Austin—Mr. Austin called to the Bar—Marriage—Letter from Amelia Opie on 'Don Juan' and Lord and Lady Byron—Skit on Jeremy Bentham.

SARAH TAYLOR was born in 1793, and received a liberal and thorough education ; Latin, French, Italian, and German, she learnt as a girl, and enjoyed the advantage of hearing excellent conversation at her father's house. Mrs. John Taylor was fond of collecting young people about her, regaling them with tea and cake, and making them play games. A contemporary of my grandmother writes to me :—" I always felt an ignoramus amongst those clever girls, and remember to this day Sally Taylor presiding over the historical commerce, and my horror lest I-should mismatch my kings and queens."

Mrs. Opie, Mrs. Barbauld, and Miss Aikin, all took great interest in " Sally," the daughter of their dear friend, Mrs. Taylor. She must have made good use of her time at school, for I have before me a small note-book, inscribed, " My reading between leaving school and marriage," which will show how the foundation was laid for the forcible style and varied knowledge which distinguished her in after life.

In a small flowing hand, the ink faded and yellow, is written:—

"Books read in the year

"1815. Alison on 'Taste;' Tacitus, 'Vita Agric.' and 'History,' Stewart, 'Philosophy of the Human Mind;' first vol. of Malthus on 'Population;' Stewart, 'Philosophical Essays;' Smith, 'Moral Sentiments;' Condorcet, 'Life of Turgot.'

"1816. Bentham, 'Traité de Législation;' Beccaria, 'Dei Delitti,' &c.; Macchiavelli, 'Istorie Fiorentine;' Blackstone, 'Comment.;' part of Tacitus.

"1817. Sir J. Smith, 'Commonwealth of England;' Horne Tooke, 'Diversions of Purley;' Bentham, 'Des Peines,' &c.; Bentham on 'Parliamentary Reform.' Finished Tacitus, Macchiavelli, 'Discorsi su T. Livio,' Lord Bacon's works entire, Middleton's 'Life of Cicero.'

"1818. Macchiavelli, 'Il Principe;' Bishop Butler, 'Sermons;' Cæsar, 'De Bello Civili;' Sallust, 'Bell. Catilin.;' Goethe, 'Iphigenie auf Tauris;' Bentham, 'Defence of Usury,' also his 'Church of Englandism.'

"1819. Hume's 'Essays;' Bridge, 'Algebra to Simple Equations;' Bentham on 'Judicial Establishments;' Cicero; Meyer 'Esprit, &c., des Institutions Judiciaires;' Bentham's 'Letters to Lord Pelham,' and 'Introduction to Rationale of Evidence.'

"1820. Bentham, 'Fragment on Government;' 'Memoirs of Cardinal de Retz;' part of 'Rudimenta Artis Logica.' Began Mill's 'British India.'

"1821. Finished Mill's pamphlet on 'Parliamentary Reform;' Helvetius, 'De l'Homme.'"

No doubt a good deal of this stiff reading was due to the influence of Mr. John Austin, with whom the high-spirited, handsome girl fell passionately in love.

Her beauty must have been very great; for Mrs.

Wilde tells me that, in 1812, when Sally Taylor, on her way to Tavistock with her brother Arthur, was taken ill at Bath—

" My mother and I started off to the White Hart Inn, put her into a sedan chair, and took her to our lodgings.

She was with us about ten days, lying on the sofa, with no dress but a riding-habit ; and I remember well how our drawing-room was besieged by the young beaux of Bath, anxious to see the recumbent beauty."

Sarah Taylor was permitted to engage herself to Mr. John Austin in 1814, and she announces the event to a favourite cousin as follows :—

" The clock strikes eleven as I sit down to scrawl a few lines to you. Forgive a short letter. After some weeks of a suspense and anxiety which have prevented my writing on this most interesting subject sooner, I am enabled, thank God ! to tell you that my doom is most happily sealed. I know you will rejoice for me and with me, when I assure you that my heart and my judgment are equally satisfied with the man of my choice, that he is all and more than I ever imagined, that he loves me dearly, and finally that I am the happiest girl in the world. John is studying for the Bar, where I hope to see him distinguish himself. He has confessedly superb talents, and will, I know, study hard for my sake ; but it must be some time before he can maintain a wife.

This will be no affliction to me ; I have no idea of impatience to be married, and I can imagine no greater happiness than to possess his affection, to write to him, and occasionally to see him.

I have great doubts, dear Mary, whether he will

entirely please you, as he is certainly stern, but I am sure you would admire his lofty and delicate feelings of honour towards our sex. At any rate, if you don't like him, never tell me so—you know I love you very dearly, and it would give me pain. So, dear, let him be all perfection, will you? If you tell me he is not, I shall doubt your word, or your penetration, for the first time in my life."

Mrs. Barbauld, to whom Sarah Taylor also announced her engagement, says :—"I have had the pleasure of seeing Mr. Austin, and though prejudiced in his favour, I was not disappointed. After tea, the conversation warmed, and we had some very pleasant argumentation on moral and metaphysical subjects." Sarah was then staying with her widowed sister, Mrs. Reeve, and Mrs. Barbauld sent her the following verses "suggested by the contrast of your situations "—

To Sarah Taylor.

"Sweet are the thoughts that stir the virgin's breast,
  When *Love* first enters there a timid guest ;
  Before her dazzled eyes gay visions shine,
  And laughing Cupids wreaths of roses twine ;
  And conscious Beauty hastens to employ
  Her span of empire and her hour of joy.

Sarah, not thus to thee his power is shown.
  More stern he greets thee from his awful throne ;
  Free called to bid thy cheering converse flow,
  And shed thy sweetness in the house of woe ;
  The solemn sympathies of grief to share,
  And, sadly smiling, soothe a sister's care.
  O'er her young hopes the sable pall is spread :
  Her wedded heart holds converse with the dead.
  To ties no longer earthly, fondly true,
  Each thought that breathes of love, must breathe of heaven too.

"Thus, Sarah, Love thy nobler mind prepares,
   Shows thee his dangers, duties, sorrows, cares;
   Thus with severer lessons schools thy heart,
   And, pleased his happiest influence to impart,
   For thee, dismissing from his chastened train
   Each motley form of fickle, light or vain,
   Builds the strong fabric of that love sublime,
   Which conquers Death, and triumphs over Time."

A. L. BARBAULD.

From her sister's, Sarah Taylor went to stay at Creeting Mill, in Suffolk, with the parents of Mr. Austin ; and her mother wrote to her from Norwich :—

"Of your being happy I could scarcely doubt, for if there is one thing finer than all others in this mortal state, it is the conviction of being preferred by the person whom we prefer to every one, and that there are such solid grounds of preference as to bid defiance to time and circumstances. In the description of fictitious attachment, the termination of difficulties is the termination of interest—to you may it bring only additional ties! We are all proud of being agreeable to Mr. Austin, and I have no fear of continuing so, for our attractions (if we have any) are not holiday suits, just as upon gala days, . but the usual appearance of our characters, as you know—who certainly ought to know us best. Mr. Staff and Mr. Roscoe drank tea with us, and the latter poured forth a stream of entertainment and friendliness, of taste, literature and politics which I heartily wished both you and Mr. John Austin could have enjoyed with us. I have been hearing to-day real eloquence, though of a peculiar kind, as you may suppose, being from Mark Wilks at the funeral of Jonathan Davey. It produced the proper effect of eloquence—that of riveting the attention of fifteen hundred people. My affectionate regards to Mr. and

Mrs. Austin, to John what you please, and everything you please, and to yourself your father's blessing as well as mine."

Mr. Fox, the eminent Unitarian clergyman, afterwards M.P. for Oldham, mentions dining at Mr. John Taylor's, jun., in May, 1816:—"Amongst the party was a Mr. Austin, a young man preparing for the Bar, of very strong and original mind. 'Who is he?' I asked of Richard Taylor. 'He is likely to become our brother-in-law.' Alas! thought I, thou art a false prophet in predicting that Sally Taylor's triumphs are at an end." Later on in the same book (Mrs. Eliza Fox's 'Memoirs'), he writes:— "I have just seen Sally Taylor, but alas! how changed —from the extreme of display and flirtation, from all that was dazzling, attractive, and imposing, she has become the most demure, reserved and decorous creature in existence. Mr. Austin has wrought miracles, for which he is blessed by the ladies, and cursed by the gentlemen, and wondered at by all. The majority say, it is not natural, and cannot last. Some abuse the *weakness* which makes her, they say, the complete slave of her lover; others praise the *strength of mind* by which she has so totally transformed her manners and habits."

In 1818, Mr. Austin was called to the Bar, having left the Army, which he entered at a very early age, and in which he served for five years, chiefly in Malta and Sicily, under Lord William Bentinck. The following year he married Sarah Taylor, and the young couple took the upper part of No. 1, Queen Square, Westminster, next door to Mr. James Mill, and close to Mr. Jeremy Bentham. Two people more unlike it would have been difficult to find—Mr. Austin, habitually grave and despondent ; his wife, brilliantly handsome, fond of society, in which she shone, and with an almost superabundance of energy and animal spirits. Life opened brightly, and in answer to a happy letter of thanks for a wedding present from the young bride, her mother's old friend, Mrs. Opie, writes :—

" Before I perform my other duties of the day (praying and washing excepted) I will fulfil the pleasing duty of writing to you. . . .

I wonder I have written so proper and virtuous a letter, as I have just been reading 'Don Juan' through (that being, not one of the duties, but of the intended sins of the day). I have long made up my mind to read it, if it fell in my way, and also to own I have read it ; as I should think it a greater vice to tell a lie about it, than to read it—if it were worse than it is. And when I heard some highly virtuous and modest women tell me they had read it, and were 'not ashamed,' and when I recollected that I had read Prior, Pope, Dryden and Grimm, I thought I would e'en add to my list of offences that of reading 'Don Juan.' I must say that the account of its wickedness is most exaggerated. Wit and satire it abounds in, with here and there tenderness, pathos and poetry worthy its distinguished author. To be sure, Donna Inez does seem meant for his wife, but I almost excuse this bitterness, though the creature should not have published it. *She*, I think, did more than becomes a wife, *whatever her provocation*—to undraw the veil a wife ought to throw over the frailties of her husband, and I think, too, she had little temptation to do it. The world's feeling would of course have been with Lord Byron's forsaken wife. Why then enter into details of his guilt which could only serve to blacken the fame of her child's father, and were not wanted to avenge her.   She was excused—every one knew the character of Lord Byron.   Why then did she, as if in self-justification, make every one in her circle acquainted with his most secret depravity?   I never can excuse Lady Byron's conduct, though I can make allowances for her as a spoiled child, and a flattered woman, who never knew contradiction till she became a wife.

Let me, dear *Austina mia,* hear from you.   I could not give you a greater proof of my affection than writing you this long scrawl, when I am writing sometimes eight or ten hours a day.   I *know* a circumstance now often written and talked of but which I never knew really happened before.   Rosalind was wrong.   For I *know* a lovely girl who has 'died for love.'   Aye! a letter came from her lover in India, saying he could not marry her, because he loved her no longer.   Three days she pined, was restless, miserable.   She then suddenly put her hand to her head, and exclaimed, 'Ah! my brain! my brain is on fire!'   To this succeeded deafness, blindness, delirium and insensibility.

On the third night she died, blood gushing from her nostrils.   Poor thing! she fell a victim, in 'the flower of youth and beauty's pride,' to man's perfidy.

God bless you, dear.

" Ever yours affectionately,
" A. OPIE."

Many diaries and letters of that time mention Mrs. Austin.   She is " My best and brightest " to Lord Jeffrey ; " Dear, fair and wise " to Sydney Smith ; " My great ally " to Sir James Stephen ; " Sunlight through waste weltering chaos " to Thomas Carlyle (while he needed her aid) ; " La petite mère du genre humain " to Michel Chevalier ; " Liebes Mutterlein " to John

Stuart Mill, and "My own Professorin" to Charles Buller, to whom she taught German, as well as to the sons of Mr. James Mill.

The following skit upon Jeremy Bentham was written about this time by Charles Austin, brother-in-law of Mrs. Austin, who had then just left the University where he shone as a man of intellect, and a brilliant orator and converser :—

"A CARD.

ORIGINAL IDEA WAREHOUSE,

QUEEN SQUARE, WESTMINSTER.

Jeremy Bentham, Codifier and Legislator to the French and Spanish nations, and the world in general, condescendingly informs Mankind and Reformists in particular, that he continues to carry on business as usual at his Hermitage, Westminster, *for reputation only*. Executes orders with everything but despatch. All sorts of Political Plans, Projects and Schemes, built. Old Plans fresh cast, corrected and re-modelled, equal to new. Words coined, Motives analysed, Intrinsic Values examined, and Moral Prejudices decomposed, and carefully weighed. Jeremy Bentham will not be answerable for any articles unless bearing the unequivocal marks of his workmanship : Originality, Unconsecutiveness, Ruggedness, and Elaborate Classification. All others are counterfeit.

N.B.—No credit given (but as much taken as can be obtained)."

CHAPTER V.

IN June, 1821, Mrs. Austin's only child Lucie was born,
and the bright hopes of the young wife were rapidly
fading. Mr. Austin was physically unfitted for the
profession he had chosen ; sensitive and nervous in the
highest degree, he could do nothing rapidly or imperfectly, he distrusted himself and was deficient in readi-
ness and self-reliance. Absolutely intolerant of any
imperfection, he recast and polished a phrase until he
could no longer find a fault. I think that Mr. J. S. Mill in
his 'Autobiography' has given an excellent and a fair
estimate of my grandfather, though no words can
describe his extraordinary eloquence when talking on
any subject that interested him. Mr. Mill writes :—

"During the winter of 1821-22 Mr. John Austin
kindly allowed me to read 'Roman Law' with him.
These readings with Mr. Austin, who had made Bentham's best ideas his own, and added much to them
from other sources and from his own mind, were not
only a valuable introduction to legal studies, but an

important portion of general education. He was a man of great intellectual powers, which in conversation appeared at their very best ; from the vigour and richness of expression with which, under the excitement of discussion, he was accustomed to maintain some view or other of most general subjects ; and from an appearance of not only strong, but deliberate and collected will ; mixed with a certain bitterness, partly derived from temperament, and partly from the general cast of his feelings and reflections. The dissatisfaction with life and the world, felt more or less in the present state of society and intellect by every discerning and highly conscientious mind, gave in his case a rather melancholy tinge to the character ; very natural to those whose passive moral susceptibilities are more than proportioned to their active energies. For it must be said, that the strength of will of which his manner seemed to give such strong assurance, expended itself principally in manner. With great zeal for human improvement, a strong sense of duty, and capacities and acquirements the extent of which is proved by the writings he has left, he hardly ever completed any intellectual task of magnitude. He had so high a standard of what ought to be done, so exaggerated a sense of difficulties in his own performances, and was so unable to content himself with the amount of elaboration sufficient for the occasion and the purpose, that he not only spoilt much of his work for ordinary use by overlabouring it, but spent so much time and exertion in superfluous study and thought, that when his task ought to have been completed, he had generally worked himself into an illness. From this mental infirmity (of which he is not the sole example among the accomplished and able men I have known), combined with liability to frequent attacks of disabling, though not dangerous, ill-health, he accomplished, through life, little in comparison with what he seemed capable of ;

but what he did produce is held in the very highest estimation by the most competent judges. . . . There was in his conversation and demeanour a tone of high-mindedness, which did not show itself so much, if the quality existed as much, in any of the other persons with whom I at that time associated."

Mrs. John Taylor writes to her daughter in 1821 :—

"Did you see the *Quarterly Review* on 'Huntingdon's Works and Life' with this passage : 'Perhaps some of our readers may think that in the days of Alderman Wood, Jeremy Bentham and Dr. Eady (whose fame is written in chalk upon all the walls), we have bestowed too much attention upon an inferior "quack."' ? It is a fine thing to know a man like Mr. Bentham, who will speak out and expose such a farrago of mystery and absurdity as the Church Catechism, and all its foolish formularies. We have lost our friend and neighbour, Crome, after a few days' illness; his pictures and his pupils are in high estimation, and will rise in value now he can paint no more."

Early in 1822, Mrs. Taylor writes to tell Mrs. Austin how ill her father had been, and continues :—

"It is great comfort to hear of your animated little being. If she should keep up to her present measure of health and activity, she will begin to walk by the time you visit Norwich. I am glad, too, that you do not find a life of economy such an insuperable bar to good society as some people imagine. I have not found it so ; but perhaps opinions differ upon the term *good society*. If things go on in their present course, lavish expenditure will go out of fashion, and retrenchment, both public and private, must be the order of the day. Men who are really superior to common prejudices seem always glad to find women who can understand them and feel with them. Your house must be eminently useful to your husband's brothers—they are all to be admired. No part of my past life gives me more pleasure on reflection than those hours which were devoted to the company of young men just entering into life, many of whom have expressed the warmest gratitude for impressions made during our confidential intercourse. What say you to the marriages of Lord Albemarle and Mr. Coke? The former, we understand, has made choice of a lady who enters into his plans of retrenchment, which he says shall not induce him to follow the fashion of abandoning his county; but to take the more manly course of shutting up the superfluous rooms at Quiddenham, and discharging all his servants save one man and two women, living in the meantime upon the mutton and other produce of his farm. But what, you will say, could induce Mr. Coke to marry a blooming girl of twenty? Just what induces many men to marry. The conviction that he had inspired her with an attachment to him which young and very amiable men had in vain sought to produce in her mind: it is not in human nature to be insensible to so flattering a distinction, especially at an age when the probability of making such impressions grows weaker. . . ."

Though the Austins were poor, the learning and glowing eloquence of Mr. Austin and the talents and beauty of his wife, made their house a resort of the most remarkable and cultivated people of that time. The knowledge, rare in those days, that Mrs. Austin possessed of Italian, and her kindness and helpfulness, made her the great centre of the Italian refugees. These were the men who in 1821 helped Charles Felix of Savoy to turn out his brother ; and the first use he made of his power was to persecute his instruments. The Chevalier de Santa Rosa, Prandi, Radice, Cocchi, Floresi (Marquis de Boyl), Ugo Foscolo, Vecelli (lineal descendant of the great painter Titian), and G. Pecchio, were some of them. The latter writes to her :—" I shall preserve sincere gratitude and an everlasting memory of you, the protecting saint of the refugees, a saint as beautiful as any Raphael has painted." Mrs. Austin exerted herself to help them in different ways. Cucchi and Radice she sent to Norwich, and interested her own family and Mrs. Opie to find them Italian lessons. I give a very quaint letter from Santa Rosa, who was exceedingly liked and respected by all who knew him, in what he truly calls his " outlandish English "—

" DEAR MADAM,   December 26, 1822.

" I like you because you are good, and because your gentle, beautiful face express faithfully your goodness. I could not easily close the list of because . . . but I won't omit this. I like you because you are most affectionate in the world to your fireside. Let, let foolish people open a large yawning when they must remain at home one whole day. I pity them, almost I despise. I know a country-man of mine, gentle and pretty creature, who one day tell so to his friend : ' Alas ! I give handsome present to people who will be able to learn me to use the twenty-four hours of every day.' Shocking ! twenty-four hours in every day. This gentleman, however, is presently a outlaw. Who would guess it !

I am a little tired of the dinner I was present to yesterday, yet that meeting was much pleasing to me. I was sitting near to Ugoni, and at the left side sweet

Arrivabene stood with much calmness. The first don't forget to talk of your *radicalism.* The second increased very much in my favour. *Il entre de plus en plus en grâce auprès de moi,* telling scripturally, and for useful interpretation, of my bad English.

I received yesterday a very dear letter from one my friend, whom I like heartily, from where we were yet at nineteenth year of life. He is a physician, very fond of his profession, humane, disinterested towards his sicks; perseverant, prudent friend; he likes children of mine as well as they should be proper things of him. His letter gives me a diligent account of those unfortunate children—diligent and favourable, much favourable; you know I wish only two things in the world. My country's deliverance; and obscure, private life amongst my wife, my tender wife, and my children. A glory; I think it vaporous dream. Affections enjoyed in peace; dreams, perhaps, but clear and delicious dreams.

I hope to see you to-morrow at two hours afternoon. Let you remember that I will be very much angry with you if you shall wait for me only one minute.

Let forgive my outlandish English, and believe me

Your faithful friend,
SANTA ROSA."

The last letter written by Mrs. Taylor to her daughter was in February, 1823. She says:—

" I should be very ungrateful if I did not thank you for your kind communications, as they keep up the idea of our darling's progress, besides so much interesting matter respecting those martyrs to the cause of freedom, for whom one must feel such powerful sympathy. This winter is an unfortunate one for Italian constitutions, and illness must be a bad aggravation of their other sufferings. No wonder they are eager to be with one who can both converse with them and feel for them. You know how desirous I was of your being accustomed to speak those languages which are now so useful. I rejoiced that you accomplished it so well. Those billets of Santa Rosa show his heart and mind. The English ones prove what difficulty attends the expression of ideas in a strange tongue, and I observe the similarity of his attempts and other foreigners with whom I was formerly acquainted. The mortification of being with such people and having no access to their minds is very great. It would now exclude you from some of your greatest enjoyments. You inquire about Cucchi; the only intelligence I have had is from Mrs. Opie. She likes him and will endeavour to procure him pupils; she thinks him more fit for the world than poor Radice, who is too sensitive and delicate. Little Henry's longings to be with Darling are natural; children are very sociable beings. Enjoy your precious child, dear Sally, while trifles amuse her. I learned from experience to regret the growing up of children. With their infantine pleasures I knew what to do, but when they begin to long for more elaborate enjoyments I have been often puzzled to know what to grant and what to deny. I suffered when a child from too strict a regimen. It led in some instances to concealment, which is always dangerous."

Through her father's position as one of the prominent Whig leaders in Norwich, Mrs. Austin became acquainted with the leaders of that party in London; the life-long friendship with Mr. and Mrs. Grote must also have begun as soon as they settled there, for I find frequent references to visits to Threadneedle Street. Jeremy Bentham was much attached to Mrs. Austin, whom he called his great-grandchild.

The old sage introduced M. Charles Comte, son-in-law of Jean Baptiste Say, to the Austins. He had been condemned to prison under the Bourbons for his bold political writings in the *Censeur Européen*, but by his wife's help escaped to Switzerland. At Lausanne he was named Professor of Law, when the French Government objected to his nomination and even threatened the Swiss Federal Council. Becoming aware of this, and not wishing to be the cause of annoyance to Switzerland, M. Comte went to England in 1823 ; he was then writing his 'Traité de Législation,' while Mr. Austin was beginning his work on 'Jurisprudence.' In 1825, M. J. B. Say went to England to see his daughter, and put his son to learn engineering with Mrs. Austin's brother Philip Taylor.

In 1826 was started the project of creating a London University, where a general system of education should be established independent of all religious teaching. The promoters of the scheme were chiefly members of the various dissenting bodies, and Liberals in politics. Mr. Austin had, after a long struggle, in which his health and spirits suffered severely, given up practice at the Bar, and he was selected to fill the chair of Jurisprudence, which it was proposed to found at the new University. Mrs. Austin was writing for many of the periodicals of that time, and was too busy to go down to Norwich to see her father. His last letter to her was in May, 1826 :—

" The last number of the 'Retrospective' is not yet in our library ; I shall soon have it, and search for your articles. You do not point out your papers in the 'London.' You'll think me squeamish, but I had rather you had let alone the review of the memoirs of the detestable Madame de Pompadour and all her vile satellites.

Give my love to your husband ; tell him I rejoice in the fame he has gotten by his paper upon Joint Stock Companies. Give a kiss to dear Lucie. . . ."

The following month Mr. Taylor left Norwich, intending to pay a long-promised visit to his eldest brother in Dublin. At Birmingham his son Philip met him, and on the way to his house at Corngreaves the horse ran away down a steep hill. The reins broke, the carriage was upset, and all the occupants more or less hurt. Mr. John Taylor was carried senseless into the house of Mr. Brewin, near the scene of the accident, where he died on the 23rd June, 1826, aged 76. Few men were more missed or more deeply mourned. Simple and unostentatious, a trusty friend and exemplary parent, his integrity and excellent understanding had given him a high position in his native city.

Some of Mr. Austin's friends—Messrs. Bingham, Macculloch, Strutt, C. Austin, and others—had started an annual review of Parliamentary proceedings, which did not live many years ; for that he wrote the article on Joint Stock Companies to which Mr. John Taylor alludes, and which is mentioned in the following letter from Jean Baptiste Say :—

(TRANSLATION.)

Paris, April 26, 1826.

" I have received, dear madame and friend, the ' Parliamentary History and Review,' with a letter from Mr. Bingham. I immediately had a notice of the work inserted in the ' Revue Encyclopédique,' which occupies itself chiefly with serious subjects, and is the only journal which has any circulation in foreign countries. I have announced it in the way I think most likely to draw attention here, for English affairs are judged differently out of your island. I do not hope for many readers in France except in Paris, or in Switzerland save in Geneva. Perhaps we may get more in Holland and in Brussels; certainly in the United States, where the language will facilitate matters. For my part, I read Mr. Austin's article on the Joint Stock Companies with the greatest satisfaction, and I am entirely of his opinion. Comte also read it with extreme interest. It is an excellent idea to have preceded the Parliamentary debates with an abridged sketch of Bentham's political sophisms. . . . The misfortunes of the Greeks arouse great sympathy in France; we are indignant with our infamous Government, which protects the Turks. The truth is, kings, nobles, and priests are doing their best to make themselves obnoxious, and are succeeding admirably. We are raising subscriptions for the unfortunate Greeks, and have already collected 100,000 francs, a great deal when you consider that the feeling of the Government is entirely the other way, and that in our country the administration has a thousand ways of annoying individuals.

CHAPTER VI.

Letter from Mr. Austin to Mr. Grote on London University Professorship—Residence at Bonn—Schlegel—Niebuhr and German society.

THE first stone of London University (now University College) was laid in April, 1827, with great solemnity, by the Duke of Sussex ; and Mr. Austin determined to go to Germany, in order to prepare himself by studying what was done by the great jurists in that country.

The following extracts from a letter of his to Mr. Grote will show with what ardour he threw himself into his work, and how conscientiously he carried out the task he had set himself :—

Mr. Austin to Mr. Grote.

DEAR GROTE,   December 9, 1827.

Since my return to Bonn in the beginning of October I have been busily engaged with my lectures, and in consequence of a great improvement in the state of my health I have of late pursued, and am now pursuing, the work with hope and ardour, as well as with my wonted assiduity. Unless I be crippled by a return of my old disease, or by the intrusion of some unexpected cause of anxiety, I shall be ready (I am confident) at the opening of the London University. The following is the manner in which I pass my day :—From eight to twelve, work ; from twelve to two, exercise ; from two to four (or half-past), dinner, rest, and reading some light book ; from thence to ten or eleven, work. Consequently I have already made a considerable progress towards the attainment of it. Taking the 'Institutes of Gaius' (a clear, concise, and elegant exposition of the Roman Law), *not* as my guide to the *rationale* of Jurisprudence, but for the purpose of helping my memory to the subjects with which it is conversant, I have nearly completed a review of it in its whole extent, settled the departments under which it could be distributed, with the order in which they could be arranged, prepared a set of *loci* for the reception of thoughts and quotations, and reduced a great number of the distinctions, the most difficult to express, to a form which I think they may retain. With my subject completely conceived and distinctly divided, with its details collected and arranged, and with enough of it *expressed* to serve me for a month or two in advance, I could enter upon my course without hesitation. And I trust that the impulse which I have now gotten will carry me onward to this point, at the least, before the opening of the University. It is only at the outset, if ever, that my lectures will be attended by hearers *not* students in the University. Although, therefore, at the outset I shall try to make an impression by manner as well as by matter, it is only at the outset that I shall be nice about style. After a time I shall even venture upon *extempore* elocution, introducing it at first with reserve, and only in the less important places, but gradually extending the use of it as I wax in boldness and fluency. Nor could I do my duty the worse for doing it less laboriously. Extemporaneous lectures are not only more flexible than written ones, and therefore better fitted to enter the apprehension of the student, but are also more likely to rouse and fix his attention by the greater earnestness and animation with which they are naturally delivered. I am so satisfied of this, that if I were not afraid of breaking down for want of the habit of extemporising, I would certainly begin my course with nothing prepared but matter and method. Even as it is, I shall not *write out at length* beyond the extent which I have mentioned, nor shall I begin to write out at all till within two or three months of the opening lecture. If I began earlier, I fear that I should be tempted to polish the expression at the expense of more important objects—just ideas, and clear, compact management. . . . For my own sake, and for the good of the London University, I wish to obtain a better knowledge of the routine pursued here than it has yet been possible for me to acquire. As my imperfect knowledge of the language would have disabled me from following the professors, and my attendance upon their lectures would have been time thrown away, I have as yet heard none. At present, however, I am almost in a state to hear them with advantage, and shall soon begin to attend them. I was present last Saturday evening at a sort of lecture (followed by tea, coffee, and conversation) which W. v. Schlegel gives once a week at his own house to the *beau monde* of Bonn ; and, difficult as the language is, I understood almost everything that fell from him. But though I have attended no lectures, a young Doctor of Law, who is a *privatim docens* (*i.e.* a professor, but not formally appointed or salaried by the Government), attends me four times a week, for an hour each time, and reads law with me. He is a friend of Mr. Niebuhr, and as good a subject as I could have hit upon. He has studied at Göttingen under Hugo, and at Berlin under von Savigny. On the whole, I think my residence here will be of great use to me. Though the Philosophy of Law is in a backward state amongst the Germans, such of their expository books (particularly on the Roman Law) as I have run through appear to me to be models of arrangement, and to abound with learning. . . .

E 2

Mrs. Austin describes the manners and customs of Bonn to her sister Mrs. Reeve and to Mrs. Grote in the following letters :—

Mrs. Austin to Mrs. Reeve.

Bonn, January 2, 1828.

Life here glides along; they smoke and eat, walk and dance; the studious men pore over researches which have neither object nor excitement to a busy, active spirit; the women cook, and knit, and higgle for "pfennigs," but one does not see the strife and the struggle, the carking care, the soul-consuming efforts to get and to spend that are the pride and the curse of England. Alas! we English pay dearly for our boasted energy, industry, activity, and so forth. Life is a toil and a conflict.

The absence of all that we know (to our cost) under the name of *patronage* here is truly wonderful, and accounts for the great attachment of the people of all classes to their King. It is really attachment, for they have nothing to hope or to gain from favouritism.

On Christmas Eve we dined at von Schlegel's, where I met the only woman I have seen in Germany who made any impression on me—Madame Mendelssohn, wife of a grandson of the philosopher of that name. She is a lovely and sweet-mannered, gracious creature, such as one would love to see anywhere. They are Berliners, and are here only for the winter. She knows but few people, and like me is not much attracted by those she does know. My husband is raving about her, and says if Jurisprudence was not his *belle passion* he should fall in love with her. I sat on Schlegel's right, she on his left; next to me the old President Jacobi, a distinguished lawyer. Professor Welcker, a very agreeable man, and Mr. Beer, a rich and accomplished Jew, and a poet, made up our very pleasant party. Schlegel, like Niebuhr, loves to talk English. My Lucie is quite well and in great favour with men, women and children. Last week she had a party of ten children, and we had great romps, teaching them English games. Of all the people I know here there is only Rittmeister Laroche, who speaks nothing but German, and as he can ride and fight much better than he can judge of language, I am not very scrupulous about my bad German with him. You would be greatly amused at him—such a genuine, rough old Teuton. My husband laughs till he can't sit at his *naïveté* and bluntness, which cover a *fond* of kindness, generosity, and gentlemanly feeling. One reads such characters in novels, but I never saw one till now. . . .

Mrs. Austin to Mrs. Grote.

MY DEAR MRS. GROTE,   Bonn, January 26, 1828.

You can form but a very inadequate notion of the pleasure even the sight of the handwriting of a high-spirited, sensible and accomplished Englishwoman was calculated to give me in this land of dowdiness, insipidity, and slavish, base prejudice as to all that regards our sex. We are apt to think we are worse treated by our *natural legislators* than any of our continental sisters, but " come here a bit " (that is German) and you shall see. My glorious man lays on to them with all the force he can muster in a strange tongue, but the Hercules is in chains, and he feels it, and grows very angry sometimes. What eternal talk must ensue between you and me before the vials of my wrath are at all spent! God will, my dearest Mrs. Grote, that you may be in a condition to encounter this charge of tongues without physical detriment!

By-the-bye, my husband told you, did he not, of his soirées at W. v. Schlegel's? They are pleasant enough, and to hear him speak his language is, be the matter what it may, pleasure and profit to a learner. They say there is only one man in Germany who speaks it so well, and that is Tieck. Among the countless feuds which divide this little town is one (I perceive) between the partisans of Niebuhr and of Schlegel, the two most distinguished men here. We have perhaps offended both by taking part with neither. I speak this only conjecturally, for Niebuhr has been as attentive to us as he is to anybody ; and Schlegel, considering we had no letter, more so than we had any right to expect. Niebuhr came to wish me a Happy New Year, and brought me his life of his father, which is interesting from the rooted spirit of democratical pride and determination it betrays. The tone in which he speaks of his ancestors, free *yeomen* (so to speak) of Friesland, will please Mr. Grote.

I am delighted with him, and only wish it were possible to see more of him. He has strong *rapports* with our friend Mr. Mill. Schlegel is as different as a man can well be—profoundly indifferent, apparently, to public affairs, but eminently agreeable and well bred. Niebuhr is complained of here as hard and dogmatical. I need not say that he interests us the most, but Schlegel is excellent company. He speaks French like a Frenchman, and English extremely well, even elegantly. He has a young Norwegian living with him and assisting him in his Oriental researches. The Government has taken a surprising affection for Oriental history and antiquities. Mr. Weber, a very clever, well-informed young bookseller here, and a good Liberal, says this is the latest thing hit upon to divert the attention of people who have leisure to think, from matters of public importance. What is grievous in Germany is that, with a few such exceptions as Niebuhr (to whom all honour for his courage), the Governments can always command the time, talents, and pens of the vast body of *gelehrte* into any frivolous unprofitable channel they will. Accordingly the history of letters affords nothing like the mass of useless labour and research which the German press is always putting forth. This is peculiarly striking in regard to a subject it seems difficult to treat without a regard had to the end—*i.e.* jurisprudence. This difficulty, however, my husband assures me, the German jurists labour, with no trifling success, to overcome; and he says many of their books appear rather more to belong to the department of Bibliography—histories of Editions, Codes, etc. Nevertheless, he is quite satisfied with what his studies here have produced to himself. He goes on with the utmost steadiness and with unvarying cheerfulness and satisfaction. I believe with all my heart, my dear and most valued friend, that you will rejoice to see his excellencies come to view and my anxieties cease. If his health does but stand, I fear nothing. Our dear child is a great joy to us. She grows wonderfully, and is the happiest thing in the world. Her German is very pretty—she interprets for her father with great joy and *naïveté.* God forbid that I should bring up a daughter here! but at her present age I am most glad to have her here and to send her to a school where she learns, *well,* writing, arithmetic, sewing, knitting, geography, and, as a matter of course, German.

We are in a state of blissful ignorance of all that can grieve Whig or Liberal hearts. My family write to me, but they say not much of such matters.

In God's name, therefore, write, my dear Mrs. Grote! not to mention that all people who write, do not write like yourself. Mr. Mill, I suppose, is not to be thought of; but if you know ever a good Christian who would —Eyton Tooke for instance—I should be humbly obliged.

Our theatre closes after one more representation.   I

pay about a guinea for the whole season, and have had
a very good pennyworth of pleasure and improvement.
The subscription to four balls for us both is three
thalers. But forgive my demands on your "precious
sight." When you can, do write again, and believe me,
with the most cordial affection and esteem,

Yours,

SARAH AUSTIN.

CHAPTER VII.

*The Austins return to London—German influence on Mr. Austin
—Mr. J. S. Mill's opinion—Letter from M. Say to Mrs. Austin
—Letter from M. de Beyle on peculiarities of Englishmen—
Mrs. Austin on the advantage of learning German—Opinion
of the London University—Charles Villiers—Contributions to
the New Monthly—Invitation from Bentham—Mr. Austin's
lectures published—Death of Bentham.*

IN 1828 the Austins returned to London, and Mr.
Austin's Lectures opened with a class which exceeded
his expectations.   Mr. J. S. Mill writes : *

"The influences of German literature and of the
German character and state of society had made a very
perceptible change in Mr. Austin's views of life.   His
personal disposition was much softened ; he was less
militant and polemic ; his tastes had begun to turn
themselves towards the poetic and contemplative.   He
attached much less importance than formerly to outward
changes, unless accompanied by a better cultivation of
the inward nature.   He had a strong distaste for the
general meanness of English life, the absence of enlarged
thoughts and unselfish desires, the low objects on which
the faculties of all classes of the English are intent.
Even the kind of public interests which Englishmen care
for, he held in very little esteem.   He thought that there
was more practical good government, and (which is true
enough) infinitely more care for the education and

* 'Autobiography.' J. S. Mill.

mental improvement of the people, under the Prussian Monarchy, than under the English representative government ; and he held with the French 'Economistes,' that the real security for good government is 'un peuple éclairé,' which is not always the fruit of popular institutions, and which, if it could be had without them, would do their work better than they. Though he approved of the Reform Bill, he predicted, what in fact occurred, that it would not produce the great immediate improvements in government which many predicted from it. . . He never ceased to be a utilitarian, and with all his love for the Germans, and enjoyment of their literature, never became in the smallest degree reconciled to the innate-principle metaphysics. . . . He professed great disrespect for what he called 'the universal principles of human nature of the political economists,' and insisted on the evidence which history and daily experience afford of the 'extraordinary pliability of human nature ;' nor did he think it possible to get any positive bounds to the moral capabilities which might unfold themselves in mankind under an enlightened direction of social and educational influences."

Mrs. Austin from the first had thrown herself into all her husband's pursuits, and in spite of her many literary occupations she had an extensive correspondence, both for herself and for Mr. Austin. In April, 1828, M. J. B. Say writes to her from Paris :—

M. J. B. Say to Mrs. Austin.

[TRANSLATION.]

MADAM AND DEAR FRIEND,

I take advantage of my eldest son's visit to London to send you the first volume of my 'Cours d'Economie

Politique,' which is just out.   There will be six vols.,
and if it please God, or the Devil, they will be published
in the course of this year and the next.   It will be seen
in this volume, and still more in the following ones, that
I consider my subject in conjunction with Social Science
in its entirety.   For the economy of society consists of
a continual interchange of good offices which Political
Economy rates at their proper value ; appraising the
things of which we may have need, and the conditions
on which we may obtain them.   I submit these views to
Mr. Austin.

All this does not prevent me from being very angry
with you for not having come to Paris now, during the
season, and seeing in what our studies of Jurisprudence
consist.   Instead of this, you are coming (*if* you come)
in August, when every one is overwhelmed with heat·
and dust, when all the schools are closed—when—when
—in short, your project lacks common sense.

Yours ever,
J. B. SAY.

A very different letter is the following from that
spirituel writer, M. de Beyle (Stendhal), which is full of
what Miss Aikin calls " airy French grace ":—

M. de Beyle to Mrs. Austin.

[TRANSLATION.]

MISTER TRANSLATOR,   1828.

I beg you to cut out any repetitions and to suppress
what may appear improper.   I am discontented with
myself, I am serious and lengthy, a caricature of the
style of Tacitus.   There are too few words for each idea ;
in the *Edinburgh Review* there are never more than
four ideas in a page.   Recounting takes up a deal of
space ; I wanted to show what it is that makes us laugh

in the 'Sous-chef,' but I read my two first pages to an Englishman and he did not understand a word. Do try and lengthen my two pages into three. Shakespeare does not know how to laugh like Molière; I love Rosalind, and I am touched by the tender Jaques in the forest of Arden—it is gold, it is diamonds, but it is not laughter. Have you ever remarked the wonderful art in 'Le Médecin malgré lui'? I advise you to read it. M. T—— rewrote his Julien six times, five different versions were rejected by the Censor. Very likely M. Joubert wrote his delightful 'Sous-chef' three or four times. Those four peasants dressed in decent clothes, which they wear so ill, and who for twenty minutes, during all the last part of the book, gravely turn over the pages of their fat account book, instead of listening to what is said, are inimitable. Do you think my readers will understand that? It seems to me that except when they read Shakespeare, Byron, or Sterne, no Englishman understands "*nuances;*" we adore them. A fool says to a woman, "I love you"; the words mean nothing, he might as well say, "Olli Batachor"; it is the *nuance* which gives force to the meaning. Read the Memoirs of Cossé, then you will understand the French faculty for laughing. Do you know Le Dictionnaire du Bas Langage? You cannot understand Molière and the "langage parlé de l'High Life" without it; but the word *low* language, what horror it would cause in a country of aristocrats! There you will find *ab hoc et ab hac*, which means "by chance," "a thing not to be attended to," "to attach no importance to." When I tell an Englishman anything funny or odd, I am obliged to explain for a quarter of an hour (what a pleasure!) to prove that I have told the truth. No Frenchman can keep a secret; we are only agreeable when we talk; we must talk: as soon as a Frenchman of good society has nothing more to say, out come the secrets.

You ask about a meeting at Granada? M. de Chateaubriand was once desperately in love with Madame de Noailles. She said to him, " What are you doing in Paris? A man like you shrivels up in a salon. Go to Jerusalem, return by Barbary and Spain, and I swear that you shall find me in the ruins of the Alhambra at Granada." It came to pass, and Madame de Noailles did not at all lose her reputation. She died some time ago, and M. de Chateaubriand wrote down the anecdote. His present mistress told me that it is in his best style. Forgive my rambling nonsense, as I don't even know your name, I write as though I had known you for ten years.

To her sister Mrs. Reeve, who was then living at Geneva for the education of her son, the present editor of the *Edinburgh Review*, Mrs. Austin writes in 1829 :—

Mrs. Austin to Mrs. Reeve.

. . . My husband has been better and worse, and better, and so on. He has now passed two months or more without an attack. This appears but a pittance of time for a man engaged in the most extensive and diffi- cult of all studies, to rearrange all his dissipated ideas and to collect the scattered and mutilated fragments of long and nearly perfected chains of thought and arrange- ment. Yet this is a longer reprieve than he has had for a considerable time. He is now going on with spirit. Many times, however, since I wrote last, he has entirely despaired of being able to commence his public career, and I have held myself in a state of constant prepara- tion for any decision he might take, and have accus- tomed myself to look steadily at the abandonment of all our prospects here for ever. Indeed, those who know what a life of prolonged uncertainty and suspense is, will not wonder at me for wishing that the worst were come and nothing left to hope or fear. Not that I do not see the terrible consequences to a hypochondriacal man of living without a fixed employment. This has embittered my gardening—otherwise such a pleasure. In gardening all is prospective. The flower seeds to be raised for next year's blooming, the strawberry runners to be laid down for next spring, the fruit trees to be pruned for next year's bearing—all are done, for I did not like him to perceive anything like *giving up*. Another year, if affairs go well, I shall make my garden much prettier to receive you in. My darling child is now returned from a visit to her grandmamma. She is quite well—grown a great girl, but just the same " herzliches Kind " (Henry will translate) — honest, simple and energetic. Her Latin, which I have kept in my own hands, goes on very fairly. She reads *De viris illustribus* nicely, and parses well. German she keeps up, reading, writing and speaking it constantly. Above all, her own insatiable love of reading keeps her little mind always active ; and her original way of thinking will save her, I hope, from a trivial or vulgar taste in reading. We have had a visit from my dear Mr. Mill, who I lament to say is a good deal broken and aged by two bad attacks of gout. He is most kind and affectionate. Have you seen his admirable book ? Henry will oblige me and serve himself by reading it with the attention it deserves. Tell him particularly to observe the part on Naming, on Abstract Terms, Relative Terms, etc. Victor Cousin has sent me his ' Cours de Philosophie.' This is a very different sort of book, but, though not so much to my taste, I love and respect the author's mind and intentions with all my heart. My prince of pupils, John Romilly, has re-commenced his lessons. We are reading an easy sketch of the History of the Roman Law—very interesting to me. I hope Henry is learning German. I am more and more convinced that *en fait de langage* it is the most important acquisition an Englishman can make. The characteristics of German literature are dispassionateness of inquiry and reality of knowledge, and these are singularly valuable to the native of a country where everything is impatiently pushed forward to answer the ends of immediate gain . . .

Mrs. Austin to Mrs. Reeve.

Park Road, London, April 12, 1830.

. . . My last account of the University, of its prospects and of ours as connected with it, was full of gloomy forebodings. I cannot say that, looking at the institution at large and for any permanent futurity, these are much removed. It is the opinion of many, I almost fear of most, that it contains within itself the seeds of dissolution. The expenditure has been lavish, the plans are ill-digested, and vibrating, like all things in which the Whigs have a hand, between the desire of being popular and the fear of being unfashionable, so as of course to satisfy neither class whom they seek to conciliate by cowardly half-measures. The Council are not united, and the Professors as a body are openly at war with the Council. With neither body would my husband ever have anything to do. Most wisely he has kept utterly aloof, having to do, as he says, solely with his class. With them he is upon the most delightful terms, and at variance with nobody. This is quite worthy of him. Since I wrote, he has received the agreeable notice that his guarantee will be continued another year, so that for another year, beginning from next Michaelmas, we are secure of the means of living. His fees for this year have amounted to £120, so that the University has not, as in the case of several of the

Professors of modern languages who have literally no classes, to make good the whole sum. These guarantees, which will have lasted for two years, will be discontinued at the end of this session. The Latin, Greek and Mathematics do very well, and pay sufficiently. My husband thinks that even if the University were to fail, he should by that time have established a reputation as teacher of Law which would always enable him to get a class somewhere. I think there is good ground to believe this. Romilly and John Mill both assure me that they know of several who do not enter now, only because the course is so far advanced, and who will undoubtedly enter another year. He has, since I wrote, two new pupils, one a Mr. Tuffnell, the other a son of Mr. Frankland Lewis, who you know is in the Ministry. A good-natured lad who comes often to see me, and is the dandy of the class (a son of Sir Alexander Johnston), says it is really very agreeable to attend Mr. Austin's class—it is such a gentlemanly one! There is the handsome and fashionable Charles Villiers, the young M.P. Charles Buller, and the three Romillys, Mr. Tuffnell, Mr. Lewis, and so on. This will enable us to fetch up our leeway, for the two last years were cruel ones, and put us sadly back in everything. We shall now get afloat again, and then, come what may, shall start clear. I am now translating monthly a certain portion of scraps for the *New Monthly*, from my favourite German prose authors. The first number they appeared in was that for April. These bits were done only for the private edification of my friend John Sterling, but he thought them worth giving to the editor. I have now, too, undertaken another trade, namely, giving lessons in Latin. My aunt Lizzie wrote to ask me whether I would consent to give lessons to the only daughter of her old friend Mr. Minskull. So Lucie and I trot down to Bentinck Street with our bag of books, and quite enjoy it. I do not fancy myself at all degraded by thus agreeably earning a guinea a week, and if anybody else does, he or she is quite welcome to avoid my society, as I inevitably should his or hers. I have had two or three pleasant evenings lately after lecture. My young friend Charles Buller's father and mother have come three times to tea, and I have had the Bellenden Kers, John Mill, John Sterling, Charles Austin, Miss Goldsmid and her brother, Mr. Wishaw, Mr. Tuffnell, Mr. P. Johnston, Charles Romilly, and Mr. Otway Cave, M.P., in three brigades to meet them. The latter, who sits for Leicester, and has great Irish property, is a constant visitor, and has a perfect furore for bringing people. Yesterday he walked in, ushering Sir Francis Burdett; now he asks my leave to bring O'Connell. Of course I let him, and am only amused at the whim. He is a violent Liberal, and having nothing to do, likes, I suppose, to sit and talk politics for ever and ever. *Au reste* he is very good-natured, and a prodigious puffer of my husband, which may have its use. John Mill is ever my dearest child and friend, and he really doats on Lucie, and can do anything with her. She is a monstrous great girl, but, though she has admirable qualities, I am not satisfied with her. She is too wild, undisciplined and independent; and though she knows a great deal, it is in a strange, wild way. She reads everything; composes German verses, has imagined and put together a fairy world, dress, language, music, everything, and talks to them in the garden; but she is sadly negligent of her own appearance, and is, as Sterling calls her, Miss Orson.

*　　*　　*　　*　　*　　*

Jeremy Bentham writes to Mrs. Austin in August, 1830, when Mr. Austin had gone to see his sister :—

Mr. Jeremy Bentham to Mrs. Austin.

August 25, 1830.

Odd as it is, I am still alive. Are we ever to see one another again? If yes, I propose, or name, a distant day—next Wednesday—to make the surer—or any day hereafter (the nearer best) that you will name. You are a widow bewitched. To return in the evening to your own abode would not be (practically speaking) possible. Myrmidons for escorting you back I have none. The bed-chamber your mother once occupied is vacant; should that not quadrate with your notion of propriety, in Bell Yard, within twenty feet of my street door, is a bed-chamber, in which you would be under the care of the wife of a tenant of mine, a perfectly decent woman. I never saw it, but it has been occupied, with marks of satisfaction, at various times, by guests of mine, more than once.

Your loving great-grandpapa,

J. B.

Mrs. Austin to Mrs. Reeve.

Dear Sister, London, April 12, 1831.

That which ought to be the greatest consolation and pleasure to me—writing to you—is become a pain. Often in the midst of some depressing event I have felt irresistibly prompted to sit down and vent all my despondency to you—then again I have said to myself, why afflict her? I have heard that you are well and happy, grown fat and handsome, *rajeunie de dix ans.* I knew that the good news I sent you of my husband's health would give you great satisfaction, knowing as you do, that that is the mainspring of good and evil to me. Would I could confirm it now! I think you do not know that when he was to begin his lectures in

November, he actually had no class, so that they were deferred till January, and he now lectures to eight. At first he bore this shock wonderfully, considering what it must be to a man who has devoted the whole of such a mind as his, and all its stores, to that one object. He did not flag or despond in the least. He merely said— what was sufficiently evident, that it was now decided that we could not live here ; that he would go through his course as well as if his class were ever so numerous, and at the end of it send in his resignation. In all this I acquiesced ; but as I could not endure that he should quit the University and England, and leave no proof of what a man the institution and the country were sending forth, for want of all encouragement, or even the most humble means of subsistence, I entreated him to publish the earlier part of his course, containing the basis of Jurisprudence, which I knew to be separable from the less generally interesting details. At first he quite rejected the idea ; but on my placing before him many arguments which appeared to me weighty, he consented, only saying that he could incur no risk, neither could he send for a publisher, but that if I would find one and negotiate everything, he would print them. You may imagine I was not slow to undertake nor to accomplish this. After two interviews, Baldwin undertook the business, and but for several untoward things they would now be out. I cannot express to you the approbation this move of mine has received from all his and my friends ; the Romillys, Street, Booth, Mill, Duckworth, Empson, Erle and many others have told me it was the best thing I ever did, and could not fail to establish his reputation. A passage from one lecture has appeared in the *Examiner*, and been copied into several provincial papers with great approbation. But what avails all this while everything here is pursued, not as a science, but merely as a craft ? We cannot live on air, but must go somewhere where our little means will support us. Plan we have none. You know how much my inclinations are with Germany. He at present seems rather to think of Paris, where he says he would devote himself entirely to constructing a complete Corpus Juris—such an one as might live for ever and be a text-book for all future codifiers. You may imagine that I could willingly make any and every sacrifice to so noble a project. I have had an immense deal to do—Lucie's entire education, nursing John, needlework, writing, etc. Lucie now goes to a Dr. Biber, who has five other pupils (boys), and his own little child. The being relieved from the constant wear and fret of seeing my dear child not half-educated is an immense thing. She seems chiefly to take to Greek, with which her father is very anxious to have her thoroughly imbued. As this scheme, even if we stay in England, cannot last many years, I am quite willing to forego all the feminine parts of her education for the present. The main thing is to secure her independence ; both with relation to her own mind and outward circumstances. She is handsome, striking, and full of vigour and animation.

In 1832, just when the Reform Bill had been carried, Jeremy Bentham died. Mrs. Austin saw him a fortnight before, and he gave her a ring, which I now have, with his portrait and some of his hair let in behind, with "Memento for Mrs. John Austin. Jeremy Bentham's Hair and Profile," engraved on it. He kissed her affectionately and said, "There, my dear, it is the only ring I ever gave to a woman."

CHAPTER VIII.

Mr. John Sterling on Mrs. Austin's translation of Prince Pückler-Muskau, and on Miss Martineau—Mr. Austin publishes his 'Jurisprudence Determined,' and is appointed a member of the Criminal Law Commission—Letters from Mrs. Austin to M. Victor Cousin—Letters from Mr. Thomas Carlyle on the state of Politics and Literature.

IN 1831 Mrs. Austin translated Prince Pückler-Muskau's book, 'Tour in England, Ireland and France,' which was published the following year, and is alluded to in the following letter by John Sterling, written from Colonaria, Cape St. Vincent :—

Mr. John Sterling to Mrs. Austin.

MY DEAR FRIEND,   July 9, 1832.

Since that evening when John Mill took me to your house and introduced me to you, I think I have never been so long as of late without either writing or speaking to you. In the meantime you must have been abundantly busy as well as myself, and I trust you are little likely to suppose that my silence proceeded from forgetfulness. Indeed, I have been in some sort conversing with you, for I have been reading the travels of that Prince Prettyman, to whose book you have shown so much more favour than you would have bestowed on the author ; and I have been also reconsidering in an old number or two of the *N. M. Magazine* the specimens of German genius, which I like much better. I do not deny that your *protégé*, the Prince, is rather lively, and perhaps as things go in Germany, a good deal of a gentleman, in spite of his bad waltzing; but his utter ignorance of the literature, morals, politics, and religion of England, is ill-compensated by some dashing sketches of scenery, and by his wearisome descriptions of the manners of a small knot of people who, so far as I ever saw, were despicable and ridiculous in the eyes of the great body of their more decent countrymen. The most disgraceful part of the business is Goethe's praise of the Tourist. You do not admire or respect him, but the ablest German since Luther, or at least since Leibnitz, does both; and I can only regard the fact as one among many evidences of the mischief of attempting to realise in life the theory, striking and seductive as it is, which all Goethe's works (so far as they are translated into English) so exquisitely inculcate. Of course the falseness of his doctrine does not, in my opinion, depend for proof on the consequences of the endeavour to put it in practice, but this is the kind of evidence which will always be most powerful with the multitudes. Long ere this you will have received a budget of my MS. It is possible that Murray (of whom my father knows something) might publish it—or perhaps a man of the name of Moxon, who seems to affect a conscience, and deserves encouragement for that decorous hypocrisy. The preface and the motto ought, I think, to convince my readers—even without a portrait—that my mustachios are in truth at least as formidable as Prince Pückler-Muskau's! It would be great fun if you were to edit me after translating him; but if you think my book a botch, pray do not soil your fingers with it. In principle I am still far more inclined to Coleridge than to any other writer I know, and I read him with ever new delight. If I had not feared to disgrace him by the homage, I would have dedicated my novel to him, as to my greatest intellectual and moral benefactor. I heartily long that you, dearest friend, and all others whom I value could join me in the common ground of love and reverence for that wise old man. Of what I have lately read I will say nothing, except that I am sorry to see Buller (in the *N. M. M.*) stationary at the point at which he stood when I first knew him—now, alas! some seven years (how spent by both of us) agone—and that Miss Martineau, with all her extraordinary zeal and talents, has given a very absurd picture of the West Indies. If, as I believe, she has no semblance of authority for the incident of the bloodhound, her delineation is positively wicked. She is ridiculously wrong as to the mode of cultivation pursued here, and her representation of the negroes' wish for the ruin of their owners is, I believe, quite erroneous, saying nothing as to whether it would be really beneficial to the slaves or not. At all events, I have seen negroes after a hurricane and she has not, and I know that it both is a calamity to them, and that they feel it to be so.

God keep you from the follies and misery of all around.

Ever, my dear Friend, yours sincerely,
JOHN STERLING.

In June, 1832, Mr. Austin gave his last lecture, and published his 'Province of Jurisprudence Determined.' In the following year he was appointed by Lord Brougham, then Lord Chancellor, member of the Criminal Law Commission. Though this turned him to a narrower field than that he had marked out for himself, he entered upon it with conscientious devotion, and carried into it profound and comprehensive views. He, however, soon found that the powers granted to the Commission did not authorise the fundamental reforms he conceived necessary, and that his opinions differed from those of his colleagues. Every meeting left him disheartened and agitated, and his health suffered considerably. Mrs. Austin brought out her 'Characteristics of Goethe,' in 1833, and 'Selections from the Old Testament,' besides writing articles for various periodicals; as she said to a friend, "I think I am the busiest woman in the world."

The chief interest of Mrs. Austin's life was Popular Education ; she had been for some years collecting facts about the primary schools in other countries, and she wrote to her friend M. Cousin :—

Mrs. Austin to M. Victor Cousin.

[TRANSLATION.]

26, Park Road,
March 5, 1833.

VERY DEAR FRIEND,

Your reports will I hope be a benediction for England as well as for France. My husband and I are always talking of them. I almost cried when I read them, to the infinite amusement of my friend Jeffrey (the Lord Advocate), who is enraged at my being touched by a report. Oh no, my dear friend, I am not a Radical, far from it ; but read the description of our factory children —unfortunate victims of our commercial greatness— and then mock at me if you dare, for being dissatisfied with a Government who permits so many innocent creatures to be condemned to nothing but suffering. Mr. Babbage, our great mathematician, quietly told me the other day, that calculations showed that in the manufacturing towns a whole population exists who are "*worked out*" before attaining thirty years of age! Such words make me shudder. Is it possible to speak thus of our brothers ; of human beings born with brains, hearts, and

souls? But I am persuaded that the remedy will not,
cannot come from the people. How many and what
cultivated intellects it needs to throw some light on this
question ! To return to our reports. Can you send me
a few more copies? It is important to get the *Times*
to notice them. I have lent all mine to members of
Parliament, who promise me that they will mention
them in the House. I have spoken to a publisher, and
we intend to bring out a translation—a cheap one—so
that the people may see what is being done elsewhere.

I write in great haste; my husband is ill and I am
overworked, but always,

Your affectionate,
S. AUSTIN.

Mrs. Austin to M. Victor Cousin.

[TRANSLATION.]

April 2, 1833.

You are an *ingrat* not to write to me and send me
copies of your Reports. If you did but know how
I am working for your glory! 1st. There will be a
slight notice of them in a note in the next *Edinburgh*.
2nd. I have met Barnes, the omnipotent editor of the
Times, and have preached to him ; ditto the editor of
the *Examiner*. 3rd. I have written an urgent letter
to Edward Strutt, M.P. for Derby. Bickersteth,
Empson, and Romilly, all the men of any note that I
know and have mentioned it to, say there cannot be a
better man than Strutt. He has my copy of the
'Prussia ;' after him it goes to Empson ; then to Sir W.
Molesworth, the young member for Cornwall, whom I
have converted—not to Radicalism, but the reverse—to
the opinion that the people must be instructed, guided
—in short, governed.

We still think of going to reside at Bonn. People all

exclaim and regret, and are *au désespoir*, and I am quite "the fashion"—but that will not enable us to live. Do you see Charlatan Brougham's speech throwing up National Education entirely. I told his friend Jeffrey what I thought of it. God bless you, my dear friend, for your good works! certainly the education of the people is the one all-important duty of rulers. Brougham's reputation is sinking faster than it ever rose. Ten thousand pities—he had such capabilities, everything but—sincere earnestness.

We are all well, write and tell me how you are, and believe me ever

Affectionately yours,
S. AUSTIN.

Thomas Carlyle, whom she had known before through the Bullers, and introduced to several of her friends, writes :—

Mr. Thomas Carlyle to Mrs. Austin.

Craigenputtock,
June 13, 1833.

MY DEAR MRS. AUSTIN,

A hurried word is all I can send you in return for your kind, good letter, which spoke to us, as all your letters do, like the voice of a Friend. Many things remind us of you ; to my Wife I believe you are literally the best of all womankind ; neither for me is there any figure in that huge city whom I can remember with purer satisfaction. This, if it be a comfort to you in your brave life-fight, is a quite genuine one. Continue to bear yourself like a brave, true woman, and know always that friendly eyes and hearts are upon you. On my own side, too, I will say that the interest you take in my poor, small and so sorely hampered toils is a great encouragement, a great increase of strength to me. It is something surely that the words out of my heart speak sometimes into such a heart, and find response there; that you find them not utterly vain, and my little Life a kind of Reality and no Chimæra. Could I one day so much as resemble that Portrait you possess of me, and persist in calling like! But alas! alas! However we will be content; *alle Frauen*, says Jean Paul, *sind geborne Dichterinnen*, bless them for it, most of all when their art comes our own way!

Your Falk, which has long been expected, will prove a most welcome present; the extracts I see in the Newspapers whet my curiosity. I might have had the original in Edinburgh; but waited for your English with the Notes.

We have heard often of your purpose to leave England, a thing sad to think of, to hear confirmed as near at hand. Yet how shall one gainsay it? Your view of the case is most probably just and accurate; your resolution on it the best. Let us not add lead to the bravely buoyant; rather than think of you as lost, I will lay schemes how we may cross the Channel ourselves, and pass some winter beside you! Were that not a scheme? After all, more unlikely things have come to pass. We shall see; we shall hope, and to the last keep hoping. *Der Mensch*, says F. Schlegel almost pathetically, *in dieser Erde ist eigentlich auf Hoffnung gestellt;* this is called the Place of Hope. Will you then, in that case, undertake to "do the hoping" for us all?

My own course is utterly dubious at this moment; the signs of the times are quite despicable in England, nothing but a hollow, barren, jarring of Radicalism and Toryism for unmeasured periods, likely enough to issue in confusion and broken crowns; in which struggle I as one feel hitherto no call to spend or be spent. Alas! it is but a sowing of the wind, a reaping of the whirl-wind. The stern destiny and duty of this and the next generation; for which duty, however, there is enough and more than enough volunteering to do. Meanwhile Literature, one's sole craft and staff of life, lies broken in abeyance; what room for music amid the braying of innumerable jackasses, the howling of innumerable hyænas whetting the tooth to eat them up? Alas for it! it is a sick disjointed time; neither shall we ever mend it; at best let us hope to mend ourselves. I declare I sometimes think of throwing down the Pen altogether as a worthless weapon; and leading out a Colony of these poor starving Drudges to the waste places of their old Mother Earth, when for the sweat of their brow bread *will* rise for them; it were perhaps the worthiest service that at this moment could be rendered our old world to throw open for it the doors of the New. Thither must they come at last, "bursts of eloquence" will do nothing; men are starving and will try many things before they die. But poor I, *ach Gott!* I am no Hengist or Alaric; only a writer of Articles in bad prose; stick to thy last, O Tutor; the Pen is not worthless, it is omnipotent to those who have Faith. "Cast thy bread upon the waters, thou shalt find it after many days." And so we look into this waste fermenting Chaos without shuddering; and trust to find our way through it better or worse.

In any case, fail not to tell us what you decide on, consider us as deeply interested in whatever befalls you. On the whole I have still a hope that somehow you will not go; at least not till we have met again.

The Faust, second part, had reached Edinburgh before I left; I read it there with such interest as you may fancy. Several years ago I had occasion to study Helena, and particularly noted that Chorus you mention. I consider the whole Play now completed as a thing wide, wide before me, and deep; into which I have not seen half way. Some new scenes bear traces of feebleness, many are very beautiful ; happily the Plan, the noble Idea, can be deciphered there, not feeble or old, but young for ever.

Charles Buller is the Free-carrier of this letter ; pray tell me of him and his, for he never writes. And now, dear Friend, *Gott befohlen !* My wife joins me in all kind salutations to Lucykin and to Mr. A. and you.

Ever your affectionate,
T. CARLYLE.

Mr. Thomas Carlyle to Mrs. Austin.

Craigenputtock,

MY DEAR MRS. AUSTIN,   July 18, 1833.

Your three beautiful Volumes were here sooner by your conveyance than they could have been by mine.* We have all read them, with pleasure, with eagerness ; for me, I could not skip even what I knew in German already, but must have it taste for me a second time in your fine clear-flowing English.

A Book more honestly put together I have not met with for many years. A discreet gentle feminine tone runs through it, with quiet lookings nevertheless into much, much that lies beyond the English horizon ; no compromise with error, yet no over-loud assertion of the truth ; unwearied inquiry, faithful elaboration ; in a word, the thing *done* that is pretended to be done : what other praise could I wish to give you ?

I perceive that Falk has been the root or nucleus of the whole, yet so much better than Falk have you made it, I almost regret you had not left him out altogether : a dull *undiaphanous*, semi-diaphanous kind of man ; one cannot see Goethe through him, only see a *huge singularity.* Some of the speeches, especially that about

---

* ' Characteristics of Goethe, from the German of Falk, with Notes.'

Schulze, I must endeavour to consider as mis-reported not a little. However, you, with your appendages and fringings, have done wonders, and actually almost (with such a deft, assiduous needle) *worked* a silk-purse out of what the Proverb says will never make one. Had but a Boswell stood in Falk's shoes, there had been a task worthy of you !

Leaving Falk (which was worth turning into English, too), I find nothing else that is not instructive, much that is gracefully so ; of your doing, nothing, as I said, that is not well done. You have fairly and clearly (and in your case almost heroically) stated the *true* principle of Translation ; and what is more, acted on it ; I hear the fine silver music of Goethe sound through *your* voice, through your heart ; you can *actually translate Goethe*, which (quietly, I reckon) is what hardly three people in England can. And so let me heartily wish you all manner of success ; and scientifically *promise* you as much as in these strange days almost any Book merely artistic in character can hope for. Finally, I said several times in words, and here again say in ink, that you may find a higher task one day, than Translating ; though I praise and honour you much for adhering to that as you now stand, and keeping far from you all ambition, but the highest, that of living faithfully. *Das weitere wird sich geben.* Stand by that ; there is nothing else will abide any wearing, let the voice of the Reviewer be high or low, and millions of caps or none at all leap into the air at your name.

I have very little time this evening ; and no business to devote so much of it even to you ; but the Pen must on. We shall eagerly expect news within those three weeks ; Jane says, the Letter is to be *hers.* She farther declares, with that promptitude which so well beseems the female intellect, that you ought to come *hither !* There is an excellent house and garden to be let (for almost nothing) within few miles of us ; and no cheaper country can be found in the whole world. Then there is such abundant room in *this* house of ours ; and it were so easy for you to come and investigate the whole matter and see us to boot. In this latter part of the proposition, I too must heartily give assent and encouragement ; it is all literally true about the *room ;* about the welcome there is still less doubt ; and then the journey were no unpleasant thing ; the rather if you held John Mill to his word, who has as good as promised to see us here this autumn. After all, what if you should really take thought of it?

In the meantime, again accept my thanks and friendliest wishes ; may all Good be with you and Lucykin and the heart to conquer all Evil !

Ever affectionately,

T. CARLYLE.

CHAPTER IX.

Sir W. Hamilton on Popular Education—Insufficiency of English legal education—Mr. Austin lectures at the Temple—Mr. Carlyle on British Reviewing, on |house-hunting—Prof. F. W. Carové, author of 'The Story without an End'—Mr. R. Southey on Mrs. Austin's translation of Cousin on Instruction in Prussia—The Provost of Eton to Mrs. Austin—Mr. Charles Buller to Mrs. Austin.

SIR WILLIAM HAMILTON, whom Mrs. Austin had asked for books and annotations on popular education, writes :

Sir Wm. Hamilton to Mrs. Austin.

MY DEAR MADAM,   Edinburgh, Jan. 14, 1834.

I expect some books from Hamburgh on the primary education of different countries of Germany, but from the rapidity with which it will be obviously proper that you bring the *Rapport* out, there is little probability of their being here in time to be of any use. The Elbe will be frozen for some time yet. My stock of pedagogical works apply chiefly to the higher departments—the learned schools and Universities of Germany. In regard to my co-operation, you may command any little assistance I can lend. But I am sensible that it must be too unimportant to allow me to take advantage of your prepossessions in my favour. If anything I can do is worth mention at all, a word in your preface will be honour enough. In fact I do not recollect any topic on which I could say anything in the way of annotation, unless it be a few pages on the history of popular education. Even on that subject I am not *well* prepared; and I do not know where any good account is to be found. I know, however, the ordinary sources, and have a few notes taken in my reading. These I will either send you (who would do this far better) or work them into a kind of narrative myself. Perhaps, however, M. Cousin is to perform this—that would be best of all. If, therefore, you persevere in your plan, you may depend on anything I can do. I quite agree with you in thinking that your translation should be made a cheap book nothing goes down now that is dear, and it is in the present case desirable that the public should be as generally interested in the question as possible. The subject has already apparently taken hold of attention, and nothing can ensure success so much as the diffusion of such information and reasoning as the *Rapport* contains. Believe me, my dear madam, with much regard,

Ever truly yours,
W. HAMILTON.

The insufficiency of the legal education of the country had for some time attracted the attention of the more enlightened part of the profession ; and it was determined in 1834, by the Society of the Inner Temple, that the principles and history of Jurisprudence should be taught. Among the most earnest promoters of this scheme was Mr. Austin's friend, Mr. Bickersteth, afterwards Lord Langdale.* Mr. Austin was engaged to

---

* See 'Greville Memoirs,' vol. iii. p. 138. Melbourne said "Bickersteth was a Benthamite, and they were all fools." I said, "The Austins were not fools." "Austin? Oh, a d——d fool ; did you ever read his book on 'Jurisprudence'?" I said I had read the greater part of it, and that it did not appear to be the work of a fool. He said he had read it all, and that it was the dullest book he had ever read, and full of truisms elaborately set forth. Melbourne is very fond of being slashing and paradoxical."

deliver a series of lectures on Jurisprudence at the Inner Temple. Had this appointment been made under different conditions it was one he would have preferred to any other, however distinguished or however lucrative. Unfortunately it was not of a kind to give him the security and confidence he wanted. He was invited to undertake the discouraging task of trying to establish a new order of things, without the certain, though distant, prospect which usually cheers the pioneer in such an enterprise. The uncertainty weighed upon him from the first. He was disqualified by nature from all work of a passing and temporary sort; and in order to labour with courage and animation, he needed to see before him a long period of persistent study, and security from harassing anxiety. His precarious health and depressed spirits required support; and he was but too easily disheartened at what he thought the want of confidence in the scheme, or in him, evinced in a merely tentative appointment. The severe feverish attacks to which he had always been subject, became more frequent, and at length his wife induced him to abandon his lectures and go to Hastings to try and recruit. She published her translation of Carové's charming ' Story without an End,' dedicated to her daughter, whose favourite book it was.

Mr. Thomas Carlyle to Mrs. Austin.

Craigenputtock, Jan. 21, 1834.

Many thanks, my dear Mrs. Austin, for your kind messages and memorials : two Notes, through the Advocate, then the dainty little book,* with another Note; all of which have now arrived safe, the last only this day week. It is an *allerliebstes Büchlein,* graceful in spirit as

* ' The Story without an End.'

in embodiment and decoration ; and we all participate in Lucie's love of it ; but fancy there will be children enough (of six feet high and lower statures) in this "envy of surrounding nations" to ask : What does it prove, then ?

I have learned lately, by various cheering symptoms, that British Reviewing had as good as died a natural death, and the Lie lied itself out ; that the most harmonious diapason from the united throat of universal British Criticism would hardly pay its own expenses. Rejoice, my dear Friend, that you can now sit apart from that distracted gulph of abominations ; and pray for those that must still swim for their life there.

We learned long ago through Mill with the truest satisfaction what turn affairs had taken with you ; that the Labourer, at length, was found worthy at least of *some* hire. The greater is now our regret and apprehension when Jeffrey informs us that Mr. Austin's health again threatens to fail. Your own health too, it seems, is bad ; you have to complain of disspiritment, now when you have need of all your strength. " Rise, noble Talbot, this is not a time to faint and sink : force faltering Nature by your strength of soul," etc. Alas ! it is so much easier said than done ; and yet in Life one must often try to do it. For on the whole, my dear Heroine, there is no Rest for us in this world, which subsists by toil. " Rest ? " said the stern old Arnauld, "shall I not have all Eternity to rest in ? "

You speak playfully of coming hither to see us. Would it were in earnest ! I think there were few faces welcomer here to all parties interested. If the Sun were north again, and the days bright, what if you should actually put it in practice ! I do not think you ever in your life saw such a solitude as this : the everlasting skies and the everlasting moors ; the hum of the world all mute as Death, so distant is it—till Wednesday nights arrive, and the Letters and Newspapers, and we find it is all going on as distractedly as ever.   Come and see it and try it.

As for myself I think I have arrived at a kind of pause in my History, so singular is the course of things without me and within me.   I have written very little for a year; less than for any of the last seven.   I stand as if earnestly looking out, in the most labyrinthic country, till I catch the right track again.   A kind of *enfant Perdu*, I believe, at any rate, yet who would so fain *not* perish and leave the breach unwon!   We shall do our best.

Write to us soon; my wife says you still owe her a long letter : there is so much we *need* to hear.   And so good-night, dear Friend,

Yours affectionately,
T. CARLYLE.

Mr. Thomas Carlyle to Mrs. Austin.

Craigenputtock,
March 20, 1834.

MY DEAR MRS. AUSTIN,

My date, you perceive, is the 20th, and your letter did not reach us till late in the evening of the appointed 19th.   We have at the utmost only two Post-days weekly here—in general, only one (the Wednesday, which answers to your London Monday); and though last week, as it chanced, both Post-days did their duty, your Express unhappily fell between them ; and so here we are.   My whole soul grows sick in the business of house-seeking ; I get to think, with a kind of comfort, of the grim house six feet by three which will need no seeking.   In return, I ought to profess myself humble in my requisitions as to that matter.   I must have air to breathe ; I must have sleep also, for which latter object, *procul, O procul este*, ye accursed tribes of Bugs, ye loud-bawling Watchmen, that awaken the world every half hour only to say what o'clock it is!   Other indispensable requisition I have none.

The house which Lucykin and you describe so hopefully seems as if it had been expressly built for us. Our answer is at once, secure it for Whit-Sunday, if it be still attainable.   Till we hear otherwise, we will still have a kind of hope that it may.   If you do so prosper, there will be various other inquiries to trouble you with, various minor arrangements to tax your kind discretion with.   For example, what *are* the fixtures, beyond grates?   We have window-curtains, Venetian blinds, etc. etc., which will be useless here, which might chance to fit them.   The measured dimensions of all the rooms and windows (if you can procure them) will bring the whole matter before us.   The general outline of the Housekin I already have, by assurance of Imagination ; a sunk story, three raised ones, the little bed-quilt of garden before the house or behind it, as it shall please the Fates. You must, on the whole, consent to consider us as a Brother and Sister in this matter ; and pray lend us your head as well as your affection.

My Dame bids me say that as to carpets (since those here, not indeed of great value, will go waste if left) nothing can be decided till we know the sizes, and, according to your judgment, the quality and cheapness. The only thing that will be certain of that sort is, perhaps, a fixture already—some sort of wax-cloth for a lobby.

I look to London with bodings of a huge, dim, most vexed character.   Never shall, with my whole heart, have as much of the " Hoping to do yourself " as you can undertake.   In me is little Hope, or only Hope of a kind that I call " desperate "—a Hope that recognises all earthly things to be *Lug und Trug ;* and yet under them, and symbolically hid in them, are *Ewiges und Wahres ;* of this same desperate Hope I have for many years (God be thanked for it!) never been bereft, nay, on the whole, grown full and fuller of it. For the present, I lie quite becalmed. Not *calm*, alas! that is a very different matter. I am doing, and can set at doing, nothing, or as good as that. No line have I written for months; only read whole heaps of Books, with little profit. In any case, befall what may, I see it to be the hest of the Unseen Guide that I should come to you, so I come *getrosten Muthes*. You, my dear Friend, and your kind, hopeful, and helpful words, fall like sunlight through the waste weltering chaos. May the Heavens bless you for it!

And so with all manner of good wishes, and as much of Hope, " desperate " and other, as may be,

Ever yours affectionately,
T. CARLYLE.

My wife, full of cares, tumults, and headaches, and I doubt also of indolence, bribes me to write this letter, not unwillingly, which you are to take as hers, and her love with it."

Carové, the author of the ' Story without an End,' to whom Mrs. Austin sent a copy of her translation, wrote her a very characteristic letter, full of high-flown German sentiment, which it is difficult to render in English.

Prof. F. W. Carové to Mrs. Austin.

[TRANSLATION.]

MOST HONOURED LADY,   Frankfurt, May 23, 1834.

The beautiful little book which you have so kindly sent me was a most agreeable surprise. The ' Story without an End ' is one of the few wild flowers which I have been able to pluck in a pleasant oasis in my jour-ney through life. I almost blush to see it so daintily adorned, as a lily of the valley would hang its head if it were transported into a richly-gilt vase. But when I read your touching and charming dedication to your child, when I see the kindly words you address to the writer of the little tale, I envied the wild flower, to be plucked by such hands, and planted by the love of a mother in the pure heart of a child. It has attained its highest and best destiny. To encourage children's hearts to love the beautiful and the good, to feed them on the flowers which fall on starlit nights like manna from the skies, caught by gentle, poetical hands and distributed to children by the light of day—this is the task you have set yourself, and it is worthy of a true and happy mother. The stars are reflected undimmed and brilliant in the crystal hearts of children ; they assimilate beautiful and noble things into their very being : later, they would only receive more or less deep impressions. I feel proud that you thought my story worthy of translation into your language. I have compared your work with the original, and see with delight that by your art my tale has had the same good fortune as Goethe's 'Faust,' translated by Mr. Hayward. One is tempted to think the translations are originals, and if placed side by side, they might be hailed as twins.

Your ever devoted,
F. W. CAROVÉ.

The same year Mrs. Austin published 'Reports on the State of Public Instruction in Prussia,' translated from M. V. Cousin, with a Preface. Sir W. Hamilton writes : "The execution of your task has done justice to its paramount importance. You must be altogether sick and surfeited with praise, but just let me say that I am entirely of your opinion in *everything* you say in your Preface."

Mr. Robert Southey to Mrs. Austin.

DEAR MRS. AUSTIN,   Keswick, June, 1834.

I have just received your translation of M. Cousin's Report, and with it your note. Our wishes and views on the momentous subject seem to be entirely accordant. I shall enter upon it fully ere long in writing the life of my poor old friend Dr. Bell.

Would that I could see how it were possible to restore the sense of duty, and the principle of religious contentment, in this distracted and corrupted nation, where the whole tendency of public life (in its widest sense) is to counteract the best principles that can be inculcated on education ! Would I could see what is to save a nation from destruction, when the prevailing opinion is that our duty to God and to our neighbour may be dispensed with, and that every one's duty is only to himself !

I shall read your book with great interest. I have never been in Prussia, but what I have seen of the Prussians impressed me much in their favour. There was a national feeling about them which promised well for the strength and stability of their country.; and their government, according to all that I have been able to learn concerning it, seems to have the welfare of the people at heart, and to be doing everything for their improvement that circumstances render possible.

You, I trust, will live to see something done by our Government in the same spirit. But there must first be more regard to religion and morality in its counsels, and then there must be men in authority who know that it is folly, or worse than folly, to erect an edifice upon the sand.

Farewell, dear madam, and believe me, with sincere respect,

Yours,
ROBERT SOUTHEY.

/ The following letter from the Provost of Eton relates
to the translation from the German of a book, which
Mrs. Austin undertook at his suggestion. She alludes
to this book in writing to Mr. Murray (Dec. 26, 1834),
as "Grecian Antiquities, or Illustrations of the Religious,
Moral, Civil, and Domestic History and Manners of the
Greeks, for the use of Schools, by Dr. Heinrich Hase ;"
and to Rev. Mr. Howes (translator of Horace, Persius
etc.) she writes :—

"I have not put my name to it, but have no objection
to tell my friends that it is mine. For the Greek I am
not responsible. The proofs have all gone through
Dr. Hawtrey's hands, as well as those of my friend
Dr. Rosen. The original is written in the worst of bad
German styles ; I hope I have succeeded in making it
more readable."

Rev. E. Hawtrey to Mrs. Austin.

DEAR MRS. AUSTIN,   Eton College, May 26, 1835.

I quite approve of your and Hase's idea about the
burning, and have inserted your alteration in the proofs,
which I had from Murray.

The only thing in the book which I am out of conceit
with is my translation of the 'Swallow.' I do not say
this to draw you into giving it praise which it does not
merit, but merely because it seems to me to be put
forward in too naked a way where its presence is not
excused by the insertion of any other translations. It is
too late now to leave it out, without cancelling a sheet.
I should have kept it for the end, had I not thought Mr.
Sotheby's translation of 'the Home' were to be inserted.
I have seen a great deal of M. de Beaumont, and think
him more like a gentleman than any Frenchman I ever

met. Generally speaking, I think the French (except the good old *aile de pigeon noblesse* and *abbés*) are as unlike gentlemen as possible.

I hope you like Coleridge's 'Table Talk.' Henry Coleridge seems to have done his work very well ; but if the judge had had the same opportunities, he would have done it better. It is surprising to read so much sound practical sense from a man who was all his life the victim of capricious and over-indulged sensibility.

I am just now going to Cambridge to endeavour to persuade my college to give me a living, to which I have all the claim which seniority, and the established custom of giving those which fall vacant to the next in rotation, can give. But it seems that twenty years' hard work at Eton, instead of the same number of years doing nothing in college, is considered an objection.

The narrow-mindedness of college idlers perhaps exceeds that of any other class of men existing.

I shall send for Cochrane's review, and read it with great interest.

Pray make my best compliments to Mr. Austin, who, I hope, finds Hastings as beneficial as at first. My sister sends her kindest regards to you and Lucie, and I am,

Dear Mrs. Austin,
Yours very sincerely,
E. HAWTREY.

Mr. Charles Buller to Mrs. Austin.

MY DEAR PROFESSORIN, London, June 11, 1835.

My speech on the Ballot was indeed most successful. The rascally reporters burked me—merely through indolence, I believe—so that I have not got my due credit in the country ; but in the House the effect was most favourable, and will do me permanent good there. Molesworth's speech was singular, but the House liked its manliness very much. Grote's was capital, in his cold, correct style. Ward's and Strutt's were also good. Nothing could be worse than our opponents' —all of them, especially Lord John's, Stanley's, and Peel's.

When Mr. Austin comes to town, I hope he will come and see us. I don't say now that we can offer him a bed ; but the old Cove dines every day at three, and Mr. Austin will every day be welcome. I am very sorry to hear from you so bad an account of his health. Do you think Hastings agrees with him ? I wish these d—d Whigs would give him a pension, or some good appointment ; but they are a spiritless, heartless *canaille*.

Believe me,
Yours most dutifully,
CHARLES BULLER, JUN.

CHAPTER X.

Mr. Austin s failing health—Moves to Boulogne—Lord Jeffrey on
  Mrs. Austin's prospects—Wreck of the ' Amphitrite,'—M. de
  Tocqueville on French Manners, etc.—Mr. Austin appointed
  Royal Commissioner to Malta— Lord Jeffrey to Mrs. Austin.

MR. AUSTIN had for some time determined to leave
England, and seek an obscure and tranquil retreat on
the Continent, where they might live upon their very
small means. Boulogne was selected, and there the
Austins lived for more than a year, Mrs. Austin busily
occupied translating von Raumer's ' England in 1835,'
which came out the following year.

Lord Jeffrey to Mrs. Austin.

July, 1835.

I take offence at you, my best and brightest ! You
do not think it possible, and you *know* that it is not.
I have never felt anything for you but thankfulness for
your kindness, and admiration for excellencies which
it did me good to think of. If I spoke too lightly of
your trials, it was but in a mistaken purpose of comfort, and partly in the hope of making you think lightly
of them too. One of the cures for despondency is to
look on life as but a poor play, and it is a remedy, or at
least an ingredient in a remedy, and no way dangerous
to those whose temperament is not misanthropical.
Rest assured, my most dear Chit, that before you are
threescore years of age, and have bowed under the load

of the successive bereavements which must be encountered in such a course, aye, and have risen again from the blow, and felt the inextinguishable spirit of love and humanity reviving in the crushed heart, and looking ahead with its old affections on a new earth and a new heaven, you will learn to smile, though more in pity than in scorn, at this unsubstantial pageant of existence ; and feel how much a deep and habitual sense of its nothingness can soften the sense of its ills. Have you not health and a great intellect, and a good conscience, and a kind heart, and devoted friends, and a fair measure of fame and admiration, and a generous disposition, and a pure taste, and a relish for all pure and elegant enjoyments : and a power of engaging love and respect whereever you go, and of valuing the sentiments you inspire ? How dull this writing is ! I think I could talk soothingly to you, if we were sitting in the clear sun on the green·downs near Hastings, or in the soft shade of my dear Kensington, for then I could see your deep grand eyes and your moving lips, and know when to stop or how to go on. But now I may be distressing you, or at all events tiring you to death. Pray forgive me—I have done.

I wish anything to prosper in which you take an interest. But no *radical* publication or radical scheme will prosper in this generation. In mere numbers and physical strength they are far weaker than their opponents (at least as long as wages are tolerable), and taking the wealth, union, and intelligence of the other party into view, the disparity is incalculable. Even in reasoning I think they are the weakest, whatever such dogmatists as your Mill and Roebuck may pretend. For my part I think the Quakers are better political reasoners than they are, and yet nobody, I suppose, seriously expects that we shall all become Quakers. They all forget that one man's political happiness is not another's, and when the Benthamites say that it is mere ignorance and prejudice that prevents their standard from being universally adopted, they forget that some dozen of other more numerous sects say the same thing, and are quite as sincere and confident that theirs is the great truth, and that it alone must prevail. As to the desirableness of meat, clothes, and fire, they are all agreed, but differ widely enough as to the best means of making them easily accessible, and will differ, as well as to the relative value of the higher elements of enjoyment for 5000 years to come. You think all this very poor and shallow, and I dare say it is, but it is not the less true that the Radicals are in a great minority, especially among the reading classes, and consequently that no Radical review will prosper or be able to pay its contributors from natural resources for five quarters.

You know I am a little heretical about education, or sceptical rather, for I do not disapprove of most of your practical views—I only distrust their effects, especially on the morality, good order and manageableness of society. I agree, however, that education should be as much extended and as much improved as possible. Not because I believe it will promote those objects—for I rather apprehend its effect will be the reverse—but because I believe it will increase the range of enjoyment of individuals, far more than it will endanger those objects.

Ever most affectionately yours,

F. JEFFREY.

P.S.—Which of your many portraits had most success in the Exhibition? I must have mine back by-and-bye."

At Boulogne Mrs. Austin made many friends among the fishermen and their wives. From the first "la belle Anglaise" was extremely popular, but her gallant conduct when the 'Amphitrite' was wrecked one stormy night on the Boulogne sands made the whole matelote population adore her.   The 'Amphitrite' was going to Botany Bay with female convicts, and Mrs. Austin, with the extraordinary energy and determination which always distinguished her, stood the whole night wet through on the beach, receiving the few survivors, and seeing that they were cared for.   She saved one woman's life by dashing into the sea and pulling her to land. One of the pilots, " Henin," greatly distinguished himself, and when he went to Paris to receive the Cross of the Légion d'honneur from the King for his gallantry, Mrs. Austin gave him a letter to the Says.   There Henin could talk of nothing but " la belle Anglaise " and her dear little girl and their courage.   The Royal Humane Society gave Mrs. Austin a diploma* for saving life, and one of the poor convicts presented her with a book which was washed up from the wreck and found on the sands.   A curious book it is to have been in a convict ship, 'The Mirrour of Magistrates.'   It was sadly torn and battered, but has been pieced together as skilfully as could be managed.

* At a Committee, holden Sept. 1833, Benjamin Hawes, Esq., F.S.A., in the chair.

It was unanimously resolved—That the grateful and sincere thanks of this Committee are justly due, and are hereby presented, inscribed on vellum, to Mrs. Austin, for the lively solicitude which she manifested for the fulfilment of the important objects of this Institution, on the occasion of the calamitous wreck of the British convict ship 'Amphitrite,' off the port of Boulogne-sur-Mer, on the night of the 31st August last ; when, by her presence of mind, perseverance, and humanity, in conjunction with that of Mrs. John Curtis, she had the happiness, under Divine Providence, to recover three of the mariners of the above vessel, who were washed on shore by the violence of the gale, and taken to the Marine Hotel in a state of insensibility.

(Signed) NORTHUMBERLAND (*President*).
BENJAMIN HAWES (*Chairman*).

The ' Humane Society's Report ' for 1834, page 79.

M. de Tocqueville to Mrs. Austin.

[TRANSLATION.]

Château de Baujy, Nov. 26, 1835.

I should be inexcusable, dear madam, not to have answered your charming letter before, but it waited at Paris for my return from a short journey. I now hasten to reply and to say how much I wish to present Madame de Tocqueville to you. I hope with her to enjoy two things not easily found united in this world—a busy intellectual, and a tranquil calm, home-life. Such is my dream ; and in order to make it a reality, I have had the audacity to choose my wife for myself. Now that the thing is done, a good many people think I acted wisely. But I do not aspire to revolutionise our habits ; many a year will pass by ere marriage, generally speaking, will cease to be anything but an "*affaire.*"

What you say about M. R. and men of his condition is perfectly true. In France, simple and elegant manners are only found among the scions of old families. Others are either vulgar or too particular and careful. This comes, I fancy, from the state of revolution, which still endures ; it is a crisis we must pass through. In the confusion which subsists, new men do not know how to distinguish themselves. Some conceive that rudeness and pushing will make them remarkable ; others, that minute attention to the smallest detail will cloak their low origin. Both are uneasy about the results of their attempts, and their uneasiness is betrayed by affected assurance. Men who are born and brought up with the habit of being by *right* in the first society, do not think of these things ; they have a natural ease of manner, and, without thinking, attain the goal the others strive for in vain. But I trust that a time will come when a model will be established of good manners and good taste, to which you will see all well-educated people conform, just as among the aristocracy there is a certain code to which all bow without discussion, and I may say, without being aware of it.

You see, dear madam, that I preserve my democratic tendencies in spite of your observations. I am an adherent of democracy without being blind to its defects and its dangers; I may say I am so because I see them clearly. I am intimately convinced that nothing will prevent its ultimate triumph, and that it is only by going with the current, and trying to direct it as far as possible towards progress, that the evils may be diminished and the possible good be developed.

I must ask your forgiveness for turning a letter into a dull lecture of political philosophy, but it was you who first started the subject, and you must take the consequences. However, let the world go as it pleases, and let me talk a little of ourselves. You say you are not coming to Paris; I am sorry and surprised. Do you really mean to spend the winter on the sands of Boulogne? Do you not know that a provincial town is the most impossible place in the world, and that there is no medium between a capital city and a desert? The climate of London does not suit Mr. Austin, dulness will drive him from Boulogne, and wherever you go you must pass through Paris. So I shall expect you, dear madam, and hope soon to tell you *de vive voix* that I am always

Yours sincerely,
ALEXIS DE TOCQUEVILLE.

In 1836 a proposal was made to Mr. Austin by the Colonial Office, through his esteemed and faithful friend Sir James Stephen, to go to Malta as Royal Commissioner, to inquire into the nature and extent of the grievances of which the natives of that island complained. He accepted an appointment for which he was peculiarly fitted, and they returned to London to prepare for sailing to Malta. It was not thought advisable to take a young girl to so hot a climate, and Lucie Austin was entrusted to the care of a Miss Shepherd, who kept a school at Bromley Bromley Common.

I have heard that my grandmother's personal merits were taken into account in the nomination of Mr. Austin ; she is not forgotten yet in Malta, for a well-known and popular Maltese, Sir Adrian Dingli, writes to me :—

"Your grandmother was very popular with my countrymen, and contributed largely with Mr. Austin and Mr. Lewis to break down a barrier raised by a clique of old English residents who had for many years successfully worked to keep the *natives* at a distance from the Government and from the so-called society. She took a leading part in the reform of the primary schools, and is still regarded here as a friend."

Lord Jeffrey wrote, on hearing of the appointment to Malta :—

Lord Jeffrey to Mrs. Austin.

Edinburgh,
My very dear Mrs. Austin,   August 31, 1836.

I am so sorry you are going to such a distance ! We thought it bad enough when you spent a summer at Boulogne, and now you are embarking for Malta ! It is difficult to get over that—and I saw so little of you this spring ! And where or what shall I be by the time you return ? Yet, if you like it, it is folly to repine, and if you think it your duty, ought we not all to cheer and applaud you ? Yes, we shall all come right, if you will only give pledges that you will be safe, and not stay away too long. I have not yet heard how long you expect to be ; and what is short at your age, may well be long at mine. But do let me know, and assure me (of what I do not doubt), that neither Turks nor Grecians, nor Knights Templars nor Corsairs, nor Italy nor Egypt or Palestine shall ever divide you from the love of your own dear England, or make you forget those who there love and remember you. No, no ; you are not of that order of beings, though I've basely doubted you of late, and feel this desertion as a sort of judgment on my little faith. As I *must* be forgiven before you go, I am bound to confess my transgressions, and shall therefore state that I have been murmuring to Empson against you, and trying to seduce him from his allegiance, by insinuating that you were leaving your true friends for lords and ladies, and giving up your heart (though large) to vanities and vexations of the spirit—nay, saying in my jealous bitterness, " Let her go to her President of the Council, her canons residentiary, her dandy peda-- gogues, her wits, flatterers and keepers of human mena-- geries, and see what comes thereof in the end ! " It was. worse, and I am bound to add that Empson resisted the infection, assured me I was mistaken, or at all events that we were sure to have you back again when the little experimental course was over, and that I tried to believe him, and had in good faith succeeded, when this fatal Maltese dispensation came entirely to humble my pride, and open my eyes to what I ought always to have seen. Pray pardon me therefore, and let this be penance and humiliation enough. I shall never again relapse into such a heresy.

I have not yet seen your Greek book, and our Bœotian booksellers cannot tell me whether it is published or not. I should have liked better to have something more characteristic of you, to look back to in your absence— your account of the Boulogne sailors, for example ; but that interesting little sketch is thrown aside, I fear, in the fever and bustle of your present preparations. At all events I have your picture, and I cannot tell you how much I prize it. I wish you had something more worthy of you to do than these translations. I shall be curious to see your 'v. Raumer,' though I have a notion that he knows more of past times than of present, and has been too little in England. Do not forget us. Empson and I shall help each other to keep you in dear remembrance, and so farewell, Brightest and Best.

Faithfully yours,
F. JEFFREY.

CHAPTER XI.

Letters to Mrs. Reeve—Voyage to Malta—Arrival in Valletta—
Condition of women in Malta—Cholera and its ravages—Mrs.
Jameson's opinions of America—Mrs. Austin to Mrs. Senior on
the action of the Government—Mrs. Austin to M. Victor Cousin
on Malta.

THE following letters, written during Mrs. Austin's
sojourn in Malta, to Mr. and Mrs. Senior, to her sister
Mrs. Reeve, and to Mr. Murray, will tell of her life better
than I can :—

Mrs. Austin to Mrs. Reeve.

DEAR SISTER,   Lazaretto, Malta, Oct., 1836.

Nothing can be more improving, animating, beautiful,
and unlike the rest of existence, than the first sight of
the interior of an English man-of-war ; the first day or
two passed in her in the midst of all her pomp and
glory, her orderly tumult, her difficulties and her power ;
but the weariness that comes on after some days is
indescribable.   Accordingly, after a ten days' passage
from Marseilles on board the magnificent frigate ' Vernon,'
nothing could exceed our impatience at the calm which
kept us hanging off the coast of Malta, nor the joy with
which we saw the steam-frigate ' Medea ' coming out of
the harbour to tow us in.   I shall never forget the effect
which her rapid undeviating course had upon me, after
ten days of tacking, watching, longing for winds that
would not blow.   It was like the course of a man who
asks no help but of his own judgment and his own

inflexible will, compared with that of a weak and dependent woman shaping her way by every changing mood. In an hour from the time she took our towing rope we were in the great harbour of Valletta. No description, and I think no painting, can do justice to the wonderful aspect. In the first place the many harbours, the way in which the rocky points throw themselves out into the sea ; then the colouring, the points a rich yellow white, the bays deep blue, and both lying under a sky which renders every object sharp, and every shadow deep and defined. The fortifications which grow out of all these headlands are so engrafted on the rocks, that you cannot see where the one begins and the other ends. The high massive walls overlap and intersect at so many points, that there can be no monotony. In the bright sunlight the shadows of all these angles cut the earth or the sea just as variously as the solid walls do the sky. Above all rose the city with its many churches. The most striking objects seen from the port are the splendid Albergo di Castiglia, the lighthouse on Fort St. Elmo, and the Barracca, a row of arches standing on a lofty point and surrounded with trees—the only ones visible. Imagine these walls and bastions, this Barracca, and every balcony overlooking the harbour crowded with people, whose cheers as we entered the harbour rang across the waves and re-echoed from side to side, with an effect that to me, who expected nothing, was quite overpowering. Till this moment I had hardly been conscious of the awful task committed to my husband ; I felt those cheers, eager and vehement as they were, as the voice of the suffering calling for help and for justice. While the officers around me were gaily congratulating me on a reception so flattering, I could say nothing, and turned away to hide my tears.

Innumerable Maltese boats were flitting about the

harbour, all painted bright green and red. Their build is peculiar ; the prow rises like a swan's neck. Most of them have a little flag, those belonging to the Lazaretto being distinguished by a yellow one. They are rowed by two men standing, who at every stroke bend forward and throw their weight upon the oar. Most of them wear the long red woollen shawl, which they get from Tripoli, girded round the loins ; their dress is a blue jacket and blue or white trowsers, and the flat straw hat of our sailors. Nothing can be gayer than the appearance of these boats, while darting through them might be seen all the varieties of man-of-war's boats, with all the characteristics of their nation about them— steadiness, precision, order, promptitude, neatness, and quietness.

As the sun sank in the cloudless sky, the guns from all the ships were fired, and the bells and hum of the city were distinctly audible. The 'Vernon's' barge took us into the Quarantine harbour, which lies on the other side of the tongue of land on which stands Valletta. At the Lazaretto we found Mr. Greig, the superintendent of Quarantine, waiting to introduce us to our rooms, for we are supposed to be infected, as the 'Vernon' came from the Levant to fetch us at Marseilles. The stillness of this very comfortable prison contrasted strongly with the scene we had left, and was a great relief to wearied travellers.

Mrs. Austin to Mrs. Reeve.

DEAR SISTER,   Valletta, Nov. 4, 1836.

If you see Lucie, she can give you a description of our entry—triumphant, I might call it, were it not rather the result of expectation of what is to be done than of satisfaction at any results. Indeed, we all felt it to be very affecting and even oppressive.

I greatly fear that all this popularity will vanish when the poor Maltese find the Commissioners don't make bread cheap and give them work; but we shall see. Their first act was yesterday to send for the leaders of the complainants.

I have already a strong persuasion that much of the disgust and discontent arises from the insolence, prejudice, and want of breeding of the English. If they bully where they are on sufferance (as on the Continent), what will they do where, as the Marchese di Piro said to me, " chaque petit employé se croit un roi." The result is that the noble Maltese families, poor and proud, depressed and insulted, have entirely retired from the society of the English, and the most complete hatred and *éloignement* prevail. Such are the elements out of which I have to make my society.

The English have all left their cards, because they must. The Commissioners are the third persons in the island, having precedence of all but the Governor (when he comes) and the Archbishop. As Sir H. Bouverie has no wife, I take precedence, if I choose to claim it, of every woman in the island; and though you may believe I shall never assert this, yet I suspect the great ladies know it, and like me accordingly. The Maltese, with few exceptions, stay away, because, as the Marchese di Piro said, they tremble at the thought of being repulsed. I have told Sir Ignatius Bonavia, the intelligent judge, to be my mediator with them, and to assure them how flattered I shall be by their visits or how happy to visit them. He and the di Piro family declare that they will be honoured, delighted, touched, etc.; all which I believe, because they are used to such different conduct. But then how will the English ladies bear this—so strong a censure, though a tacit one, on their conduct? Very likely there are causes of disgust on both sides; but I suspect intolerance of all foreign manners and habits, combined with the *prepotenza* of masters, have been carried to great lengths, and have done as much mischief as any acts or system of misgovernment.   You may imagine that I am not on roses.   I regard my Maltese servants as (probably) spies.   I *know* that every word we utter, and every act we do, is watched and reported with the intense interest of hope and fear.   So, my dear sister, my grandeurs have their usual concomitant of *gêne* and anxiety.   I hope by implicit civility, caution, and kindness, to get through my difficult task ; but it *is* difficult.

Mrs. Austin to Mr. Nassau Senior.

DEAR MR. SENIOR,   Valletta, Jan. 12, 1837.

We should be very glad to afford two or three intelligent, inquiring men here an opportunity of referring to some of the English Parliamentary Reports, particularly any on Pauperism or Education, or any of the subjects from which they can expect useful suggestions.   You will do Malta and the Commissioners a great service.   Mr. Lewis has lent Dr. Sciortino, a very clever advocate and leading *Liberal,* your ' Preface to the Foreign Reports.' No country can stand in greater need of enlightenment than this, where marriage is so criminally and disgustingly early and so dreadfully prolific.   I have seen a husband of fifteen ; mothers, under twenty, of four or five children are not rare ; and the recklessness seems to increase with the misery.   One cause seems to me that domestic servants are almost all men ; in our house, five out of six are men, and I cannot help it.   As the cotton spinning and weaving has so greatly declined, there is no employment for girls, and mothers strive to marry their daughters at all events.   One said to me, " Ma che farò delle mie zitelle ?   Con un marito mangiano un pezzo di pane, o bianco, o nero.   Se no, prenderanno la cattiva strada."* All this is true except the *pezzo di pane*, which even *nero* is not always to be got, especially for eight or ten new-comers. I was told to-day that a boy of fourteen who was going to be married had given it up on hearing that the Commissioners had made a law against marrying under twenty. I said, "I hope you didn't undeceive him."

Tell Mr. Stephen I received his wife's kind note, and thank both him and her cordially. Tell him I am assured by several Maltese gentlemen that they think the people would not refuse to emigrate if they could be sure that they would have priests, doctors, etc., with them, and live under the same government and protection as here. It seems they have always imagined they were to be abandoned to their fate. Even these gentlemen seem to have no other notion of colonizing. They call emigrating leaving wife and children for an indefinite time, and going to Egypt or Greece to find work. They are so quiet, sober, frugal and docile, that I should think they would make excellent settlers, if willing.

Such a state of extreme and hopeless destitution can hardly be conceived. The failure of the cotton manufacture—partly caused by the exclusion of Malta cotton from Spain, partly by the introduction of English here—has taken from the people of the Cazals their only means of living, save agriculture ; and how insufficient that must be, you may guess. Lewis and I had half a mind to write to some influential or rich men in England to get up a subscription with a view to allay the present intense suffering. It would have a very good effect on the minds of the people here, as a proof of sympathy ; but Sir H. Bouverie, when I spoke to him, objected, certainly on the soundest principles, to do anything to keep up the

* But what am I to do with my girls? With a husband they will at any rate eat a bit of bread, either white or black. Otherwise, they will go to the bad.

habit of depending on Government or others for aid. I still think, however, a voluntary subscription would do little harm in this way, the Government always steadily refusing succour, as it ought.

A Maltese told me the other day he did not believe it possible that *any Englishman* could have gained the confidence of the people to the degree Mr. Austin had gained it. I allow for flattery ; but yet it is clear they have confidence in the Commission.

The moral and intellectual destitution of the people is dreadful. No schools in the Cazals, no *tolerable* education for the middling classes ; an university whose first professor receives £25 a year, and to which no attention is paid by the Government ; no press, no place for discussion, no intercourse with the English of an amicable and instructive kind—what wonder if they are ignorant and childish ?

The only thing I *cannot* understand is how life is sustained under such circumstances. What I remark is this, When it is a question of laughing at the Maltese, no words can be found contemptuous enough for their poverty. When it is a question to inquire seriously into their state—to give at least pity, attention, reflection, if not aid, then it is all exaggeration ; they are not worse off than the Irish, perhaps not than some of the English. Their landlords ought to help them. The Maltese gentry won't support their poor—reasons for stopping the ear and steeling the heart. I am afraid it is too true that many of the pretty, graceful girls we see about are very insufficiently fed. I find many striking resemblances to the Irish ; there is one great difference— all will suffer any privation to appear decently dressed at church and in the streets ; and this laudable feeling disguises their poverty.

I ventured to send through my sister a petition to Mrs. Senior on behalf of some of the poor girls who make lace. I hope by another packet to send her a little specimen of their embroidery, the beauty and cheapness of which may recommend it. It is chiefly done by daughters of decayed families. Pray give my kindest regards to her. Let us hear of you all, and don't forget your little knot of friends here. Can you tell me anything of John Mill? Remember how precious news of our friends is to us. Our very best regards to Mr. and Mrs. Stephen.

Yours ever,
SARAH AUSTIN.

Mrs. Austin to Mr. Murray.

DEAR MR. MURRAY,   Sliema, June 20, 1837.

I am filled with amazement and alarm at seeing my translation of Ranke advertised as forthcoming.* You have a very erroneous idea of my life in Malta if you imagine I can put pen to paper for anything not immediately connected with the island. From the moment we landed I considered myself as bound to devote my time and thoughts, and whatever little power of usefulness I may have, to the poor neglected Maltese ; and I trust whenever I leave them, be it soon or late, not one among them may be able to say I have eaten their bread and not given them in return my whole time and mind and strength, such as they are. Were they ten times greater, there is ample occupation for them, and they should equally be at their service.

---

* On the 1st of August, 1836, Mrs. Austin had written to Mr. Murray, junior, as follows :—" I forgot to come to an arrangement (with your father) about Ranke. It is just possible, though not likely, that I may find some leisure time at Malta, and I wish to know whether I may regard his desire to have a translation of Ranke as certain." Again (Sept. 19th, 1836) she writes : "We are off to-morrow, early. I take Ranke. Mr. Lewis has the 2nd and 3rd vols. When I see what I can do, I will write you word."

I am sure you understand and respect this feeling, and will not be angry at my delay. When I tell you that in sending out notices that I should be at home every Wednesday evening during summer, I found I had above 250 to direct, and those only to heads of families, you may conceive what it is to keep up the intercourses of civility with such a society, and that consisting of persons whose pride, wounded in various ways, is extremely susceptible, and who value attention above everything.

Added to this are the concerns of the poorer classes. I have been endeavouring to establish a bazaar for the sale of various works of art and ingenuity in which the Maltese excel. . . . But no one who has not been here can understand how entirely it is like having to manage for a lot of children. The Maltese have many excellent qualities : but nothing, absolutely nothing, has been done to cultivate them, and of course they are ignorant, prejudiced, and helpless. The cure for this is not to abuse and despise, but to teach, help, and encourage them. I am racking my brain to invent new works and to improve old, and am at home to all comers upon business. And thus my life goes.

Among other things which I find sunk in the profoundest neglect is Art. There are, or have been, materials for collecting a most interesting museum. Of all who have governed the island, no one seems even to have dreamt of such a thing. Now I fear it is too late. The numerous remains found have been destroyed or dispersed.

I have rashly, and in my zeal to save from ruin at least the design of a curious and admirable work, embarked on a speculation about which, perhaps, my nephew has spoken to you. In the cathedral at Città Vecchia I was struck with some very fine antique *marqueterie* in the choir which seems to have passed wholly unobserved ; and having found a very deserving and able artist, who is perishing for want of employment, I set him to make drawings of the figures. They (the drawings) have come out such as to far surpass my most sanguine expectations, and I take upon me to say that a set of more exquisite illustrations of early art can hardly be found. They are, too, so far as I am able to learn from reference to books, nearly unique, as drawings from figures in *marqueterie*—or, as the Italians call it, *intarsia :* most of the remaining specimens of that kind of work are in arabesque. There are about twenty ; among them a Nativity, which might be a picture by Mantegna for grace and expression, a magnificent St. Michael and the Dragon, St. Barbara, St. Margaret, St. Agatha, Mary Magdalene, etc., wonderful for grace and beauty.

Seeing that this was a work of high antiquity, I made a great stir in the chapter to find out the history of it, and after many difficulties, my excellent friend the Dean found in the Archives of the Dominicans the original contract, between the Chapter of Malta and the Sicilian artists, dated 1488, and written in Latin and Sicilian. This, with a whole history of it, I mean to print. . . . Mr. Camana—the artist—is to lithograph his drawings, and to colour one, at least, after the original. Were I not afraid of being utterly ruined, I should add outlines of the Byzantine pictures, and of two most beautiful crosses of wrought silver, which the order brought with them from Rhodes. The French carried away seven cartloads of silver of the most exquisite workmanship from this church.

And now, my dear Mr. Murray, you are in possession of the whole matter. I do not ask you to help me out of my scrape, if scrape it be, but if you can do anything towards it without risk or injury to yourself, I am pretty sure you will, both for my sake and because you like to do a handsome thing for literature and art.

God knows, these poor people want a patron of spirit and liberality. If I were rich I would ask nobody's aid, and even as it is I will sell my gowns rather than this poor artist shall be disappointed.

. . . . Many other things might be said and written about Malta. If I were a reporter of what I see and hear, and not "*La Signora Commissionaria*," as they call me, I could write you a book cheap at £1000. Not only am I the only Englishwoman the Maltese ladies will admit on a footing of intimacy in their families (warned and disgusted by the insolence they have met with), but people of all classes talk to me with the utmost freedom. Then the pictures I could give, and must give, if I gave any, of colonial manners! This is what England and the world ought to know ; but it is so completely out of my line to deal in personalities that I could not do it, even to answer a great end.

Altogether, Malta is thoroughly peculiar in its physical aspect, its architectural splendour, its wretchedness, in the traces which successive Eastern and Western civilization have left, and which one detects in familiar trifles. . . .

If you knew the misery here, dear Mr. Murray, the misery of the middling and higher classes, you would not wonder that I trouble my friends. Farewell.

Yours very sincerely,
S. AUSTIN.

Mrs. Austin to Mr. Murray.

Sliema, near Valletta,

DEAR MR. MURRAY,   Oct. 18, 1837.

. . . . I must write a line to tell you that my projects are all changed. I find that Mr. Hyzler,* a very admirable artist here, of whose talents I sent some specimens

---

* A friend of Overbeck, with whom he studied in Rome.

to England, has in progress a much more extensive work. With the most meritorious industry and perseverance, he is exploring and drawing the remains of art in Malta — frescoes, oil-paintings, sculpture, tapestry, works in gold and silver—everything. I have been with him and Don Annetto Casolani, one of the Canons of the Cathedral, to see the fine frescoes in the crypt or underground churches in Città Vecchia, and was truly amazed at the quantity of neglected works of great beauty that exist. Mr. Hyzler means to publish his work in numbers ; there will be about three hundred illustrations, all wholly new, never drawn or engraved, and forming a complete series of art from the twelfth century downwards. The beauty of the drawings cannot, I am persuaded, be exceeded, and Mr. Hyzler's profound knowledge of the history of Christian art secures the excellence and trustworthiness of the descriptions. My inlaid figures, therefore, will form but a small part of his work.... I should like to see your name attached to it ; if not, I know you will give me your advice. I say *me*, for I have so identified myself with these poor people, that I feel as interested in their affairs as if they were my own. . . .

Yours, dear Mr. Murray, in great haste,

S. AUSTIN.

On January 6, 1838, Mrs. Austin again writes (from Valletta) to Mr. Murray :—

"You were quite right in imagining that your first letter was lost. I regret to say it never came to hand. Your second was as kind and as satisfactory as I expected it to be. I have communicated its contents to Mr. Hyzler, who is extremely pleased at it. . . . This history will be illustrated by antiquities found, and actually existing, in Malta, arranged chronologically. They will consist chiefly of the following :—

1. Paintings in frescoes, some of extreme antiquity, existing in the crypts and underground churches used by the early Christians, cut in the solid rock, on which the frescos are painted.

2. Paintings on panel, beginning with some very early Byzantine. Among them is the *Tritico*, which was always carried to sea in the galley of the Admiral when the Knights went out to fight the Mussulmans.

3. Intarsia, or inlaid wood (date 1480), in the choir of the Cathedral at Città Vecchia.

4. Carvings in wood.

5. Sacred utensils, such as fonts, pixes, etc. ; among them the silver crucifixes brought by the order from Rhodes—a splendid specimen of alto relievo in silver.

. . . . Do me the favour to consult Mr. Head.* I take him to be the very best judge of art, and the most learned man in its history, of any man in England, and I would wish for your sake and mine that he should know all this project, and give you his opinion. Hyzler will, of course, write in Italian, but I am ready to give him the benefit of my translating.'

. . . . I see you persist in booking me for Ranke. I should be too happy, but, as I told you, I can hardly write a letter. To mend the matter, I keep school every day for the monitors of the Normal School. I am a dreadful beggar, and so hardened that I don't mind asking you for a copy of any easy, simple little historical work. These boys, and very clever boys too, have been taught to read fluently Italian and English, understanding *nothing* of either. Do me the honour to come to my children's ball on the 10th. I shall have at least five hundred people of all ages, from the Arch-

* Edw. Head, Assistant Poor Law Commissioner.

bishop, aged eighty, to babies. Our house was under the Knights, the Auberge d'Arragon, and I have two drawings-rooms, thirty-six by twenty-six, and thirty-six by forty-two, adjoining, and opening on a vast corridor, so there will be abundant room for you all.

The little black-eyed things are very pretty and very happy. We never dine out or give dinner-parties, and I find this sort of party pleases the poor Maltese more than anything. My best regards.

Yours always,
S. AUSTIN.

Mrs. Austin to Mrs. Reeve.

DEAR SUSAN,   Sliema, Malta, August 9, 1837.

Heat interruptions, but above all a shock that really unfitted me for anything, have kept me from writing. I must tell you this tragical history. One of the persons whom I know the best and like the best here is a Mrs. Sammut, wife of a Dr. Sammut, whom I never saw, he having, for the sake of securing a small pension, gone on board an English man-of-war as surgeon two years ago. They had just lost a beautiful little girl when we came, and Mrs. Sammut only began to recover enough to go out. She had eight children. The two eldest daughters, both married, had been the most admired girls in Malta ; the grown-up single daughter was an excellent and charming girl. From the first appearance of cholera, poor Mrs. Sammut was overwhelmed with terror ; her daughter, Mrs. Dedminno, and she came together to see me one evening, looking like spectres, and I said then, " If they are attacked, they will die." The daughter was attacked, struggled a week, and died, leaving a baby. Last Monday, what was my horror (knowing the mother) at hearing that Carmela was attacked and dying. On Wednesday morning she died. But imagine

that on Tuesday, the father—the most doting of fathers
—returned, after his two years' exile from his family ! I
had sent on Tuesday to ask Mrs. Sammut to send me
her two little children, and I cannot describe to you how
affecting it was to hear them talk of the presents papa
had brought from England for mamma and Carmela.
Poor Carmela said on Tuesday, "As soon as I am up
again, I shall take papa to see Mrs. Austin." From the
first, I have endeavoured to make my large house and
fine situation useful to convalescents, and thus I have
had two young men who had just escaped, and several
poor girls, who had been passing the last two months
under the combined influence of rigorous confinement
to the house, insufficient food, and incessant fear and
gloom. This feeble, abject terror, this inability to look
death in the face, was always despicable to me ; it is
now odious. Under its influence I have seen mothers
refuse to go near their children, husbands their wives.
I have seen one of eight brothers (in the upper classes),
not *one* of whom would approach their father's death-bed.
In short, every variety of atrocious selfishness. These
are the people who die. For myself I never feared ; I
am not very solicitous to live, nor do I think myself very
obnoxious to this sort of complaint. As to cure, it is
anything, everything, nothing. Nobody knows. Everything succeeds—everything fails. I have kept on my
course, eating the same, riding in the much-dreaded
sereno every evening, bathing in the sea (prohibited most
emphatically, I cannot guess why) every day—in short,
altering nothing ; and but for the dreadful heat I should
be perfectly well. To-day is terrific. You have not the
faintest idea what *sun* means. The rocks in my little
bay where I bathe, if only a hand's-breadth is out of the
water, are so hot you cannot touch them. Yet it is
seldom stifling as in London. You sit still, and the
perspiration runs off in a continued stream. Then the

sea-breeze comes, rustling the leaves and rippling the sea, and you are refreshed. The trying days are those of the *scirocco* or the *libeccio ;* and once in a few years they are reminded that Malta is in Africa by a blast of the simoom.

August 15.

I add a word to say that we are all alive. We have lost about 4000 people off our little rock ; you may think how thankful I am Lucie is not here—God help her ! I trust she is gone, or going, to Coed Dhu. The thought of the wood and the river makes me *thirsty*. But I must not forget our oranges, figs, melons, water-melons, peaches, nectarines, grapes, all so fine, so plentiful—and our boats on the blue sea. If made the most of, Malta might have many attractions. This is a sad letter ; pray send me something cheerful.

The following letter from Mrs. Jameson, who was an intimate friend of Mrs. Austin, is interesting :—

Mrs. Jameson to Mrs. Austin.

Philadelphia, Dec. 27, 1837.

This, my dearest friend, is the third letter I have written to you since I received yours, dated last March. Now until I reach England I have no chance of hearing from you or of you, or where you are or how you are. The hope that when I arrive in London I may meet you there, comes over me sometimes with a feeling of delight which makes me dread disappointment. I must not give way to such a hope, for which, in truth, I have no foundation, except the expression in your letter that it was not likely you would spend another winter in Malta. How much we shall have to tell each other— what histories ! My budget is full of all manner of things in *my* way—and yours ? Your path is among deeper waters: I go paddling about among sunny shallows, afraid of venturing beyond my depth; and *you* launch into the wide sea of human interests, politics and governments, fearless and assured in principle, and when earth is left behind, looking to the stars of heaven. What have you been doing—you who are *never* idle, and who continue to crowd into a given time more good to others and yourself than any one I have ever known? Where·ever you are, however you be, and whatever you do, how I wish I were with you! I am preparing to cross that wide, dark, wintry Atlantic, and shiver a little at the thought; but the thought of home, my own dear people who make my home, and dear familiar faces and fire-sides, and hearts on which the aching head can rest itself—all these rise up before me, and the voyage, with all its manifold miseries, seems but a step across a summer brook. I left Toronto before the breaking out of the disturbances, luckily; for though I think the lamentable folly of the people in being led by a few men into premature resistance could end no otherwise, yet I have sympathies with them. There has been much error and misrule on the part of our Government, and the magnificent capabilities of Canada seem, as yet, little understood. If any one can do good, it will be Sir Francis Head, a truth-telling, large-minded, strong-headed man, the first, I apprehend, whom they have had in the Upper Country that united liberality and decision. Sir John Colborne, whom I also know, I admired as a fine, true-hearted soldier; as for Lord Gosford, I must own I rather wondered how the deuce he got *there.*

After all, Harriet Martineau has left little to say; her book, as far as I can judge, is the truest of books, though I do not always agree with her views—which may, indeed, proceed from my own ignorance. There are people here who would willingly roast her before a slow fire and eat her up afterwards, I believe ; but among candid and intelligent people there is but one opinion— that the book is a fair book, though containing some mistakes in facts. I have no idea myself of writing anything, except on the only subject I do understand, *i.e.*, the state of art in this country, which is more interesting than you could easily imagine. This, and my tour among the Indians, will be the subject of my next perpetration. I am now staying with Fanny Butler, who is certainly the most gifted creature it has ever been my lot to meet with, take her altogether. Health and strength, intellect and genius, the most robust temperament, the most fearless, uncompromising love of truth. Put these together, with youth, riches, happiness : don't you think this is a group of bright ideas ? That there may be some little flaws, that in this "*superflu d'âme et de vie*" there should be, at times, a little *too muchness*—all this, though it makes me tremble a little for her future, takes nothing from the admiration with which I regard her, for thus in the consistent, complete *human* being, it must be, and ought to be, and it will be all *fined* down in due time. Her child, though fair, has a Kemble face, and is a little curiosity—doted upon, of course, and not less admirably managed. This is all I will allow myself to say at present, for I feel as if I were talking to you, and pour all out as if my paper were boundless and my time infinite. My dear, dear friend, how I wish I could but know how you fare ! But however that may be, you love me still, and do not forget me—of that I am as certain as of my own exist- ence and my true affection for you. God bless you and keep you, my dear and good friend !

I am,

Yours affectionately,

ANNA.

Mrs. Austin to Mrs. Senior.

DEAR MRS. SENIOR,　　　　　　Valletta, March 7, 1838.

My commissions for silk and mittens are so numerous and business so thriving that I need not encumber you with anything more unless you wish it. The Queen's commission for eight dozen pairs long and eight dozen pairs short mits, is more than I can get executed with the perfection I wish while I am here. Lady Lansdowne and others are always writing for them. As to the turban, Lady L. admires hers so much that she has written to order a dress for Lady Louisa. That, with a scarf for the Queen, will keep my best hands occupied.

Mr. Senior's letter was a great treat. You can have no idea how barren society here is of all that makes society worth having. I shall find myself ages behind in everything relating to books and news when I come among you. But I hope we are of some use, and that is the best thing.

Tell Mr. Senior our revenue is very flourishing. I send him an answer to an attack on the Commissioners, which appeared in the *Times*, and was reprinted here. This answer is by Dr. Sciortino,* an advocate, altogether the ablest and best man we have found here. He was one of the leaders of the *extrême gauche*. He, even in England, would pass for a man of great ability, of course cramped by want of advantages.

I cannot understand the course adopted by "our friends the Radicals" in England. Above all, I wonder at Mr. Grote. I cannot imagine what Molesworth can mean by his motion about Lord Glenelg. Is it to please Lord Brougham? At this distance it looks like madness—particularly to us. A Maltese *ultra-Liberal*,

---

* Sir W. Reid (when Governor of Malta) said, "I know no society in which Sciortino would not be a distinguished man."

to whom I mentioned it, said if it were carried it would be the greatest calamity for Malta, for that Lord Glenelg was the first Colonial Minister who had shown a disinterested regard to the good of the island.

I want to get something in the way of a statistical table, as I have a notion of getting the village school-masters to keep a kind of register. Births, deaths, and marriages *are* registered; but I want to see the number who emigrate, who go to school, etc. If Mr. Senior has anything that would serve as a pattern, I should be very thankful for it. The Commissioners are too busy.

Ask Mr. Senior to tell Mr. Stephen (to whom I have not time to write to-day) that 1,100 Maltese have emigrated since last November, all, or nearly all, I imagine, to the opposite coast. The people are much more occupied, beggars diminished, the island generally more cheerful. Governor's Carnival Ball the fullest ever known. I am very busy (as usual) with schools, work-people, artists, etc.

I bore ᛫you with Malta, but what can I say else, except that I am always,

Yours faithfully attached,
SARAH AUSTIN.

Mrs. Austin to M. Victor Cousin.

[TRANSLATION.]

DEAR M. COUSIN, Valletta, April 25, 1838.

I take advantage of Mr. Lewis's departure for London to break a silence which has lasted far too long. He will tell you of us, and of our little island, which owes so much to him, and of our reforms; but he also wants to hear you talk of Plato and Greek literature, of philosophy and politics. Make him tell you about his translations of Müller's 'History of the Dorians,' and Boeckh's 'Athenian Public Economy.' If you want to know about the political and administrative reforms my husband and his colleague have effected here, you must ask Lewis ; I shall only mention my *Fach* (speciality), which is, as you know, my dear and venerated master, public instruction. It did not exist at Malta. There was one school for boys and one for girls in the town of Valletta. In obedience to the recommendations of the Commissioners, twelve more are to be established in the villages, six for each sex. Our famous book serves as our guide,* but we follow humbly at a distance. I am occupied in making an abridged translation (into Italian) *al uso di Malta.* Alas, what concessions we are forced to make ; it is impossible to make the Maltese pay a *grano*† a week ; they would not send their children to school. The remedy for this—compulsion—is not to be thought of. As to the obvious and economic system of sending young children of the two sexes to the same village school, equally impossible. You must know Malta to understand what *il nostro decoro* means. It is an obstacle to everything except vice.

Then, my dear Councillor of State, imagine the condition of a people forced to learn four languages— (1) Maltese, a kind of bastard Arabic, which has never been reduced to any system or written down, so they conceived the brilliant idea of teaching children to read in a foreign language (Italian), and the consequence is a whole generation who read fluently without understanding a word. (2) Italian, the written language used in the courts, the pulpit, the theatre, etc. (3) English, the language of the governing class ; I need not tell you how necessary a knowledge of this is to all who are not absolutely independent of us. (4) Arabic. This island swarms with inhabitants, and emigration is perpetual.

---

* 'Report on the State of Public Instruction in Prussia,' by M. V. Cousin, translated by Mrs. Austin (with a Preface).

† Three granos make one farthing.

The opposite coast of Africa and the Levant offer the easiest and most profitable outlet, for though the poor Maltese are far behind us in civilisation, yet they are in advance of Africa or Asia.

So you see what we have to do. But I have never been discouraged ; the Maltese are very docile, sharp and intelligent. How much there is to say about this little half-Arab nation—corrupted and degraded to the last degree by the worst government in the world, that of the Order ; neglected and despised by the English, ignorant, superstitious, and devoured by every kind of prejudice ! They must not be left in such a condition. Good-bye, my dear friend and master,

Ever yours,
S. AUSTIN.

CHAPTER XII.

The Austins return to London—Mrs. Austin to Dr. Sciortino on
Maltese affairs—Letter to M. Victor Cousin on education in
England—Translation of Ranke's Popes—Mr. Gladstone on
popular education—Mr. Macaulay's review of the translation
of Ranke—Mrs. Austin on the change of Ministry, and her
daughter's engagement.

IN July, 1838, Mr. and Mrs. Austin left Malta, the
Commission having been brought suddenly to a close
by Lord Glenelg's successor.   No reason was assigned,
nor was Mr. Austin's abrupt dismissal accompanied with
a single word of recognition for his services.   He had,
however, the satisfaction of seeing every measure he
recommended adopted by the Colonial Office,* and he
always looked back with great satisfaction to his connection with two men for whom he entertained so sincere
a respect as Lord Glenelg and Sir James Stephen.

The following letter is written to Dr. Paolo Sciortino,
a lawyer at Malta, for whom both Mr. and Mrs. Austin
entertained a great friendship :—

4, Queen Street, Mayfair,

DEAR DR. SCIORTINO,   August 2, 1838.

A hundred times on our journey I was tempted to
write to Malta, to tell my dear friends again and again
that I should never forget them nor cease to feel the
liveliest interest in everything that concerns them.   At
Milan my first care was to find out some one who could

---

* Sir W. Reid (when Governor of Malta) said, " All that is
valuable in the code of Law here was done by Austin and Lewis." ·

give me information about the state of education in Lombardy. I found a Signor Racheli, a benevolent and intelligent man, who is at the head of a large *instituto* there, and he introduced me to the Abbate Ambrosio Ambrosoli. The latter is a priest such as all men must venerate—liberal, enlightened, and devoted to the public good. Having obtained from them all the information I could, I thought I could do nothing so serviceable for dear Malta as to put them in correspondence with the *Capo d'Istruzione Publica* there. I therefore explained to them fully our excellent Rettore's situation and views, and entreated the Abbate to write to him. Unless you knew the state of parties here, as none but an Englishman can know them—unless you knew how all the Ministers' interests are enlinked together, you could form no idea of Lord Glenelg's *virtue* in having disobliged, and almost offended, at least a dozen old friends, powerful supporters or colleagues, merely to do an act of justice to Malta, which nobody will appreciate.

I hope you saw Mr. Spring Rice's declaration that they were determined to do full justice to Malta. I have seen him three times. I dined there last Sunday, and told him many things he did not know. On Saturday I dined at Lord Lansdowne's, and met Lord Minto, Colonel Fox, and others. Colonel Fox, who knows Malta well, expressed great approbation and pleasure at what had been done, and a strong conviction of the great improvability of the Maltese. . . .

Mrs. Austin to M. Victor Cousin.

[Translation.]

4, Queen Street, Mayfair, Dec. 31, 1838.

It is a great pleasure to me, my dear friend, to see those *pattes de mouches* which I have missed for so long. Another pleasure has been reading your admirable

speeches in the *Morning Chronicle* of to-day.   I
recognise you, and I recognise all the sentiments that
I am so proud to share with you.   It is in vain, dear
friend, to try and uphold religion, her own ministers are
her assassins.   To find oneself between bigots or atheists
provokes despair, and one does not know which to hate
the most.   Let us talk about schools.   You know
that an absence of two years has broken the thread of
my knowledge of schools here.   But I do know that
there is a remarkable movement to which I want to call
your attention.   There is a certain party of young men
(clergymen and others), all Tories and High Churchmen,
who have, it seems, had the sense to see that the schools
of the National School Society (which as you know
have long represented the bigoted party) are bad
enough and ridiculous enough to discredit their
supporters.   From what I hear they are going to try
and reform the church schools, to insist upon better
instruction, and to try and place them on a par with the
best liberal schools ; always retaining religion (Anglican
of course) as the principal thing.   These gentlemen
appear to me to have faith in their religion and not to
be afraid of a little secular teaching.   The man who is
at the head of this movement is Mr. Gladstone, a
Member of Parliament, who is regarded as the probable
successor of Peel, *i.e.* the leader of the Tory party.   I
believe that he and I shall suit one another.   But I
have a strong idea that this is only part of a whole.
The Radical party is evidently effete—not two of them
are of the same mind—they all want to act according
to their own private notions—they will accomplish
nothing.   But by incessantly menacing the Tories they
will, *through them,* attain what they would have been
powerless to do by themselves—and what the Tories
never would have done without their threats.   By the
first opportunity I shall send you the last report of the

Poor Law Commissioners. You will find two interesting papers; one by Dr. S. Smith on the causes of fever in large towns, and one by Dr. Kay, on the workhouse schools. I believe that they will become the best schools in England, for the evident reason that their managing board has not to attend to the recommendations of a parcel of idiots. As to my little island; there it was not a question of writing, but of acting. And I acted. I will not tell you how I worked, but the fact is that there are now ten village schools, where there was not one. I believe things would have remained as they were, had I not searched for and found the masters and opened the schools in person. My poor little *Saraceni!* we could only smile and gesticulate to one another. Since my return I have been trying to get a professor of English for the *Liceo*, and have insisted on his being a Catholic. I gained the complete confidence of the Maltese as soon as they found that I did not aim at converting them. They generally distrust Protestants, and I must confess they are not far wrong.

At this moment I am translating Ranke's ' History of the Popes.' It has been done so badly into French that Ranke was forced to disavow it. I suppose the translator was an ultra-Catholic, but he cuts a poor figure.

Good-bye, dear friend, keep well for the good of humanity.

Your faithful friend,
S. AUSTIN.

During the winter of 1838–39, Mr. Austin was very ill. Mrs. Austin was busy in collecting facts concerning Education. She wrote to Mr. Gladstone, asking for documents ; and he answered :—

Mr. Gladstone to Mrs. Austin.

6, Carlton Gardens,
Feb. 16, 1839.

DEAR MRS. AUSTIN,

Together with Mr. Horner's translation of Cousin's 'Report on Holland,' for which I beg to offer my best thanks, I send to you two sets of papers which will show a good deal of light on our recent proceedings with regard to popular education. One of them I thought you might wish to forward to M. Cousin. I have to regret that a paper on Diocesan Training Seminaries is out of print, and that I am therefore unable to forward copies.

Allow me to request your continued and, if possible, active interest in furtherance of these designs.

I remain, dear Mrs. Austin,
Your faithful Servant,
W. E. GLADSTONE.

Mrs. Austin to Mr. Gladstone.

DEAR SIR,   Feb. 18, 1839.

I am extremely obliged to you for the documents you have sent me, and yet more for accepting the sympathy and good wishes—in default of better things—of so humble a fellow-labourer in "*la sainte cause*," as Cousin always and truly calls it. If my co-operation were worth anything, it might not be loss of time to try to convince you to how great an extent you might count upon it, and where I should hesitate, and why. But these would be fruitless discussions. All I *can* do (and that belongs to my sex) is this, To try to persuade some who think differently from you, and who fancy that you are parted from each other by walls of adamant and not by slender and partial partitions, to give an attentive, respectful, and *grateful* ear to your projects, and to see whether it is really demanded by the cause of rational education to reject so much zeal, charity, and knowledge.

I had the pleasure of making two inexorable Liberals waver, and at last confess that, indeed, there was a great deal that was good in the scheme.

My fear is, my dear Mr. Gladstone, that your own earnest and, to me, affecting view of the duties and rights attached to the character of Christian teacher, leads you to over-estimate, and, alas! greatly, the aid we have to expect from the clergy. Shall I say more?— that they will thwart you—not all, God forbid, but many. Having lived much among Radicals and "Liberals" of all sorts, I shall find it difficult to persuade you how sincerely it has long been my conviction that a Church, such as you conceive it, is really the nursing-mother of all its children, and its clergy the natural, inevitable, and desirable heads of instruction; but have we not seen them at work? and after that, can we trust them? If you are strong enough to provide motives and checks, you may do two blessed acts,—reform your clergy and teach your people. As it is, how few of them conceive what it is to teach a people.

With regard to the thing which makes the great clamour—the exclusion of Dissidents—I think little of that; that is not your affair, or the Church's. If the State gives money, that is another thing. It must give to all, and for all, from whose pockets it is taken. That is just. The time was over too long before you or (even) I were born, when the spirit of faith had given place to the spirit of questioning, for us in our day to find any remedy. And the remedy will not be found, at any rate, in the sort of ignorance which now lies at the lowest bottom of our society. *All* must be taught. But I am preaching a sermon to you—of all things the least needed. The subject is most tempting.

You must think of the poor girls—and pity them. I think a girl can hardly, save by a miracle, escape destruction from bad training ; a boy may struggle through it. If either wants to be specially sheltered and fortified and restrained, it is the ones in every way weak. You must lay this matter to heart. Pray excuse me.

Most truly yours,
SARAH AUSTIN.

Mrs. Austin to M. Victor Cousin.

[TRANSLATION.]

DEAR FRIEND AND MASTER,   London, Feb., 1839.

There is not time to collect all I should like to send you by M. C., but here is a book that will interest you, and above all a report by Dr. Kay. He is a most useful man about public instruction. I think I told you that I went with him to one of the workhouse schools. There were 1,100 of these poor little creatures very well lodged, and taught by five Scotch masters who seemed to me to do their work admirably. It is well worth seeing.

My schools at Malta are flourishing, about 1,000 boys and 500 girls are being taught, where before our arrival there was not one. This is consoling. And in truth I need consolation. My husband's health is worse than ever, and I cannot describe my life to you, never an instant of repose. I am surrounded by friends and acquaintances who esteem me, and I have my daughter, a handsome and talented girl ; but I dare not think of the future.

Do send me your 'Abélard.' Have you seen the notice in the *London and Westminster Review ?* I send you the speech of Lord J. Russell (last night's debates). It will interest you. I have seen young

Gladstone, a distinguished Tory who wants to re-establish education based on the Church in quite a Catholic form.

He has, however, clear ideas, zeal and conscientiousness. We get on extremely well together; he was with me for two hours, for I am regarded as quite an authority about public instruction, and am friends with all who take that subject to heart. Send me everything you can about your normal schools, Lord Granville will forward the packet.

Ever yours,
S. AUSTIN.

Besides writing on Education, Mrs. Austin was hard at work translating L. v. Ranke's 'History of the Popes,' which had been so badly done into French that, as she says in her Preface, it "is not only full of particular inaccuracies arising from ignorance or carelessness, but is infected with the sectarian spirit from which the original is so remarkably and so laudably exempt." Professor Ranke wrote to Mrs. Austin :—

" My book needs to be set right in the eyes of all but German readers, after the unconscientious treatment it has received at the hands of a Catholicising French translator. I look to England to redress the wrong done to me in France."

Macaulay, who was to review the original book, asked Mrs. Austin to let him have her sheets to read.

" I am," he says, " prompted purely by selfish motives. Being but indifferently skilled in German, I wished, in reviewing a most important German work, to have the help of a very good translation. I shall be exceedingly obliged to you for the sheets whenever it may be quite convenient to you. I am very slowly reading Ranke's book a second time, at the rate of ten or fifteen pages a morning while I dress. The movement and din of this strange whirlpool, London, allows me no more time for German, and having once got some hold on the language, I do not choose to let it go."

Mrs. Austin writes to her Maltese friend :—

DEAR DR. SCIORTINO,   May 10, 1839.

I was going to condole ·with you on the change Ministry on the appointment of Lord Stanley as Colonial Secretary. Now all is changed again, or rather all is in suspense and confusion. Before this reaches you, you will know the result by the French post. My notion is that the country will not like to see the Queen, poor child! oppressed, and that she will show the firmness that is in her blood. Perhaps this may end in a re-organization of a Whig Ministry. Certainly some change is wanted. I am now interrupted by the entrance of Lewis's cousin, Sir Alexander Duff Gordon, to tell me that one of my anxieties is over —that my husband is paid. The sum fixed is £1,500 a year, consequently £3,000 ; and this is paid by England, my dear friend, as it ought to be. Without this, though in my conscience I think Malta might well have thought it due to him, I could not have enjoyed it ; for poor Malta is very near my heart, and I could ill bear any good fortune at her expense. So the Commission has cost you, dear people, only our expenses ; and how moderate they were I need not tell you. I must tell you how new and strong a motive I have for some little aid to our small means. This same Alexander Gordon has fallen in love with my dear child, and Alexander has nothing but a small *impiego*, his handsome person, excellent and sweet character, and his title (a great misfortune). This £3,000 will enable us to help them when they marry. Now you will understand my anxiety when I heard the Tories were coming in—the Tories who hate all such men and such reformers as my husband. On occasion of Lord Brougham's attack on my husband, the ferocity of which I cannot describe to you, I went (my husband being ill) to Lord Glenelg, to talk to him about the social and religious state of Malta. He behaved like a true man of conscience, humanity, and enlarged sympathies, and confirmed me in all I thought of him. Lord Normanby, too, behaved very well, and my excellent friends, Lord and Lady Lansdowne, of course. He studied the Ordinance, and comprehended the whole case. In short, I had great consolations. But my poor husband was made so ill he could not leave his bed, and I had to do strange things for a woman, *contro il nostro decoro* (against our decorum), certainly; but a woman fighting for her husband is always in the right.

CHAPTER XIII.

THE following letter to Mr. Gladstone preceded the publication of the pamphlet 'On National Education.' Mrs. Austin never cared about appearing before the public in her own person, and although often pressed to "give us something of your own" by her many friends, was generally content to translate.

Mrs. Austin to Mr. Gladstone.

DEAR MR. GLADSTONE,   May 27, 1839.

I am going to take the strangest liberty with you, which, however, if you can understand the feeling that prompts it, will not, I trust, displease you. About four years ago I received from Paris a quantity of official documents relating to public instruction, which, being both unpublished and extremely unattractive, appeared to me most unlikely to reach the eye of any English readers. I was therefore tempted to give such an *aperçu* of them as I could, in the form of an article in a review. The review in question ('Cochrane's Foreign Quarterly') died at its birth, and my article was buried with it. Some people interested in the subject have from time to time urged me to reprint it separately, a suggestion I never attended to till very lately ; when, on looking it over again, it seemed to me that there were suggestions in it worth preserving, and that the result of the deliberations of the French Chamber was a thing to be regarded, if not imitated.

I therefore gave it to Mr. Murray, and have been adding a few notes. But now, seeing the violence and bitterness with which the subject is, I will not say discussed, but handled, by the Press, I take fright. I have always shrunk from appearing before the public in my own person or behalf, as the author or champion of any opinions whatever.

It is, I truly assure you, no feigned humility when I say that I never felt that I had the least pretension to instruct the world, nor the least call to amuse it. On the subject of the education of the people, I did indeed once venture on a few words, but only under cover of a great name. If I spoke then, it was out of a heart filled with sympathy for those on whom lies the burthen of the heat of the day, with indignation at all who neglect, at all who delude them, and seeing no remedy but this. I think for the same cause I would bear martyrdom if it would do any good ; but I am, after all, a woman ; and I cannot bear, without a good reason, the coarse and disgusting hands of the daily press to be laid upon me. I feel that I am *not* a partisan, nor a bigot, nor an infidel, but I may and must express opinions which may be misstated and distorted to any or all of these forms of evil, and my courage is tottering. In this state of mind I can think of nothing but the comfort it would be to me to have one word of advice from you. You will not agree with all I have ventured to say, but you will, I trust, find little to object to, and that little not offensively urged. Will you read the few pages which I will ask Mr. Murray to send you ? Will you tell me whether the party to which you in a wide sense belong are likely to attack me with the sort of rancour I see and hear now so much afloat on all sides. God forbid I should confound you with those who use such poisoned weapons. I judge you as I wish to be judged by you, and I look to you and the small knot of friends with whom you act with an anxious hope you can hardly imagine. But you will know better than I what may provoke less candid judgments than yours.

You will see a sort of prophetic longing for that very movement in the Church which you have excited, and, if I do not flatter myself, some notions of the duties of a minister of religion not wholly unlike your own.

Forgive me, dear sir, for this (I repeat) strange appeal to your kindness. After it, need I say with what sentiments and respect and trust

I am yours,
SARAH AUSTIN.

Mr. Gladstone to Mrs. Austin.

6, Carlton Gardens,
June 18, 1839.

DEAR MRS. AUSTIN,

I much regret the delay which has taken place in returning your proof sheets. Those up to page 112 came to me almost immediately after your note, and I read them immediately, and waited for the remainder. I received them only last evening.

Let me now make a remark on the note, in which you have alluded to suggestions made by me, in very kind and flattering terms. I fear it would be of little use if I were to remark that they are much beyond my merits; but on one particular point I am about to suggest a modification. As the admission of candidates into holy orders is the sacred and sole prerogative of the governors of the Church, we, or any inferior agency, can hardly be said to look to *procuring* their entrance: but this we hope, to raise men to such proficiency and merit that the bishops may find them fit for the ministry.

After this observation let me say that I find your point of view upon the whole subject is different in a considerable degree from mine, and that perhaps the chief part of my duty towards you consists in saying whether you have so handled your subject, in your own sense, as to entitle you to the most delicate and respectful treatment. To such a question I can have no hesitation in replying affirmatively.

I cannot quite prevail on myself here to close my letter without adverting to the general subject; and yet, besides my general dread of its controverted parts, I am at present more than ever disqualified from doing justice either to you or to my own impressions. But the very great sympathy with which I receive most of your sentiments induces me to say a word. You are for pressing and urging the people to their profit against their inclination : so am I. You set little value upon all merely technical instruction, upon all that fails to touch the inner nature of man : so do I. And here I find ground of union broad and deep-laid, and I should indeed rejoice to see a portion of your benevolent energies lent, as I am sure they would freely be, to aid in the work of popular education within the bosom of the Church.

As to that subtle and ulterior question which respects the duty of the State at a moment when it seems to be losing in great measure the capacity and even the idea of duty properly so-called, I can tremble and hope, but little more. I more than doubt whether your idea, namely that of raising man to social sufficiency and morality, can be accomplished, except through the ancient religion of Christ ; or whether, overlooking what severs professing Christians, we can secure a residue such as shall produce an adequate effect upon the heart and affections of man ; or whether, the principles of eclecticism are legitimately applicable to the Gospel ; or whether, if we find ourselves in a state of incapacity to work through the Church, we can remedy the defect by the adoption of principles contrary to hers. On these questions, or forms of the same question, I am quite unable to fix myself in the affirmative conclusion.

But indeed I am most unfit to pursue the subject; private circumstances of no common interest are upon me, as I have become very recently engaged to be married to Miss Glynne, and I hope your recollections will enable you in some degree to excuse me, and

Believe me, with much regard, most truly yours,

W. E. GLADSTONE.

L. v. Ranke to Mrs. Austin.

[TRANSLATION.]

HONOURED MADAM, Berlin, Oct. 1839.

I must thank you for sending me the sheets. I have now all but the Introduction. The great care with which you have translated my book gives me the greatest satisfaction. I hear myself speak English much better than I could ever have learnt it. I see that you have used the latest edition. Of course I have not yet been able to compare everything, but wherever I have opened the pages I perceive care and conscientiousness, and I am well satisfied. My journey to Brussels and Paris has delayed the publication of the third volume of the new edition, but it will appear almost immediately. I beg you to observe this, as I have added a good deal in the third volume. I send you the academic treatise which you have heard about : it will probably be too long to add to the Appendix, already very bulky ; but perhaps may be turned to some other purpose. At the end you will see that I touch upon the debated question of Tasso's relations to Leonora d'Este. Since then some pamphlets by Count Alberti have appeared, dealing with this subject, which may lead to other results.   As far as I have yet seen, in those that have reached me, I perceive nothing which changes my opinion in the least.   Pray thank Mr. Milman and Mr. Hallam for their kind messages, and accept my best thanks and high esteem.

Ever yours,
L. v. RANKE.

Mrs. Austin to Dr. Sciortino.

Kensington, May 28, 1840.

It is impossible for me to convey to you any idea of the life of incessant toil, care, interruption, and agitation I have been leading.   Of the former—the toil—I send you, dear and excellent friend, some small evidence.*

My husband has for some time been considerably better than during the winter.   To our inexpressible joy and comfort he was able to accompany his dear girl to church, and to surrender his right in her to her husband at the altar.   It has been a great pang to me the parting from her, and a solemn thing, as the end of one period and mode of existence and the beginning of another. But if my husband is restored to health, I have all I desire.   My son-in-law is a model of sweetness, simplicity, and uprightness, and we are happy in committing our child to such hands.   We start for Carlsbad in a few days.   My husband desires me to assure you that he has never for an instant lost sight of the 'Report on the Consiglio Popolare.'   He has constantly meditated on it ; and the result has been some important alterations, and, as Lewis thinks, improvements in his recommendations.

In June, Mr. and Mrs. Austin started for Carlsbad. Before leaving she writes as follows :—

* 'History of the Popes.' Ranke.

Mrs. Austin to Mr. Murray.

DEAR MR. MURRAY,   June 1, 1840.

I enclose my acknowledgment* that all my claims upon you are acquitted, and I cannot do this without a less formal document acknowledging the uniform kindness and courtesy which make all transactions with you smooth and agreeable. I sincerely hope your interest will be promoted by this undertaking—the more largely the better I shall be pleased. I am told I ought to have made some stipulations as to a second edition. I am, however, entirely satisfied to leave that contingency in your hands; you know my circumstances and my motives for what I do, and I would not be so unjust to my own thorough persuasion of your always doing what is just and generous as to seem to doubt that you will do for me all that it would be fair in me to wish.

As to future undertakings, we had better wait till I get to Carlsbad. I shall see Von Savigny and other of the great men of Germany; I may hear of something new and promising, or at least discuss the old. Whatever I hear, you shall know it, and have the option of publishing whatever I do. This I need hardly say. I· have already two or three things in my head, and 'Count Egmont' I shall certainly finish, but that is a small affair as to bulk.   Most truly yours,

S. AUSTIN.

Mrs. Austin to Dr. Sciortino.

DEAR DR. SCIORTINO,   Carlsbad, August 19, 1840.

We have made some interesting acquaintances here, among them General Leysser, the President Speaker of the Lower Chamber of Saxony, who, on occasion of the

* An acknowledgment of the final payment for the translation of Ranke's 'Popes.'

little revolution of Dresden, took the command of the insurgent peasants, kept them in order, and mediated with the Government. In short, preserved the public peace. He is an enlightened, humane man, and much attached to his admirable little country and its mild rulers. It grieves one to see such a country so utterly at the mercy of its powerful neighbours, especially that country which all others abhor in proportion as they know it— Russia. I never believed, as you know, that the Maltese could desire to transfer themselves to Russia, but now that I know more of both, the idea would drive me mad. You know, dear friend, whether I was blind to the mis- conduct of my country and countrymen! But I assure you the worst of us are angels compared to these re- morseless savages, who have no idea of truth, honour, or humanity. Here I have had an opportunity of hearing *details* from Austrians, Russians, Saxons, and above all from their victims, the wretched Poles. Countess Potocka, a most noble woman, who reminds me of a Roman matron, said to me, " The most cruel thing is that their barbarities so far exceed the imaginations of civilised people, that the simplest relation of our woes seems falsehood and exaggeration. You *cannot* believe us." I give you one example. The Emperor is forcing the Greek Church on the Poles, who are fervent Catholics. The poor women who refused to conform have been pre- vented from giving suck to their infants till they would go to the Greek Church! Just analyse the head and heart that could conceive this infernal measure. Educa- tion studiously withheld and prohibited, all the Polish universities shut up, young boys suddenly seized and carried off to remote parts of Russia, leaving not a trace. There are many mothers of the first families in Poland who have thus been robbed of their sons, and cannot gain the smallest tidings where they are. Name, language, religion—all changed.

The people here have the mild, good-natured, and somewhat indifferent (*molle*) character of their nation— very honest, dull, and without aspirations. The censorship on books is complete ; that is, *all* are forbidden except those specially allowed—an *index expurgatorius* reversed. But foreigners can get permission for any ; and the *Allgemeine Zeitung*, a most excellent paper, circulates freely. The truth is, there is no demand for more than the Government grants. General Leysser told me that occasionally, when Austrians come to Dresden, he has proposed to them to go to hear the debates in the Chamber. They said, "That must be excessively dull ; are there no gambling-houses here ?"

M. Michel Chevalier to Mrs. Austin.

[TRANSLATION.]

DEAR MADAM,   Paris, Nov. 15, 1840.

I have returned to Paris. I adore this Babylon for the sake of its inhabitants, the *élite* of France, who after all are so charming, although they have cut off their lace ruffles and cuffs, and diminished their high red heels. Your letter awaited me, a charming letter such as only a Frenchwoman can pen, and which has delighted me by proving that I am right in claiming you as a country- woman. You say you are attracted by suffering, that feeling was the loadstone to my heart. Men, generally speaking, are not attracted by sorrow ; that is reserved to your sex ; that it is that converts noble women into humble sisters of charity, and makes of you *la petite mère* of humanity. In this also the Frenchwoman is superior to all others—another reason for your being one.

But allow me to say, that from the first time I saw you, I was bound to you by an unconquerable instinct which draws me towards superior natures, towards those angels who occasionally descend to our earth. This has been, madam, a source of great and pure pleasure to me, but it has also caused me much pain and raised me many enemies. This very love, this search for privileged natures is, in me, inseparable from a contempt for the vulgar and common herd. I wish them well, I work to promote their interests ; in France I even pass for a democrat. The little I have written bears the stamp of devotion to the cause of the amelioration of the people. But on the understanding that the populace should have nothing to do with my life, and that mediocre men (and women) should not annoy me by their contact. That class of people are to me as though they did not exist, and I let them see it. I admit that this is a fault, and one I have in vain sought to subdue. But when I see a really fine character, I not only esteem, I adore. You see now what made me seek to know you, and why I was so happy in your company ; I confess this fault in my character which has made me so many enemies, and will make me many more. One must confess to somebody. Catholicism was far-seeing in instituting such a practice. Confession lightens many a burden and makes life easier, but the only confessor I admit is a woman ; and when the canons of the Church refused to you ladies the right of exercising this function, they showed a singular misconception of human nature. Do you remember that I told you at Carlsbad we should not have war? I still think so; only Lord Palmerston must not send us any more notes like that of the 2nd November. The English Cabinet should not pour oil on the fire when we try to throw water. The note of the 2nd is the work of a fool or a madman.

Ever yours from my heart,
MICHEL CHEVALIER.

CHAPTER XIV.

Mrs. Austin's 'Fragments from German Prose Writers'—Letters
   to M. Guizot on behalf of some inhabitants of Boulogne—
   Sydney Smith's opinion of Guizot's 'Washington'—M. A. de
   Vigny to Mrs. Austin—Mrs. Austin undertakes translation of
   Ranke's 'History of the Reformation.'

MRS. AUSTIN was all the autumn preparing her book,
'Fragments from German Prose Writers : with Notes.'
Her husband, who derived considerable benefit from the
Carlsbad waters, went to Dresden, and she, in February,
to London, to see her daughter.

Mrs. Austin to M. Guizot.

3, Pont Street, Belgrave Square,
Jan. 29, 1841.

I should hardly venture to trouble you again, dear
M. Guizot, but I have a petition to present. And now,
perhaps, my excuse is worse than none. But you shall
hear, and you will forgive me.

When I lived in your city of Boulogne, my only friends
were my poor neighbours on the port, the *matelote*
population, pilots, fishermen, and their wives. I was
admitted into all their *fêtes de famille,* and into all their
sorrows, and it is enough to say that I found in their
admirable qualities and in their cordial attachment, compensation for what we call civilised society. I have just
received a touching proof that neither years of absence,
nor all the bad efforts of bad or evil men to make us
believe we are born to hate and injure each other, can

efface from the heart of one woman the memory of the tears another had shed with her and for her. One of the most unhappy and forlorn of wives and mothers has recollected her old friend in England. You saw the account of the sad accident at Boulogne, by which eight persons out of a boat's crew of eleven perished. The boat belonged to a man named Delpierre (but always called Caton), the *doyen* of the pilots, a man upwards of sixty (I think), *décoré* for his many services, lame in consequence of having broken his leg in the performance of his duty, brave, quiet, sober, good-natured, an excellent husband and father. Even when I was there (in '35) he was almost worn out in the service, and, at his earnest request, I had the impertinence to add my poor solicitations to M. Cousin to try to get him a *débit de tabac* as a *retraite.* Alas, poor fellow, he has found rest in the element he had braved so long. He and his son, a fine, brave, handsome boy of nineteen, perished together. I cannot tell you with what anguish I think of the wretched wife and mother. She was so passionately devoted to them. I remember once standing with her alone at the end of the pier, when her husband and this very son, then a child, went off to Dover with despatches, in a frightful sea, just at sunset in a December evening. I stayed by her to watch the little boat as long as we could descry a trace of it on the dark and stormy waters, and her face is before me now, as she turned away and said to me, "C'est tout ce que j'ai au monde." I was so alarmed at her state that I went home and stayed with her almost all night. The other pilots' wives whom I begged to go to her only said, " Madame Caton ne sait pas se faire une raison. Elle est toujours à se tourmenter." And now all her blackest misgivings are verified. Strange how these dark shadows rest for years on the soul ! She was the only woman I saw possessed by these terrors.

But, dear sir, what am I doing?—Writing as if you had nothing to do but to read my womanish letters. Well, what I *want* to say is, that she sends to ask me if I have any friend at Paris who would solicit for a pension for her. She is very ill and quite forlorn. I do not think, with her passionate temper, she can live long.

Can it be? and can you spare one minute from graver things to recollect it? She would think it a homage to the virtues of "Monsieur Caton," as she always called him, with a sort of veneration I honoured in her. I used to show that *ménage* with such pride to all my English friends— the pretty, neat cottage, and the *décorations* and medals under a glass case, carefully displayed by the wife. And as if death had not weapons enough in his armoury to strike us and those we love, we must forge them for him!

I hope you are satisfied with Sir Robert Peel's speeches, and, tolerably, with the Duke's. I can assure you they have excited unutterable joy and satisfaction here. Depend upon it, Sir Robert speaks the language of the whole middle class of England—of nearly *all* England. Nobody but partisans, bound hand and foot, ever attempted to defend the Note of the 2nd November. Miss Berry, who sees everybody of all parties, told me she had heard but one opinion—one feeling of indignation. We all pray for you, revere you, and love you. That is the real *English sentiment.* Will you believe me? You know I do not flatter my countrymen ; but there is, I am confident, no rancour against France here ; and if that dear, naughty child, the French nation, would have made a little less noise, this would have been more evident.

In Germany, indeed—*ah, c'est une autre affaire*—but even that will wear out. The French can conciliate any people if they will.

Forgive me, dear sir, this torment of impertinence. At least let me not add to it, or allow you to think that you are bound to take the least notice of it, except for my poor suppliant's sake ; and even for her, if I have trespassed too far, forgive me, for the sake of my loyal attachment to France, and allow me to add of my affectionate and profound respect for her best son and citizen.

SARAH AUSTIN.

Mrs. Austin to M. Guizot.

DEAR MONSIEUR GUIZOT,   Feb. 19, 1841.

The benefit you have conferred on the sorrowing wife and mother is so great that it seems almost impertinent to say anything about the unspeakable pleasure you have given *me*. And yet I must thank you for myself as well as for her. How often have I lamented as you do, how often declaimed with even female impatience on that fatal ignorance of each other which renders nations obnoxious to all sorts of exasperating influences and mischievous prejudices ! But, alas ! we must wait. The great stream of knowledge will not roll on the quicker for our regrets, be they ever so passionate ; for our labours it will. Do not laugh at my "our." I mean it to comprehend, not only the best and wisest of statesmen and the person who would form a very ridiculous *dual* with him, but the humbler creature that cherishes a kindly feeling to his "foreigner" brother, that tries to allay an evil passion, or to clear away a noxious prejudice.

God be praised ! we have some such brethren and fellow-workers, and in time shall have many more. The periodical Press, that awful engine, will in time find its level ; at present its authority is wholly factitious, exaggerated, and false. The Press is so imposing ; men naturally believe in it implicitly for a long time. But they *find it out*. Nothing but truth stands. There remains, however, with nations as with individuals, the great difficulty, the passions. There are states of mind, or rather of temper, in which truth cannot be heard ; even facts are not seen, not looked at ; and here the demons of the Press *attendent les hommes ;* into these burning hearts they pour their infernal combustibles. However, we *have* made great progress.   The old idea of *a Frenchman* is really extinct, and though we see that they have some faults, and perhaps believe they have more, we *all* recognise their grand and charming qualities.   Your *jeunesse* seems to me difficult to *put into harness.*   It seems to me (if it is not presumptuous to say so) that it does not make any rational estimate of life.   What life *is for?* What it *can* and what it *cannot* give ?   What to aim at ? What to acquiesce in ?   Your young heaven-stormers do not settle these points with themselves so well or so soon as our less vivacious and less ambitious youth.   So it seems to me ; and here is a great element of disquiet.

Poor Madame Caton and I will pray for you ; and you will not disdain her prayers, though they should be addressed to the Mother of Mercy.   Thank you for your kind expressions to myself.   If the most cordial and respectful attachment can deserve them, I do.

Yours, dear sir,
S. A.

Mrs. Austin to M. Guizot.

DEAR MONSIEUR GUIZOT,   Feb. 22, 1841.

I have sometimes been inclined to retort upon you your " *C'est une méprise,*" and to tell you you were an Englishman.   But *on se trahit,* and the grace with which you added a delicate kindness to a substantial benefit, forces me to renounce all claim to you as a countryman. I need not attempt to describe the pleasure you gave me, because you understood it when you wrote those few most kind lines which arrived after I had sent my letter. Of course, I sent off the letter to Boulogne instantly.

Now I must give you a message from that jovial son of the Anglican Church, Sydney Smith.   He said with great earnestness and emphasis, " Tell M. Guizot that I have just read his 'Washington,' and that in my life I never read anything evincing more taste, tact, sense, judgment ; and that is precisely Lord Grey's opinion." I don't know if this is worth much to you, but they are fastidious critics, and you may like to hear their opinions. I dined on Saturday at Lord Langdale's. I had seen him last at the House of Lords, where I heard the Queen's Speech, and we looked with blank astonishment at each other at the *omission.** He spoke of it again on Saturday with great contempt. We talked of you, and he said, "Tell M. Guizot it is not the fortifying Paris— nobody would care about that—it is the armament, the seeing France put on a war establishment. That is what makes people uneasy, and will keep them so." I tell you this, dear sir, because you may like to know what is thought by friends of peace and of good government. But *nobody* accuses you—nobody thinks you a "*barbare.*" Everybody sees that it would be impossible to govern the chafing, impatient courser without allowing him some rein. I assure you that there is the most universal confidence in your intentions and in your wisdom, and that the extreme calmness of the English people rests mainly on that confidence. Everybody believes that you will do *the best you can.* As to the character of those you have to manage, people differ widely according to the strength of their prejudices. You may like to know that my brother, Philip Taylor, who has long been established as an engineer at Marseilles, writes that every opinion he hears is pacific, and that the citizens of Marseilles complain bitterly of being misrepresented by the Press. All his workmen are Frenchmen, *and even*

---

* Lord Brougham in the Upper House, and Messrs. Grote and Hume in the Lower, referred to the omission of all mention of France in the Queen's Speech, and censured the manner in which that Power had been treated by our Government during the late complications. See W. N. Molesworth's 'History of England,' vol. ii., p. 43.

Provençaux (I hope you accept the compliment), and it is impossible to find greater harmony and attachment. I am sorry M. Cousin talks about "*le bas empire*." All that is nonsense. Who can find the least shred of analogy? Who does not see that France cannot move hand or foot without shaking Europe from end to end? Who doubts her enormous power to do mischief to all her neighbours? I dislike these attempts to pique the *amour propre* of individuals or nations by allusions and phrases, especially when they are false and absurd. Pardon : these are hard words for a woman ; but when the welfare of millions is at stake, I am subject to *emportements*, which are not pretty. Again and again accept my most cordial thanks, and believe me, with the most respectful attachment,

Yours,
S. AUSTIN.

The author of ' Cinq-Mars ' writes one of those inimitable French *billets* which are so hard to render into any other language :—

M. A. de Vigny to Mrs. Austin.

[TRANSLATION.]

Paris, March 26, 1841.

Most assuredly, Madame, it is impossible to find more charming coquetry than that of England as represented by you, and there is no Syria one would not abandon with delight for a person who becomes so amiable after succeeding in all her desires. She exactly resembles that lovely lady of the Court of Louis XIV., who sent a message to her lover, "Let him understand that I have been unfaithful to him, but I do not bear him any malice."

It has taken time to find the coat-of-arms of Bayard. They were only discovered in the Royal Library the day before yesterday ; and I wished to draw them for you myself. As an artist I am not, like Bayard, *sans peur et sans reproche,* but you will not be able to reproach my exactness. Mr. Reeve will tell you that Barbier, whom he will see at my house this evening, is ever your true and loyal friend. I always see your portrait hung above any other in his room, and we often talk of the absent one it represents.   Your devoted

A. DE VIGNY.

Mrs. Austin wrote to Professor Ranke, intimating a desire to translate his 'History of the Reformation.' He answers :—

Prof. v. Ranke to Mrs. Austin.

[TRANSLATION.]

HONOURED MADAM,   Berlin, April, 1841.

When, last summer, I had your translation of my book on the Popes lying before me, I undertook to compare it with the original, and to write fully to you on the subject. I read the end last, that being fresher in my memory, and was delighted to hear my thoughts speak in the ringing tones of the purest English. This change, for which I must thank you, caused me a kind of illusion. It appeared to me almost as though I had written it myself. I did not carry out my intention. It has been said with truth that it is *my English self;* and who cares to study himself, when the world for so many centuries offers so much that is infinitely greater? Again, my University labours, and the new and large work I am engaged in, engrosses all my powers and all my attention.

In the meantime, the notices I have seen, and particularly the intention of Mr. Murray, which you tell me of in your last letter, give me extreme pleasure. I am as glad as though the reception were personal to myself, and shall for ever remain grateful to you, my honoured friend, who have been the means of procuring such a reception of my book. I admire the courage which prompts you to desire to translate the book on the Reformation. You will have to face five, perhaps six, volumes, in which German interests are entirely preponderant. But I cannot deny that I should like you to undertake it. Everything must be studied from its source. If the great development of the Reformation is to be understood, people must be at the pains to study the conditions of Germany at that time, without which it would never have been accomplished. This includes an appreciation of the whole history of that period which reacted upon the conditions of Germany.

Mrs. Austin to Mrs. Grote.

Carlsbad, Bohemia, Aug. 24, 1841.

. . . . Our visit at my beloved Tetschen afforded us many opportunities of learning something of the *statistiques* and condition of the country. To judge from Count Thun's own dominions, one would be inclined to judge very favourably of the state of the country. The cottages are better, cleaner, and more adorned than in almost any part of Germany I have seen ; the roads good, and great appearance of activity. But they all tell you, and wherever you go you hear, that "*Unser* Graf stands alone." He hardly ever goes near Vienna, lives among and for his *Unterthanen* (subjects), and you meet him miles from the castle, in all weathers, on foot, wearing a blouse and bareheaded, yet looking always a most imposing *ritterlich* (knightly) man. His son, my dear Francis, is still more beloved—indeed adored ; and no wonder. Combined with his father's sense of what is *due* to his dependents, he has a truly Christian or, if you will, democratic feeling of brotherhood with the meanest—a persuasion that they are not where and what they ought to be ; and this gives to his manner to them an ineffable sweetness and benignity. His mother said to me, "If there is a child or a dog in the house, it will not quit Franz."

The younger son, Leo, struck my husband extremely. As he is in the judicial career, he and the Professor "cottoned" together, much to their common satisfaction. Countess Thun told me that Leo wrote about Austin with unwonted satisfaction. This is one of the many occasions which make me feel bitterly what a great teacher is lost to the world. To see that noble-minded young man, full of knowledge and of high aspirations towards a useful career, drinking in his words, was to me nearly as melancholy as agreeable. A few—and how few!—will know, and when it is too late will say, what it was to hear him expound. His audience here is of the feminine gender—Lady William Russell, Mademoiselle Schopenhauer, and Mrs. Hamilton Gray. Cummer, dear, we are certainly *looking up!* These women have beaten all the men who have been here out of the field for general knowledge and powers of thought and conversation. Mademoiselle Schopenhauer and my husband discussed the *light* questions of the "existence of evil" and the "eternity of the world," as soon as they met; last night came Lady William to ask him to throw light on the Schelling and Hegel controversy, which she is looking into.

What you say, dear Cummer, is very true: life is, to most, an uneasy pursuit. I, however, have been so disciplined in living *au jour la journée* that I have not even a place to hanker after; I go where the winds and the waves drive, and try to make the best of the spot where I am. Generally speaking, I succeed pretty well. I am glad you like my book.* It has great success in Germany.

Your ever affectionate

S. A.

* ' Fragments of German Authors.'

CHAPTER XV.

IN Germany Mrs. Austin began to keep a diary for the amusement of her daughter, Lady Duff Gordon. Unfortunately she did not continue it for any time, or at all regularly. Part of the diary appeared in *Macmillan's Magazine* in 1877 ('German Society Forty Years Ago').

" *June* 1841.—In the steamer from Mainz to Bonn was—*inter alios*—an individual of the genus *Rath.* He sat opposite to us at dinner on the deck, and first attracted my attention by the following reply to his neighbour, a man who appeared to entertain the profoundest admiration for him : 'Oh, yes, there are lots of *theorists* in the world, only too many. *I* represent *den gesunden Menschenverstand*' (sound common sense). Delighted at this declaration, I raised my eyes, and saw a face beaming with the most undoubting self-complacency. He went on to detail certain schemes of his for the good of his country—Oldenburg, as it seemed. My husband began to interrogate him about Oldenburg, and I said all I knew of it was from Justus Möser. The worthy Rath looked at me amazed, and said this was the first time he ever heard Justus Möser mentioned by a lady. I said so much the worse; there is an infinity of good sense in his writings. Yes, but he never expected to hear of his being read by a lady, and that I was evidently the second representative of sound common sense in the world, ' worthy to be *my* disciple,' added he with emphasis.

"*Sept.* 1841.—In Dresden I met the Grand Duke of Saxe Weimar, who told me the following anecdote on the authority of his mother-in-law the Empress of Russia :—When Paul and his wife went to Paris, they were called, as is well-known, le Comte and la Comtesse du Nord. The Comtesse du Nord accompanied Marie Antoinette to the theatre at Versailles. Marie Antoinette pointed out, behind her fan, *aussi honnêtement que possible*, all the distinguished persons in the house. In doing this she had her head bent forward. All of a sudden she drew back with such an expression of terror and horror that the Comtesse said, ' Pardon, madame, mais je suis sûre que vous avez vu 'quelque chose qui vous agite.' The Queen, after she had recovered herself, told her that there was about the Court, but not of right belonging to it, a woman who professed to read fortunes on cards. One evening she had been displaying her skill to several ladies, and at length the Queen desired to have her own destiny told. The cards were arranged in the usual manner, but when the woman had to read the result, she looked horror-struck, and stammered out some generalities. The Queen insisted on her saying what she saw, but she declared she could not. ' From that time,' said Marie Antoinette, 'the sight of that woman produces in me a feeling I cannot describe, of aversion and horror, and she seems studiously to throw herself in my way !'

"The Grand Duke told very curious stories about a sort of second sight ; especially of a Princess of S——, who was, I believe, connected with the House of Saxony. It is the custom among them to allow the bodies of their deceased relations to lie in state, and all the

members of the family go to look at them. The
Princess was a single woman, and not young. She had
the faculty, or the curse, of always seeing, not the body
actually exposed, but the next member of the family who
was to die. On one occasion a child died ; she went to
the bedside and said, 'I thought I came to look at a
branch, but I see the tree.' In less than three weeks the
father was dead. The Grand Duke told me several
other instances of the same kind. But this faculty was
not confined to deaths. A gentleman whom the Grand
Duke knew and named to me, went one day to visit the
Princess ; as soon as she saw him she said, 'I am delighted to see you, but why have you your leg bound
up ?' 'Oh,' said her sister, Princess M——, 'it is not
bound up ; what are you talking of ?' '*I* see that it is,'
she said. On his way home his carriage was upset and
his leg broken.

"*Nov.* 1841, *Dresden.*—I went to see '*Figaro's Hochzeit,*'
not '*Le Nozze di Figaro.*' If you have a mind to understand why the Italians can never be reconciled to
Austrian rulers go to see '*Figaro's Hochzeit.*' A Herr
Dettmer, from Frankfurt, did Figaro, a good singer, I
have no doubt, and not a bad, *i.e.,* an absurd, actor.
But Figaro, the incarnation of Southern vivacity, *espiè-
glerie* and joyous grace ! Imagine a square, thick-set
man, with blond hair and a broad face, and that peculiar
manner of standing and walking with the knees in, the
heels stuck into the earth and the toes in the air, which
one sees only in Germany. I thought of Piuco, a young
Maltese, never, I believe, off his tiny island, whom I
last saw in that part. I saw before me his *élancé* and
supple figure, his small head clustered round with coal-
black hair, his delicately turned jetty moustache, his
truly Spanish costume, the sharp knee just covered by
the breeches tied with gay ribbons, and the elastic step
of the springing foot and high-bounding instep. What

a contrast!—and what can Art do against Nature in such a case? Then the women ; I had seen Ronzi de Begnis in the Countess. What a Countess! What a type of Southern voluptuous grace, of high and stately beauty and indolent charm! Imagine a long-faced, lackadaisical-looking German woman, lean and high-shouldered, and with that peculiar construction of body which German women now affect. An enormously long waist laced in to an absurd degree, and owing its equally extravagant rotundity below to the tailor. 'Happy we,' says Countess Hahn-Hahn, 'who, with so many ells of muslin or silk, can have a beautiful figure.'

"Now as a set-off I must say what Germans can do ; and what I am sure we cannot in this our day. I went to see Schiller's '*Braut von Messina.*' I expected little. The piece is especially lyric rather than dramatic. The long speeches, thought I, will be dull, the choruses absurd. The sentiments are pagan. What have Spanish Sicilian nobles to do with a Nemesis, with oracles, with a curse like that on the House of Athens, with sustained speeches, the whole purport of which is '*incusare deos.*' Well, I was wrong. In the opening scene, Mlle. Berg has to stand for a quarter of an hour between two straight lines of senators and to make a speech—*rien que cela.* Can anything be more difficult? Yet such was the beauty of her declamation of Schiller's majestic verse, such the solemnity, propriety, grace, and dignity of her action, that at every moment one's interest rose. I cannot at this moment recollect ever to have seen an actress who could have done it so well. Rachel, with all her vast talents as a declaimer, would have been too hard for the heart-stricken mother. Emil Devrient's *Don Cesar* was quite as good. His acting in the last scene, where Beatrice entreats him to live, was frightfully good. The attempts at paternal tenderness, instantly relapsing into the fatal passion ignorantly conceived, made one's heart stand still. One saw before one the youth vainly struggling with the hereditary curse of his house—the doomed victim and instrument of the vengeance of an implacable destiny. Anything more thoroughly heathenish than the play I cannot conceive, and I question whether an English audience would sit it out. We should find it our duty to be shocked. The audience last night were probably attracted by Schiller's name, and knew that such 'horrid opinions' once existed in Greece, and that a poet imitating Greek tragedy might represent Greek modes of thinking. In short, we did not feel ourselves the least compromised by the Queen of Sicily's attack upon the gods. The chorus is, as in duty bound, a pacificator ; the amount of comfort, it is true, often is, 'It can't be helped ;' but this is so nobly and beautifully expressed that one is satisfied."

Mrs. Austin to M. Guizot.

DEAR M. GUIZOT,   Dresden, December 20, 1841.

Never were men gifted with the spirit of large and enlightened humanity more wanted than now. Men's hands are at peace, but their hearts are full of bitter hate, jealousy, rancour, and envy. The explosion of last year was *but* an explosion. The combustible materials were all there. The war-cry of Germany surprised some people in France ; it surprised not me, who could have predicted it exactly. I have ventured formerly to say what I knew of the temper of Germans towards France —to some Frenchmen. They took it as an offence offered by an Englishwoman. What can one do but hold one's tongue ? M. Thiers will not tell you, nor anybody, all he saw and heard, nor how he was repulsed, nor the immeasurable humiliations he had to undergo. Even the account of his interview with the King of Prussia, which I have read in the *Revue de Paris*, though not flattering, is a very different version from what I had from a lady nearly connected with the Royal Family of Prussia. That the Princes of Germany have made the most of this *Deutsch* and anti-French enthusiasm, was to be expected, and the *Rheinlied* and all that is become tiresome and absurd. But if the feeling had not been intense and universal, the Princes could have made nothing of it, and the *Rheinlied* would have appeared to everybody a very poor song. No, dear sir, years of moderation, of forbearance must efface the fatal impressions left by *a government of conquerors,* not worse, perhaps, than any other such ; but all such are bad, or at least galling and offensive, and *that,* as Princess Hohenzollern said to me, is what men never forget, though they do the physical sufferings of war. But if such are the sentiments of Germany towards France, they are not an atom more friendly towards England. The only difference is, that the hostility towards us is more one of locality and class ; being directed against our commercial preponderancy, it rages in the manufacturing districts and classes. In Austria one hears little of it, nor in what is called good society anywhere, rather the reverse. But the journals sufficiently show the bitter jealousy and animosity of the middling and industrial classes. They, for their misfortune and ours, are now taking up, with all the zeal of discoverers or proselytes, the anti-social doctrines on trade, which the majority in England so long professed and acted on, and which the ruling class still acts on. All the most perverse views on the relations of nations are put forth here as a sort of religion, and are called patriotism. The beautiful cosmopolitanism which so distinguished Germany from the national bullies of France and England is decried as mean and abject. Every calamity that happens in France or England is enlarged upon with a sort of delight ; prophecies, in which " the wish " was evidently "father to the thought," of decline and dissolution are continually put forth, and, as relates to England, are mixed up with the abundant exaggerations of her actual power and wealth. All this saddens the heart. Malignity and evil passions are bad enough, but the hopeless thing is to see the *reason* in such a state that an accumulation of capital and skill, which it must ever require ages to produce, should be regarded as a thing which men are interested in destroying! As if they were not there for the world! As if the very prosperity of a manufacturing country did not prove the wide diffusion of productions which all desire to have! Alas, alas! My husband is writing (to my infinite joy) an article for the *Edinburgh Review*, on a book by a Dr. List, which has made a great noise here. He is the apostle of the exclusive or, as it is called, protective system. To be sure we can only cry, "Meâ culpâ, meâ culpâ!" So much more easy is it to propagate falsehood than truth; so much more easy to excite bad feelings than good ones. I write to you—and that is the charm—as if France and England were one country, persuaded as I am that they have one interest, and that, whatever your countrymen may think, the English are the only people at the present time capable of appreciating them, simply because they are equals, and look neither up nor down. This constitutes an enormous difference from all other countries. Germany possesses a *class* of men superior in mental culture, *on a given point*, to all others. But not only is the range of each man limited, the *diffusion* of knowledge is not comparable to that with us. Above all (you will not laugh), the condition of women, their intellectual and moral station, is so immeasurably lower, that it must take a long time to bring them up to our level. Of course I use "our" for our *two* countries. Imagine that here, in this courtly little capital, it is the universal custom in what they call society for the men to go into a separate room, or if there is none, to assemble in a corner, while the women sit round the table or in a circle. No man thinks of talking to a lady. I have told them that I am not accustomed to be insulted in this way, and that after such men as M. Guizot have not disdained to speak to me as if I were not quite a fool, I will not take such an assumption of superiority at the hands of little chamberlains, etc. Not that I want or value their conversation, but my English blood boils at seeing myself so degraded. We in England are *oppressed*, but not condemned. The advantages attending these small states, this intimate and really paternal relation between princes and people, are many and striking: the harmony, for instance, between this good King of Saxony and his people is edifying ; *but* the vast and expansive life of Paris and London is wholly wanting, and with it, how much is wanting ! We, the advanced guard on the march of civilisation, have all the rough work to do. Among us the fearful struggle of suffering man with the world, which he thinks he can alter so as to suit it to himself, is going on, and must go on, till the matter is worked out by reason and experiment, and till he finds *what* he can change and what he *must* endure. In Germany, this is to come ; but it will come to all in turn. Meanwhile how fearful are its appearances with both of us ! Yet even for this, I repeat, we can better understand and appreciate each other. France and England are *men* of the same growth and strength. How much of the future destiny of the world depends on them and on their amity ! Here I feel it. In almost all companies and parts of Germany, I, "the *natural enemy*" of France, find myself her defender—scolded and wondered at for being so. In Berlin, whither we mean to go, I expect to find even more of this, judging from the numerous Berliners I know. Prussia is a *new* power (relatively to us), and has the *susceptibilité* of a *parvenu*.

They have a perfect right to estimate themselves very highly ; but they set no bounds to their pretensions, and are *offusqués* at those of all other nations. Their enthusiasm for their King has sadly declined. He committed the great blunder of talking too much, exciting vague and large hopes, and now they say he does nothing. They call him the *redselig*, as opposed to his father the *hochselig*. In Berlin this sort of *Wortwitz* is universal ; their *calembourgs* are poor and blunt attempts at imitations of French *mots*, which nobody can imitate. There is an ecclesiastical movement which will do the King no good. Bunsen is sent to England to concoct an Established Church, hierarchy, or something like it. It is a great pity, for everybody believes the King to be both good and *plein d'esprit*, but not wise nor firm. The poor Poles seem to hope something from him. What, they hardly can tell you. But they are in a state to catch at straws.

I sometimes cannot help admitting to myself that, considering my husband's vast and peculiar powers, some way of making them useful to the public might have been found by a Government discerning of true and rare merit, though his health did not allow him to keep time in the routine of official business. These little princes, whom we call "beggarly," etc., etc., are ingenious in providing harbours of refuge where such men can work for the world, in whose vortex they cannot live. He would have been satisfied with the merest subsistence if he had been treated with the respect and deference he deserves. But which of those men of expedients, to whom philosophy is ridiculous, could be expected to imagine such a thing ? What is to come I know not, but I think any change good that delivers the country from sneering sceptics of all that is too high and too great for them, like Lord Melbourne and Lord Palmerston. I hope you have reason to be better pleased with the present people.

Lord John closed his career with honour. He is a loss.

Farewell, dear sir, with every sentiment of affection and respect,

Yours,   SARAH AUSTIN.

Mrs. Austin to Mr. Murray.

Dresden, March 22, 1842.

Now, my dear Mr. Murray, you must give me an attentive ear, or rather eye, and, an immediate reply, to what I am going to say. You may recollect that I spoke to you about the 'Puss in boots' of Otto Speckter, and I think showed you two of the designs; they are at Lady Gordon's if you want to refresh your memory.

Yesterday I received a parcel from Rudolf Besser of Hamburg, containing a complete set of the plates as a gift from Speckter, and the enclosed letter, which Mr. John Murray must read to you. Therefore you must say whether or not you will treat with Speckter for the plates, and with me for the text. I am going now to write to him, and shall say that he had better send a complete copy of the plates to some one in London authorised to show them and to treat on his behalf. I have spoken to Tieck about them. He says he received them at Potsdam, and that the King and Queen of Prussia were delighted and diverted with them, as he was himself—indeed, it is impossible there can be two opinions on their merit and genius. But in case you think of the thing, you had better show them to E. Landseer as the most competent of all judges.

My own share in the matter is of course inconsiderable, but I really cannot help recommending you warmly to think of the work; the designs are quite bewitching, and as a Christmas book, I should think it must have a great success. There are twelve plates, and a frontispiece of cats which is inimitable.

I would give a list of the subjects, but I have sent it to the young Princes and Princesses of Saxony to look at. If you mean to undertake it, you will negotiate *directly* with Otto Speckter, Hamburg, for the plates, and will be so good as to tell me what you propose to give me for my share. I had rather have said nothing about that, but our transatlantic friends have taken good care to curb any flights of generosity of mine, and I must break off other work to do this : you will not wish me to make any such sacrifice. John E. Taylor tells me you speak of me with kind and cordial interest, and I do not doubt it. The consciousness that I carry with me the respect and good wishes of my friends, as well as *my own* respect, supports me, and will support me under this unexpected tide of calamity.

You may perhaps have heard that a letter dated Weimar (as a blind), which appeared in the *Times*, and, I am told, attracted a good deal of attention in London, was written by me. If you have *not* heard it, I entreat you not to speak of it; I have no inclination to figure as a newspaper writer. But as several people guessed it, it may perhaps have reached your ears. I have had very high compliments upon it. I have myself never seen it in print, but I hope a copy is kept for me. That, and many other things, will perhaps one day see the light in a more permanent form. I am much urged by the Germans to write upon Germany. This is a high compliment from them, for they are much dissatisfied with all that has been written, especially in France — more perhaps with the praise than the censure. M. de Brunnow, brother of the Russian Ambassador in London, and himself a writer, is very urgent with me.

A few remarks on the Gallery which I sent to the *Athenæum*, and which people have guessed to be mine, were immediately translated, and inserted in one of the most considerable journals. In short, I am very conscious that my opinion has a weight here which it does not deserve. It would be more to *my* purpose if the exaggeration were as great in England. As I declined going to Court—my husband too unwell—the Queen sent for me. I had a private audience of two hours, and have seldom had a more agreeable conversation. Her kind and cordial manner put me in a moment at my ease, and her sense and information *forced* me to listen and to talk with interest. As I sat on the sofa by her side, discussing every kind of subject, I forgot all except that she was a very agreeable and sensible woman.

Tieck and I are great friends. Pray remember me to Mr. Grüner ; tell him he promised to write.

In the next number of the *British and Foreign Review* you will see an article of mine (if you care to see it), some of which will, I think, amuse you. I am pretty far advanced with one for the *Edinburgh Review* on changes in manners in Germany. As to translating the ' Rome in 1833,' the idea was suggested to me by an exceedingly clever man, who lived there four years and married a natural daughter of Prince Henry of Prussia, who permanently resides there. He assured me that it was the *only* faithful and lively picture of *actual living* Rome. Of this I cannot possibly judge, but I *can* judge of Dr. Franck's capacity, and of that I think most highly ; it is certain the English never get behind the scenes. It is a very small book, and my idea was to unite to it a new and much admired work on Venice, called ' Sospiri,' and one on Naples and the Neapolitans by Dr. K. A. Mayer (2 vols.), also just published and greatly praised. One of the best journals says of the last, " it introduces us into the varied life of the people, the Neapolitans, in their most peculiar and intimate ways of thinking and living, and contains information concerning preachers, churches, popular festivals, theatres," etc. The author lived there many years. The three might make 3 vols.

But I conceive the sort of disgust at the name of Italy, however good and however new the matter.

Lastly, Dr. Liepmann, *ci-devant* historical tutor to the Czarewitch, came to me the other day to say that a Dr. Echtermeyer, of whom he thinks very highly, had a project of writing a history of German literature, expressly for England—at least, for foreigners (*i.e.* non-Germans)—and wished to consult me. I let him come, and gave him this advice: To write a view of his scheme, together with some account of his pretensions and former pursuits, and I promised that I would forward it to you. Perhaps it may accompany this. I have inquired about him ; he is a young man, but there is a great persuasion of his capacity. Everybody to whom I have spoken says he would do it well—and he is not a Dresden man. If you agree about it, and it is good, I would, if you like, translate it.

I have set a friend of mine (a lady) upon writing down her recollections of *what she saw* of the scenes of war in Dresden, especially in 1813. The anecdotes of Napoleon and his troops, of the King, etc., which she sat telling me one evening, made me feel that we islanders never have any idea of what passed under the eyes of these people, and I exclaimed : " Why don't you write all this ? " She said, " Oh, no ; she never thought of such a thing." But two days after, she called and said she had resolved to do it, and to call the book ' Ein Kriegsjahr in Dresden.' I shall see what it turns out, and, if you like, will keep an eye on it for you. I thought of it for a magazine, but *nous verrons.*

I must conclude this long scrawl. I am hoping to see my dear children and grandchild on the Rhine, which cheers me much. We are all in admiration of Sir Robert Peel. " Staats Minister " v. Lindenau made me a long visit yesterday, and we talked over English affairs, in which he is greatly interested. He is a truly admirable man, and worthy to estimate Peel, whom he greatly reveres. M. de Lindenau is very kind, and gives me every sort of information and documents about Saxony. I am going to have the wages and expenditure of labourers in every district of the kingdom.

Pray regard this letter as strictly private, at least all about myself. What I tell you as a friend kind enough to be interested for me, would be ridiculous *self-glorification* to others. Best regards to Mrs. Murray and your family.

Yours most truly,
S. AUSTIN.

Mrs. Austin to M. Victor Cousin.

[TRANSLATION.]

Bonn, June 5, 1842.

We ought to have been here in April but—there is always a but in my life; I think I told you my husband intended to write a reply to a book which has obtained a great success in Germany, 'Über die National Oekonomie,' by Dr. List—a book containing everything that was most false, most anti-social, and detestable about the commercial relations of nations. Mr. Austin had commenced an article for the *Edinburgh Review*; it was announced and expected. The three first months of the year passed by (like so many others) in attacks of illness and fruitless attempts at work, so that at the moment when we ought to have started, he was obliged to work almost night and day, and I also, for I copied every word. However, here we are, though we only left Dresden on the 21st of May. We go to Carlsbad in August, and if my husband proposes to return to Dresden, I really think, for the first time in my life, I shall oppose his project. Is life so long that one can afford to throw away years ? To vegetate, without any sphere of usefulness, any interchange of ideas, any society ? Mr. Austin needs a different atmosphere. He

talks of Berlin ; and we have received very flattering
invitations from there. But I have a great dislike of
the disparaging intellect and the bad puns that pass for
wit in Berlin. How are you ? Have you seen Mr.
Grote ? Write to me, and accept the best love of

GROSSMÜTTERCHEN.
(LITTLE GRANDMOTHER.)

Mrs. Austin to Mrs. Grote.

DEAR FRIEND AND CUMMER,*   July, 1842.

Thank you for your beautiful little " *Andenken*," and
more for thinking of me so far off and so long asunder.

But I cannot accept any gift as indemnity for a letter,
which I still look for with eagerness. I know how little
a letter can contain of all you have to say, but that little
will be very precious to your old friend. When we may
meet again seems wholly uncertain. My husband will
not hear of attempting to live in London on our present
income, and though I long so much for a home and a
resting-place that I would willingly try a cottage in the
country in England, I fear it would not suit him, and I
am not quite sure if, after all, it would suit me. Pleasures
one cannot reach are better at a distance which make
them wholly out of the question, and if I felt I *could* get
at my children and my friends, perhaps my longing
would be more painful, at least more *irritating* and less
stumpf than it is now, when seas and mountains are
between us. Mrs. Jameson made my mouth water by
the mention of a cottage at Ealing for £22 a year. I
wonder what it is like. We have been paying three
times that for lodgings at Dresden, and not good ones
—indeed, there are few good. Still, I cannot deny the
enormous differences on the whole, arising partly from

* " Cummer," a Scotch word, from the French *commère*, used
by the two ladies in writing to each other as a familiar sign of
intimacy.

the cheapness of things, and yet more from the habits of the people. I was there perfectly on a level with anybody you please—visited and received as well as the ladies of princely houses and royal alliances, and what did it cost?—The whole winter not the price of one London dinner! Their blood and connections signify nothing, it is true, but I mean that as to society, one could go no higher, and some of them were charming, distinguished, accomplished women. The Queen, who was extremely kind to me, not the least so; Princess Reuss, a cousin of the Duchess of Kent, who lived exactly as I did, extremely lively, amusing, inquiring, and full of anecdotes; Madame de Lüttichau above all, a woman of incomparable nobleness, grace, and expansion of mind, and a heart full of all goodness. *She* is an acquisition for life and death, for there cannot come a time in which I shall not feel the better for having known her, loved her, and lived with her as I did. She has dreadful health—the fate of so many I love. But Dresden is utterly barren of public interests and of the sort of society they create. For my husband, there would have been absolutely nothing but for the accident of a very clever Prussian, Dr. Franck, being there; with him he walked and talked.

M. de Lindenau is a Turgot, stunted and checked by want of space and of vital air; but he is hardly to be got at, and his calls on me were considered miracles. I have great hopes of seeing him here; he half promised me to come if he can get a holiday. We shall stay to the latest day consistent with my husband's taking the waters—of Carlsbad, I suppose. It is not certain, for Cousin has been taking enormous pains to persuade us that Emms or Plombières are as good. But my husband means to consult an eminent physician here about Plombières. Cousin wants to meet us there, and of course it would be a great pleasure to meet him, and a great advantage to be spared crossing Germany again now that we are on the Rhine ; but it would be absurd to give up the unquestionable good of Carlsbad for a chance. If George Lewis could have gone there with us, as he intended, my husband would not have hesitated. I shall find there two of the people I love and honour the most—the Archbishop of Erlau and Lady William Russell—at least, I trust she may still be there, and he has written to me to ask me our time, that he may not miss us.

Cousin's unwearying and uncooled friendship is extremely touching, and I have lived long enough to know all its rarity. Fourteen years ago we met here by chance, and since that time never has he varied from the most cordial attachment. Our adversity and absence from England has enabled me to take the standard of many friendships, and this standard will abide with me.

Among those who have come like the purest gold out of the furnace, I must mention my dear John Mill, and the excellent and *unprofessing* Lewis. I don't mean to say they are alone, but they are pre-eminent.

I hope Mr. Grote will read my husband's article on List's book, and you, too, dearest Cummer, spite of petticoats, which in this country extinguish the idea of such inquiries. He wishes much to review John Mill's book when it comes out. I want him *first* to write an article, such as he, and only he, could, on Prussia. In this case, however, he says he must go and spend the winter at Berlin ; and this I cannot, spite of all invitations, compliments, and cajoleries, bear the thought of. Everybody (Germans included) hates Berlin, as the abode of every sort of false and arrogant pretension. Nevertheless there are so many *really* eminent men that there must be some good society.

Your affectionate
S. AUSTIN.

CHAPTER XVI.

Diary of Mrs. Austin in 1842 and 1843—Dresden—Berlin—Literary Society there—The Grimms—Ranke—Anecdotes of Berlin Society—Of Niebuhr—Mr. Grote to Mr. Austin.

ANOTHER entry in Mrs. Austin's diary in Dresden is a funny illustration of German manners :—

" *Feb.* 1842.—Two days before we left Dresden, as I was dressing to go out, Nannie, my maid, came into my room and said two ladies wanted to see me. She said she had never seen them—they said I did not know them. I sent to say that I was sorry but I could not receive them as Madame de S—— was already waiting for me. Nannie came back with the answer that they would wait in the anteroom—they only wanted to speak to me for a moment. Annoyed at being forced to commit a rudeness, I hurried on my gown and went out. In the anteroom were a middle-aged lady and a young one. I broke out into apologies, etc. ; upon which the elder lady said in German, 'Pardon me for being so pressing. I only wished to give my daughter strength for the battle of life.' I was literally confounded at the oddness of this address, and remained dumb. It seemed her daughter wished to translate from the English. After a short explanation she turned to her daughter, and pointing to me, said, ' Now, my dear, you have seen the mistress, so we will not keep her any longer.' And so they went. I threw myself into a chair, and, alone as I was, burst into an uncontrollable fit of laughter. This is as good a piece of Germanism as is to be found in any novel. Even my Dresden friends thought it quite amazing."

In November, 1842, she writes at Berlin in her diary—

" 22nd.—Tea at Schellings', a very agreeable party. Two Grimms and Mdme. Grimm, Ranke, Steffens, Countess Bohlen, Perz and wife, de Savigny, and others. I was more struck with the Grimms than with anybody. I talked to Wilhelm, taking him for Jacob. He told me of my mistake, and I said it did not signify, the brothers Grimm were one thing. Presently Jacob came and sat by me ; I told him I had been forewarned that he would run away from a stranger and a woman—an Englishwoman. . On the contrary, he was polite, cordial, and willing to talk. He told me he was preparing a new edition of the German Mythology, and was especially occupied about spells. I mentioned to him the Indian spells given in Meadows Taylor's novels. His exterior is striking and engaging. He has the shyness and simplicity of a German man of letters, but without any of the awkward, uncouth, ungentlemanlike air which is so common among them. His is a noble and refined head, full of intelligence, thought, and benevolence. Wilhelm is also a fine-looking man, younger, less imposing, less refined, but with a charming air of good nature and sense. His wife is very pleasing. Ranke is a little, insignificant-looking man, very like a Frenchman—small, vivacious, and a little conceited-looking. It seems the audience expected a scene—we were to fall into each other's arms. On the contrary, we appeared to be of one mind—viz., to meet with the utmost coolness and indifference. Mdme. Schelling said he was, what he seldom is, abashed. He thought people were looking at him, and therefore he hardly spoke to me. Schelling was a most polite and effective host, and his wife did the honours better than any German woman I have seen. We women were not entrenched behind tables—fixtures against the walls, as is usual, while the men huddle into corners to talk. I was less plagued about my authorship than I expected: altogether it was pleasant, cordial, and promised agreeable things.

"*24th.*—Dr. Julius called. He is evidently extremely disgusted with Berlin and with all in it except the King, of whom he says the Berliners are not worthy.

"My maid Nannie told me a curious illustration of the position of servants here. The maid of our landlord has, it seems, a habit of running out and being gone for hours without leave. On Sunday evening last she had leave. Monday and Tuesday, ditto. Wednesday she took leave, and did not return till after ten. Her mistress asked where she had been, and she refused to answer: 'If I won't tell you, you can't hang me for it.' Another day, the master, who is lame, came down into the kitchen and asked her to run upstairs and fetch his spectacles for him. 'Oh, I am washing dishes,' said she. The droll thing is, that they say they are only too glad to have this steady and obliging person because she is honest—a thing almost unique here, as it seems.

" *30th.*—Ranke called to talk to me about the translation of his 'Reformation in Germany.' Strenuously resisted all idea of abridgement. His articulation is bad, his manner not pleasant nor gentlemanlike. He is not so good as his books. Some people are better.

" *Dec.* 17*th.*—Went to Savigny's. Nobody was there but W. Grimm and his wife and a few men. Grimm told me he had received two volumes of Norwegian fairy-tales, and that they were delightful. Talking of them, I said, 'Your children appear to me the happiest in the world ; they live in the midst of fairy-tales.' 'Ah,' said he, 'I must tell you about that. When we were at

Göttingen, somebody spoke to my little son about his father's "*Mährchen*." He had read them, but never thought of their being mine. He came running to me, and said with an offended air, "Father, they say you wrote those fairy-tales ; surely you never invented such silly rubbish ? " He thought it below my dignity.'

"Another story of Grimm's :—

"'When I was a young man, I was walking one day and saw an officer in the old-fashioned uniform. It was under the old Elector. The officers still wore pigtails, cocked hats set over one eye, high neck-cloths, and coats buttoned back. As he was walking stiffly along, a groom came by riding a horse, which he appeared to be breaking in. "What mare is that you are riding ? " called out the major with an authoritative, disdainful air. "She belongs to Prince George," answered the groom. "Ah——h ! " said the major, raising his hand reverently to his hat with a military salute, and bowing low to the mare. I told this story,' continued Grimm, 'to Prince B., thinking to make him laugh. But he looked grave, and said, with quite a tragic tone of voice, "Ah, that feeling is no longer to be found ! "'

"Savigny told a *Volksmährchen* too :—

"'St. Anselm was grown old and infirm, and lay on the ground among thorns and thistles. *Der liebe Gott* said to him, "You are very badly lodged there ; why don't you build yourself a house ? " "Before I take the trouble," said Anselm, "I should like to know how long I have to live." "About thirty years," said *Der liebe Gott*. "Oh, for so short a time," replied he, "it's not worth while," and turned himself round among the thistles.'

"*Jan.* 1843.—Berlin is too large and too small, too new and too old, too bustling and too quiet, dull and not venerable. I could go on multiplying these contradictions, but it is better to make them intelligible. It is large enough to make the distances inconvenient and costly in time and money. You cannot, as in Dresden, run all over the town in an hour. The distances, too, are wearisome—long, straight streets of shabby, monotonous houses. It is large enough to contain such a population as to furnish incessant interruptions and distraction —eternal visiting, a host of lions, all sorts of *devoirs sociaux*, etc., etc. On the other hand, it does not afford that most precious of heaven's gifts—liberty. If you have the smallest pretension to be *vornehm* (fine), you can only live Unter den Linden, or in the Wilhelms-strasse.

"Social life does not exist in Berlin, though people are always in company, and one is, as Ranke said, *gehetzt* (hunted). In the fashionable parties one always sees the same faces—faces possessed by *ennui*. The great matter is for the men to show their decorations and the women their gowns, and to be called *Excellency*. Generally speaking, it strikes me that the Prussians have no confidence in their own individual power of commanding respect. Much as they hold to all the old ideas and distinctions about birth, even that does not enable them to assume an upright, independent attitude, not even when combined with wealth. Count G——, a man of old Saxon nobility, with large estates and the notions and feelings of an English aristocrat, tells me that he is completely *shouldered* in Berlin society, because he neither has nor will have any official title, wears no orders, and, in short, stands upon his own personal distinctions. The idea of going about the world stark naked as to one's mere name, Mr. Pitt, Mr. Fox, Mr. Canning—a German would be ashamed!

"Till a man is *accroché* on the Court by some title, order, office, or what not, he may be fairly said not to exist. The Germans are becoming clamorous for freer institutions; but how much might they emancipate themselves! A vast deal of this servility is perfectly voluntary, but it seems in the blood. They dislike the King of Hanover as much as we do ; but when Madame de L—— whispered to me at a ball, ' *Voilà votre Prince et Seigneur,*' and I replied in no whisper, '*Prince oui, mais, grace à Dieu, Seigneur non,*' she looked frightened, and so did all the ladies round her—and why? He could do them no more harm than me.

"The other day I went up three pair of stairs to call on a nice little Professor's wife. Arrived at the top, I rang the bell, and out comes a great hulking maid, who looks down upon me from a height of three or four steps. 'Is Madame G—— at home?' Answer (stereotype), ' I don't know ;' after a pause—' Do you mean the Frau Professorin?' 'Yes, Madame G——.' On this out rushes a second maid, looks half stupid, half indignant —'What, do you mean the Frau Geheimräthin?' The joke was now too good to drop. I said again, ' I mean Madame G——, as it seems you do not hear distinctly ; take my card to Madame G——.' I was admitted with the usual words, ' Most agreeable,' and found the very pleasant Frau Professorin Geheimräthin, for she is both, whose servants seem ashamed of her name. Yet it is a name very illustrious in learning.

"*Jan.* 18*th.*—At a dinner-party we talked of Niebuhr, Varnhagen von Ense's article, etc. Von Raumer said, ' I went to his house one evening at Rome, and we *nearly* succeeded in boiling some water for tea, but not quite.' Niebuhr told him that it was a serious thing to associate with Amati, the keeper of the Chigi Library and a great archæologist, because he frequented a wine-shop, the *Sabina,* where the wine was very dear.

"When the late King was at Rome, Niebuhr did the honours so badly that the King was quite impatient. He showed him little fragments of things in which he could take no interest, and none of the great objects. One day Niebuhr spoke of Palestrina. ' What is that ?'

said the King. 'What! your Majesty does not know that?' exclaimed Niebuhr in a tone of astonishment. The King was extremely annoyed, and turning round to some one, said, 'Stuff and nonsense; it's bad enough never to have learnt anything, without having it proclaimed aloud.'

"' Niebuhr's ideas about his own importance and his excessive cowardice were such,' said B———, 'that at the time of the Carbonari affairs, he actually wrote home to the Prussian Government that the whole of this conspiracy was directed against himself.'

"Dr. Franck told me a story of which I never heard before. Voltaire had for some reason or other taken a grudge against the prophet Habakkuk, and affected to find in him things he never wrote. Somebody took the Bible and began to demonstrate to him that he was mistaken. '*C'est égal*,' he said impatiently, '*Habakkuk était capable de tout!*'

"Bettina von Arnim called, and we had a *tête-à-tête* of two hours. Her conversation is that of a clever woman, with some originality, great conceit, and vast unconscious ignorance. Her sentiments have a bold and noble character. We talked about crime, punishment, prisons, education, law of divorce, etc., etc. Gleams of truth and sense, clouds of nonsense—all tumbled out with equally undoubting confidence. Occasional great fidelity of expression. Talking of the so-called happiness and security of ordinary marriages in Germany, she said, '*Qu'est-ce que cela me fait? Est-ce que je me soucie de ces nids qu'on arrange pour propager?*' I laughed out: one must admit that the expression is most happy. She talked of the Ministers with great contempt, and said, 'There is not a man in Germany: have you seen one for whom you feel any enthusiasm? They are all like frogs in a big pond—well, well, let them splash their best, what have we to do with their croaking?'

Some things she said about the folly of attacking full-grown, habitual vice by legislation, prison discipline, etc., were very true, and showed a great capacity for just thought. But what *did* she mean, or what did Schleiermacher mean, for she quoted him, by saying, '*Le péché est une grâce de Dieu*'? There are things said to make people stare. She read me an extract out of a letter of his, speaking of two people who had what one would call a criminal attachment for each other. He wrote, 'As I have always held that those whom God has joined, man should not keep asunder;' taking these words in the completely opposite to what we do, *i.e.*, that persons who don't love each other are joined by the world only, but those who do, by God. If this were known in England! And he so pious, so eloquent a divine!

"*Jan. 20th.*—M. and Mme. de Savigny came in, and the conversation fell on the Italians. Mme. de Savigny spoke highly of them, saying they were not more given to cheating than their neighbours, and had a fund of inexhaustible good-nature and obligingness, and *sehr gewandt* (very clever). M. de Savigny also said they found means to accomplish everything they desired. She spoke of a young Abbate who had been much with them at Rome, and of his serviceableness. Savigny said he had studied theology at the 'Sapienza,' and had the best testimonials to his assiduity and progress. His learning may be judged of by the fact that he believed the whole Bible to have been written by St. John. Somehow the Abbate got sent to Venice. He was enchanted at this; his curiosity was awakened, and he thought he would see the world. So he wrote to M. de Savigny to say he wished to come to Berlin. After making many inquiries about the relative dearness and cheapness of things, and many other particulars, he asked, '*E la prego di domandare al Vescovo di questa città, se trovero mezzo di vivere allegramente dalle messe per i defunti ?'* (And I beg of you to inquire from the Bishop of that city whether I shall be able to live jovially on the proceeds of masses for the dead).

"This strikes me as a charming story."

1842–43 was a busy year for Mrs. Austin. She wrote an article on H. Steffen's 'Autobiography' in the *British and Foreign Review*; one 'On Changes in German Manners,' for the *Edinburgh Review*; many letters to the *Athenæum*, and one to the *Times* on Germany; an article on Ritter von Lang's 'Memoirs,' and one 'On the State of Germany from the French Revolution to 1815.' 'Stories of the Gods and Heroes of Greece' (by Niebuhr), came out in 1843 under Mrs. Austin's name, but they were translated by her daughter, Lady Duff Gordon.

Mr. Grote writes to Mr. Austin from London :—

DEAR AUSTIN,   London, February, 1843.

I am very glad to hear that you are employed upon an article in the *Edinburgh* on the subject of Prussia. The English public is greatly misinformed upon the subject now, and you have the best opportunities for collecting such matter as·will improve and rectify their views. I presume you will derive much assistance in the way of suggestions from this recent French publication which has appeared, so very virulent against the Government; it is a perfect *Prusso-mastix.* The difficulty in a country where the Press is fettered, must consist in finding out what can justly be objected to in the working of the Government. I have no doubt that the French book is very unduly vituperative.

I have resumed my History, and find it the greatest object of interest and delight now remaining to me. The prospect of public matters, as far as present progress is concerned, presents little which interests me, and still less which I contemplate with any satisfaction, either in England or abroad. Intellectual curiosity and activity is now the great pleasure and occupation of my life, and is likely to become more and more so. In July next, I have determined to leave business altogether, and I shall then devote myself exclusively to the prosecution of my History, which I find a very long, though a very interesting, business.

G. GROTE.

Herr Julius Hübner to Mrs. Austin.

[TRANSLATION.]

MY DEAR MRS. AUSTIN,   Dresden.

The above illustration will show that I have received your charming gift,* but I cannot illustrate my thanks, which are heartfelt, either in words or drawings. I think you know me well enough to be sure that I shall treasure your present. I begged Miss Taylor to thank you immediately I received it, but ashamed at having delayed so long in writing, I seize the opportunity of the departure of my friend and colleague Schnorr, and director of our gallery, to send you these few lines. Your information about the London Exhibition was most welcome, and I hope to send a picture next

* A china bowl.

N 2

year—"Hannah bringing the little Samuel to Eli." I hope it may please you and your compatriots.

Yours ever devoted

JULIUS HÜBNER.

THE MAGIC BOWL.

CHAPTER XVII.

Mrs. Austin to M. Guizot.

Carlsbad, April 20, 1843.

I COULD hardly believe my eyes, dear sir, when I read,
in Henry Reeve's letter from Paris, that you wished to
hear from me.

He may perhaps have told you something of our wan-
dering and chequered life. I often *come before myself,*
as the Germans say, as if I were constantly acting
Cinderella, alternating between our poverty and the
privations it occasions, and the society of kings and
queens, Court fêtes, and the strange necessity of being
sort of personage: ridiculous contrast! But I cannot
help it. The Germans lay a sort of claim to me, and I
cannot without affectation refuse their civilities. One
thing at least I have gained—an insight into German
opinions, habits, and character such as, I believe, few
foreigners, and, indeed, few Germans, possess. I say *few
Germans*; for, in spite of all the talk about German
unity, one member of this vast family does in fact know
very little and cares very little, except where his own
interests are threatened, about the other. Dresden and
Berlin are connected by a railroad—in ten hours you
pass from one to the other. They are both members of
the *Zollverein,* both Protestant, both *northern* (which is

much); well, you would never believe how totally ignorant I found such men as Savigny, Eichhorn, and other politicians of the character of the public men of Saxony; of the relation of the King to his people; of the character and training of the young Princes. Everything I told them seemed new; and the only time I ever heard a remark on what was going on in the neighbour country, was when Savigny said to me, " Voyez-vous ce qui se passe en Saxe? *Les Chambres se forment.*" " Si, je le vois," said I, "avec la plus grande satisfaction." In Berlin this might be imputed to the arrogant pretensions and scornful character of the people, who affect to look down upon the rest of Germany as centuries behind them (and upon none more than some of their own fellow-subjects, the Westphalians for example); but it is not confined to Berlin. The subjects of each State, however small, have their eyes pretty much turned to their own Court and their own institutions. Not to talk of Austria, I am convinced that if I went to Stuttgart, all I have to tell about Berlin would be quite as new to nine people out of ten as if it were about London or Paris. Indeed, more so; and for obvious reasons. The only ground on which the German periodical Press enjoys any freedom is the foreign. From our papers and yours they extract largely; but very little information as to what passes at home is to be got from them. You have no doubt seen and deplored the strange and contradictory proceedings of the King of Prussia about the Press. These are indeed the " fantastic tricks " which " make the angels weep." That one man should imagine he can play with the mind of a great nation as a boy plays with a bird he has tied to a string, now let it flutter a little way, then pull it back again, now toss it into the air, then bring it down to the ground! I accuse you in my heart of the downfall of Savigny. He saw that a man who had attained to the highest eminence in science and letters had become a consummate statesman, an unequalled Minister. He mistook his vocation, and now, with the usual injustice of mankind, his great past merits are entirely forgotten in his present degradation. One of the evils of this sort of government is the bandying about of the blame attached to an unpopular measure. Every one of the Ministers who signed that *Ordonnance*, in private washed his hands of it. Is this loyal to their master? I trow not. But he *will* have all the power and all the merit—so there is no help. Enough, enough. I am sure you hear all this better from M. de Bresson. Only don't imagine I think the King ill disposed. I believe him to be kind-hearted, good-natured, impressionable, *spirituel*—in short, a clever, excitable, amiable, vain woman. If you like to hear more, I will empty the whole sack at your feet next winter. The state of the public mind in Prussia is deeply interesting, especially in the provinces.

We passed through Dresden a fortnight ago. We heard a debate on the Press in the Lower Chamber. It's the fashion to laugh at these miniature Parliaments. I looked at this one with great respect and a sort of *motherly* (English) tenderness. What is more, I ventured to speak up for it to one of the most excellent and judicious women in the world, the Princess Johann, mother of the future King. I had a long *tête-à-tête* with her, and one with the Queen. They are anxious, as well they may, for they must feel the *contre coup* of every shot in Prussia. I love and honour them and their husbands enough to feel it impossible not to speak out *the truth*. The Chambers are not always right, as you may suppose. " Je le crois bien, Madame," said I, " mais enfin le peuple veut être écouté—la question est, Où et comment on les écoutera. Puisque je vous aime, je bénis Dieu que la Saxe ait une constitution. Elle a moins de chemin à faire." I was surprised at my own audacity, but it is all true. I *do* love them. I *am* convinced that changes are coming, perhaps storms. I *do* think that those will fare best who have already a legal arena for discussion. Will you believe the end? I kissed her hand and begged her pardon, and she thanked me with tears in her eyes. With the Queen it was nearly the same. Good people, they desire nothing but to do right. But how is one to convince them that a King is no longer a father of a family of *children*—or a schoolmaster?

I am just returned from hearing Mass and *Te Deum* sung in honour of the Emperor's birthday. Here indeed *unser Kaiser* has *beau jeu.* The devotion to the blood of Hapsburg, or rather to the progeny of Maria Theresa, is as unquestioning as their religious faith. There is something (*convenons en*) touching, generous, self-forgetting in this *canine* attachment. The trifle that the Emperor is a helpless idiot makes no difference. Not that the people don't know it. But what then? He is "*unser armer Herr.*" I have had a surfeit of *Aufklärung*, dear sir, and am refreshing my spirit in the midst of Austrian good-nature, credulity, innocence, folly, and honesty. Do you not sigh for a dose? When I think what it is to govern restive English and restless French, who would not be Metternich? Ah, rather, who would? To have no better comfort at the close of such a life than to say, "*Après moi le déluge*"! What an empty, barren heart! what a yet unfledged soul! On what wings is it to reach Heaven? One word more about statesmen. I did not see an approach to one in Berlin. *Geschäftsmänner* as many as you please—able and sufficient. Out of England (which I always except for fear of partiality) I have seen three men who struck me as endowed, in a greater or less degree, with the sort of mind and character which are required in a statesman. Their names are Woronzow, Lindenau, Guizot. You must not be offended that I mention two comparatively obscure men with one so illustrious. By your side they are a sort of " village Hampdens ; " for what is a Governor of the Crimea, or a Minister of poor, weak, cramped Saxony, in comparison with *the* Minister of France ? But these two men have the large liberal curiosity, the profound interest in all that is going on everywhere that can affect the progress of mankind ; they have the unprejudiced view, the impartial judgment, which reminded me of *parts* of yourself—I say parts, for my dear M. de Lindenau is timid. However, such as he is, I saw nothing comparable to him at Berlin.

We are coming to try if we can live at Paris. I am not without fears as to the result of the experiment. M. Cousin is encouraging ; M. Chevalier represents Paris as very costly. I must try. I have never wanted luxuries, and now I want them less than ever. What I know is, that I had rather live ill at Paris than well anywhere else, except London. If it will not do, then I shall propose some place not far from England—perhaps in my favourite Normandy. Berlin is a *ville de province*—a very remarkable one, if you please, but nothing more. Where do you see Rhineland, Westphalian, or even Silesian nobles? They go to Düsseldorf, to Münster, to Breslau, not to Berlin, unless they have special business.

Farewell, dear Monsieur Guizot—*lieber Excellenz*, as we say. With the most affectionate respect,

Yours faithfully,

S. AUSTIN.

Mrs. Austin to M. Guizot.

Boulogne,

DEAR MONSIEUR GUIZOT, June 7, 1843.

You won't be affronted when I tell you who is the important personage that has constantly prevented my writing to you—my little granddaughter. I am the most foolish of grandmothers, and am never so happy as when all my schemes are disconcerted and all my things thrown into confusion by this little creature. I have not yet finished the last of some letters which I have sent lately to the *Athenæum,* in the humble hope of clearing away a few national prejudices. I cannot— that is to say, I will not—write *a book* about Germany, because I could not *ignore* all the great social questions which that country suggests in such abundance, and I do not choose to betray or offend. But one subject is, in all countries, open, and in all, to my mind, far more interesting than any other—the condition, habits, and character of the *people.* More and more do I find all my sympathies going over to those upon whom the burthen of life rests so heavily; and not only *in spite* of their ignorance and their faults, but *because* of them. The absence of real active sympathy between the different classes of society in England must come to an end. What that end will be—good or bad—He who can turn and soften hearts only knows. I find the same cordial welcome as ever from my " Matelot " friends— rough hands held out, shouts from the boats, and, more than all, the touching confidence with which the bereaved and the unhappy came instantly to claim my sorrow and pity. They are a fine, energetic race, and appear doubly so after my good Germans, who are somewhat sleepy, it must be owned.

As to the life you lead, I have the most lively conception of all its disgusts, which are a thousand times worse than its fatigues. But I have such a profound persuasion that there is nothing which can give so much value to life as the fulfilment of great duties, the conscious obedience to a high vocation, that I can hardly regret it for you. It seems to me that Sir Robert Peel's position is much worse. I am sure you sympathise with him. How can men so placed *not* feel the deepest interest in each other? I am persuaded the difficulty of governing will go on to increase, both in extent and in intensity. How can it be otherwise? Traditional authority is gone, and Reason, which should replace it, alas! alas! how feeble is it still! Can you explain the sort of epidemy of nationality which now reigns? The Irish have almost ceased to talk of religion. The quarrel is Celtic and Saxon, as it seems. I am just come from reading and hearing a great deal about the various branches of Slavonic nationality, which are making themselves heard in the Austrian Empire—after centuries of dead silence. A new journal, published at Leipzig, *Vierteljahrschrift aus und für Ungarn,* gives one a curious insight into the conflicting Magyar and Slavonic nationalities there, their mutual hatred, and common hatred of their German masters. To what does all this lead? To improvement? or to new discords, wars, and consequently barbarism? I rather hope the former. It is, at all events, extremely interesting. France is perhaps the only country so perfectly incorporated as to have no fermentation of the kind to go through.

With the most affectionate respect,

Yours,

S. AUSTIN.

Mrs. Austin to Mrs. Grote.

Boulogne, June 10, 1843.

Your handwriting and your welcome, dearest Cummer, were the first that greeted me on my arrival at this threshold of England, and gave me a home feeling I have long been a stranger to. How vividly the past came back to me! and how much and agreeably I was touched that this first welcome to very old haunts should come from you! I should have written instantly, before I slept, but, as usual, I was entangled in other things, and did not like to write only a line to say "Thank you." My husband is delighted to be again in

France, which is after all his *pays de prédilection.* I suppose we shall remain here till late in the autumn. I hope so, for I am in no hurry to undertake another move, and it is a great comfort to me to feel myself so near to England. You know more of Paris than I do ; my mind is in a state of utter suspense and doubt as to what it will turn out as a residence for poor people. I hear the most contradictory accounts, but there remains the fact that Guizot, Villemain, etc., lived upon 10,000 francs a year, or less ; married, and with children. By-the-bye I have had the kindest of letters from M. Guizot, to whom I had never written since our going to Paris was decreed, because I had a horror of seeming to lay claim to his recollection and attentions. The more charming was the cordiality with which he offered them. But of course one can see little of a man who has to manage France. My own wishes, however, point much more to *rest* and a cottage in England, than to new experiments on society, new ground to take up in life. I have been not unlucky in that way, and am far from sharing my dear partner's disgust with mankind, odious as many sides of them are ; but I have had enough. As to my coming to England, matters stand thus. I shall certainly not leave Lucie, and she will probably stay here till the end of July. At all events I shall find you at Burnham or somewhere. What you say of reviewing the phases and the progress of one's own mind often comes home to me. How much should we have to interchange on this most interesting of all subjects ! knowing as we do each other's *points de départ,* and all that has since occurred to modify our opinions. Mine are greatly modified, partly by " objective," and partly by "subjective " causes. I remain however true to that intense sympathy with the obscure and suffering classes from which I have never in any moment varied. If I do not deceive myself, that is evident even in the

slightest trifle I write, and gives, indeed, their only value
to such things. .·. . . .

Your most affectionate

S. AUSTIN.

Mrs. Austin to Mrs. Grote.

London, Oct. 25, 1843.

. . . . I have had various treaties with booksellers on
the carpet, which have ended in one, ratified with
Longman, for a translation of Ranke's 'Reformation.'
This is an awful undertaking, and I could doubtless
gain much more money and fame by lighter work. But
you know my dislike to encounter the public in my
own person, my distrust of myself, and my liking for
steady *respectable* work. I have therefore put my head
into the yoke very willingly. I welcome the forced
absorption in drudgery as a potent reason against
painful meditations. My nouns and adverbs keep me
out of myself, and the honest pride of earning is also a
resource against the worst pictures of poverty, though
indeed I feel them little in my own person. My views
of life, dear friend, are very much carried out of and
beyond this world—not indeed with any very defined
dogmatic faith, but with a sort of reliance that encourages me in a thorny and weary path. How natural
it is to take refuge *somewhere* from the world ! Farewell,
dear friend. Let us not forget all the thoughts and
feelings we have shared, nor lose the hope of a tranquil
retrospect of them together. . . . . .

Your truly attached Cummer,

S. A.

In 1844, Mr. Austin was elected by the Institute a
corresponding member of the Moral and Political Class.
Earnest appeals were again made to him at this time to

publish a second edition of 'The Province of Juris-prudence.' Letters from friends, and even from strangers, arrived, lamenting the impossibility of getting a copy, and setting forth the ever-increasing reputation of the book. To give a mere reprint would have been easy enough, and it is what any one else so encouraged would probably have done; but Mr. Austin had dis-covered defects in it which had escaped the criticism of others, and with that fastidious taste and scrupulous conscience which it was impossible to satisfy, he refused to republish what appeared to him imperfections.

"It belonged to the nature of his mind to grapple with a question with difficulty, almost with reluctance. It seemed as if he had a sort of dread of the labour and tension to which, when it had once taken hold on him, it would inevitably subject him. He was frequently urged to write on matters which he had studied with an earnestness second only to that which he had devoted to his own peculiar science—such as Philosophy, Political Economy, and Political Science generally. He usually evaded these applications; but to the person with whom he had no reserves he used to say, 'I cannot work so; I can do nothing in a perfunctory manner.' He knew perfectly his strength and his weakness. He could work out a subject requiring the utmost stretch of the human faculties with a clearness and completeness that have rarely been equalled. But he had no mental agility. When he gave himself up to an inquiry, it mastered him like an overwhelming passion. Even as early as the year 1816 he spoke to me, in a letter, of 'the difficulty he found in turning his faculties from any object whereon they have been long and intently employed to any other object.' And for the same reason, when his mind had once loosened its grasp of a subject, it could with difficulty recover its hold.

At the time when a second edition of his book was first demanded, he was occupied in the business of the public, to which it was with him a matter of conscience to consecrate his undivided attention. That he had long meditated a book embracing a far wider field I well knew, but I feared that this great work would never be accomplished, and would have gladly compounded for something far less perfect than his conceptions. But I saw that nothing could shake his resolution, and I never willingly adverted to the subject. Whenever it was mentioned, he said that the book must be entirely recast and rewritten, and that there must be at least another volume. His opinion of the necessity of an entire *refonte* of his book arose in great measure from the conviction, which had continually been gaining strength in his mind, that until the ethical notions of men were more clear and consistent, no considerable improvement could be hoped for in legal or political science, nor, consequently, in legal or political institutions." *

That my grandfather entertained the project of recasting his great work is apparent from part of a letter written in 1844, to Sir William Erle, the companion of his early studies, the beloved and faithful friend of every period of his life :—

. . . I shall now set to work in good earnest, and, if my unlucky stars will allow me a little peace, I hope I shall turn out something of considerable utility.

* Preface by Sarah Austin to ' The Province of Jurisprudence determined.'

I intend to show the relations of positive morality and law (*mos* and *jus*), and of both, to their common standard or test; to show that there are principles and distinctions common to all systems of law (or that law is the subject of an abstract science); to show the possibility and conditions of codification; to exhibit a short scheme of a body of law arranged in a natural order; and to show that the English Law, in spite of its great peculiarities, might be made to conform to that order much more closely than is imagined. The questions involved in this scheme are so numerous and difficult, that what I shall produce will be very imperfect. I think, however, that the subject is one which will necessarily attract attention before many years are over, and I believe that my suggestions will be of considerable use to those who, under happier auspices, will pursue the inquiry. There are points upon which I shall ask your advice.

Yours most truly,
JOHN AUSTIN.

The Austins took an apartment in Avenue Marbœuf, and soon collected all that was most remarkable in Paris round them. Yet she writes to a friend:—" I shall never feel at home in Paris—not even so much as in Germany. I see a vast number of eminent men, and, as far as that goes, it is interesting and amusing. But I shall never learn to breathe freely in the moral atmosphere of France. One main thing is the want of veracity, of which they all accuse one another— I fear, with reason. I never heard anything like what the public men say of each other. In all this Guizot stands alone. I see him often and intimately, with only his mother and children, and I respect and love him more and more. But how they abuse him ! "

CHAPTER XVIII.

M. A. Comte on Women and Social Philosophy—Baron Alexander v. Humboldt to Mrs. Austin—M. A. Comte and his Official Position—Madame Sophie Germain—Mr. J. S. Mill on M. A. Comte, M. Guizot, and the *Edinburgh Review*—Grammar and Plain Needlework—Mr. T. B. Macaulay to Mrs. Austin.

AMONG the eminent men who frequented Mrs. Austin's *salon* was the founder of the doctrine of Positivism, M. Auguste Comte. In 1832 he was officially attached to the Polytechnic School, and afterwards filled the post of examiner of candidates for admission. He was dismissed in 1844, and Mrs. Austin used her influence with M. Guizot to try and get him replaced. He writes to her :—

M. Auguste Comte to Mrs. Austin.

[TRANSLATION.]

MADAM,   Paris, March 4, 1844.

On returning home late last night, I found the charming letter, a payment for my little packet which I certainly did not expect.* The attention which you promise to bestow on this work only augments my gratitude for your assiduity at my initial lectures.

The important observation contained in your letter gives me, madam, an opportunity of clearing myself

* 'Discours sur l'Esprit Positif,' Févr. 1844.

of a half-reproach, which would grieve me if I thought I had deserved it—my supposed tendency to an insufficient appreciation of the value of women in general and yourself in particular. Although I am firmly convinced that the social status of your sex is essentially different from ours, for the eventual happiness of both, I nevertheless believe that I have rendered with the keenest satisfaction full justice to the moral as well as the intellectual qualities which are purely feminine. This subject, I may remark, will be more fully mentioned in the great special treatise on Social Philosophy which I am going to begin this year. The general condition of women in modern society, coupled with their peculiar organisation, renders them, in many respects, specially apt to appreciate a complete philosophical revolution. Indeed, one would be inclined to be extremely suspicious of any system of philosophy, particularly social, which was not profoundly sympathetic to women. Without going back farther than to our great Descartes, I can never forget that, in spite of the abstract and austere character of his leading conceptions, which do not sufficiently touch upon social questions, women were really the first to understand and to protect him. This arose from their being fortunately placed in a position at once impartial and less hampered with philosophic prejudices. Perhaps one ought not to count the celebrated Christina among these generous patrons, her conduct was probably determined by her rank as a sovereign ; but there can be no doubt about the constant zeal and the disinterestedness of the amiable Princess Palatine, who from the first fully appreciated the great mental revolution inaugurated by Descartes. As to myself, madam, I can honestly say that among the fifty persons, more or less, in Europe whose sympathy I have during twenty years been striving to obtain, as the principal guarantee and the noblest recompense of my philosophical labours, I have always counted on a large proportion of women. Besides this kind of general confession, I must tell you how much honoured and touched I am by the decisive approbation which you have thought fit to accord me, in spite of inevitable divergences of opinion. Although I have not had the pleasure of conversing with you as much as I should wish, I trust that you credit me with enough taste and discernment to have already understood your eminent moral and intellectual qualities. I have thanked our dear friend, John Mill, for procuring me such a pleasant acquaintance, which has resulted in a noble and cordial exchange of thought and sentiments, at least on my part, with you and your illustrious husband. In spite of my very solitary life, I have had various opportunities of knowing some extremely distinguished women, but till now you are the only one, madam, in whom moral delicacy and mental elevation are so happily united. Hitherto the women whose intellectual superiority placed them above the rank of *blue stockings*, had a deplorable tendency towards the aberrations of *femmes libres*. Allow me, madam, to express the intense satisfaction it gives me to see the happy union of two qualities I regard as absolutely indispensable, but which to-day are always in contrast. This unfortunate alternative between two kinds of eccentricities, each equally repugnant, and arising from the conditions of our present social position, renders me the more disposed to admire that happy disposition which, without affectation, is free from either.

Accept, madam, the assurance of the sincere and affectionate respect of your devoted servant,

A. COMTE.

Baron v. Humboldt, the old friend of Mrs. Austin's brothers, to whom she had written from Boulogne, on her way to pay a short visit to her daughter in London, answered her suggestion of a translation of his ' Ansichten der Natur,' in the following whimsical letter :—

Baron Alex. v. Humboldt to Mrs. Austin.

[TRANSLATION.]

Sans Souci, June 7, 1844.

I am extremely culpable, madam ! While on your way through France, on your arrival at Boulogne, you wrote me a most charming letter, as is your wont— without even being aware of it—a letter full of kindness for the antediluvian traveller, who tells of the rocks whose formation he watched. You must think me a savage of the Orinoco, an inhabitant of those Asiatic steppes which I imagined I had described before I saw them. I have not answered your kind note before, because, in the first place, notwithstanding the celebrity of your name—of which you seem to be unaware—I did not wish my answer to be lost for want of a precise address. Secondly, because, after so much hesitation, I felt I deserved your anger. So I wrapped myself in silence, a stratagem which has the advantage of bestow- ing an appearance of graceful timidity. This subterfuge of old age availed me nothing ; your indulgent kindness has recalled me to the paths of virtue, and I need not even have recourse to the commonplace excuse of hard work, or allege the disappointment of not having seen you in Paris. I will not invoke the mighty shade that they say still occasionally pays nocturnal visits to the tomb of the faithful dogs on the summit of the historical hill where I dwell. You know, madam, how to make life sweeter ; I have your pardon, that great word has been pronounced by you in a letter written to the ex- cellent Madame Alex. Mendelssohn. I am happy to be

able to offer you my thanks and the affectionate devotion, which will only end with my life.   As though the
trouble which His non-puritanical but anti-papistical
Holiness Von Ranke gives you was not sufficient, you
want to plunge into my Savannahs, into my foaming
cataracts, into the catacombs of that Indian nation
whose language has only been preserved in the mouth of
some old parrot or Aturis.   Our historian, Ranke, since
he has espoused a virgin of the Thames, has given up
our language, without having made much progress in
yours.   This no doubt contributes to his domestic
happiness.   Honest Raumer, whose political tendencies
agree better with mine, has landed safely in the land of
Troll.   I hope he arrived in time to enjoy the tremendous
riot at Philadelphia, and to profit by the religious
liberty proclaimed by the flare of incendiary torches.

After Ranke should come 'Ansichten der Natur.'
You will never find a book offering the same advantages,
notes longer than the text, information how in the
tropics rain is followed by fine weather, and sentiment
induced by the sight of sand, rocks, river-foam, palm-
trees, and wild sheep.   This Teutonic sentimentality,
which has stood me in such good stead in my own
country, would be ridiculous in the land of Positive
Philosophy.   I cannot believe that you wish to translate
me, glad and pleased as it would make me.   Luckily
you can find no title for my pre-Adamite work.   Alas!
you have got some one in England whom you do not
read, young Darwin, who went with the expedition to
the Straits of Magellan.   He has succeeded far better
than myself with the subject I took up.   There are
admirable descriptions of tropical nature in his journal,
which you do not read because the author is a zoologist,
which you imagine to be synonymous with bore.   Mr.
Darwin has another merit, a very rare one in your
country—he has praised me.

If I tell you that the "tyrant of these parts" never mentions your name without an expression of attachment and high esteem, you will think that I flatter my King, and that Bettina, savagely treated as she has been in the *Quarterly Review*, has every reason to call the chamberlains "sneaking beasts."

Ever yours, with love and respect,
ALEX. V. HUMBOLDT.

The following letter was written to Mrs. Austin in London. As soon as she returned to Paris in August, she invited Comte to come and see her, and, as will be seen by his answer and by Mr. J. Stuart Mill's letter, did what she could to help him :—

M. Auguste Comte to Mrs. Austin.

[TRANSLATION.]

DEAR LADY, Paris, July 22, 1844.

Although you have perhaps heard from Mr. Austin, whom I immediately informed of the decision on my case, or from our dear friend, John Mill, to whom I wrote a detailed account, yet I take the opportunity to recall myself to your memory. The Minister of War has exercised the admirable firmness he showed from the first, as I told you at Paris. In vain he has exhausted, in my favour, every possible resource against the insufficient rules, which he had not time to change in order to protect me. In addition to the personal good-will and esteem of the Marshal, whom I did not know before, I shall eventually, thanks to this crisis evoked by abominable malevolence, obtain the consolidation of my official position, which there is even a talk of making permanent, in order to preserve me from future cabals. But I do not conduct the examinations this year, my place being filled as though I were on the sick-list—

although the Minister refused to dismiss me. The pecuniary loss is the same, but the results are far different, and everything points to the hope that in a few months I shall be safe from all danger, save the loss of a year's income, which will naturally go to my substitute who does the work.

After having finished your business in London, I hope your family affections will have left you leisure to realise your project of translating the memorable 'Posthumous Discourse of Sophie Germain,' which should, it seems to me, inspire all you ladies with a strong fellow-feeling of interest, as being, I conceive, one of the finest works that have ever been produced by one of your sex, till now so little occupied by this elevated and rational philosophy.

I have every reason to believe that M. Guizot has spoken to his colleague, the Marshal, in my favour—I know that you asked him to do so. The Marshal was already well-disposed towards me, partly by his own appreciation of the iniquitous persecution which obliged me to invoke his official aid, partly by the unanimous declarations of my Polytechnical superiors, who all testified in my favour.

Count for ever, my dearest lady, on the affection and respect of your most devoted,

A. COMTE.

Mr. J. S. Mill to Mrs. Austin.

India House, January 18, 1845.

... About poor Comte's affairs, he has himself written to me very fully, and informed me of the final close of the whole matter, so far as his restoration to the examinership is concerned. I am glad on every account that you interested yourself with Guizot for him, and that you mentioned my name in the manner you did, although it would hardly have been warrantable in me to take any direct measure of the same kind, as my acquaintance with Guizot is so very slight. It may be useful to Comte on future occasions to have given evidence to Guizot of our interest in him. He himself seems to bear up bravely against his misfortune. I perceive he has considerable hope that when a vacancy occurs in any one of the several other Polytechnic offices, the opportunity may be taken of repairing the injustice done him ; and I hope the occasion may occur soon, as I have much doubt about the success of his other plans. The private lessons in mathematics may answer, notwithstanding their high price, but not, I fear, if he relies at all upon the rich English. What do you think of his Review project? To me it seems a very doubtful one ; and I fear, too, he will be disappointed by the very little help I shall be able to give him in writing for it, although I will do all I can. About Comte himself I have formed very much the same opinion that you have, both as to his good and bad points of character. He is evidently (either from character or the tendencies of a solitary thinker, little appreciated by the world), most obstinately bent upon following his own course, regardless not only of giving offence (which might be a virtue), but of compromising his means of livelihood. He piques himself exceedingly upon being the only Frenchman who speaks out his opinions without any compromises or reserves, and he has gone so far in that course that I think he would do himself more harm than good now by swerving from it. At all events, I am certain he will not abate one jot of his "franchise philosophique," and therefore there is not much use in advising him to do so. He is a man one can only serve in his own way.

What you say about Guizot and his family interests me exceedingly. A man in such a position as his, acts under so many difficulties, and is mixed up in so many questionable transactions that one's favourable opinion is continually liable to receive shocks, and I have for many years been oscillating in Guizot's case between great esteem and considerable misgivings. Nothing I ever heard of him tells so much in his favour as the feeling you express about him after familiar intercourse. If he was an angel he would be sure to be misunderstood in the place he is in. I do not know whether to wish or to deprecate his being thrown out of it, which seems now so likely to happen.

I have been chiefly occupied lately in writing an article for the *Edinburgh Review* on the "claims of labour." I never knew a time when so much nonsense, and mischievous nonsense, too, was afloat on that subject, and I thought it a most useful thing to enter a protest against the intolerable mass of pseudo-philanthropy now getting into vogue, and to commit the *Edinburgh Review* at the same time (if possible) to strong things in favour of good popular education and just laws. I am afraid, however, that some of the strong things I have said on both sides will frighten so timid a man as Napier, and that he will not dare to print them unmodified. He always, of himself, seems to like my articles, and evidently always hears so much said against them afterwards, by the octogenarian clique, Rogers, Sydney Smith, etc., whom he looks up to, that he has now, I think, a constant terror lest I should get him into a scrape.

Is there any chance of the article on Prussia soon, or of a book rather than an article, or of a reprint of your husband's former book, with the second volume which he projected? I feel certain that a book with his name would be read by numbers of people to whom it would do good, and nothing but books seems to do good now. The time for writing books seems to have come again, though unhappily not for living by doing it.

Ever affectionately yours,
J. S. MILL.

The first two volumes of the translation of Ranke's 'History of the Reformation in Germany' had come out in 1845, and Mrs. Austin was busily employed on the third.

Mrs. Austin to her sister, Mrs. Reeve.

Paris, February, 1845.

With a bad cold, and a head heavy and weary with proof-correcting, at past ten o'clock you will not expect much from me. I hope you will not *lâcher prise* of the governess affair. All the current notions are so insane, smatterings of this and that. Do you, my dear Susan, stick hard to English grammar and plain needle-work, two things now *untaught*, and the intellectual and moral effects of which are not to be over-rated. I think the taste for fancy-work very corrupting (to the exclusion of wholesome sewing). Why *don't* you write about these things? What is the use of sending your most excellent and true remarks to me—the most convinced of all people? Write, write I would, if I had one minute to spare. I will as it is; but just think what I have to do—500 pages still of Ranke; then things occur which I am obliged to *vent* on the *Athenæum*.

On my last Thursday, Mrs. Hunter Blair, Madame de Triqueti, Baroness de Peyronnet, and Baroness Stockhausen (the three former English) walked in dressed for the Embassy ball. Two or three men from Vienna and elsewhere were absolutely confounded at their beauty; and really I don't think I ever saw four such handsome women together, and no other there save myself.

Pray don't *cultivate* Hopie too much. Janet, I hear, continues deaf to all suggestions about learning her letters and the like. I must come and teach her, I think; indeed, I am nowise anxious about it—I mean the teaching ; about the coming, anxious enough. I want to see my new grandchild and my dear girl with her two babes.

Mr. T. B. (afterwards Lord) Macaulay to Mrs. Austin.

Albany, London,
Feb. 27, 1846.

MY DEAR MRS. AUSTIN,

Many thanks for your kind letter. I must beg you to convey to M. Cousin my acknowledgments for his politeness. I have read his speech with great interest, though with less interest than I should, no doubt, have felt if I had been well acquainted with the history and system of the university. I am truly gratified to learn that so eminent a man thinks well of me. But I am afraid that I should sink fast in his estimation if he knew how little I have troubled myself about metaphysics since I was a lad at college, and how profoundly sceptical I am about all the great metaphysical questions. You must be mistaken, I think, in saying that he owes me a grudge about Descartes. I could swear that I never wrote a line either praising or blaming Descartes. It would have been very foolish and presumptuous in me to do so. For I know scarcely anything of Descartes except at second-hand.

I should very much like to visit Paris during the full season. I have often been there. But, as I could go only when our Parliament was not sitting, my visits have been paid in September and October. I therefore know the quays, boulevards, streets, churches, gardens, and coffee-houses extremely well. I am acquainted with every picture in the Museum. I have also a shamefully vivid recollection of the cookery and wine at the Rocher de Cancale and the Frères Provençaux. But of the society of Paris I know next to nothing. In general, I have been as much alone there as if I had been in the Isle of Skye. I used to put a book in my pocket and to sit reading four or five hours together in the garden of the Tuileries or of the Luxembourg. In fact, all my knowledge of good French society has been acquired in London. Nothing would give me more pleasure than to see, under your guidance, something of the interior of agreeable Parisian houses. I fear, however, that these are not times for such schemes. No English Member of Parliament must dare to think of a holiday before August. Again, thanks for your kindness. I need not tell you how much you are missed here, and by how many.

Believe me ever, dear Mrs. Austin,
Yours most truly,
T. B. MACAULAY,

CHAPTER XIX.

Letter from Comte A. de Vigny to Mrs. Austin—Education in
France—Small Waists—Contempt for the King—Pope and
Milton—Political Probity—Letter from Sir Robert Peel to Mrs.
Austin—An Article on Germany—Belgium—Mrs. Hudson the
"Railway Queen."

THE author of 'Cinq Mars,' already mentioned, wrote
to Mrs. Austin, who had left her apartments near the
Champs Elysées for one in Rue Lavoisier :—

M. A. de Vigny to Mrs. Austin.

[TRANSLATION.]

June 6, 1846.

To begin with, your brother will not arrive to-day.
Then, music is far more heating than the serious
conversation of my friends, among whom is Barbier, who
expects you. From all this I conclude that you can
do nothing wiser than come to me, in those Elysian
fields, which once you loved so well. I promise you
draughts as cold as you can desire, and ice of every
description, even in our conversation, which shall be
consecrated to rigid Puritanism. If you desire it, we
will believe you are eighty, and destitute of all charm or
attraction. To crown all, I will say as many disagreeable
things to you as you like. What can you want more ?

Should your brother by some extraordinary chance
arrive, be so kind as to take his arm and introduce us to
him, so that he may see whether we know how to love
you. Mind you remember that to pass along the quays

and over the bridges, even in a carriage, to go to the Faubourg St. Germain is the greatest danger you can encounter in such a torrid zone as this.

Watch over your existence, and for prudence' sake come here at nine o'clock, and leave at four after midnight.

Your slave waits. I am writing my wishes and my grave advice standing. Meditate on them.

Yours with all my heart,
A. DE VIGNY.

M. B. St. Hilaire to Mrs. Austin.

[TRANSLATION.]

Environs d'Agen,
August 10, 1846.

DEAR MADAM AND FRIEND,

Since the 22nd July I have been here, and shall remain until the end of the month. I am entirely alone, save a visit twice a week from my friends at Agen. But I have Aristotle, and hope to finish the translation of another volume of Pyschology before returning to Paris ; I have also Homer, Milton, and Pope, whom I admire for his excellent common sense, his delicate criticism, and the beauty of his language ; and Aristophanes, who sometimes makes me blush, but to counterbalance his *gaillardise* I have some ponderous volumes of St. Thomas.

Alas! among the people here, no one can write or read, save the little shepherd of fourteen years old. This is unfortunately the rule in France, in spite of the law of 1833. England is, in this, infinitely more advanced ; statistics prove it. You have results and no laws ; we have laws, but till now no results. Our two countries have an immense deal to learn from one another. All that has occurred during the last two months has filled me with admiration and respect for your statesmen and your political system.

I am quite of your opinion about the stalwart Norman women, and I cannot express the horror and terror (I assure you the words are not too strong) with which I have always regarded the small waists one can span with two hands. I admire waists like the Venus of Milo and the huntress Diana, and women who resemble them. Real grace can never exist without strength. One of the finest sights I ever saw was on a market day at Barfleur, near Cherbourg. Four or five hundred women were there, and certainly, without any exaggeration, two hundred were magnificently handsome. Without any wish to offend your patriotism, a great part of the beauty and strength which distinguishes your race came from our Normandy. What you tell me of the private life of M. Guizot is not new to me. I know his private and domestic virtues, but his political virtue! I do not wish to annoy you, but with the late elections he is continuing the career begun six years ago. I pity him sincerely, and I suspect that in his own heart he pities himself. The last assassination, real or pretended, is more deplorable than the others. It has become a kind of pastime to shoot at the King. The neglect to answer a letter is thus revenged, like Lecomte, or a bankruptcy is averted, as in the case of Joseph Henry. The royal person, if not the royal office, has fallen into contempt; this is what sixteen years of such government has produced. You need not look for any other cause for the horrible attempts on his life, which would soon cease if public opinion really entertained for His Majesty those sentiments which the head of the state, the father of a great people ought always to inspire.

How long do you remain at Sandgate? I need not say that you may always count on

Your most devoted

B. St. Hilaire.

M. B. St. Hilaire to Mrs. Austin.

[TRANSLATION.]

Environs d'Agen, Sept. 4, 1846.

. . . I am quite of your opinion about Pope; he has no poetical sentiment, but infinite *esprit;* I think him superior to our Boileau in depth of thought, and even in style, if I may venture to judge an English writer. I began Milton's 'Comus' a month ago; I shall take it up again, on your recommendation, and intend to try and translate it in order to learn the language. Please say many things from me to Monsieur Alexandre and Madame Lucie.

Your ever devoted
B. ST. HILAIRE.

M. B. St. Hilaire to Mrs. Austin.

[TRANSLATION.]

MADAM AND DEAR FRIEND,   Paris, Oct. 8, 1846.

Your letter was most welcome. I returned three days ago, in improved health and with another volume of Aristotle done. Like you I dread some terrible catastrophe. No one understands what our Government is aiming at, and every one agrees with M. de Lamartine that some great blunder has been committed. We know but too well the probity of our rulers, and are therefore inclined to throw the blame on them in such a doubtful question. Nothing will make us believe that men whose loyalty and honour all Europe has admired, men like Sir Robert Peel, Lord John Russell, and Mr. Cobden, would stoop to falsehood. Here, on the contrary, it is the common official weapon, and he who uses it most skilfully is most admired. I must add that M. Guizot, pardon me, but I know it as a fact, has caused his adherents to spread the report that England has behaved dishonestly, and that he is only revenging himself.

I trust your visit to England has done you good; my holiday would have been sad enough but for my work. I have returned positively intoxicated with Homer. Never before have I read, translated, and enjoyed him so much. I admire many writers, but how far does Homer surpass every one! Ah! why do you not know Greek? Does our compact still hold good? I assure you that I intend to learn English. If you see Mr. Grote, tell him I am beginning his book, and shall write to him soon.

Your most devoted
B. St. Hilaire.

In 1846, Sir Robert Peel's Ministry was defeated on the second reading of the Irish Coercion Bill by a majority of 295 to 219. On June 29th, Sir Robert Peel announced to the House that he had resigned office, and that Lord John Russell had undertaken to form a new Administration. Mrs. Austin always considered the speech Sir Robert made on that occasion one of his noblest efforts; and when she sent him the third volume of Ranke's ' Reformation,' she wrote and expressed her admiration of his conduct about the Corn Laws. He answered :—

Sir Robert Peel to Mrs. Austin.

Madam, ·   Feb. 4, 1847.

I thank you for your kind attention in sending for my acceptance the third volume of that valuable work for which the great mass of the British public are indebted to your labours.

I thank you still more for the gratifying assurances

that you convey to me, that you rightly appreciate the motives which have induced me to sacrifice official power and to sever party ties in the firm belief that paramount considerations of the public welfare demanded the immediate and resolute disregard of other and very subordinate ones. I ought indeed to take little credit for any sacrifice, for the return to domestic life and the enjoyment of political independence are more than ample compensations for anything I have lost.

Beyond this, the cordial approbation of hearts and intellects like yours is a reward which no evasion of difficulties or dextrous management of party could have ever secured.

I have the honour to be, madam, with sincere esteem for your character, and gratitude for your services to literature,

Your faithful servant,
ROBERT PEEL.

Mrs. Austin to M. Guizot.

Blankenberghe près Bruges,

DEAR AND MOST HONOURED SIR,   August 6, 1847.

Why I have not written before is a long story. The pith of it is a luckless article for the *Edinburgh Review*, promised, and at length sent, for the next number. I had had this long in hand, or *in petto*—too long—have got far too much material, and taken too much pains, so that I rather think I have spoiled it. I grew weary and discouraged ; and if I ever happen to fall short in my internal supply of hope and cheerfulness, I get none from without. My dearest partner has not, and never had, enough for home consumption, much less to give to his neighbours. Another bad thing is that the subject-matter (Germany from 1790 to 1806) forces me into a sort of hostile attitude *vis-à-vis* of France. Ah, now you are alarmed ! But let me dispel your fears by saying that it is France warlike, invading, victorious, *ergo* detestable, as all such countries are, with which I have to do—the France of Napoleon. The more I read and think of that man, the more execrable he appears to me, and the more I am persuaded that he did France more mischief than one would think it possible for a single man to do to so great a country. I speak very boldly, for I don't know how ill you think of him ; though I am sure, from necessary inference, not well. On the other hand, everybody, I suppose, is agreed that the thrashing of Germany was "the making of her," to use an excellent vulgar phrase.

This is a tolerable place enough—a beach without a pebble between this and Holland ; but the Belgian *Wesen* does not please me. One tries hard to be cosmopolitan, and not to think oneself better than all the rest of the world ; but I have heard you say, "Il n'y a que la France et l'Angleterre" ; and if you add Germany, I am afraid I shall be forced to say the same. We have many great ladies here who seem to be afraid of nothing so much as to be supposed to understand a word of their own language ; my efforts to speak Flemish pass for a sort of insanity. The truth is, my philological soul finds great solace here in the study (if I may call it so) of this *Mittelding* between German and English. It is very amusing ; but the language is like the people ; only the people are a half-way between *French* and German, and unluckily seem to me to combine the coarseness of the latter with the impertinence (what Madame Guizot once called the "*délire d'égalité*") of the former. The French are insubordinate but *d'égal en égal,* well-behaved and gracious ; the Germans are uncouth and coarse, but give respect unto whom respect is due : take away the two *buts* and you have a Belgian. I see two of their newspapers and no other. They are, of course, extremely discontented. The loudest complaints are respecting the great and increasing pauperism, with which they reproach the Government. It is curious, but melancholy, to observe every country busied in solving the insoluble problem—how to have a perfect government in the midst of a very imperfect people, that very people at the same time exercising a powerful control over its government. How we all turn round and round upon this like squirrels in a cage !

I heard from Lord Lansdowne two or three days ago. What with Education and Ireland, he says he never had so much to do in any year of his life. So much the better for us that he can do it; I think he is *ce que nous avons de mieux.* He wants only the energy that great ambition gives. He says, " We shall have a parliament of railway kings." And now, I pray you, what can be worse than that ?—The deification of money by a whole people. As Lord Brougham says, we have no right to give ourselves pharisaical airs. I must give you a story sent to me. Mrs. Hudson, the railway queen, was shown a bust of Marcus Aurelius at Lord Westminster's, on which she said, "I suppose that is not the present Marquis." To *goûter* this, you must know that the extreme vulgar (hackney coachmen, etc.) in England pronounce "marquis" very like "Marcus."

My husband has been working on an article on International Law. I know you will read it with interest.

Always yours,
S. AUSTIN.

CHAPTER XX.

The French Revolution of 1848—M. B. St. Hilaire on the Aspect of Paris—Letter from Dr. Whewell to Mrs. Austin on the French Revolution—Her Answer—M. B. St. Hilaire at the Luxembourg—Fighting in Paris—MM. Cavaignac and de la Villemarqué—Cousin and B. St. Hilaire—A Working Man's Library at Bow.

AFTER passing some time at Rochefort in the Ardennes with Sir Alexander and Lady Duff Gordon, the Austins returned to Paris, only to be uprooted by the Revolution of 1848.   The letters of M. B. St. Hilaire to Mrs. Austin in London give a calm yet vivid picture of those events, in which he bore a considerable part :—

M. B. St. Hilaire to Mrs. Austin.

[TRANSLATION.]

MADAM,   Paris, March 4, 1848.

Your letter gave me the greatest pleasure ; it was delightful to see your writing once more.   The aspect of affairs here is more serious and sadder than during the first flush of triumph.   This arises from two reasons—the financial crisis, and the electoral struggle which has already begun.   The fall in the funds, the suspension of several great industries, and the straits of the operatives out of employment are causes for legitimate anxiety, which need not, however, be exaggerated.   The good sense of the working classes raises hopes that the condition of things will soon improve.   The old Republican party are committing a grave fault by showing they desire to control the elections; public opinion, though pretty tranquil, will not submit to dictation, and this may prove a source of trouble. Add to which, the electoral law is unfortunately most complicated and difficult of application.

The worst symptom is a feeling of anxiety, in which the strongest minds cannot help sharing. I am not surprised at the blindness of our last King. What a position he has lost! No one here even remembers him. A reign of seventeen years has not left a trace. You may believe me when I speak thus of him, for you know what I have told you for many years. Write to me sometimes; I pass nearly all my time at the Hôtel de Ville.

Your ever devoted
B. St. Hilaire.

Dr. Whewell to Mrs. Austin.

Trinity Lodge, Cambridge,

My dear Mrs. Austin, March 9, 1848.

I have just heard that you are in England, and cannot refrain from sending you a line to express my satisfaction at this among all the miserable events of the last three weeks. We have been perpetually casting our thoughts to you in the Rue Lavoisier, while all the sounds of wreck and ruin have come to us day after day, and fervently hoping that you were safe and unmolested. We know well the grief you would feel at the fall of some of the great persons of this deplorable drama, and at the prostration of so many years of labour in building up the edifice of peace and order, and we hoped that you had no more special trouble of your own to grieve for. The great kindness which you showed us at Paris made us take to the place more than we should otherwise have done ; and so we were better able to follow the story from one part of the city to another, and from one person to another, than we should otherwise have been ; and all this was mixed with recollections of you, because to you we owed so much of it. I hope we shall hear that all the Guizot family are well and tranquil under this change. M. Guizot must be supported by his knowledge of the general respect in which he is held, and I am glad to hope that Madame Guizot may find a tranquil haven after the storms of her Paris life. I am puzzled how to write to my Paris friends ; but I suppose one ought to take it for granted that they have cordially accepted the Republic ; but that is so new a *tone* that it is not easy to fall into at once. I suppose we shall by degrees come to an understanding. Mrs. Whewell joins me in kind regards. I hope Mr. Austin is well.

Always most sincerely yours,

W. WHEWELL.

Mrs. Austin to Dr. Whewell.

8, Queen Square, Westminster,
March 12, 1848.

DEAR DR. WHEWELL,

Thank you cordially for thinking of me amidst the havoc and ruin of a country. One felt one's own nothingness in an earthquake that was overthrowing and swallowing up, not only thrones, dominations, powers, but all the best hopes and dearest interests of the good men and true friends we had learned to love and esteem. And even these seemed little compared to such a fearful triumph of the evil principle—the complete abasement of moral and intellectual under animal force. Never in the whole world, I think, were so many men of supposed sense and talent so utterly and stupidly and obstinately wrong. Nay, dear sir, let us say it to one another, if not to the incredulous world, " The Lord *had* hardened

Pharaoh's heart." Nothing else will account for such a superhuman blindness and stubbornness. On the Monday even, fourteen men—Lord Normanby for one—went to implore him to give way, and were received with jokes ; but the Opposition were no better, and are rightly served. The torrent soon dashed over them.

I would never affect to congratulate anybody on the Republic ; they would not believe you—they do not believe in it themselves. One can only, I think, express *deep regret* (which all feel, except, perhaps, a handful of reckless adventurers) and fervent but not sanguine wishes that good may come out of the gigantic evil. I have written to poor M. de Lamartine, and could truly say that we all admire his efforts and pray for his success. But for him, God knows what might have been done ! And still, who can predict ?

M. Guizot is well, and I left his dear old mother firm, resigned, and heroic. I am house-hunting for and with his dear children, which occupies nearly all my time. Best regards to Mrs. Whewell.

Most truly yours,
S. AUSTIN.

I positively *dread* letters from Paris. The Circourts are gone without notice, and without saying whither.

My husband says, " I cannot think with patience of any Englishman exulting in this awful ruin. It is worse than foolish—implying gross insensibility to the sufferings of others. I don't wonder at any perverseness in so insane a coxcomb as Carlyle," etc., etc. I think these words are altogether to your taste, as they are to mine.

M. Guizot's present address is 46, Bryanston Square ; but we are in hopes of housing him very soon.

M. B. St. Hilaire to Mrs. Austin.

[TRANSLATION.]

Commission du Pouvoir Exécutif, Paris,
MADAM AND TRUE FRIEND,   June 5, 1848.

You must have thought I was dead ; and, indeed, this long silence is almost worse. To give you an idea of the life we are leading, I will say that since we have been at the Luxembourg, for nearly three weeks, I have not yet found time to go to my own house, nearly next door, Rue de l'Odeon, 35. We work night and day ; and I bless God that He permits my health to resist the strain.

I suspect that you do not much approve of our work. If I had the time I would explain our situation, which is far from being an easy one, and I hope I should induce you to share our hopes. I am unofficially attached to the Government, dividing the task with my friends Garnier-Pagés and Daguerre. Write to me soon ; the opinion of England is of great importance to us. I have not seen Cousin for the same reason that I have not written to you.

Aristotle and philosophy are abandoned for Madame la République.

Your most devoted
B. ST. HILAIRE.

M. B. St. Hilaire to Mrs. Austin.

[TRANSLATION.]

MADAM AND DEAR FRIEND,   Paris, July 2, 1848.

We are all safe and sound. Cousin is pretty well ; I have not been wounded, although I was under fire several times. The only one of our friends who is hurt is Bixio, whose place I took at the Hotel de Ville. A ball has gone through his right side ; it has been extracted, and we hope to save him.

The terrible crisis * we have just traversed had been imminent for four months. All our efforts were directed towards its prevention ; a month sooner the insurgents would have been victorious. But we had time to prepare our forces ; and although the struggle has been bloody, the issue was never doubtful.

My health has resisted the forced labour of the last four months—days and nights passed without any rest ; even my eyes have not given me any uneasiness. I have never had ten minutes to myself ; philosophy, poetry, friendships, private business—all has been neglected ; but the Republic and liberty were well worth the sacrifice.

I have refused to enter into a Ministerial combination as Minister of Public Instruction ; my colleagues did not inspire me with sufficient confidence. The Chamber was disappointed at my refusal, but my friends and people of sense think I was right. Forgive my long silence ; give me news of all your family, and believe me,

The most devoted of all your devoted friends,

B. St. Hilaire.

Mrs. Austin to Dr. Whewell.

8, Queen Square, Westminster,
Dear Dr. Whewell,   August 4, 1848.

It is quite clear to me that the French are utterly without the moral force and the capacity for corporate action which alone can enable a people to *withstand,* " Mes compatriotes ne valent rien excepté un fusil à la

---

* The insurrection of the Red Republic in Paris, suppressed by the army under Marshal Cavaignac, after immense slaughter on both sides.

main," writes a lady to me. Now they submit quietly, or rather gratefully, to martial law ; and as long as Cavaignac is prudent enough not to *call* himself king or governor, they will let him do as he pleases.

I forget if you know my excellent, honourable, and pious young friend, the Vicomte de la Villemarqué, who published the 'Chants Bretons.' I send you a letter of his. One from Cousin—curious—I wrote to him in the first agonizing day of terror, and said, "Wherever we are, we shall have a nook for you, if you will accept it." He interprets this into asking him to emigrate. The passage about the difficulty of his political attitude in this country will make you smile. How little they understand us ! You see what he says about St. Hilaire. I cannot express my grief that he should have seen it to be his duty to serve under or with such men—he whom I thought the *most* honest man in all France. I made bold to write him a letter of remonstrance. I told him I dreaded for him "that last infirmity of noble minds, the belief that some sacrifice of principle on his part might be useful to his country." I implored him to think that God wanted not *his* help to govern His universe, that the government of his own soul was the only one absolutely confided to him, and a great deal more such vain entreaty. Vain, indeed ! I have heard from him twice, but there is no more *épanchement* possible between us at present. It is *a second Spanish marriage.*

I suppose you, like everybody else, know the *secret*— that M. Guizot wrote, and I translated, the article on the state of Religion in France in the last *Quarterly*. I believe we shall soon go to work again.

Now I must talk to you of a very different letter—one of which I am very proud. It comes from a number of hard-handed men, earning from 10*s.* to 4*l.* a week, in a manufactory of railroad carriages at Bow. I went to see them and their library, and, at my request, Mr. Murray was so kind as to send them a munificent present of books. I asked only for any rejected copies he might have. Now, dear Dr. Whewell, you will not laugh at me when I say that this letter caused my eyes to fill with tears. So much gratitude for so small a thing, and after all not due to me—such a yearning for the sympathy and approbation of their "betters"—such a sense of the value of instruction! How is it that those who have the power do not draw near to these brave hearts and excellent heads, and win them as they might? What a true dignity and politeness is there in their manner of addressing me!

Would it be too much to ask you, dear Dr. Whewell, to send them a book—one of your own, I mean—and to descend from the intellectual heights in which you dwell to give a word of encouragement to these our less favoured brothers? Think of the effect of a *word* of approbation from the Master of Trinity!—a sign that the moral culture they aspire after will be a bond of union between them and the highest philosopher!

These six hundred men have founded their own library, without the least guidance. I looked it through, and there is not an objectionable book. I found Locke and Reid, Shakespeare and Milton, Walter Scott, and almost all our best classics. Is not this cheering? When we meet in London again, you must go and see the poor fellows at their *vulcanic* work.

With the greatest respect and regard,
Yours,
S. AUSTIN.

CHAPTER XXI.

Decree against MM. Louis Blanc and Caussidière—Mr. Hallam's forecast about Prince Louis Napoleon—M. J. J. Ampère on the Republic—Madame Récamier—The National Assembly and the President—Letter from Mrs. Austin to Dr. Sciortino — M. B. St. Hilaire on M. Guizot and M. Thiers' Books—Letter from Mrs. Austin to M. Victor Cousin on the Principles of the French Revolution.

M. B. St. Hilaire to Mrs. Austin.

[TRANSLATION.]

MADAM,   Paris, August 27, 1848.

I have heard about you from Cousin, but it would be very kind of you to let me hear from yourself. The state of affairs here is very strange, and we do not yet see how we are to improve them. The necessary thing is to inspire confidence, and the decree against Louis Blanc and Caussidière is a step in the right direction. A month ago we asked the Government to make up its mind ; it has hesitated far too long, and the public peace has suffered. Paris, in the midst of these serious questions, is exactly as you left it. No one would imagine that we are in a state of siege, if from time to time the most monstrous measures—transportations without trial, newspapers suspended, etc.—did not recall it to our minds. We have not yet had any serious discussion on foreign affairs, or even internal questions. It is singular that public opinion has not yet asserted itself. The unhappy fate of Italy has not awakened us ; events in

Germany have taught us nothing. It is incomprehensible. Let us hope that freedom of thought will soon return to France.

What do you think of us? Do you believe the mediation will be a success? Here we doubt it, although we wish it. Cavaignac is a strong supporter of peace; that is all very well, but I am not sure whether he realises its inevitable conditions. We had an interview with him the other day, but obtained no further information than we had gathered from his speech, so I suspect that he had nothing more to say.

I have been named President of the Commission on Primary Instruction. The first thing is to extend the law of 1833, so ably analysed by you. I am extremely preoccupied with my work, which is of great importance, and I should be glad if I had the chance of talking it over with you. I hope you are well. How is Mr. Austin?

Yours ever,
B. St. Hilaire.

Mr. Hallam to Mrs. Austin.

Dear Mrs. Austin,   Clifton, Oct. 2, 1848.

It is so long since I have heard anything about you, that I must trouble you with a few lines of inquiry. Let me know your plans, and especially what hope I may entertain of meeting you in the early part of the winter. If you have any idea of going to Bowood, I should much like to fix the same time.

I have had a letter from Guizot lately, who has, as you of course know, been settled for some time in his old quarters at Brompton. He takes a gloomy view of France; but can a wise man hope much, at least for the present? I cannot but look at the extraordinary favour shown everywhere to Louis Napoleon as a new element of revolution. It is easy to say, as we have been told for many years, that there are no Bonapartists. I believe this was true as to the superior classes ; but in the people, and especially in the Departments, I suspect that the attachment to the name and memory of Napoleon has been a deep and enduring sentiment, not counterbalanced by any other, except among the Legitimists. Neither the Orleans family nor the Republic having any hold upon the peasantry or rather small proprietors. The universal suffrage has brought into importance this popular sentiment ; and though something now may be ascribed to the notion that young Louis has been persecuted, I shall consider that every vote given to him for President of the Republic as given to him for Emperor ; to which, if he commits no great blunder by his own incapacity, he will be pushed in a short time. On the other hand, we see no element of strength either in the Republican or the Royalist parties, except that where possession goes for a great deal, and the apprehension of the *red* republic will lead men to rally round that which exists. I beg my best regards to Mr. Austin.

Very faithfully yours,
H. HALLAM.

M. Jean Jacques Ampère to Mrs. Austin.

[TRANSLATION.]

DEAR MADAM,   Paris, Oct. 13, 1848.

Two absences from Paris and two illnesses have alone prevented me from writing to you long ere this ; since then, what events have happened in the world ! Where is our poor Germany ? Where is Berlin, which we knew as so philosophic and so literary ?—now given up to such hideous disorder. What will become of Austria after this victory gained in the cause of order by the natural friends of German-Austria?   And we, where are we drifting to in this Bonapartist phantasmagoria which has been evoked by universal suffrage?   The only thing that seems certain is a universal disposition to be rid of the Republic at any cost, and as quickly as possible.   It would, perhaps, have been wiser to have kept it as it already existed—to have organised it on a reasonable basis, and not again to play at the dangerous game of restorations.   But, wrongly or rightly, the great majority in France do not wish for a republic—not even a reasonable republic.   France does not believe in such a one, which, since the 2nd of June, I have always maintained to be possible and, I conceive, desirable.   However, the will of a nation is a thing to be considered ; only how is it to be carried out?   We can but guess at it, without understanding the process by which the goal is to be reached.   There is a jump to be made in the dark ; let us hope that in making it France will not break her neck.

I ought to have mentioned the subject before which lies far nearer my heart than politics, and which you ask about—the sorrows of Madame Récamier, and of her eyesight.   Many griefs, and cruel ones, have fallen on her, but this last has been the worst, from which she has not yet recovered, and which will leave an indelible trace.*   We have hopes for her eyes, but they are slow in being realised.   She is extremely touched by your sympathy and your remembrance of her, and has charged me to thank you, and to send you, from her, a small volume almost entirely composed of quotations.   She has dedicated herself to the memory of M. Ballanche, and thinks that you will like to read the words of one whom you knew how to appreciate.

J. J. AMPÈRE.

* Death of Chateaubriand.

M. B. St. Hilaire to Mrs. Austin.

[Translation.]

MADAM AND DEAR FRIEND,   Paris, Dec. 28, 1848.

I cannot let the year pass without sending you a line. In spite of our parliamentary battles, I have continued my philosophical labours. You will see what I have done by the volume which I hope Mr. Quain has delivered safe into your hands. In a few days I hope to send you a little pamphlet on 'True Democracy,' that I have written for the Academy of Science. But I am most anxious to get back to Aristotle ; I have still twenty-five volumes before me.

You will have seen our struggle with Cavaignac. Opinions here are divided, and I should think that must be the case in England, if the affair has excited any attention. My intimate conviction is that the Republic, and society with it, would have been wrecked, had it been entrusted for four years to such imprudent hands. The country was of the same opinion, but the National Assembly was against us. The Assembly is to-day in a delicate position, and we are working hard to smooth the difficulties between it and the President. Louis Napoleon's position is a strong one, thanks to the immense majority he had. I have had an interview with him, and I think he possesses a quality we stand much in need of—calmness. His head is not turned by success, and his intentions seem honest. People here are beginning to be hopeful, and although the Ministry is not quite what one would desire, it will suffice for its duties, and we shall do our best to aid it. Faucher is in the Cabinet, as you will have seen. Cousin is not very well. Some day we will come to England and see you.

Your ever devoted
B. St. Hilaire.

Mrs. Austin to Dr. Sciortino, Malta.

Weybridge, Feb. 18, 1849.

Though it is long indeed since I had the pleasure of hearing from you, I reckon with the same serenity as ever on your attachment to us, and I am sure you will wish to know what has become of us in the mighty convulsion which has shaken Europe. We were in Paris through the whole of that horrible scene—infinitely more contemptible than horrible, when you saw with your eyes, and heard with your ears, that *nobody* of any class wished, approved, or even could endure the change, except the small band of ruffians who were allowed to bring it about. The French have no popular institutions, nor any wish or taste for any. A great central power which is to be overthrown now and then, is what they understand and like.

I came over to England in March, time enough to see a very different scene; where the people stood up like men, and said at once what was their determination.

Your affectionate friend,

S. AUSTIN.

M. B. St. Hilaire to Mrs. Austin.

[TRANSLATION.]

MADAM, Paris, Feb. 24, 1849.

I was most happy to receive your letter, I had expected it so long! M. Guizot ought to be very grateful to you; had any other hand undertaken to interpret him, I am sure your compatriots would not welcome his book as they are sure to do.* Here, I am sorry to say it has had no success; I do not speak of our democrats,

---

* 'On the Causes of the Success of the English Revolution of 1640–1688,' etc., by M. Guizot.

but among the most sensible and calmest men of his own party. For my own part, I should have been glad if from his exile he had been able to cure the ills of an ungrateful country. But nothing of the sort. M. Guizot was arbiter of our destinies for eight years. Alas! what has he done with them? His book contains no advice, it is a bitter criticism which proves that he despised the society of which he was the leader. We were also disappointed in the style.

Do not judge the book of Thiers by the two sheets you have, they are the weakest. A quarter, at least, of the rest is occupied in combating the Commissions and Socialism, and in explaining taxation. The doctrine it teaches is sterling, and the style, though careless, has inimitable qualities. I believe that it is to be translated in Belgium and England and published in a cheap edition. Here it is already on sale in four diverse sizes, and is found most useful in combating the anti-social doctrines which now afflict us.

I assure you that the exiles * can return when they like; no one will trouble them, unless they provoke animosity. The past is absolutely forgotten. It is not thoughtlessness on our part, but indulgence and good-nature.

Your devoted
B. St. Hilaire.

Mrs. Austin to M. Victor Cousin.

[Translation.]

Dear Friend,   Weybridge, March 8, 1849.

In writing *for* you, I have delayed writing *to* you. On Tuesday I got your article, and wrote at once to the editor of the *Examiner* to say how glad I should be to

* M. Guizot and his family.

make an abridged translation, if he had no one more capable of doing it. I have not yet heard from him, but my article is nearly finished. If you have another, I will send it to the *Spectator*. I suppose you have seen the notice in the *Times?*

But I warn you, my dear friend, that English readers will not understand your expression, "*the principles of the French Revolution.*" If you mean the principles of constitutional monarchy, of representative government, of responsible ministers, etc., then they are rather the principles of 1688 which are under discussion, and which were triumphant and adopted in England a century before the French Revolution. If you mean more than that, people will tell you that the fault committed by France was in not being contented with such liberties. This will be a difficulty with English reviewers. I point it out to you because I foresee the objections that will be raised.

It seems to me that you are perfectly right, as against the three fallen dynasties ; but I do not think that you have succeeded in justifying France. Surely, by firmness, constancy, and union, some better way than revolution might have been found of controlling them ! You will admit that William III. was remarkably autocratic, and that our nation had no particular reason to be pleased with the four Georges? A true friend of France will always say to her, Have patience and determination, and you will obtain the triumph of true principles, without overturning all government.

There is my opinion ; I give it for what it is worth. Apart from this, your paper is full of admirable matter, admirably said, and unanswerable.

The post is going. I shall do an article for a magazine besides a review.

Yours ever affectionately,
S. AUSTIN.

CHAPTER XXII.

The President—Italy and Austria—M. J. W. Decaisne on Madame Récamier and M. Lamartine—Rome and the Holy See—Public Instruction in France—Mrs. Austin is given a Pension by the Queen—Visitors at Weybridge—Madame de Maintenon—Letter from Miss Berry to Mrs. Austin on Madame Récamier—England a suggestive Country—Letter from M. B. St. Hilaire to Mrs. Austin—Letter from Mrs. Austin to M. Victor Cousin comparing English and French writers.

M. B. St. Hilaire to Mrs. Austin.

[TRANSLATION.]

MADAM,   Paris, April 4, 1849.

. . . Things here are improving. Our President is judicious and firm, but he does not show himself enough, which is a mistake, as he must gain by being known. What strikes most people in him is his honesty, a rare quality among political men.

Poor Italy ! What a disgraceful spectacle ! How low she has fallen, to die without striking a blow.* It was expected here, and so caused but little excitement. Austria appears to act with moderation, and if she continues to be prudent, we have nothing to say. It seems that Prussia refuses the Empire ; she is right, her time has not yet come ; if she contents herself, for the

---

* Marshal Radetzky defeated the Sardinian army at Novara on March 23, 1849. Then came the abdication of Charles Albert, which deferred the emancipation of Italy for ten years.

present, with moral ascendency material greatness will be sure to fall to her share.

I do not know whether the Republic will improve us, but you know my optimism, and I think that our morality, which had sunk so low under the late government, is already improving.

Your most devoted,
B. ST. HILAIRE.

M. J. W. Decaisne to Mrs. Austin.

[TRANSLATION.]

Paris, April 8, 1849.

Nothing, dear madam, could give me more pleasure than your kind remembrance of me. If our dear friend, Madame Récamier, has always appeared to me the most perfect type of French grace and elegance, you always represented English goodness, kindness, and sound sense. We are beginning to settle down, confidence is returning, and will, I trust, bring prosperity with it. I see indications of this, but I only say so under my breath, for few people are hopeful, and I am called an *optimist* when I hazard a prediction of renewed prosperity. But I do believe in it and the future will prove whether I am wrong. Our unfortunate and beloved Madame Récamier is sinking. The death of M. de Chateaubriand was a fatal blow. A second operation has succeeded no better than the first and she is condemned to total blindness, her eyesight is irretrievably lost. Amid all her misfortunes she has preserved her wonderful grace and unfailing gentleness, but the inimitable charm of that delightful *salon* is gone. M. de Lamartine has fallen, sadly fallen, from the sublime height on which the Revolution placed him ; his wife is ever the model of devotion and abnegation, but there also it is as though a thunderbolt had fallen. M. Léon Faucher desires to be remembered to you, and I beg you will say many things to your beautiful daughter, and to Sir Alexander and to Mr. Austin.

Ever your sincere friend,
J. W. DECAISNE.

M. B. St. Hilaire to Mrs. Austin.

TRANSLATION.]

MADAM AND DEAR FRIEND,   Paris, July 8, 1849.

. . . . Since the victory of the 13th of June, and the taking of Rome,* everything is improving here. Our "Montagnards" have been as ridiculous as they are odious, and if we are moderate and calm, our triumph is assured. I drew up the proclamation of the Legislative Assembly ; if it has come under your notice, you will see what republican language I have put into the mouths of our conservative majority. I am beginning to believe that the Republic is established, and that force or stratagem would have hard work to destroy it. The President appears to be sincere in supporting it, and in three years he will probably be re-elected after some necessary modifications of the constitution. The Roman affair is by no means at an end, spite of our dubious conquest. It is a serious thing to have 50,000 French troops in the heart of Italy ; add to this that the Pope is inimical to our principles, and I do not see how we can force him to accept them, as he did not ask us to replace him on his throne. I believe that the clerical power is at an end ; but is the Holy See enlightened enough to resign itself to the loss of temporal power ?

* By General Oudinot.

It seems doubtful, according to what poor Rossi * told me.

I am on the commission to examine the law of public instruction. M. Thiers is our president; but can you believe that the object of the law is to again place instruction in the hands of the clergy? You, who know France, you can judge of the wisdom of such an attempt. We have seen some queer things under the Republic, but certainly none so extraordinary as this. Should this unlucky project succeed, it will pave the way for an interminable series of revolutions. It is waste of time to preach in the name of, and to advocate, order, for the sake of organising anarchy.

I hope the Assembly will be prorogued in August, and the first use I shall make of my liberty will be to pay you a visit.

Your ever devoted,
B. St. Hilaire.

Mrs. Austin to M. Guizot.

Weybridge, July 27, 1849.

. . . . I received two days ago from Lord John an announcement that Her Majesty had been pleased to grant me a pension of £100 a year on the Civil List. If I had been disposed to *faire effet*, I should have rejected it with disdain like Miss Martineau, and called it robbing the people, etc., etc. But I have done no such thing. On the contrary, I told Lord John that though I could

---

* Pellegrino Rossi. Born at Carrara, 1787. Exiled 1815. Was named Professor of Civil Law at Geneva in 1819; afterwards went to Paris, where he held the chair of Political Economy and then that of International Law at the Collège de France. In 1829 he published his 'Traité du Droit Pénal,' in which he endeavoured to reconcile Bentham's utilitarianism with the principles of justice. Was appointed French Ambassador to Gregory XVI. in 1845. Became Prime Minister to Pius IX. in 1848, and was assassinated the same year in Rome on November 15th.

not have taken it on the score of *want*, I accepted it with pride and satisfaction, as a proof that my humble labours had been thought useful. I hope you will not despise me for my baseness.

Among all the false friends and pernicious teachers the poor people are cursed with, I know none who do more to cut at the root of improvement than those who persuade them that money given to intellectual labour is taken from their necessities. Of course I do not speak of the value of mine, which may be small enough ; but of the principle. I am quite sure of your joy, and that of my dearest children, at this little accession to my means, and compliment to my humble works.

I fancy you all at dear Val Richer, tranquil and at home. May God's blessing be upon that home.

Ever faithfully yours,
S. AUSTIN.

In August M. B. St. Hilaire went over to pay the Austins a visit at Weybridge. Mrs. Austin wrote to her sister, Mrs. Reeve :—

" He saw in London, baths and washhouses, model lodgings, Blue Coat, City of London and Borough Road schools ; ' Cymbeline ' at Sadler's Wells, and the annual *fête* at Spicer Street—all sights illustrative of the physical, moral, and intellectual state of the people, and all very satisfactory. I think in so few days it would have been difficult to do more."

Mrs. Austin to M. Guizot.

DEAR M. GUIZOT,   Weybridge, August 31, 1849.

You must have been astonished at my long silence— at least I flatter myself so.

Weybridge has been a perfect *tourbillon* of visitors,

coming and going, and as all, or nearly all, were foreigners, my whole time and existence has been in requisition as *cicerone.* M. St. Hilaire, who leaves us to-morrow, has been here above a fortnight. Each of our guests has brought us his contribution of new ideas. M. de Haxthausen especially, one of the most remarkable and interesting men I ever met with, and whose knowledge of Russia and the East is, I think, unequalled in extent and depth. He is the nobleman of *uralt* Westphalian race, under whose protection young Paul Lieven travelled.

I think M. St. Hilaire will carry home some useful notions. He is so good and upright a man, that if he saw the truth, I think he would act up to it. My husband's conversation has been a kind of perpetual lecture on politics, political economy, etc. I send by him to Madame Lenormant a copy I have just received, of my little attempt to describe Madame Récamier. You will find yourself quoted (anonymously) and will, I hope, pardon an allusion to your dear mother. As to Madame de Maintenon—one cause of my delay in writing has been that I was myself waiting for an answer from Mr. Empson; I have received it, and it is to the effect that it is against the rules of the review (as I suspected) to publish a critique of *any* incomplete work, and that we must wait till the whole is published before anything can be done. Will you, dear sir, be so good as to communicate this to the Duke de Noailles? At the same time let me repeat my misgivings as to my ability to do it justice. I find on talking with M. St. Hilaire, that his view of her character is even more favourable than that given by M. de Noailles, and I also find, to my own shame and regret, that I cannot divest myself of sentiments and prejudices against her, imbibed long ago, and which I feel I am not sufficiently acquainted with all the points of the subject to defend.

To satisfy my own conscience, I must go into a thorough *study* of her character. My husband's opinion of her is much like my own. I need not say with what gratitude I should receive any hints you would give me about this extraordinary person. I wish to be *just*, and indeed I feel that any doubt of my own justice would oppress me so that I could not write. Right or wrong, I have always *believed* myself right. Pray don't laugh at my pedantry.

I spent an hour *tête-à-tête* with the Duchess of Orleans. I think I never came near a more perfectly balanced mind. *Our people* are firmly persuaded that her son will reign ; why, they can hardly tell, but so it is. Somebody had told her that the English people felt a malignant joy at the misfortunes and degradation of France. She asked me if this was true ; you may guess my reply. Who is it that invents such calumnies ? I take upon me to say, nothing can be more false.

S. A.

Miss Berry to Mrs. Austin.

MY DEAR MRS. AUSTIN,   Richmond, August 31, 1849.

I am very glad to see our poor friend Madame Récamier in such good hands as yours. I am only sorry that your acquaintance with her began so late in her career, and that you had not seen her, like me, in all the various phases of a life so varied in circumstances and situations, although so little in its character and disposition.

I saw her first in Paris at the Peace of Amiens, and in the strange hodge-podge of society which Paris then presented. She was the beauty *par excellence*, and her house the show house of Paris, fitted up in all the minute expense and bad taste of the day.

I am ashamed of having been so long expressing to you how much we shall rejoice in your visit, and be

pleased to receive your French friends, provided only
that they are made aware of the two old sybils that they
are to meet.

You must let me know what day the end of this week
or the beginning of the next you are likely to come, and
to believe you will always be welcome to

Your sincere friend and humble servant,

A. M. BERRY.

Mrs. Austin to M. Guizot.

DEAR MONSIEUR GUIZOT,   Weybridge, Sept. 7, 1849.

I can only repeat what I have told you—that there is
nothing I shall not always be ready to lay aside when
you do me the honour to claim my help. I shall have
the greatest pleasure in translating *anything* you write,
and a peculiar satisfaction in giving to my country the
opinions of the man in all the world best qualified by the
natural bent of his mind and character, as well as by his
studies and his experience, to form a sound and useful
judgment of it. I am far from thinking that anything
great is to be achieved by mere imitation ; the project of
imitating institutions, which, like those of England, are
almost all the offspring of slowly developed circumstances, is peculiarly absurd and hopeless ; but I am
entirely convinced that no man can be qualified to
legislate for what is called a free country (or a country
aspiring to be so), without a very attentive and profound
study of England. England is the most *suggestive* of all
countries to a legislator ; but who knows that so well as
my dear M. Guizot ? I long to see what your residence
among us may have suggested to you. I have been
made to think much of these things lately, by seeing the
effect produced by England on M. St. Hilaire, who spent
a fortnight with us, and has just returned to France.

Spite of all I had said and written to him, I saw he was
wholly unprepared for the absence of all visible interven-
tion of the government.   The immense variety of local
powers ; the extent to which the people are acquainted
with and possessed of those powers ; the quiet and (as it
seems) self-regulating movement of the whole complex
machine ; the almost unconstrained and rarely-abused
individual liberty—he was in constant amazement ;
perhaps indeed these things are more striking in a village
than in London.   My last words were "go, and tell what
you have seen," and indeed he is well-inclined to do so ;
but will anybody hear him ?

Your most affectionate and faithful

S. AUSTIN.

M. B. St. Hilaire to Mrs. Austin.

[TRANSLATION.]

MADAM AND DEAR FRIEND,   Paris, Oct. 1, 1849.

On my return from Weybridge, I spent three weeks
with my friends at Agen, and I can assure you that
the profound impression made upon me by all I saw in
England has been communicated to every one I have
seen.   Cousin is so pleased with my letters (*à l'Ordre*)
that he wants me to collect and publish them.   Thanks
to you, to Mr. Austin, and to Lady Lucie, I have been
able to learn a greal deal in a short time.   Some people
have thought my descriptions exaggerated, but I soon
brought them to reason.

Thanks, a thousand thanks, for having been the cause
of my taking this journey.   Remember me to all your
family, and tell little Janet she need not fear that I shall
forget her.

Your devoted friend,

B. ST. HILAIRE.

Mrs. Austin to M. Victor Cousin.

[TRANSLATION.]

DEAR FRIEND,   Weybridge, Oct. 13, 1849.

. . . Up to a certain point connoisseurs in style would accord the supremacy you claim for your compatriots; but you pretend too much, and your pretensions will be questioned. Your list is too long, and contains names to which we think we can find parallels. We shall cite you Swift against Rabelais; Addison is certainly superior to Labruyère in grace and simplicity; while Fielding is behind Lesage in nothing. But enough, and only to show you what objections you will raise. It will be asked whether you are really so intimately acquainted with those great masters of prose, Defoe and Bunyan; whether you really understand the perfections of the style of Hobbes and of Berkeley sufficiently that you should place them below the French writers you mention. Again, there are people, and I am one of them, who find a finish, a variety, a wonderful harmony, and a power of description (all accomplished with the simplest and most familiar means), in the style of Goethe, which place him, in his line, on a level with any writer that can be named. I leave aside all considerations of matter, and only talk of style.

You are quite right in saying that some of your writers are incomparable for the mixture of grandeur and *naïveté* which you characterise so well, and had you stopped there, every one would be of your opinion. But there are other merits; who, for instance, among your historians has a narrative style equal to Hume? I do not wish to enter into discussion, but I affirm that it would be doing you an ill service to translate what you have sent me.

Ever, dear friend, your affectionate

S. AUSTIN.

CHAPTER XXIII.

Letter from Mr. H. Crabb Robinson to Mrs. Austin on Mrs. Opie's Memoirs—Mrs. Austin to Dr. Whewell on the "fatal facilities of the French Language"—M. B. St. Hilaire fears a "*Coup d'état*"—Letter from Mrs. Austin to M. Guizot on finishing the Translation of his Book—Elections in Paris—Mrs. Austin's Estimate of Lord Palmerston—Letter from M. B. St. Hilaire to Mrs. Austin on Popular Education—Speeches by Mr. Cobden, Sir W. Molesworth, and Sir R. Peel—Death of Sir R. Peel—Lord Palmerston, Prince Metternich, Princess Lieven, and M. Guizot.

Mr. H. Crabb Robinson to Mrs. Austin.

30, Russell Square,
MY DEAR MRS. AUSTIN,   Nov. 4, 1849.

. . . Carlyle has been led by vanity to degrade himself more than any man of our age, by the public defence of slavery as an institution. John Taylor and your family generally are examples of quiet independence and contempt of that yielding to gentility which is the great disgrace of the age, and the support of the Church.

When I think of the French and the Americans, I am humiliated at the variety of my frustrated hopes, and take consolation in Schiller's ' Worte des Wahns.'

At Bury I looked over Mrs. Opie's Memoirs—and that with interest. The obviously unequalled attachment of Amelia Alderson to Mrs. John Taylor—that was the name I always heard pronounced with great reverence by Catherine Buck. This was a few years before I heard Mrs. Barbauld speak of Susan and Sally

Taylor with such warmth; the naked names do not offend you, I daresay. In the Life there is a studied omission of the name of *Clarkson*, who was really the great figure at the anti-slavery congress or gathering. I do not understand these things—they are not worth understanding, I daresay. I have made a note to read a memoir by you in *Fraser* of Madame Récamier, the most quiet, graceful old lady I ever saw. If in advanced life she practised art, she effectually concealed it. Best remembrances to Mr. Austin.

Very truly yours,
H. C. ROBINSON.

Mrs. Austin to Dr. Whewell.

DEAR DR. WHEWELL,   Weybridge, Jan. 8, 1850.

I should not have let one post depart without my thanks and my husband's, and our answering good wishes, if I had not been in a state of almost breathless haste to finish my task for M. Guizot.* I had not a moment's interval, as you will have imagined, between the completion of the article for the *Quarterly* and the beginning of the pamphlet. They are not long; but I think nothing ever cost me so much trouble. It is certainly more difficult to translate French than German into *good* English—easier perhaps into certain combinations of English words. The "fatal facilities" of the French language, the many expedients for giving an air of meaning to no meanings, are all laid bare when one comes to translate—Cinderella's ball clothes drop off, and leave her dirty and ragged. One finds to one's consternation that it is not only words, but ideas (that is, distinct ideas) that one has to furnish; this is the case

---

* Mrs. Austin was translating M. Guizot's book 'On the Causes of the Success of the English Revolution of 1640–88,' which came out in 1850.

with all modern French. The constant use of large sweeping abstractions, as active or passive in every conceivable event, gives an unutterable vagueness to thought.   Suppose Mr. Macaulay talked of what the Revolution of 1688 did and suffered ; the translator has constantly to ask who ? which of the agents ? etc., etc. ; but you know all this better than I.   Then the article for the *Quarterly Review* was not interesting, I thought, to the English *public*—only to US *du métier ;* and I had to dress it a little—as much as I dared.   I felt as if you and my dear Mrs. Whewell would be likely to guess one interpretation.   My head and heart were full of Cambridge, and a little of all the mingled and delightful feelings I had experienced there seemed naturally to flow through my pen.   M. Guizot, however, heartily approved.   The pamphlet you will perhaps see in the original, as well as the English, which I hope you will receive from Mr. Murray.   You will understand the labour it has cost me.   I wished to do it justice and even more than justice ; I wish I could have put into it a little more of practical utility, for, you see, *even he* suggests nothing positive, nothing as even a *beginning* of permanent institutions.   Is it not pitiable to see 30,000,000 of people now occupied in ascertaining how much, or rather how little, sense one trifling young man has ? *Ils en sont toujours là.*   What M. G. says of the worship of democracy is true enough.

All these things fill me with the deepest anxiety on one point—the point on which the permanency of our institutions and our salvation as a nation turn.   Are our higher classes able to keep the lead of the rest ?   If they are, we are safe ; if not, I agree with my poor dear Charles Buller—*our* turn must come.

Now Cambridge and Oxford must really look to this. The recent deaths seem to bring to view a great scarcity of men able to lead.   Why is this ?

Mr. Austin thanks you very much for your recollection of him and his tastes ; he has read your paper with great interest. You know, I believe, what a *Lockite* he is, but that does not lessen his admiration for the striking and elevated tone of your speculations. I have read the essay with great delight, though you choose to assume that I shall not care for it. What indeed can be so interesting ? All the other subjects that we call serious, how small and transitory they seem when compared to these which reach into infinity—a little beyond aristocracies and democracies !

Yours ever, dear Dr. Whewell, with cordial respect and regard,

S. AUSTIN.

M. B. St. Hilaire to Mrs. Austin.

[TRANSLATION.]

MADAM AND DEAR FRIEND,   Paris, Jan. 19, 1850.

Affairs here do not improve, and confidence does not return. The publication of that unlucky paper of the Elysée has raised absurd fears of a "coup d'état." For my part, I do not think they have much foundation, but they are generally credited. The majority in the Assembly is, as usual, undecided about dividing into two parties or remaining united. The question is the elimination of the Legitimists, who have already formed a separate clique, and voted more than once with the "Montagne." I think that when we have voted the budget, which cannot take place for another three or four months, events will be hurried on with terrible rapidity. In June or July I foresee a great catastrophe, unless some happy accident intervenes, of which I have little hope.

I have nearly finished the publication of my book on gymnastics. There are 700 pages, and songs, of which I have written words and music.

Your devoted friend,
B. St. Hilaire.

Mrs. Austin to M. Guizot.

Weybridge, Jan. 21, 1850.

Before we start, I wish to let my dearest Monsieur Guizot know that I have finished. I take for granted you have sent me *all*, and that we conclude with the word "success"—the *refrain* of the beginning—as it ought to be. The last pages are just gone, and, if the printer is expeditious, we shall exceed by very little the day you appointed. I forgot to ask you and Mr. Murray if you had any desire to put my name in the titlepage. I have not the least objection—on the contrary, I shall feel it a very high1 honour. On the other hand, you know I am not anxious for it on any other ground. I never cared for *renown*, and as people know that I can translate, there is no new glory to be acquired, except from my humble alliance with you. How shall I thank you enough, my kind and honoured friend, for those few words, the purpose of which I understood so well? Would that I could tell you they had produced any active result! but the thing goes on in the same manner. My husband gets books and exhausts their whole contents, turning every part of his subject over a thousand times in his mind ; but though the head works, the hand is absolutely inert. And then he takes refuge in a sort of *découragement*—as if there were nothing to be done for mankind.

He is greatly disquieted about France. He says things appear to him blacker and more threatening than when there was fighting in the streets. Our Protectionists are, as you see, playing the same game as your Legitimists—only not in the midst of such imminent perils. But people seem uneasy.

I am eager to hear what you think of Mr. Senior's article on the revolution. I have not yet seen it, my copy is lent to a *journeyman carpenter.*

I cannot conclude without thanking you most sincerely and cordially for the great satisfaction I have had in translating your admirable discourse. It is perfectly and throughout *treffend.* I only wish I could do more justice to the eloquence of it, but the march of our languages is as different as that of the ideas which sway the two countries, and you must be resigned to lose some of your vivacity and point.

Yours,
S. AUSTIN.

M. B. St. Hilaire to Mrs. Austin.

[TRANSLATION.]

MADAM, Paris, March 18, 1850.

Your letter has given me great pleasure, and the violets were a sweet remembrance of Weybridge. They had not lost their scent in the journey.

The Paris elections have astounded the party, so-called, of order, which is not the party of courage. The unfortunate law of public instruction, the uncalled-for destruction of the trees of liberty, and a few other follies of our police have brought about this result. The Parisian populace have replied to silly provocations by still sillier elections. It is almost impossible to see how we are to emerge from this chaos. It seems as though the government was obstinately bent on absolute resistance, in which case it is lost. Meanwhile the principal actors keep behind the curtain ; they hold the strings of the marionettes, but do not even dare to assume the burden of affairs. We shall have to return to the Odilon Barrot and Dufaure colouring, perhaps laid on a little stronger. Nothing else will save us ; the masses will not allow the Republic to be destroyed.

Cousin is well ; he is preparing a third volume on public instruction. I am finishing a pamphlet on the same question, and shall then go back to philosophy with intense joy. Love to little Janet. I hope Mr. Austin is well ?

Your devoted
B. St. Hilaire.

Mrs. Austin to M. Guizot.

Weybridge, Whitsunday,
May, 1850.

Dearest Monsieur Guizot,

I cannot tell you the comfort I have in thinking of your tranquillity about your daughters. One is ashamed, in days like these, when the decomposition of society seems impending over us, when races of men seem doomed to destruction, to talk of what happens to ourselves as the special work of Providence. Yet there are events in which the immediate finger of God seems visible ; and the marriage of these dear children at such a time, and under such circumstances, strikes one as a *compensation.* The world owes you many a one, my dear M. Guizot, but it has none to bestow that you would value like this.

You may imagine the consternation into which we are thrown by the recall of your ambassador. My husband is miserable about it, and is not gentle in his language about Lord Palmerston. You know what I always said, "He is the evil genius of England." I think that opinion is now becoming pretty general. You see what a miserable figure he has forced his colleagues to make.

This is worse than all the rest, for never had we such urgent need of the honour and reputation of our public men, and these (one, at least) were so unspotted. It is impossible to explain to any foreigner who does not understand England as you do, how such men and such a people can submit to the caprices and the unprincipled folly of an insolent and malignant man. But you will see the terror of a protectionist ministry, and the immense difficulty of forming any other. Still, I think, things cannot long go on thus. I quite understand the indignation of the French; but is it really true that a war with England would be popular? Most assuredly, the feeling here is widely different. Nobody desires war; most people detest it.

I wish I could look forward with any confidence to a visit to Val Richer. I shall hardly be able to restrain my eagerness to see you *en patriarche.* How joyous it would be to see the *five* children around you! Mine are talking under my window, and baby's little voice *me donne des distractions* even while I am writing to you. When I feel what these ties are, I take heart for the human race. Let the *bouleversement* be ever so complete, there are things which no sophistry and no violence can ever destroy. Family affections are indestructible, and while *they* subsist there remains always the *nucleus* around which society *must* reconstitute itself on a sane and natural footing. I am heartily glad you are going to resume your history.

I go to-morrow or the next day to spend a few days at Mr. Hallam's. You know how I love and revere him God bless you, dearest sir and friend, and increase your happiness with your days.

Your most faithful

S. AUSTIN.

M. B. St. Hilaire to Mrs. Austin.

[TRANSLATION.]

MADAM,   Paris, June 18, 1850.

I hope to see you towards the middle of August. I am very tired, and have great need of a little repose. The aspect of our affairs contributes not a little to my lassitude. I am deeply afflicted by all I see, and I fear an imminent catastrophe. The business of the three millions is dishonourable, and the electoral law is a lie. Until we can get an honest government my poor country will not be cured of its many ills.

I have heard that there is an article on the " Vraie Democratie " in the *Athenæum ;* have you been so good as to occupy yourself with my little work ? I continue my translation of ' Aristotle ' every morning before going to the Chambers ; and Mr. Chase's, which you so kindly sent me, lies on my desk from 5 till 9.30. I have found him a learned, faithful, and intelligent expositor, but he thinks too much of his contemporaries. I had rather see him cite " Plato " by the side of " Aristotle ' than Butler and others.

Cousin is well ; he is finishing some small things, and will then, I hope, finish his great work on Plato.

> Your ever devoted,
> B. ST. HILIARE.

Mrs. Austin to M. Guizot.

                                          Weybridge,
DEAREST MONSIEUR GUIZOT,   July 3, 1850.

You have, I am sure, read the two debates (Lords and Commons) with intense interest, and with partial approbation and admiration. I am only now reading the House of Commons debate, having been in London, and extremely occupied while it was going on. I am struck with Cobden's speech. He is a man I do not like or esteem, but he has a wonderful command of plain, direct language, and, when he happens to be right, his speeches are admirable. Sir William Molesworth spoke and acted excellently. Several men went to ask his advice, and what he meant to do. He said, "I shall tell no one. I shall vote as. my own conscience directs, but the responsibility of each man's vote, in so critical a moment, must rest with himself." What do you think of his speech? My husband says by far the best was Sir Robert Peel's. Alas! and here we sit, not knowing whether he is still alive, or whether our poor country is robbed of this most precious of her sons. My husband is quite dejected. He says if Peel is gone there remain only the Duke of Wellington and Lord Lansdowne who have any authority in the country, and how long can we hope to retain them? My husband thinks Lord John's speeches far worse than Lord Palmerston's, and calculated to do great mischief. Everybody speaks of Lord Palmerston's as the most wonderful effort of oratory, considering his age, the heat, and all there was to increase his difficulties. During five hours he never faltered, never recalled a word, never drank a drop of water, and left off with the very same intonation of voice as he began with. How lamentable that such powers are so employed! People seem to think that, in spite of the *triumph* of the government, the system of foreign policy has received a severe and salutary check, and that even he will not risk another such struggle. If there were any bounds to human credulity, one might be amazed at hearing sensible men (as I did) talk of "all this being the result of a conspiracy." I asked in vain what means you and M. de Metternich and P^sse· Lieven and Co. possessed of influencing the minds and opinions of the English public, for I maintain that the *public* was against the government.   Nobody can answer, yet they continue to assert it.   We are very much ashamed of the vulgar, blustering tone of the speeches on that side.   I beg you to believe so.

I hope things go on tolerably in France.   There is really nothing amiss in the state of the country ; if there were but a government that commanded confidence, all would soon come right.   Wonderful elasticity of France !

I hear you are in Paris.   I shall be glad to think of you with the spud in your hand in the garden, or engaged in the sempiternal Patience in an evening.   The intervals I permit you to employ on history.   How happy you must be in the midst of all those dear children !   All here are as usual.   Little Maurice climbs the hill with rather more visible rapidity than we descend it.   The creature has attached himself with a sort of passion to his grandfather, which is very charming.   I have no news, and can think of none but the saddest—the fatal accident to Sir R. Peel.   Mr. Hallam was greatly distressed, as you may think.

Adieu, dearest sir,
Your most affectionate
S. AUSTIN.

M. B. St. Hilaire to Mrs. Austin.

[TRANSLATION.]

MADAM AND DEAR FRIEND,   Paris, August 12, 1850.

I am going to Bagnères de Bigorre for a month, and thence to Agen.   In October I hope to be with you.   I told Cousin what you say ; he has a great wish to see England, but the political reasons which influenced him last year still exist.   He will not go to see the King, and he would not like to be so near without going to Claremont.   The only way out of the difficulty is to stay in France.   He is on the superior council of Public

Instruction, where he will necessarily play a great part, although he is profoundly disgusted with politics. Things here are in a very bad state, and I doubt their improving before 1852. The conduct of the Government and of the Opposition are equally calculated to precipitate a crisis. Our political character is unformed, and I do not see who is to mould it into shape. How fortunate is England! How far in advance of other nations! I understand your pride; I wish I could feel the same for my own country, but my conscience forbids it, in spite of my fervent patriotism. The letter of M. Guizot on education is excellent, although his conclusions are rather cloudy. I, of course, approve it all the more because it shows how right I was in opposing such a detestable law. Give my love to little Janet, and tell her I will teach her how to play at ball. I never let a week pass without a good game at ball—I am passionately fond of it. . . .

Ever your devoted
B. St. Hilaire.

CHAPTER XXIV.

Mrs. Austin on John Locke's Tomb—Shakespeare and Locke—
M. B. St. Hilaire's Admiration of England—A Critic's
Pleasure—State of Germany—The Durham Letter—Sir James
Stephen—M. B. St. Hilaire on the Protestant Demonstrations
—Note of the 18th January, 1851.

Mrs. Austin to M. V. Cousin.

[TRANSLATION.]

DEAR FRIEND,   Moreton, Essex, Sept. 14, 1850.

I write to you in the parlour of a small inn, where we
have passed the night to be near High Laver.   I feel an
absolute necessity to write and tell you of our pilgrimage.
How I wished for you when we first caught sight of the
tomb of Locke!   We passed two days at Stratford-on-
Avon; I cannot describe it properly to you.   The
memory of Shakespeare lives in every stone in the road,
and fills every corner.   The room where he was born,
the tomb where he reposes, the old grammar school
where he learnt to read, the little path which he trod
when going to see Anne Hathaway, and the cottage in
which she lived.

Yesterday we were at Peterborough, and then passed
two hours at Ely, where the noble cathedral is being
restored.   We saw it under the guidance of Dr. Peacock,
whom you will know as a great mathematician.   At

Harlow we left the railway and came here in a carriage. We drove straight to the church, and stood before John Locke's tomb, let into the south wall. In the church-yard there are several tombs of the Masham family.

Wishing to copy all the inscriptions, I went this morning with a village lad across the fields, and we passed near the rectory, an old-fashioned house sur-rounded by fine trees, with a charming garden, and a rivulet meandering through it. I asked my guide whether he thought that the rector would object to my calling upon him. He said, " Oh no, he was an old and learned man." We found him in the garden with his young curate. The rector came forward with old-fashioned courtesy, begging me to honour his manse by a visit. He was singularly dressed, and his long white hair reached to his shoulders. To cut my story short, this venerable and kindly old man was mad—perfectly harmless, retaining his love of reading and of philosophy, and with the manners of a gentleman of the old school. His one passion is Locke. You may imagine how well he received me. While waiting for my husband to join us, he showed me all the editions of Locke's works, the register of the death of John Locke, bachelor, and told me his recollections as a child of Oates. The house was pulled down about forty-five years ago.

We heard divine service—the same that Locke and his illustrious friends once listened to. Opposite to us was their pew ; nothing had been changed. Afterwards we drove to Oates ; nothing is left but the laundry and two magnificent lime-trees. There we found Mr. Ingersol, a young farmer, who inherited it from his uncle, and who pointed out to us the locality of the old house. Every-thing, as you see, was favourable, the weather was beautiful, and, although not picturesque, the country round is pretty.

To return to the tombs. Sir Francis Masham, who

died in 1722, is buried inside the church; but his admirable wife, who soothed the last moments of Locke, where does she lie? There is not a trace of her; perhaps she left Oates after her husband's death, and is buried near her father at Cambridge.* But we found the tomb of Damaris Cudworth, her mother, with an inscription, which tradition assigns to Locke. It is beautiful, and quite what he would have written.

In the churchyard are the tombs of the first Lord Masham and his wife Abigail, the favourite of Queen Anne; of General Hill her brother, and Mistress Alice Hill her sister, and of the second Lord Masham and his two wives Henrietta and Charlotte. Against the south wall of the church is a square raised tomb inscribed "JOHN LOCKE, ob. A.D. 1704." Above is a marble tablet bearing the Latin inscription written by Locke himself. (You shall have copies of all the inscriptions.) Beside the principal entrance to the church there is a small door on the south side, close to which is a grass grave immediately under and parallel with the wall Here, village tradition says, lies a faithful servant of the Masham family, now remembered only as "Luke." He used to hold this door open for his master and mistress, and when he died they buried him at his post. A few steps only divided the tombs of the great philosopher and the faithful Luke.

Now I must go to bed; to-morrow morning we return to my dear cottage.

Ever your affectionate friend,
S. AUSTIN.

---

* Dame Damaris Masham (daughter of Ralph Cudworth, D.D.) is buried at Bath, where there is an inscription to her memory in the abbey church.

Mrs. Austin to M. Guizot.

DEAREST SIR AND FRIEND,

Weybridge,
Sept. 17, 1850.

. . . We had never seen the north of England, so on the 23rd of August we left home, and have been to Gloucester, Worcester, Malvern and Warwick. We spent a Sunday quietly at Stratford-on-Avon, hallowed by the greatest *human* manifestation of God's power. I forget if you have seen the lowly roof under which Shakespeare was born, or the stone under which his ashes lie. Few things in my life have touched me more than the standing in the room which heard the first wail of that sweet and mighty voice that echoes round the world. The church where he lies is singularly harmonious and beautiful, and the service in it no less so; and the thought that there he listened to the words I was hearing gave them a new solemnity. In St. George's Chapel, Windsor, there is a special prayer for "the Knights of the most Honourable Order of the Garter." I think it would be more to the purpose to have a form of thanksgiving for the creation and inspiration of Shakespeare. In default of it I made one for myself.

Our little tour ended with a pilgrimage to the grave of Locke. By the side of a humble, sequestered village church, now attended only by rustics, there lies the man whose clear and potent intelligence was second only to his spotless virtue. His tomb is inscribed,

JOHN LOCKE. Ob. 1704.

Above it is the tablet with the Latin epitaph written by himself, and which I daresay you know. We heard service in the church where he had sat by the side of his incomparable friend Lady Masham, listening to the same words of hope and peace.

I cannot tell you how tranquillising and elevating all this was. There lay the long mouldered ashes of the man ; but his love of truth, his confidence in her power, his love of mankind, his clear intelligence, his gentle piety, seemed to radiate from his modest tomb, and the simplicity and serenity of his character seemed to breathe in the whole place. I thought of you, dear sir, and wished for you. You would have seen how wisdom can move and attach the hearts of men through all time, how they triumph over time and death. Is it not a sublime thought that a few feet of obscure earth can be made dear and holy to the good of all ages, by being the resting-place of such a man as Locke? It is true that, seeing what we see, one is sometimes inclined to think he has thought and written in vain, but we must hope as he hoped, and trust as he trusted.

Your faithful and attached
S. AUSTIN.

M. B. St. Hilaire to Mrs. Austin.

[TRANSLATION.]

Bagnères de Bigorre, Sept. 17, 1850.

Ah! madam, how interesting your trip must have been, and how I should have liked to join in your reverence for Shakespeare. England does right to nourish admiration for one of her greatest sons. In our poor country of revolution we have no time for such pious and gentle creeds. The birthplace of Molière is barely known at Paris, and hardly a signature of his has been kept.

My admiration for England increases when I read your history. When I read of Cromwell and Charles II., after Elizabeth and Henry VIII., I am astonished at the rapid growth of your progress and wisdom. France, alas ! has still much to learn. I see nothing stable in the future. Instead of serving his country, the President is begging for votes ; the various hypocritical divisions of the Chamber, none of whom dare say what they really want ; the legal violence of the great party of order ; the absurdities of the demagogues—all this promises ill. Meanwhile the political morality of the nation suffers. Your Revolution of 1688 bore good fruit ; ours of 1830 has produced nothing, thanks to those into whose hands its guidance fell. I can only look to Providence to deliver us out of the mess we are in. The Republic is, however, better established than people think, and in spite of what our friend Cousin says, every day increases my faith. He laughs at me—it would be easy to turn the tables against a monarchy of eighteen years. For the moment we shall not have a *coup d'état*, and I hope that in 1852 the nation will be wise enough to choose another President, perhaps the Prince de Joinville, should he wish it.

What do you, at a distance, think of the state of things here ? Every one conspires against the Republic, at Wiesbaden, at Claremont, at Cherbourg, and at Versailles. The Republic laughs ; she is "bonne fille," but some day she might frown, without, however, ceasing to be just.

I have finished the eleventh canto of the ' Iliad,' and have begun the twelfth ; you see I am getting on. I hope Mr. Austin is well.

Your ever devoted
B. ST. HILAIRE.

Mrs. Austin to Dr. Whewell.

DEAR DR. WHEWELL,   Weybridge, Sept. 24, 1850.

You will be able to tell me something about Mr. Dowé. My husband knows nothing of man or book. The title is unpromising and sounds quackish and prophetic, but the book may have merit. I have told Cousin that, alas! we abound in people who make theology, philosophy, poetry, art, philanthropy, serve the cause of radicalism—of that general tendency to sacrifice the superior to the inferior elements of society—which is the epidemy of our times.

Jupiter nods. You directed my letter, Mrs. A., *Woodbridge.* A Mrs. Austin opened it, was perplexed, *comme de raison*, thence it went to Brandeston Hall, my brother-in-law Charles's house, where "Trin. Lodge" sufficed to put them on the right scent. I write immediately, though I cannot answer. But as the writing to my niece, Meta, for the book you want, and receiving her answer, will make a further delay, I give myself the pleasure of this little reproach, or triumph, or whatever you like that expresses the unlooked-for pleasure of finding that a great man can make a small blunder—a thing which critics especially relish. It is a long time since we met, and you may believe that a couple of days at Cambridge would be an immense gain and pleasure to me. B. St. Hilaire comes to us next month. He is as much out of heart as M. Guizot about France.

My German friends are not in better heart. I don't know how you found things. I am very glad Kreuznach answered to Mrs. Whewell. My best love to her.

I shall write again anon, and will now only say how truly I am, dear Dr. Whewell,

Yours,
S. AUSTIN.

Mrs. Austin to M. Guizot.

DEAR M. GUIZOT,   Weybridge, Nov. 30, 1850.

You seem to have floated over another of the whirl-pools or falls that lie in your course. I wish I could think it the last. I saw, however, that our good friend

B. St. Hilaire was just as far from any feeling of security this year as the last, and I conclude he would think favourably of things, *if he could.* I think his visits to England have done him great good. He has both learned and unlearned a great deal. Did he tell you that M. Cousin had resolved to accompany him, and at the last moment *retracted?* I suppose you are much agitated by what is passing in Germany; even we are so. A witty Berliner wrote to me some time ago, " Der König ist schon lang nur ein Studium für Pathologen " (The King for a long time has only been a subject for the study of pathologists). Did any one ever see such letters and such speeches ? I never asked you, *of course,* what you thought of M. de Radowitz. From the little I had seen and heard of him, my impression was that he was somewhat of a humbug. Perhaps I am wrong. I am curious to hear how he is judged. I have had a very long and very interesting letter from my dear and revered old friend, M. de Lindenau. He has been in South Germany. His impressions about Austria are very favourable. He tells me wonders of the total abandonment of the old system, and says that Schwarzenberg aims at no less than to be the Richelieu of the Austrian monarchy, in which, adds M. de L., I heartily wish him success, supposing always that it is to be a constitutional one. All that he says about the Slavonian and Magyar populations corresponds with all that I saw, heard, and thought when among them. But I will get the passage copied and send it to you. You know how entirely unprejudiced, how calm, how experienced, and how sagacious he is ; his opinions may therefore have value for you. I am thankful to think of you with two more creatures to love—especially babes : nothing is so completely delightful and refreshing as their society. Even the germs of evil which appear in them, their *naïf* selfishness, their little violences and tempers, have a *gentillesse* that disguises the cloven foot.   My Maurice is just in perfection, joyous and amusing, making every day fresh acquisitions and displaying new talents.   While I watch him and listen to his little *ramage*, I want nothing else in the world.

My husband is tolerably well—as well as a body subjected to the attrition of such a mind, revolving on itself, can be.

I wanted to send you a little thing I wrote about Locke's grave, but I have not a copy of the *Athenæum* containing it.   Cousin has, if you care to see such a trifle. There· are two parts, October 5th and 19th (I think) There are things in it that will charm you, especially the epitaph on Mrs. Cudworth, written by Locke.   What would that serene and exalted soul feel at the spectacle of the frenzy that rages in England now?   Is there anything in France or Germany more absurd or more unreasoning?   One would think the Pope were landing with 50,000 crusaders and a staff of inquisitors.   Obviously he and his bishops can act only by persuasion, and if that does not succeed without a hierarchy, neither will it with one.   The Pope and Cardinal Wiseman committed a foolish impertinence, which ought to have been met with calm remonstrance.   Lord John Russell's letter * is almost universally condemned, in spite of all you may read in newspapers, and is indeed a most wonderful production for a *statesman.*   It comes most opportunely at the moment the Irish constituencies are being increased *tenfold* by the new Act.   I heard a letter

* The so-called 'Durham Letter,' written by Lord J. Russell on Nov. 4, 1850, to the Bishop of Durham, about "the late aggression of the Pope upon our Protestantism."   Dr. Wiseman had been created a Cardinal, and appointed the first Archbishop of Westminster, in a document couched in grandiloquent style.   This manifesto was followed by the publication of a pastoral from the new Cardinal, equally pretentious, which thoroughly aroused the anti-popery feeling in England.

from Ireland yesterday, saying that the present frenzy and Lord John's letter would make it more difficult to govern Ireland than it had ever been. This anybody might have foreseen ; but his adherents call it "a good party move "—a sentiment as wise as it is moral.

Have you seen Sir James Stephen ? I am curious to hear what he says to all this. He cannot approve it, I think. Sir James is a man about whom there are very different opinions. Ours is, as I think you know, very favourable ; but his manner gives an impression of want of frankness ; and he was unpopular in the Colonial Office, spite of his great and acknowledged ability. You will find it worth while to converse with him—I should say, a good deal. His official experience must interest you, and his conversation is very original. I am much attached to them both. She is a sweet, noble, *innocent* creature. Some Englishwomen retain all their lives a sort of *naïve* innocence that makes me feel quite corrupt by their side. But it is not given to all to ignore vice when they see it, as you once said your sainted mother did. She would have delighted in Lady Stephen. It is no want of understanding in her ; she has great sense, but she cannot believe the world is what it is.

I am your most affectionate
S. AUSTIN.

P.S.—Dr. Whewell cannot say enough of the merits of Sir J. Stephen's lectures on Modern History given at Cambridge.

M. B. St. Hilaire to Mrs. Austin.

[TRANSLATION.]

Dec. 30, 1850.

I cannot, dear madam and friend, let the year pass without recalling myself to you and all your family. You see that things here are not going on satisfactorily.

The Assembly has voted two measures which I entirely approve, but which may provoke a conflict; it has asserted its authority, and it has done right. But the executive power may consider that it has been slighted, and commit some fresh blunder in attempting revenge.

Your Protestant demonstrations, I see, still continue; an insult is always resented, and the Pope's bull was nothing less. I can understand that you are tired of the anti-Papist agitations, but the Pope has only got what he deserved; I cannot pity him when I see the grievous harm he and his party do to us. With you public opinion is vigilant and energetic; there lies your power and your force: public opinion does not exist here, and that is one of our greatest evils, or rather it is the source of all our evils. Until public opinion is educated and disciplined, our governments will behave as they choose, and new elements of disorder will be perpetually renewed.

Your most devoted
B. St. Hilaire.

M. B. St. Hilaire to Mrs. Austin.

[Translation.]

Madam and Dear Friend,   Paris, Jan. 20, 1851.

I only received your letter of the 17th this morning, and went at once to call on your nephew; he was out. I am sorry to have missed Mr. Reeve, for I wished to lay before him the opinions I hold with all the moderate Republican party. The vote of the 18th, which put a stop to the Empire, is a triumph for us; our principles form the neutral ground, or, more correctly speaking, our party, by the mouth of Cavaignac, was arbiter of the situation. You may rest assured that this vote, in spite of the calumnies with which it will be assailed, has for the moment preserved order and public peace. Any attempt at establishing the Empire would infallibly, in a few months, have brought about the Red Republic with all its horrors. Thiers has, at last, to my infinite relief, understood this. For two years I have been trying to convince him, and I am thankful that he has listened to reason. The President must be Republican, that is to say, *honest*, and he must abide by his oath. The time had come to make him see this.

Cousin is hard at work editing his political speeches, and writing an introduction which will create a sensation when it comes out.

Remember me to Mr. Austin and the friends I have made through you.

Your devoted
B. ST. HILAIRE.

CHAPTER XXV.

Letter from Mrs. Austin to Dr. Whewell on his Translation of Auerbach's ' Professorin '—His Answer—Letter from M. B. St. Hilaire on the Accession of the Tories to Power—Letter from Mrs. Austin to M. Guizot—M. B. St. Hilaire on the State of France—The Death of Mrs. Taylor—M. B. St. Hilaire to Mrs. Austin on the policy of the President, Louis Napoleon, and announcing his own imprisonment in Mazas.

Mrs. Austin to Dr. Whewell.

Dear Dr. Whewell,   Weybridge, Jan. 23, 1851.

My silence must have seemed like black ingratitude, and that is not a very comfortable thought to me, who value your recollection of me—not to mention your book—at so very high a rate. I was from home when your charming ' Professorin ' * arrived, and after my return I was *écrasée* under a load of letters to answer, and an accumulation of books to read which were to be restored on a given day. I waited, absurdly, till I had read the book before I would thank you for it, instead of despatching my thanks as heralds to my opinion. I cannot tell you how captivating I find it. There is a homely freshness, a *genuine* simplicity, mixed with intimate and delicate touches of feeling far superior to anything I ever read of Auerbach's. I suspect he owes a great deal to you, for you are at ease in the most vernacular language, and find wonderful equivalents for words and expressions that others leave in despair. There's an English story founded on the same dissonance—is it not by Mrs.

* ' The Professor's Wife,' by Auerbach, translated by W. Whewell.

Sullivan ? Of course you know it. But it is far from having the charm of Lorlie.

I send you St. Hilaire's version of the present crisis. M. Anisson thinks him quite wrong, and so does my husband ; but he ought to be heard, for whatever he does is honestly done. I suspect they want what they will never find—a sincerely Republican governor.

Since I began this note I have received also the enclosed letters from M. de Circourt and M. Decaisne. I send them *all.* Make out of them, if you can, the present state of things or of minds in Paris.

The whole thing seems to me utterly baseless and, if I may make an awkward word, cementless.

Auerbach's sentiments about the English are, I fear, all but universal in Germany. Let me thank you once more for poor Lorlie, who is the type of so many a vain attempt to make others happy by self-devotion. Do you know her more vulgar and less amiable sister, Lenette, in Jean Paul's 'Siebenkäs'?

Pray remember me most affectionately to Mrs. Whewell, and believe me, dear Dr. Whewell,

Most cordially yours,
S. AUSTIN.

Dr. Whewell to Mrs. Austin.

MY DEAR MRS. AUSTIN, Trinity Lodge, Jan. 26, 1851.

I hoped that you would read the 'Professorin' before you wrote to me, or rather that you would write to me after you had read it, that I might know what you thought of it ; and certainly I have great reason to be glad that you did so, when you can find such pleasant things to say of the translation. *Your* praise on such a point is of first-rate value. I am glad you like my Lorlie. She was my companion all the summer, and part of her story was written at every place where I stayed—several pages on the top of the Faulhorn, 8,000 feet high.   It is much the prettiest of Auerbach's stories, and I think the greatest favourite in Germany. They have made a play of it.   I was somewhat consoled for Auerbach's bad opinion of the English by seeing how plainly he is quite ignorant of us, and takes his view from our writers, coloured by his own notions about religious observances.   Do you suppose that the work by a person of great pretensions, which the collaborator attacks, alludes to Bunsen's 'Church of the Future'?   I was much amused with the manner in which Auerbach makes it the summit of the Englishman's insolence to criticise German philosophy ; about which I suspect A. knows as little as he does of English life.   We English are as stupidly servile in looking with reverence on all German philosophy, as we are stupidly conceited about our social institutions and manners. I was much interested with the letters you sent me— on account of their private as well as public bearing. I am quite sorry for Circourt.   I do not see how the French are to get out of their present difficulty, but it is one not peculiar to them, though aggravated by the circumstance that their last revolution was the most absurd of revolutions.   It has always been hard for the Assembly, and the Ruler of a Constitutional Government, to settle into their positions of equilibrium.   The Ruler has to learn that he is no Ruler ; and the Assembly has to learn to allow him to be something : hard lessons which neither Germany nor France can yet learn.   I think Germany a more melancholy spectacle than France, for they have not only put out the conflagration, but seem to be extinguishing all traces of domestic fire.

Mrs. Whewell values much your kind recollections of her ; and I am, if you will allow me to be,

Affectionately yours,
W. WHEWELL.

M. B. St. Hilaire to Mrs. Austin.

[TRANSLATION.]

MADAM AND DEAR FRIEND,   Paris, Feb. 25, 1851.

The accession of the Tories is most disastrous for France, and I hear on good authority that the President is anxious. Latterly the English Press has erred in taking his part so strongly, he does not merit sympathy, and public opinion here resented such exaggerated praise. In his dealings with the Assembly, as well as with the Republic, the President is in the wrong, and he has been frank with neither. His own reputation and the public peace have suffered in consequence. He was a conspirator before the nation elected him to the eminent post he now occupies, and he retains the habit. The small riot of last Saturday ought to show you what he is and who are his friends. It is grievous to have such a government, which one is forced to despise, and which will inevitably bring about a catastrophe.

You, in your happy England, you change your Ministries, but your national interests are always honestly and energetically guarded. Whigs or Tories, England knows that she can trust her rulers; if not always wise, they are always honest and patriotic. The shame and the danger of our Ministries of transition is a thing England will never experience.

You see that to me things do not appear *couleur de rose*, and although the Republic gains ground every day, I am very uneasy lest your new Cabinet should attack the President. He is capable of stirring up the maddest popular passions in order to smooth the way for declaring the Empire, which is his object. He is utterly wanting in principle ; in one word, he is a knave.

I think the Duchess of Orleans is very wise in asking your advice, and I thank you for contributing to the amelioration of those children who may one day be our salvation.   Exile will teach them much that they never would have learnt here.

You may be sure that Weybridge will see me as soon as I can escape from the fiery furnace of politics.   Remember me to Alexander and Lady Lucie, and tell little Janet I shall teach her French.

Your devoted friend,
B. St. Hilaire.

Mrs. Austin to M. Guizot.

Weybridge,
March 23, 1851.

Dear Monsieur Guizot,

Lucie has not been in good health all the winter. The first time she returned to Weybridge after their departure, the whole village, where she is much beloved, was struck by the alteration in her looks.   For nearly a fortnight she has been labouring under a fearful attack of bronchitis—incessant cough, high fever, and all the most terrible symptoms.   Last Thursday I began to feel as if in a black dream ; but, God be praised ! it is now dispersed.   For three days past her recovery has been steadily advancing.   She is permitted to speak and to take a little food, and nothing, we are assured, remains but the necessity for extreme care.

Alexander has let the house in Queen Square, and nearly concluded an agreement for one at Esher.   We have long been trying in vain to find one for them nearer to us.   This is a great overthrow of my plans and hopes, and will make our life here quite another thing.   But I cannot complain.   It is clear that London does not suit them, and the house at Esher offers many advantages.   Indeed, I first discovered it in going to call on a lady * whom you know there.   She and her

* Duchess of Orleans.

two sons have been suffering from *grippe*, but not seriously. I saw them all three not long ago. The lady and I are engaged in a correspondence on the difficulty of finding books on English history, in which the matter of religion is treated "avec élévation et impartialité"—in a manner fit for the young, and especially for *them*. I fear, as I told her, she must not look for those qualities of a historian *here*.

I am sure you are shocked at what is passing. Dr. Wiseman has played a very *wicked* and reckless part, and Lord John Russell has been scarcely less mischievous to the country. The Whigs are under a cloud. Everything turns against them. Lord Holland has cruelly injured and diminished his father's reputation. Mr. Macaulay is convicted of calumniating Penn with extreme levity. All these things have a sinister effect. If we had a rash or unpopular sovereign, I don't know what would happen. *She* holds us all together at present, and if ever life was precious, hers is.

Germany loudly threatens another revolution. And France, *your France*, my dear Monsieur Guizot, is she recovering from her wounds? God grant it.

Give my love and heartfelt blessing to my two darlings, and say that in my prayers for my own child I do not forget them. My husband is well, and sends his most affectionate respects. And for me, dearest sir and friend, I am, as ever,

Your most affectionate

S. Austin.

M. B. St. Hilaire to Mrs. Austin.

[Translation.]

Madam and dear Friend,Paris, May 4, 1851.

I saw Cousin yesterday at the Institute; he had received your article, which pleased him much, though

he said you had become rather Tory, which astonished
me not a little. He is less likely than ever to come to
an understanding with the former adherents of Louis
Philippe ; and the fusion patronised by M. Guizot is, you
may be sure, politically speaking, the grossest error
that can be committed. I, as a Republican, am delighted, for when the choice is limited between Legitimate Monarchy and the Republic, France will not
hesitate long in making her decision. You complain
of the state of things in England ; what can I say of
ours? At the eve of an expected crisis, the President
insists on maintaining his fancy Ministry, and insists on
imposing his choice for a permanent one. How right
you are in praising the honesty of your Queen. That is
the great quality ; and if we only had an honest man at
the head of affairs, everything would go on quietly. But
Napoleon, like his two predecessors, aims at personal
government ; he will cut his own throat, and poor
France will be the sufferer ; according to the well-
known saying, "Quiquid delirant reges," etc. The condition of our policy and our administration is shameful
and a source of extreme danger ; our financial situation
is deplorable, the floating debt will soon exceed 700
millions. Work diminishes daily, agriculture is in
such a disastrous condition that the farmers are
praying for a bad harvest. As yet the people are quiet,
but this apparent tranquillity is not to be trusted ;
believe me, we shall not traverse this crisis without
a severe struggle, and our rulers are wanting in
the wisdom and firmness which might lessen if not
avert it.

I very much fear that there will be no vacation, and
that I shall not be able to leave Paris. In the present
condition of the Chamber, the Revision* will not be

---

* Of the law forbidding the re-election of the President.

voted, and the only alternative is violence. France will even be deprived of other candidates or competitors, for the princes * will not be recalled. Had my friends listened to me, the Republic would have been magnanimous and wise. Berryer has behaved abominably, and in spite of my defeat, I am glad to have spoken against a measure which may be fatal to France.† Remember me to Mr. Austin.

Your ever devoted
B. ST. HILAIRE.

M. B. St. Hilaire to Mrs. Austin.

[TRANSLATION.]

DEAR MADAM AND FRIEND,   Paris, June 9, 1851.

What do you think of the Great Exhibition, and particularly of our part of it? By what I hear on all sides, the idea of Prince Albert has been a splendid success. I have a strong desire to see it, and should like to induce Cousin to go with me. He is much struck by all the accounts he has heard, particularly from Thiers. But you see the state we are in. The speeches at Dijon must have enlightened you as to the President's character. If he has any honesty left, he must be prepared to retire in 1852, unless he intends to try a *coup d'état*. If the party of order were wise, they would begin to prepare the way for another candidate. The most suitable man would certainly be General Cavaignac.

Cousin has been very unwell lately. He is thinking of taking up politics again. His last article produced such an effect here that his success encourages him to attempt another. Had Barrot been in the Ministry,

---

* Of the House of Orleans.
† Exile of the House of Orleans.

Cousin would have spoken on the question of Revision, but with Faucher he will not open his mouth, although Faucher's conduct lately has been praiseworthy.

I am hard at work at my Sanscrit Philosophy, and have read a considerable portion to the Institute.

Your ever devoted friend,
B. St. Hilaire.

M. B. St. Hilaire to Mrs. Austin.

[Translation.]

Madam and dear Friend,   July 25, 1851.

I am entirely of your opinion that the Exhibition is one of the great events of the nineteenth century, and that I must try and see it. I shall come, if only for four or five days. You will see me fall like a bombshell into the hospitable cottage at Weybridge.

The Elysée is losing ground every day in the esteem and affection of the people.

I hope you admire the parliamentary and constitutional behaviour of your friend Faucher? He takes no notice of the formal vote of censure, and keeps his place as Minister. With you, such a man would be dishonoured, but our political usages are unformed, and we tolerate such conduct.

Your ever devoted
B. St. Hilaire.

Mrs. Austin to Dr. Whewell.

Dear Dr. Whewell,   Weybridge, Oct. 2, 1851.

Thank you most cordially for your sympathy; your hopes were, alas! in vain. My dear sister-in-law departed from us on the twelfth of last month. The death of a woman of seventy-two is so much in "the order of things," so little an event to speak to the imagination, that any expressions I could bring myself to use about her loss would seem like exaggeration.

But she had filled the whole scene of her gentle, loving, modest, and wise activity with the blessings of her rule, and she cannot be withdrawn without a chasm that nothing can fill.

My brother's resignation is the most gentle, humble, and childlike you can imagine. He is thankful for all he has had, accessible to all sympathy and comfort, anxious not to be troublesome, quietly hopeful of the future.

I shall tell him of your inquiries. He has not only a great reverence for, but a great attachment to you, and always says, "Dr. Whewell has always been very kind to me." I have half a mind to ask you if I might try to persuade him to escort me to Cambridge some day or other.

I am shocked to hear that Mr. Carlyle has permitted himself to mention me. This clatter over poor John Sterling's grave is very painful to those who knew and loved him—spite of his weaknesses and defects—for his generous heart and affectionate temper. As to Carlyle, I don't think you *at all* too hard. *J'abonde dans votre sens.* I think him one of the dissolvents of the age— as mischievous as his extravagances will let him be. We have indeed some pernicious men. I agree with the *Quarterly Review* about Kingsley and Maurice. I don't know what Carlyle has said of me, but assuredly I cannot conceal my indignation at his misuse of great talents.

Yours ever, dear Dr. Whewell,

With the greatest regard,

S. AUSTIN.

[TRANSLATION.]

MADAM AND DEAR FRIEND,   Paris, Oct. 29, 1851.

I saw Cousin yesterday at Bellevue, who is so ashamed at not having accompanied me to England that he authorises me to use force next year. I promise you that it shall not be my fault if you do not see him. He is coming back to Paris, driven by the bad weather and politics. The strange conversion of the President has alienated from him the whole of the so-called party of order, without procuring the adhesion of our side. The law of the 31st May will be repealed if the Government insists on it, but the price will be a heavy one—the contempt of the nation; and after the events of the last two years, it will be the last drop in the President's cup. M. Louis Napoleon is playing the game of the Prince de Joinville, who ought to be the sheet-anchor of the party of order in less than six weeks.

Do you see that Faucher, the new Cato, has named himself at one jump Commander of the Legion of Honour? In his electioneering rounds, this most modest of men orders his entry into the towns to be saluted by the firing of cannon. What do you say to all this in England? What a figure we make in Europe—to what depths we are fallen! Do not laugh at us, but pity us. Faucher little knew the knave he had to deal with; he thought to lead him, and he has become a blind instrument.

While at Agen, I took up a new trade, that of a master of gymnastics. I gave daily lessons to five or six little girls and to their fathers, and instructed a mistress, whom I left in my place; and what is a greater triumph, I introduced gymnastics into two religious communities, the Sacré Cœur and the Filles de Marie.

This is indeed philosophy in action and movement. I have the satisfaction of having done some good, and probably straightened more than one weak spine which was inclined to be crooked.

Remember me to Mr. Austin, and tell little Janet to play at ball every day.

Your ever devoted
B. ST. HILAIRE.

M. B. St. Hilaire to Mrs. Austin.

[TRANSLATION.]

MADAM,   Paris, Dec. 4, 1851.

Your kind letter reached me at the moment when I was leaving the prison of Mazas, where, with a good number of my colleagues, I was imprisoned for signing the act proclaiming the fall of the President. I have just left Cousin, who is gone to the Sorbonne, after vainly attempting, with me, to cross the bridges to go to Barrot. There is fighting in all Paris. I am deeply touched by your offer, and I assure you that Weybridge tempts me strongly, but I cannot leave my country until it is tranquil; I must suffer and, if necessary, die for her. Remember me to every one.

Your devoted friend,
B. ST. HILAIRE.

CHAPTER XXVI.

Letter from Mrs. Austin to M. Guizot on the State of Affairs in France and at Vienna—Mrs. Grote's visit to Paris—Letter from M. B. St. Hilaire about the Paris University—Letter from Mrs. Austin to Dr. Whewell on the threatened Expulsion of M. Cousin from the Sorbonne—His Answer.

Mrs. Austin to M. Guizot.

Dearest Monsieur Guizot,   Dec. 5, 1851.

My heart is so much with you that I cannot help writing, though I know not what good that can do you. I have long and deeply rejoiced that you would not suffer yourself to be induced to enter a field on which no honour was to be won—take what side you might. I never for an instant doubted of the wisdom of your determination, now apparent to all men. You are in a region which this new storm cannot reach, except through your patriotic affections. That is my great consolation.

The spectacle which France presents now is very painful, but so it has been for a long time past. Going back to the Taiti business, when the malignity and chicanery of your enemies first became outrageous, I could never see anything encouraging. *Franchement*, a country that will accept *any* government and maintain *none*—what can be done for it? It is now the fashion to say that " le gouvernement parlementaire ne vaut rien pour la France." If that is true, as it may be for aught I know, it is because a loyal Opposition seems impossible. What would you not have done for the consolidation of a representative government if you had been fairly met and faithfully supported? I do not ask you to tell me if you are satisfied with the new order of things, if *order* is the word. Tell me that you are not unhappy nor alarmed, and I shall be content. Let it be what it may, what it replaces is not to be regretted. If it is to be only a *réchauffée* of what failed in the hands of a giant, we may all easily turn prophets. My own discouragement about France arises more from the political character of the people (of all classes) than from anything else. Every government seems a new toy, soon to be pulled in pieces and broken. At all events, you, best and noblest of friends, have not spared them constant and serious teachings. If they will not hear, you, at least, have a clear conscience.

I have had a good deal of communication lately with Vienna. There, another sort of madness seems to prevail. It is impossible to divine what the Government intends. The most curious suspicions attach to people, especially Englishmen. That they should hate us is natural; that they should suspect English gentlemen who bear the greatest names of being *spies*, etc., dishonours nobody but themselves. God knows no *spying* is required to discover the pranks played "before high Heaven" by *our* Spirit of Mischief! What a moment to choose for invoking the direct action of the mob on the government of any country! I feel that we have no right to talk of the toleration of bad or incompetent rulers, while we tolerate such a man as that. He is, of course, popular with the mob; but to what use does he mean to put this popularity? I hear his colleagues look grave—and well they may.

Per contra, if you see the *Times*, take the trouble to read in the number of the 3rd the account of the management of the Duke of Bedford's estate. It is merely an agricultural letter, but what a picture of the loftiest aristocracy lending itself to all the details of the moral and material improvement of the lowliest classes of men ! What habits of order ! What talents for business ! These are the men who *quietly* preserve societies from ruin.

Mr. Senior has brought home one of his journals written while at Naples. He seems to have conceived the lowest possible opinion of the people, and, as a consequence, of the government. He is pretty well.

My dear daughter has made me uneasy, but she is much better ; the children admirably well. My husband very well—charmed with the correspondence of Mirabeau and Comte de la Mark. I have undertaken, after long and earnest entreaties on Mrs. Sydney Smith's part, to arrange and edit Sydney's letters and lesser writings. You know his faults, but he was in the highest degree brave, sincere, loyal, generous, and a lover of truth. These qualities in a Churchman deserve to be recorded.

Your most affectionate
S. AUSTIN.

Mr. Grote to Mrs. Austin.

DEAR MRS. AUSTIN,   Dec. 10, 1851.

Mrs. Grote is still at Paris, and talks of remaining there till the end of the month. She has been in no way personally disturbed or alarmed by what has been going on. Her lodging is 108, Champs Elysées. Very luckily she was not on the Boulevard des Italiens, otherwise I do not know what would have become of her on Tuesday the 4th, when the soldiers killed people right and left, the peaceable far more than the warlike.

I have heard from her about every other day, but never at any great length, or with much detail. She has committed to writing a sort of budget, which is to be sent home by Mrs. Blackett, and she is too tired to be able to write the facts over twice. She says generally that nothing can be conceived so awful as the state of feeling in Paris, the stupefaction and terror which reigns there. She has seen shoals of people (she says) and heard copious details. One paper which I received from her this morning I enclose for your perusal. It is drawn up by some Frenchman whose name she dares not mention, and describes certain feats of the soldiers in the "Blutbad" of December 4. Pray send it back to me when you have read it. She mentions some facts (which I do not think have passed into the newspapers) about the treatment of the Deputies when they were arrested—about fifty in number, I believe, and *not Republicans*, therefore having some claim on English sympathy—persons who, before the 2nd December, counted as the most respected politicians in France. These men were confined in the barrack all the afternoon of the 2nd, and all the night. They had to sleep on the floor, or in chairs, in their clothes. On the ensuing morning they were handed off to Vincennes in the transport vans designed for criminals ; there they were detained all that day, some of them longer. Their wives did not know what had become of them for twenty-four hours or more. Dufaure was one of these.

I would not be at Paris, as Mrs. Grote is now, for any sum which could be tendered to me. Not because of any personal fear. To an Englishman of common prudence there is no ground for fear, but from the perfect heart-sickening which this tremendous event has given me, and against which I find it hard to bear up, even here, with my books around me. I did not expect to live to see anything so like the brutal setting up of an ancient tyrant in a Grecian city. My best regards to Austin.

Yours sincerely,
G. GROTE.

Mr. Grote to Mrs. Austin.

DEAR MRS. AUSTIN,					Dec. 13, 1851.

I am very sorry I cannot come to you to-morrow, as I have already engaged myself. I return St. Hilaire's letter, which is painfully interesting, and highly honourable to his feelings about his country. If there be any one portion of France more to be deplored than another in regard to the *régime* now inaugurating, it is the writers and thinkers of the country : men who, above all things, require an atmosphere of freedom. I anticipate an enslavement of speech and thought only paralleled by that of the Empire ; and I farther anticipate, what even the Empire did not do, a more complete surrender of all public education into the hands of the priesthood than ever existed before. St. Hilaire, and the Liberal men about the University Council, will feel this most painfully. What is now beginning is "l'ère des Césars," according to Romieu's language.

The President's *coup d'état* is exactly the parallel to the insurrection of June 1848—equally brutal and guilty, only having the means of maintaining itself afterwards, as being the insurrection (for it is nothing less) of the chief man and the organised force of the country.

I had a letter from Mrs. Grote yesterday, guarded in its communications, but just in the same melancholy tone as to passing events. She says that Horace Say has received a warning that if he does not mind his doings it will be worse for him. She says that for a whole day it was fully believed that Léon Faucher, as well as Thiers, had been sent out of the country. She says that she really does not *dare* write all she hears. The quantity of people she sees is greater than her strength will sustain ; in fact, it seems that the English in Paris are the only persons now exempt from personal terror, and recipients of the breathings of Frenchmen who do not dare to communicate with one another. If I have any information to give, I will certainly communicate with Henry Reeve. I think the *Times* has done itself great honour by what it has said upon this late affair. I trust Austin is better. It is not surprising that he has been struck down by so dreadful an event.

Yours very sincerely,

G. GROTE.

M. B. St. Hilaire to Mrs. Austin.

[TRANSLATION.]

MADAM AND DEAR FRIEND,   Paris, Jan. 18, 1852.

I take advantage of Dozon's departure for England to write a few lines which will not pass under the odious eyes of the police. I can tell you nothing of our affairs, for you know more than we do, thanks to your admirable newspapers, so unlike our poor rags, censured, cut, and altered when they are not sequestered. I do not suppose that any nation ever submitted to so extraordinary and, at the same time, so shameful a regimen. But I repeat I have nothing to tell ; all is said, and excellently said, by the *Times.*

Rémusat told me before he left that his first visit in England will be to you : he meant to wait for a time before going, but I do not think our police will allow the poor exiles to stay in Belgium.

The University is to undergo important changes—some say it is to be done away with altogether. Our positions are all compromised, but till now we have not been molested. Cousin's substitute, Jules Simon, has committed an imprudence, which brought about his dismissal, and caused that of Cousin to be talked of. The latter has implacable enemies among the clergy, who to-day are all-powerful. The trap which is, to all appearance, prepared for several of us is the oath exacted by the Constitution. Of all the articles, that is the one which has excited most opposition. These are terrible moments; it is not possible that things can go on like this, which is the only comfort for cowards. Numerous as they are, the Government has not yet succeeded in obtaining any allies, and its irritation at being thus left solitary is shown by the proscriptions. What do you say to this ghastly comedy? What is the opinion in England? Blame our poor country, but pity it more than you blame. To be so little able to manage her affairs after sixty years of revolutions! To what a depth of ignorance and incapacity have three centuries of absolute monarchy brought us!

M. Guizot was at the "Institut" yesterday; he looked very well. I do not know what he thinks of the condition of things. I hear various accounts, but I cannot believe that it meets his approval.

Cousin is well; he is entirely absorbed by Madame de Longueville, whose declared lover he is. In a few months he hopes to take up 'Plato' again, in which I try to encourage him. He owes it to himself and to philosophy.

Your ever devoted Friend,
B. St. Hilaire.

Mrs. Austin to Dr. Whewell.

Weybridge, March 27, 1852.

There's a philosopher (V. Cousin) for you! You may suppose, best of masters, how I scolded and scorned him in my answer. I said, "Je vous trouve lâche vis-à-vis de la vieillesse," and so I do. The truth is, my poor old friend has a passion for making *impressions* of all sorts, upon "*les jolies femmes*" above all. We all know that it is charming to be admired, and more charming to be adored ; but what I can't understand is, how a man lives to sixty without preparing himself to relinquish the privileges of youth. However, to do him justice, he has been the truest and most constant and affectionate of friends to me, who never adored him, and have told him more disagreeable truths than most people. But do we not burn with indignation at seeing him, after forty-two years of such services to science and letters (I beg your pardon), stripped ? His chief income was 10,000 francs as member of the Conseil d'Instruction Publique—gone. The 6,000 francs as Professor at the Sorbonne he will also lose (*destitué par prétérition*), unless he lectures.

I began my answer, " Assurément que vous professerez et mieux que qui que ce soit au monde " ; and told him, what is true, that I wish I could be there to see and hear his reappearance, and to tie up his poor throat, and *dorloter* him a little.

But now, our dear and honoured Master, this is a case for your weightier hand. He honours you as he ought. It would be *ganz ausserordentlich schön* if you would write him a few lines of, not condolence, but sympathy, and such things as you know how to say and to *feel*, and administer to him a cordial that shall dispose him to rub up his armour and gird it on. You know, too, that expulsion from the Sorbonne (building) is hung over his head—all his beautiful library !

Yesterday, M. Alexandre Thomas came down to see me. I was in bed all day, having had a kind of relapse the night before, so did not see him. My husband says he is profoundly desponding about France—thinks the people *worn out*. Only M. Guizot preserves an equal mind, expects little, but does not despair. I rather frightened my husband on Thursday, and as nobody can find a cause, my doctor says it is excitement, and that I see too many people—*one* a day on an average. What a miserable state of the nerves and circulation ! To-day

I am better, and in very brave spirits ; but though these vary *extremely*, you will understand that the *fonds* remain the same. I am under no illusion and no terror. I wish I felt sure that my extreme serenity and cheerfulness about death rested on a better ground. I feel so *much love* and *trust*, and so *little fear*—and yet why ? Is this anything more than constitutional ? For, as for merits or claims—oh ! as grounds for reliance—they are out of the question, and I am not sure that my faith in any scheme of Atonement would explain my serenity. It seems to me rather a foundless trust in the Source of all good—such as His Son reveals Him to us. I wish I could *talk* with you about this.

Yours most faithfully,
S. AUSTIN.

Dr. Whewell to Mrs. Austin.

Trinity College, March 30, 1852.

It was very kind of you, my dear friend, to send me V. Cousin's letter, even though the privilege brought with it the task of reading the epistle—which is not a very easy matter. But it was still more amiable of you to think that I might gratify the dear old Eclectic by expressions of interest in his future and labours. I dare say he will not derive much pleasure from my doing so, but that you should try to procure him such pleasure as my encouragement could give, was one of those kind thoughts which make us love you. Accordingly, inspired by your suggestion, I have sent such a letter to him. It so happened that I had with me at the time a French man of letters just about to return to Paris ; and to him I committed my exhortation to Cousin to continue his speculations, pointing out some questions on which we should all, in England and France, listen to him with deference. I was glad to learn from my friend that Cousin is supposed to be so rich as not to be seriously distressed by his losses, even if they should come upon him as they threaten. With regard to his fear of age, which is a more inevitable evil, if it be an evil, I hope your exhortations will not be wasted on him. It is no doubt a little mortifying to human conceit that we must leave the world to a new generation; but it appears to me more mortifying because it interrupts what we do than what we enjoy; we have done so little, and matters seem to be going on so ill. But we must make up our minds to this, and " trust the Ruler with the skies," and with the earth, too ; and really *trust* Him—believe that He is ruling well, and will do so when we are no longer actors in the scene. Only I think there is nothing presumptuous in hoping that we may know a little how it does go on ; follow the later scenes of the drama, and see the *dénouement* to which it is tending. This is a kind of consolation which cannot deceive us, for we shall have this, or we may humbly hope, something better. I trust it will be long, my dear friend, before you have to seek for the consolations which belong to the close ; but I must say that an entirely filial spirit of resignation, hope, and love is what I have seen with most satisfaction in the cases of others who were dear to me, and what I most desire for myself. Any special view of the manner of acceptance only leads to this. This seems to lead us beyond the bourne directly.

May God bless you and restore you, is the prayer of
Your affectionate friend,
W. WHEWELL.

CHAPTER XXVII.

Qualities of French and English Men and Women—M. B. St. Hilaire refuses to take the Oath and withdraws from Paris— Letter from Mrs. Austin to Mr. Senior describing Ventnor— Letter from Mrs. Austin to M. Guizot on the Volunteer Move- ment—M. B. St. Hilaire a Gardener—Correspondence with Mr. Gladstone on National Education.

M. Guizot to Mrs. Austin.

[TRANSLATION.]

DEAR MRS. AUSTIN,   Paris, April 18, 1852.

Thanks for sending M. Dozon to me; he found you decidedly better, and the tone of your note shows me that you feel stronger. So I am content. For I send you declaration for declaration; you love me, I love you. You must take care of yourself, avoid all fatigue, and get quite well. When you can, without tiring yourself, do give me a few lines just to say how you are, until we meet either at your house or here. I shall be delighted to see you again. You possess the great qualities of your nation, and, in addition, you are sympathetic and expansive, which are rare qualities in your country. Madame de Staël used to say that the best thing in the world was a serious Frenchman. I turn the compliment, and say that the best thing in the world is an affectionate Englishman. How much more an Englishwoman! Given equal qualities, a woman is always more charming than a man.

I intend going to Val Richer about the 15th of June, and passing five months there, to work and to rest. I am getting on in life, and do not know how many more years may be granted to me. I shall die with my head and my hands full of projects and of works begun, but there are two or three I really wish to finish. We pass away so rapidly that we hardly have time to leave a mark on the sand of this earth: at all events, let us leave as complete a one as possible.

Remember me to Mr. Austin, to Lady Gordon, and to Sir Alexander.

Ever yours, with all my heart,

GUIZOT.

M. B. St. Hilaire to Mrs. Austin.

[TRANSLATION.]

MADAM AND DEAR FRIEND,   Paris, May 15, 1852.

I shall have the pleasure of seeing you sooner than I expected; in three weeks I shall be with you. I have refused the oath, preferring anything to such humiliation; at the end of the month I send in my resignation. It is rather hard after twenty-seven years of hard work, and at my age; but I assure you, my friends need not pity me much, for I am not at all out of heart; like Cousin, I am unmarried and a philosopher. I shall leave Paris, but have not yet settled where I am going; I shall bring my new address to you in person. Cousin tried to persuade me to take the oath. I think my dear master was wrong, and consulted my material good more than my honour, and, I may add, the interests of philosophy. He, as you may have seen, has asked to be put on the retired list, in order to avoid the oath; but as he has been named honorary Professor, it may still be demanded of him, and he has decided to refuse it now, as he did before. You may have seen the deplorable affair of M. Arago? He would have done better to take the oath in silence.

Your ever devoted,
B. ST. HILAIRE.

M. B. St. Hilaire to Mrs. Austin.

[TRANSLATION.]

[Les Pépinières, près Meaux,]

MADAM AND DEAR FRIEND,   Sept. 21, 1852.

I have settled myself here, and all I regret are a few of my Paris friends, whom I shall now see but seldom. Every fortnight I go to Paris to work for the *Journal des Savants.* I am taking up gardening seriously, and have more vegetables and fruit than I can use ; but I mean to have some flowers, too, and trust to you to send me some seeds. We are evidently going to have the Empire ; it will be proclaimed on some anniversary of December—either the 2nd or the 20th. It is rapid work ; the uncle took four years. But, in spite of what Victor Hugo said, it seems that people are greater now.* All the better ; the faster the pages are turned, the sooner the book will be finished. But what an abominable book it will be ! I do not mean Hugo's ; he says what every one thinks, but their mouths are closed by the police. If the pamphlet that has been printed in London could be introduced and circulated freely here, the President's position would be made rather uncomfortable. My views on all that is passing are even stronger than Victor Hugo's, and I do not think I exaggerate. I cannot understand your thinking my last letter was sad. If it were not for my poor eyes I should be the happiest of men.

* " Après Napoléon le Grand, faut-il que nous ayons Napoléon le Petit ? "

I include in this a letter of introduction for M. Véra, Professor of Philosophy. He is going to England, and hopes for employment, as he knows English. I think he does wrong to emigrate without being absolutely forced.

I am quite of your opinion as to Cousin's infatuation ; we know but too well, out of the memoirs of those times, what that famous aristocracy was. I do hope that Madame de Longueville will soon come to an end, and make place for Plato, the second edition of which will certainly take him five or six years.

Remember me to all your family.

Ever your devoted friend,
B. St. Hilaire.

Mrs. Austin to Mr. Senior.

Bonchurch, Isle of Wight,
Oct. 30, 1852.

Dear Mr. Senior,

I feel as if I must continue our conversation of Weybridge. I am here in the house of the kindest and most hospitable people in the world. The Rev. J. White, who is *à peu près Seigneur* of Bonchurch, exercises the practical and not the rhetorical functions of a Christian minister, and gives, lends, helps, and comforts, though he does not preach.

We shall live in Ventnor, a dull and *triste* little town. Was anybody ever born in Ventnor? or does anybody really *live* there? Every human being seems to me to lodge or let lodgings. How very disagreeable and factitious this is—the country and no country life! How much, had it so pleased the doctors, should I have preferred Penzance or Falmouth—some place with a body and soul of its own!

I have been reading with great satisfaction Madame de Peyronnet's article on De Maistre. I don't think she has got to the bottom of De Maistre; but how well, firmly,

and pointedly she writes! what an entire absence of the
feeble or the mawkish!   Measure her style against that
of any man's article in the same review, not to speak of
the ineffable slipslop of such historians as Miss Pardoe
etc. By-the-bye, who is the reviewer " Cardinal *Infanta* "?
One has heard of Pope Joan, but who is *she ?*

I suppose the Irish article is Lord Monteagle's.   I
have just, for the first time, run through Thackeray's
' Ireland.'   Slight and book-making as it is, there are
good things in it ; but what struck me was the contrast
to your present description.   Pray let the world have it.

Yours ever,
S. AUSTIN.

Mrs. Austin to M. Guizot.

Ventnor, Isle of Wight, Nov. 18, 1852.

What an age has passed, dearest sir and friend, since
I had the comfort of beholding your handwriting ; what
an age, too, since I wrote to you!   The last circum-
stantial account I had of you was from our dear Mr.
Hallam, who returned, as I knew he would, delighted
with his visit ; and with his usual goodness he came
down to Weybridge to tell me about it.   Here, under
the shelter of the huge wall of rock which divides me
from England, I look upon the sea and strain my eyes
to descry that France which lies beyond it, and in which
you and some few others are all that I could wish to
behold there you may be well assured, for who would
not willingly avert their eyes from the ruin and the
shame of a great nation ?   Above all, *the shame !*   Even
if one could believe that the disgraceful bargain, in which
honour and freedom have been bartered for tranquillity,
would succeed.   I wish you would empower me to
silence impertinent people who insist to me that you
approve all that is going on, and are an adherent of Louis

Napoleon. Just before I left home I met at Mr. Hawes's (who had a house at Weybridge) one of those hangers-on of fine ladies who *colportent* their news, and I nearly horsewhipped him (being in my chaise and *armed*) for asserting this. He declared that he had seen full evidence of the fact in letters to Lady Palmerston, with whom he had been staying. I have not the least doubt that Lady Palmerston asserts this to everybody, for you know how she loves you ; but I would not allow Mr. Hawes to listen to the calumny—much to the discomfiture of the dandy reporter. I can fully understand, for that my husband and I also feel, that the objects of your greatest indignation must be the men who undermined and pulled down a government which, as Mr. Austin is always repeating, "had all the conditions of progress and amelioration, and afforded not the slightest *pretext* for violent resistance, and if they suffered alone, one would regard it as a piece of Divine justice. But there is something too ungentlemanlike in the actual proceedings to please you, I am sure. Even tyrannies are susceptible of a noble or of a "blackguard" tinge. Ah, *how* noble were all the aristocratic or despotic leanings of him whom they have now borne to his thrice-honoured grave !* How full are all our hearts at the thought of his unswerving devotion to this England of ours—how intense is the grief, the gratitude, the reverence ! Yes, I will say it again, as I said when Peel died, Blessed are they who live and die for England, for there awaits them such a heart-homage as I think no nation ever yet paid. When I think over this, and feel it, as I do, I am half inclined to murmur at fate that did not give you to England, and England to you. There you would have had even your *earthly* reward. I hope you saw Lord Lansdowne's speech, and remarked the solemnity of his

---

* Duke of Wellington.

exhortations to the country to defend itself. This advice will at length be listened to, spite of all the foolish paradoxes of Cobden and Co. The Duke's voice will now be heard "trumpet-tongued" from his grave. *I* was never inclined to believe in a danger of the kind till now; but all my French correspondents agree in representing it as very real, if not imminent. People have imagined it too great a *mistake* to be committed, but that is a poor dependence ; you, *who know us*, will have no doubt as to the ultimate result. But these things ought to be impossible on the face of it, and I daresay it soon will be. The young men of the country have come forward with great alacrity, and gone through their drill with great earnestness and success—so I hear from all sides. I should not despair of raising a very active, intrepid, and formidable regiment of sharp-shooters of the gentle sex, if need were. Lamentable that this spirit and these determinations should have to be appealed to now! and yet I declare to you I see no more of the old antipathy than I did before, only, as my maid, a blunt North-country girl, says in a very resolute tone, "No, they shan't come *here*."

God bless you, ever dear and honoured friend,

Yours faithfully,

S. AUSTIN.

M. B. St. Hilaire to Mrs. Austin.

[TRANSLATION.]

Les Pepinières,

Dec. 22, 1852.

MADAM AND DEAR FRIEND,

I have become an expert gardener, and having always been used to hard work, I cultivate my acre of ground without any fatigue. I shall become a peasant, but Aristotle and Philosophy will not be losers.

In a fortnight, Cousin will publish his volume on

Madame de Longueville. You will like his preface ; he excuses himself most charmingly for taking up such light studies, and as an expiation he promises a work on Théodicée,* a summing up of his whole system of philosophy. He points out what there is to admire and what to blame in the 17th century, and makes a distinction between the reign of Louis XIV. and the century, which was, I think, much needed, especially in these times. He had an idea of suppressing this portion, but I insisted on preserving it ; he must remember that he is not only a writer and a man of letters, but a statesman and a philosopher.

Remember me to Mr. Austin, and believe me
Ever your devoted friend,
B. ST. HILAIRE.

Mrs. Austin to Mr. Gladstone.

DEAR MR. GLADSTONE, Ventnor, Jan. 4, 1853.

It would be more becoming, perhaps, if I were to begin this by presuming that you have forgotten me, and by offering you all the apologies due from a stranger ; but I cannot play the hypocrite even so far. The cause which procured me the pleasure and honour of your visit long ago has too strong a hold on your heart to allow you to forget the humblest of your fellow-labourers.

I must express the unspeakable satisfaction with which Mr. Austin and I, in our distant winter quarters, have contemplated the formation of the present Administration. We, though brought up in the intensest Whiggery, have lived too long and too much out of the party warfare of England, and have been too near witnesses of terrific political convulsions, not to have modified many opinions and questioned many axioms.

* The exposition of the theory of Divine Providence.

Above all, my long and almost daily intimate intercourse with M. Guizot, the spectacle of his combats and his fall, could hardly fail to excite grave doubts of the expediency of appeals to the people. "La belle invention que le suffrage universel, et comme les auteurs doivent être contents et fiers," writes a friend of his.

As I know what strong sympathy, respect, and regard he feels for you, I take it for granted you feel no less for him—so impossible does it seem to me that he should not attract those whom he wishes to attract. You may therefore like to see a letter I had from him lately, giving a pretty complete view of his opinions about his unfortunate country. Presuming that it will interest you, I will take care that it is sent to you. It is now in Lord Lansdowne's hands.

I dare not begin to speak of Education, yet surely I may—I must—congratulate you. Since we met, what a progress, what indications of a growing appreciation of the value of self-culture, of the dignity of self-control! The old difficulty indeed subsists, but I cannot believe that, with so sincere and earnest a desire for the one great result, it will be insurmountable. I trust to you. Surely Christianity is broad enough to furnish a basis on which to found the education of a nation which, whatever be its diversity of opinions, certainly will not consent to have that basis withdrawn.

Poor France, poor Germany! What is the result of their so excellent-seeming systems? You see it is of no use "to give the meat before you give the hunger." An ounce of education demanded is worth a pound imposed. This, you will observe, is a voluntary recantation on the part of the zealous translator of Cousin. I cannot say it costs me much, for it involves the recognition of the unspeakable superiority of England.

Yours, dear sir, with every sentiment of respect,

SARAH AUSTIN

Mr. Gladstone to Mrs. Austin.

DEAR MRS. AUSTIN,   Downing Street, Jan. 21, 1853.

I read with deep interest the letter you were so good as to address to me.

I am glad indeed that the present Government has your sympathy. Its formation has at least been, I believe, an honest work on the part of all who have contributed to it. The subject of Education, in which you feel so deep an interest, will, I hope, make sensible and *early* progress under its auspices.

I need not say that M. Guizot's letter will be full of interest for me; it shall be carefully returned.

The scandalous delay of my answer may, I hope, be excused by the fifteen days' polling which have just filled up the interval since I received your letter.

I remain, dear Mrs. Austin,
Very sincerely yours,
W. E. GLADSTONE.

Mrs. Austin to Mr. Gladstone.

DEAR MR. GLADSTONE,   Ventnor, Jan. 22, 1853.

I send you my dear, revered friend's* letter. It is one of the most valuable of the many he has favoured me with. I take for granted *you* never believed, if, indeed, you heard, the reports of his adhesion to the present shameful order of things. I wish I could think the example of English statesmen would have more effect upon the few in France who deserve that name. But from what I hear, the furious personal hates by which I saw them divided, subsist still; they cannot unite their forces even against *such* a common danger. When I

* M. Guizot.

was in Paris, Cousin said to me that he should be "des-
honoré à tout jamais" if he put his foot in Guizot's house
(his old friend and colleague), and would hardly believe
that I had met the Duke of Wellington and Sir Robert
Peel at Lansdowne House.   Judge therefore whether I
am not sensible of the value of personal concessions for
great public ends.   They are in all their motives and
tendencies the *very reverse* of compromises of important
principles for private ends, though it seems there are
people stupid enough, or wicked enough, to confound
them.   As to Education, we have yet to find the right
agent, or rather—for I believe it to be no other than
religion—how to apply it.   The part of the child's heart
and reason accessible to its influence is not yet found, or
imperfectly.   But an advance is made.   I take for
granted you have read Mr. Wilson's report of the Vaux-
hall Factory, which is full of valuable suggestions.   There
are several great social problems which I should like to
give to those men of his to deliberate upon.   My belief
is that even on such questions as universal suffrage—the
most dangerous one in our horizon—much better sense
would be elicited from them than from some of your
House of Commons declaimers.   And this is the
immense superiority of England !   I think you rulers of
England must be penetrated with affectionate respect
for the people you govern.

How often has poor M. Guizot expressed to me his
envy of English statesmen !   How deeply he felt the
demonstrations of attachment to Sir Robert Peel !
What a contrast to the recompense of his own labours !
Forgive my yielding to the temptation of what seems to
me like a faint shadow of a conversation with you ; and
believe that few wishes for your success in all that you
wish to accomplish can be more sincere and fervent than
those of your faithful and obliged,

SARAH AUSTIN.

I re-open my letter to add one word about Education. There is a point to which I extremely wish to call your attention ; and whenever you have ten minutes to spare, I will say as briefly as I can what has struck me in consequence of some very curious facts collected and communicated to me by one of the Government Inspectors—Mr. Norris. I believe you will find that there exists a great demand, as well as most unexpected resources, for a new and most valuable class of schools. Under the same superintendence as the existing Primary Schools, Mr. Norris finds the working people are actually paying *a million a year* to private schools ; the rate of schooling being from 4*d.* to 1*s.* a week. They pay at this high rate, partly from a sort of pride, partly because they fancy the instruction must be better, though it is often much worse. "But," said a man to Mr. Norris, " you know, sir, they can't teach much for 3*d.* a week."

Now is your time. The country is prosperous, the people in good spirits, and alive to all sorts of schemes of improvement. Now, dear Mr. Gladstone, give us a scheme for excellent *burgher schools*, to which the people shall " pay a good price," and have in return as much as their money can procure. This matter has been on my mind a year, and if I had been able, I should have written something about it ; but if you will take it up, I shall be happy about it.—S. A.

END OF VOL. I.